WHAT RI
THE SU

CW00495499

Wartime North Shield
backgrounds to this compelling novel about two very diffe...
young women growing up through dramatic times. Poet and biographer Kathleen Jones's move into fiction should be celebrated by readers and writers alike.' Wendy Robertson, best-selling author of Sandie Shaw and the Millionth Marvel Cooker, Land of Our Possession, and Kitty Rainbow.

'I found The Sun's Companion an engrossing read, hard to put down. If you like to "disappear" into the world of a book, you'll find this a satisfying read. Jones paints a comprehensive, moving (but never sentimental) picture of life in north east England during the early years of the war, achieving what only very good writers can do: she makes the familiar seem unfamiliar.' Linda Gillard, author of House of Silence, Emotional Geology, Untying the Knot.

'I'm not entirely sure how to describe this novel other than to say I loved it! . . I don't think I've ever read anything that has immersed me so thoroughly in time and place. These people must be real and I'm sure if I go and visit the area, these farms will actually exist! Utterly gripping and I didn't want it to end.' Debbie Bennett, best-selling author of Hamelin's Child and Edge of Dreams. IEBR Review.

'Kathleen Jones uses her skill as a biographer and researcher to fill the pages of this novel with vibrant historical detail and a thoroughly engaging story. It kept me reading long after I should have turned off the bedside light!' Amazon Review

'This is an extremely well-written book, and exceptionally enjoyable. It's difficult to put it down once started. Thank you for a

refreshing, historical fiction book that is also entertaining.' Dawn Edwards, Kindle Book Review

'Full of drama, intrigue and heartbreak.' Natalie Braine, Orion

'Kathleen Jones really understands the art of story and how it works. Her effortless-seeming prose had me completely engaged.' Pauline Fisk, Goodreads

'Wonderful! I felt I was not so much reading the book as living it.' Amazon Reviewer

'It is written with such passion and attention to detail that I slipped away easily into the worlds of Tamar and Anna.' Pink Fox.

THE SUN'S COMPANION

Nemesis is the name given to our sun's unidentified, dark, companion star, blamed for extinction events and other solar catastrophes. Nemesis was the figure of judgement in Greek mythology, who meted out the fates deserved by each individual from which none could escape.

A Book Mill Publication
Published by The Book Mill 2014

A CIP catalogue record for this book is available from the British Library.

ISBN 978-0-9574332-6-7

The Book Mill is an imprint of Ferber Jones Ltd., Bongate Mill, Appleby, CA16 6UR

Printed by CreateSpace

The Book Mill

THE SUN'S COMPANION

Kathleen Jones

PART I

DEPARTURES

1935 – 1937

'Come away, O human child!
To the waters and the wild
With a faery, hand in hand,
For the world's more full of weeping than you can understand.'

W.B. Yeats The Stolen Child

CHAPTER ONE

1935

'Tamar Fell's a bastard! Tamar Fell's a bastard!' Bertie McAffery was jumping up and down on the pavement in front of her, ginger hair flopping over his forehead, mouth pulled wide, screwed into a goggle-eyed gurning face as he taunted her. It was a warm afternoon and the bridge was crowded with children who'd come to watch the bigger boys dive into the river. Some of them took up the chant and soon they all seemed to be singing: 'Tamar Fell's a bastard! Tamar Fell's a bastard!' And then they began to recite a cruder rhyme – one that she hadn't heard before. 'Her mother's a cunt, who went with a runt, and she's another who'll go like her mother!' Every word was like a nail hammered into Tamar's brain, forcing her to shout, 'I'm not! I'm not! That's not true!' It wasn't just what they were saying, but the injustice of it that hurt. It was true that she didn't have a father – he'd died before she was born – but Sadie was Mrs Fell and wore a wedding ring and Tamar wasn't illegitimate, whatever people said.

Tamar screwed her fists up tight until her whole body trembled with the effort. She would be fourteen next year – almost grown up – and it was very unladylike to fight. But she knew from past experience that words had no power against bullies like these. Her only hope was to keep her head down and ignore them. At that moment it seemed to Tamar that she'd spent her whole life keeping quiet in order to avoid trouble. She couldn't remember a time when she hadn't felt anxious and wary. She burned to defend herself, to inflict some pain in revenge for the pain they inflicted on her, but she knew that if she lost her temper it would be a victory for her persecutors. 'They're just riff-raff!' Sadie had once said when Tamar tried to confide in her. 'Show them you're above it. If you fight back you're descending to their level.'

As she turned to walk away, Bertie made a rude sign with his fingers. Tamar knew that it was obscene, though she didn't really understand why.

Her friend Dora said, 'You're not going to let him get away with it, are you? Tamar, you're so wet!'

Bertie heard her and stuck out his tongue, shouting, 'Scaredy cat! Scaredy cat!'

Something snapped inside Tamar's head and she rushed at Bertie, taking him by surprise. He jumped up on the parapet to get out of the way. All the children were screaming now – 'A fight! A fight! Go it Bertie! Belt the bastard!' There was a red mist forming in Tamar's head. The boy's ankles were in front of her as he balanced on the parapet of the bridge. He was laughing at her. Hardly aware of what she was doing, she grabbed his toes and wrenched them backwards, digging her nails into his skin. He gave a tremendous shout, struggled to keep his footing and then, as Tamar pulled at his ankle, overbalanced and fell – not onto the pavement or into the deep pool beneath the central arch – but down, down, nearly fifteen feet into the shallow, rocky waters of the river below.

There was a terrible silence. Then a blonde haired girl was in front of Tamar shouting, 'You've killed him, that's what you've done. It's murder and you'll go to prison for ever and ever.' People were already rushing down the steps beside the bridge and Tamar could see that a man had jumped into the water and was pulling Bertie's limp body from the river. She had killed him. The pain in her stomach was almost unbearable. How could she have done something so stupid? So terrible. It was unendurable. Tamar looked at the shocked, accusing faces around her and turned and ran.

~~~~~~~~~~~~~~~~~~

Anna sat alone in the front row of desks feeling the hostile eyes of the entire class on the back of her neck. No one would speak to her and she didn't know why. Yesterday her best friend Elke Haagen who usually sat beside her had put up a hand and said,
~~~~~~~~~~~~~~~~~~

'Please Fraulein Muller, I request permission to sit at the back because of the unpleasant smell here.' And to Anna's astonishment, Fraulein Muller had told Elke that she could move her seat. Then Heidi Baumgarten in the desk on Anna's right put up her hand and by the end of the morning, Anna was sitting alone. She noticed that Fraulein Muller didn't look at her after that, and none of the other girls would talk to her in the playground. After school she walked home slowly on her own.

Elke Haagen was standing at the gate as she passed. 'Go away,' she said as Anna approached. 'I can't be friends with you anymore.'

'Why?' Anna asked indignantly. 'What's wrong with me?'

'My dad says you're a filthy Jew.'

'But I'm not!' Anna protested. 'You know I'm not. It's ridiculous!'

Elke shrugged. 'My dad says Weissmann's a Jewish name, and we don't like Jews. They stink.'

Anna knew that this was true. They'd been taught in school that Jews were ugly and unclean, the parasites of society and a source of corruption. But surely this didn't apply to her, or to her family? Her father had never mentioned anything about being Jewish, and her mother was English and went to the Lutheran church. At home that evening Anna waited for a suitable opportunity to ask her parents, but it never came. There was a strange atmosphere of anger and hostility. Her grandmother was upset. A letter had arrived telling her that Uncle Josef's shop had been vandalised in Freiburg. 'I don't know what things are coming to,' she said through her tears.

Things had begun to go wrong at the beginning of the summer. Willi Becker had come home on leave from the army, smart and important in his new uniform and he'd brought a kind of metropolitan glamour with him from the bierkellers of Munich. Most of the girls at school fancied him, except for Anna, who'd known him and his brother Klaus since they'd all been at Kindergarten together. The family lived next door and were as familiar to her as brothers and sisters. But Willi had changed. Anna noticed that he didn't talk to her any more, scarcely looked in her direction, though he flirted outrageously with some of her friends, particularly Elke. There was a carelessness, an arrogance, about him that Anna found distasteful. She heard him saying that he thought his father was a liberal fool and that the old burgers of the Stadtrat who ran the town were going to have a shock. Then Granny Weissmann, who'd nursed him as a baby and given him dried apple rings and cinnamon pastries whenever he came into her kitchen, came back from the Bäckerei and said that just as she was going in, he'd pushed rudely past her. She'd slipped and fallen in the doorway and he'd stepped over her and walked on as if she wasn't there.

'Well!' She kept saying, cradling her bruised elbow in her other hand. 'What are things coming to?'

Willi had been with Herr Becker when Anna and her father met them in the market square a couple of weeks ago and Anna's father had asked him, very kindly, how he liked the army. Willi pretended not to hear and walked off without replying. Herr Becker clapped his hand on her father's shoulder and said, 'I'm sorry. Young people . . . you know what they're like.' And he shrugged, shamefaced before he followed Willi. But then Anna noticed that Frau Becker didn't come and talk to her grandmother anymore and when she walked into town she walked on the opposite side of the street.

Anna also noticed that her parents had begun to argue more often. Not the noisy unresolved quarrels Anna was used to when her mother moaned about not being able to get soft white bread, the lack of plumbing and having to live with her mother-in-law and not having enough money. These were serious arguments conducted in hushed voices. Once Anna overheard her father say in English, 'There is nothing for us in England. It is not possible. Our livelihood is here.' There were tearful scenes that froze the instant Anna entered the room and whenever her parents were together the atmosphere seemed tense.

At school some of the boys had begun to appear in little black shorts and brown shirts until, one by one, almost all of them were in uniform. Only two boys in Anna's year were still wearing their ordinary clothes. One day these boys were called to the head teacher's office and they didn't come back. Someone whispered that they'd heard him saying 'We want only patriots here.'

Today, sitting alone at the front of the class, Anna felt nervous and vulnerable. Something was happening that she didn't understand and didn't know how to control.

In the break, Anna stood in a corner of the playground wondering how long she was going to be able to endure this enforced isolation. She'd known all these children since kindergarten, gone to youth camps with them, visited their houses. Soon, surely someone would tell them the truth and then they would realise how unjustly they were treating her? A group of boys came towards her laughing, but Anna knew instinctively that they meant to harm her. With rising panic she saw the boys spread out so that she couldn't escape. She realised too late that she was caught in the angle between the toilets and the boundary fence which was too high to climb. She was trapped.

They came so close she could smell the sweat on their bodies as they pressed her back against the rough wood. Anna kicked and bit and lashed out with her elbows in an attempt to evade the hands that tried to pin her down. But someone wrenched her arm behind her back and then two of the bigger boys caught hold of her by the hair and dragged her into the toilet block. They weren't proper toilets, just a wooden seat with a hole in it and a chute that carried everything down to a muck heap which was eventually taken away and spread on the fields. When Anna had been a small child, she'd been terrified of those black holes, nauseated by the smell and desperately afraid that some demon would rise up and pull her down into the suffocating filth beneath. The boys picked her up, twisted her arms and pushed her head down the chute so that the smell of shit rose like a taste into her mouth.

'That's where Jews go,' they shouted and then chanted. 'Jew, Jew, Jew.'

Anna was exhausted with struggling. Just as she thought she would pass out with the stench, Klaus Becker, Willi's brother, came into the toilet. He was one of the older boys now – almost old enough to leave and work on the farm with his father.

'Let her go,' he said quietly. 'That's enough.'

To Anna's relief they released their hold on her arms and she was able to struggle to her feet, coughing and spitting.

'Out,' he said to the boys with such a menacing tone that they left the toilet meekly. Anna began to stammer out her thanks but stopped as he turned to face her and she saw that the expression on his face was not sympathetic at all, but ugly. Klaus kicked the door shut behind him so that Anna couldn't get out, moved towards her and began to unbuckle his leather belt.

'Now I will show you what we do to Jews!' he said.

Tamar ran and ran through the dusty streets until she had a stitch in her side and her head ached. Ugly pictures kept appearing in her brain; Bertie McAffery's pale white body lying in the river; the shocked expressions on the faces around her. What would they do to her? Why, oh, why had she lost her temper like that? When the church clock struck six Tamar reluctantly dragged herself back to the lodging house where she lived with her mother. Sadie would be home from work. She would know what to do.

The front door was open and Sadie was standing on the step, looking anxiously out into the street. There was a policeman beside her. Tamar wondered what would happen to her now. Her heart was pounding so much she thought it would burst out of her chest.

Sadie looked grave. 'What have you done?' she asked, inclining her head towards the policeman. 'He says you pushed a boy off the bridge. It doesn't sound like you at all.'

'I tried to thump him. He was standing on the parapet . . and then he just fell over. I didn't mean to kill him.' Tamar burst into tears.

Sadie put her arm around her and gave Tamar a quick hug. 'It's all right,' she said gently. 'He broke his leg and he's got concussion, but he'll live.'

As Tamar sobbed against Sadie's shoulder, relief burned so fiercely inside her head that she felt dizzy.

'She doesn't look as if she'd hurt a fly,' the policeman said. He seemed surprised.

'They were calling me names – horrible things.'

'What kind of names?' the policeman asked.

It was the question Tamar had been dreading. 'They said I was . . .' She hesitated, looking at Sadie. But Sadie nodded encouragingly and Tamar had to go on. 'They called me a bastard. And there was a horrible rhyme they kept repeating.' Her face felt hot and swollen from crying.

Sadie's arms tightened around her. 'It's all right.' Her voice sounded strange. 'You don't have to say any more. It's all over now.'

Behind Sadie's shoulder, Tamar could see the landlady, Miss Simpson, hovering in the kitchen doorway.

'I think you'd better come in,' she said in a very sharp tone of voice. 'Standing out there on the step like that! I don't know what the neighbours are going to think.'

Sadie pulled a face only Tamar could see, then she turned to the policeman and said, 'Won't you come in?' as if he was a Sunday guest. She ushered him into the parlour asking 'Would you like a cup of tea?' Then she turned to Tamar, saying over her shoulder: 'You go up to bed, you look all in. I'll bring you something later.'

Sadie went into the parlour with the policeman. Tamar sat shivering on the stairs. She heard Sadie telling him what a gentle girl she was – she couldn't understand it. But of course it was an accident. Then she heard Sadie saying how difficult it was to bring up a child alone, her voice thickening as if she was about to cry. Through the crack in the door she could see the policeman patting her shoulder and hear him saying 'There, there, my dear' in a rather embarrassed kind of voice. As he stood up to go, Tamar slipped upstairs, took off her outer clothing and climbed between the sheets. Shortly afterwards she heard the front door thud shut and then raised voices in the kitchen. One of them Miss Simpson's. When Sadie came upstairs with a mug of Ovaltine and a plate of toast she looked flushed and her eyes were sparking.

'Is it going to be all right?' Tamar asked.

Sadie nodded. She sat down on the edge of the bed and her shoulders drooped as if she was tired. 'You mustn't mind what people say, Tamar. I know it's hard, but words can't hurt you. Just say "sticks and stones" to yourself when people call you names. Sometimes you just have to close your ears.'

'Will this mean we have to move again?' Tamar asked.

A strange shadow passed over Sadie's face. 'Of course not,' she said firmly. But her voice sounded weary. And then she shrugged. 'If we do, it won't be because of you.'

When Klaus let her go, Anna lay motionless with her eyes shut while he fastened his shorts and clattered the door to behind him. Then, slowly, she pulled herself to her feet. Her whole body shook. She cleaned the blood and slime from her legs with paper and put on her pants which had been thrown into a corner. The logical part of her mind still functioned, she realised with surprise, was still capable of decisions. 'I'm still alive,' Anna said out loud. Her voice sounded detached, oddly calm.

Lessons had restarted when Anna went outside and the yard was deserted. She took her coat and bag from her peg in the cloakroom and went out of the school gate. For the next hour Anna wandered the streets, the space between her legs raw, her stomach aching. She could feel painful bruises beginning to appear on her arms but her mind was numb and she was unable to answer any of the questions that came into it. What was she to tell her parents? How could she explain that she couldn't go back to school?

Feeling lost and miserable, Anna wound her way up the path towards the upper pastures, still rimed with frost, and wandered, shivering, through the pine forest that clothed its lower flank. Partenkirchen lay below her like a fairy tale town bathed in afternoon sunshine. She could see the Gasthof that her parents owned, the Becker's farm next door and the street of more imposing houses where the doctor and the wealthy burghers lived – Wilhelmstrasse, which was also the home of the two Miss B's who gave Anna lessons in English and painting.

Anna had lived in Partenkirchen all her life, except for a few months when she was five or six and her mother had taken her to stay with her grandparents in England. Her mother talked about it sometimes, nostalgically.

'Do you remember the time we took you to the Spanish City?' she would ask, and when Anna shook her head, she would sigh and look sad. Anna could remember walking along a street holding a candy floss in both hands carefully trying to bite into it without getting any of the pink sugar stuck to her nose or in her hair and walking straight into a lamp post because she couldn't see where she was going. She could still see the blackness behind her eyes, feel the hot bump on her forehead, and she could remember being taken by someone to stand outside a big stone building to wave at her mother, who was peering out of a window on one of the upper floors. Anna had not been told at the time, but knew now, that this was just after her mother had lost the baby who would have been her brother – a six month still birth. These two incidents were all Anna could remember of her stay in England, the rest was a blank space.

It disappointed Anna's mother, who was homesick and lonely. Mrs Weissmann found the German language difficult and had never learnt more than a few essential phrases, consequently she had few friends and those almost wholly among the small English community. To everyone in Partenkirchen, she was always 'the Englishwoman', a designation that set her apart – but one that she was proud of. Anna, only half English, felt she was being pulled in two directions, part of a mysterious battle that was being fought between her parents. Anna couldn't remember a time when she hadn't spoken German. She thought in German, dreamt in German. If it hadn't been necessary to speak English to her mother at home, she would quickly have forgotten it. Mrs Weissmann had been horrified to find that, by the time she was ten, Anna had begun to forget what she considered was her daughter's native language. So, three years ago, Anna had begun to go twice a week after school to the two English ladies who lived in the big house on the corner of Wilhelmstrasse. Miss Bateman and Miss Beatham.

Barbara Beatham, thin and tall, wore long, heavy woollen skirts even in summer, Edwardian blouses with leg o'mutton sleeves and tight, buttoned jackets braided at the cuffs. Hester Bateman was almost as wide as she was tall and even more eccentric than her companion. She ventured out in tweed knickerbockers, a man's Tyrolean jacket and long woollen socks, with what she called a gamekeeper's cape thrown over the whole. It was a bizarre sight watching them walk along the street together – Barbara taking elegant strides, Hester lurching from side to side in an attempt to keep up. Anna gave them English nicknames to fit their initials – Honey Bee and Bumble Bee. The Two Bees. One of them – it would have been impolite to ask which – had come to Partenkirchen for a weakness of the lungs, to stay at the sanatorium perched above the town. The other had come to keep her friend company. Finding that the climate suited their health, they had stayed. There was family money, Anna's father had explained, that made it possible for them to live without having to work.

Their house was as extraordinary as its occupants. In direct contrast to the heavy, hand carved wooden furniture of Anna's own home, theirs was flimsy and delicate. There were silver ornaments, photographs, bone china figurines and shelves and shelves of books. Every afternoon they had English tea from a silver teapot, drunk from shell-thin porcelain cups, and ate scones with butter and French preserves. Almost everything was sent out from England in Fortnum and Mason hampers. Sometimes they would give Anna half a dozen hot scones wrapped in a napkin to take back to her mother. At first, Miss Beatham taught Anna about English literature and the grammar of the written word. Then quite by accident Miss Bateman had seen one of her drawings – a piece of paper with a rough sketch of the houses on the main street with their long verandas and deep, carved eaves, that Anna had tucked into the back of an exercise book and forgotten.

'Who did this?' Miss Bateman asked and when Anna admitted that she had drawn it, became quite excited. She made Anna draw the bowl of flowers on the table, watching over her shoulder as Anna moved the pencil swiftly across the paper. She and Miss Beatham pored over the quick sketch for a long time. 'You have a considerable gift,' Miss Bateman said at last. 'A natural, unspoilt talent for observing and recording.'

Hester Bateman explained that she herself was actually a water-colourist and had gone to a college in London to study art when she was young, but had been unable to finish her studies. 'It was a waste,' she said. 'Your talents must not be wasted.' So the two Bees paid a visit to Anna's family. Her mother was curiously against it.

'She's supposed to be improving her English,' Mrs Weissmann said. 'What use is art?'

But Anna's father was supportive. 'If she has a gift, then she should be encouraged. Though where we're to find the money, I don't know.'

But soon it was agreed that, in addition to the English class, which would continue to be paid for, Miss Bateman would give Anna lessons free of charge in drawing and water-colour and art history. Books were dragged out of trunks and pored over on the polished tables – paintings and colours that Anna had never dreamed might exist. She had never seen anything other than a couple of prints her mother had on the living room wall, or illustrations in story books.

Gradually the English literature began to slip, two days a week became three and soon she went every day after school for an hour, to read, talk, draw. Miss Bateman lent her Ruskin's Elements of Drawing and Anna began to work her way painfully through the exercises, hatching and cross-hatching, line and form, light and shade, the principles of perspective. Anna's life had suddenly been filled with urgency and excitement. Summer was her least favourite season because she had to help her family in the Gasthof and there was little time for drawing or painting. But in the winter when the snow clogged the roads and the days shortened, she could spend hours in her room wearing woollen gloves with the finger ends cut out, copying the pictures in the books lent to her by the Two Bees. Her life had swung in a happy rhythm. Until now.

Anna heard the chimes of the school bell echoing up the walls of the valley. It was time to go down. Instinctively she walked in the direction of Wilhelmstrasse but as she turned into the street, she saw Willi Becker and his friend Hans Muller standing outside the Bees' house. They were wearing their uniforms and smoking cigarettes, standing with their backs to her, facing the other end of the street – the direction she usually took when she came from school. Anna stood quite still. She couldn't explain why, but she had a feeling that they were waiting for her. Quietly she turned back, slipping out of sight behind someone's winter wood pile. She would have to go home another way.

When she reached the Gasthof, she opened the door slowly and dragged herself into the warm kitchen. She felt so cold her bones ached with it and her stomach felt hollow. Anna hoped that neither her mother nor her grandmother would ask any questions about her day at school. But the chair beside the stove, usually occupied by Anna's grandmother, was empty, and her mother was standing at the table with her heavy winter coat on. Two bags bulging with clothes and a number of other articles parcelled up in brown paper were stacked beside the stove.

'Keep your coat on, Anna.' Mrs Weissmann said tersely, and went on cutting slabs of rye bread, reaching a sausage down from its hook on the ceiling and slicing it between the thick, dark wedges.

'Where are we going?'

'Never you mind.'

'Where's Gran?'

'She's gone to Freiburg with your father to see Uncle Joe.'

'What's happening?' Anna asked, holding her hands in front of the stove to warm them. There was something in the nervous haste of her mother's actions and the way she spoke that alarmed Anna and made the pit of her stomach flutter. Had the family discovered what had happened to her? For a moment Anna thought she was going to be sick with shame.

Mrs Weissmann was wrapping the sandwiches in oiled paper, but she paused and turned wearily towards Anna. 'We're going on a visit to your other grandparents. But you mustn't say anything to anyone.'

'We're going to England?' Anna was incredulous. 'Today? Aren't we going to wait to say goodbye to Papa or Gran?' She was horrified.

'Anna, please don't be difficult, not today. We can't say goodbye to anyone.' Her mother's voice was sharp with desperation. 'I can't explain. We have to go and we have to go now.' As she grasped Anna by the arms and pushed her towards the door, Mrs Weissmann's hands were shaking violently.

'Wait!' Anna said, her mind whirling with confused thoughts. 'There's something I have to get.' She twisted herself out of her mother's grasp and ran up the steep wooden stairs to her bedroom – a narrow loft above the kitchen. She stood for a few moments in the quiet room, breathing hard to quell the panic that made her head too dizzy to think. Then she opened a drawer and took out her sketch book and pencils and from the shelf above it a book of Renaissance prints that had been a present from Miss Bateman. She pushed them both inside her coat, tightened her belt with fingers curiously numb and clumsy and took a long look round the room that had been hers for the last thirteen years.

Mrs Weissmann's voice called urgently up the stairs. 'Hurry, hurry!' She sounded desperate with anxiety. Everything was confused in Anna's head like the whirling flakes inside the glass snowstorm that stood on her bedside table. It had been a present from her grandmother for her seventh birthday. Anna reached out and put it in her pocket, feeling the weight of it swelling the fabric out into a huge bulge against her hip. When Anna came down again, her mother grabbed her arm and swept out of the house, letting the door thump to behind them without even locking it. She pulled Anna along the street so fast she could scarcely keep her feet. Past the end of Wilhelmstrasse and down towards the railway station. There were soldiers standing in a little group just outside the entrance and Anna felt her mother hesitate. The hand gripping Anna's arm trembled. Anna had never been aware before of so many soldiers, so many policemen in Partenkirchen. Her heart almost stopped beating. Was this something to do with her? Was this what her mother was so afraid of?

'Say nothing,' her mother whispered. 'Just walk past.'

To Anna's relief the soldiers didn't even turn their heads as they passed through the turnstile onto the platform where the small branch line train sat smoking and belching.

'Ask for two tickets to Nuremberg,' Anna's mother breathed into her ear. 'Quickly!'

'Zwei Fahrkarten nach Nürnberg, bitte,' Anna said obediently, passing over the money her mother gave her.

They scrambled aboard the train with only seconds to spare before the carriage shuddered and groaned and began its slow, grinding descent from the mountain valley to the plain below. There, they had to change to a mainline express and at Köln they changed again for a destination Anna couldn't even pronounce. The train was so crowded it was difficult to get through the door and once inside, impossible to find a seat. They sat on their bags in the corridor, squeezed against each other by the cram of people.

'Don't talk to anyone, no matter what they say to you.' Anna's mother said, her manner so severe that Anna became really frightened. 'And if you have to speak at all, speak only in English. Only English do you hear?'

Anna's mouth was so dry she could only nod, and for the rest of the long journey she kept silent. Every now and then, some official or other would force his way into the carriage to look at their tickets and Anna's mother would wave her passport in front of him saying 'English, English' and they would nod curtly and move on. Anna slept a lot, particularly when it became dark and the rhythm of wheel on rail lulled her into unconsciousness, slumped against the rough woollen shoulder of her mother's coat.

Once when the train stopped she was sleepily aware that there was shouting – some sort of argument. Anna opened her eyes and saw two guards pushing an elderly man in a dark hat and woollen overcoat. One of them snatched the bundle he held under his arm and threw it out of the door. He was protesting, pleading and then the other guard hit him, hard across the face. Anna's mother, realising she was awake, put her hand over Anna's eyes and pulled her closer, holding her very tight. There was more shouting, the sound of the train door banging, someone crying, and then the train jerked and began to move again.

'We're going home, Anna,' her mother murmured. 'Home.'

Anna didn't reply. Home to her was a small town in the clear light of the Alps. Every puff of smoke from the funnel was taking her further and further away from everything she loved.

CHAPTER TWO

Just as Tamar began to descend the stairs, the tread croaked under her foot, forcing her to pause in mid step, her legs trembling with the effort of holding still.

'For god's sake be quiet!' Sadie hissed over her shoulder and Tamar shivered with fear and shame.

The staircase tipped away from her as steeply as a railway embankment, down towards the gloom of the hallway. The bottom step seemed impossibly far. At the foot of the stairs the pale winter sun made two coloured hop-scotch squares on the floor through the stained glass above the front door. Once they were outside that door they would be safe, but the old black linoleum treads, spattered with candle grease and capped with rubber, complained at every step. Tamar tried not to imagine what would happen if she tripped. In her head she saw the suitcase burst open, her mother's shoes in their little cotton bags, the crystal spray bottle of Milles Fleures, powder jars and tortoiseshell-backed brushes rattling, bouncing and banging down the stairs like dinner gongs, summoning all the other lodgers to witness their attempted flight.

This was not the kind of adventure that happened to any of the girls in her School Friend magazine, where all the girls had names like Kitty or Sylvia and went to boarding school in Tunbridge and had exciting holidays in the south of France. None of them ever lived in cheap lodgings or had mothers who argued about the rent. Tamar had heard part of the conversation on the landing the night before. 'Two weeks owing!' That had been said very sharply. Then there was some murmuring in her mother's voice and then Miss Simpson's strident Yorkshire accent again. 'If you can't pay by Friday you're out. We don't want your sort here!' Tamar had covered her ears with the eiderdown to block out the rest. She knew what was coming and she dreaded it.

Sweating with effort, Tamar was carrying a small brown suitcase and the round leather hat box, taking care not to let them bump against the banisters. Her mother, Sadie, struggled with two larger suitcases, one in each hand and a bag looped around her wrist. She was cursing in a vicious undertone because the corner of the case had snagged her only decent pair of stockings. They would have to be darned, and Sadie hated darned stockings.

'They tell people you haven't any money, as surely as if you'd shouted it across the street,' she said. Tamar knew it was important when you moved to a new place to create the right impression and Sadie had dressed very carefully in her best grey two piece with a matching little velvet toque and veil pinned to the side of her head with a cherry-red hatpin.

The stairs stank of bleach and dogs – two horrible brown and white terriers yapping and scratching on the other side of the kitchen door. But they were nearly at the bottom now. Tamar could see through the open parlour door and read the glass-framed text that hung above the pedal organ; 'The Lord Observeth Everything – The Lord Knoweth Everything', embroidered in large elaborate letters on black linen. Tamar hoped it wasn't true. Reflected in the glass, she could also see old Mrs Simpson dozing in the arm chair. She was wearing a navy wool afternoon dress and a fairisle cardigan to hide the patches under her arms where the sweat had eaten holes in the fabric, and her lap was piled with the old rags she coughed and spat into. 'Is that you back, Ella?' she enquired querulously in a voice thick with bronchitis. But Miss Simpson wasn't there. On Thursday mornings she met her sister in town and they went to the cemetery to put flowers on their father's grave before having lunch in Emsleys.

The voice called again, but Sadie didn't answer. She put the cases down on the door mat, turned the handle gently and then went out, motioning Tamar to pull the door to behind them. Tamar didn't need to be told to close it with only the faintest click, as the tongue of the lock slid back into the latch. 'Thank God the old bat's deaf,' Sadie said. She turned purposefully along the street in the opposite direction to the parlour window.

The wind stung Tamar's legs between her socks and the hem of last winter's coat. Her toes hurt where they scraped against the paper scrunched up inside her new shoes. Sadie always bought them a size too big to allow for growth, but it made walking painful until Tamar got used to it. She didn't bother to ask whether anyone was collecting them. Tamar had been through this experience often enough to know what to expect. Their departures were solitary, clandestine affairs. Only rarely had one of the 'uncles' been there to collect them.

When Tamar looked back at her childhood she remembered a succession of Uncles, men who came to take her mother out, who fixed them somewhere to live and took Tamar to the Fair, or the afternoon matinee and bought her candy floss and dolls that wet their pants and made a mewling sound when she turned them over. 'Say thank you to Uncle Richard,' Sadie would say, giving her a little nudge between the shoulder blades. 'Be nice to Uncle Richard.' It was wonderful while it lasted, but then there would always be some sort of crisis. This time had been no exception. There had been a letter that left Sadie distraught and too unwell to go to work. Then delivery vans brought flowers and boxes filled with tissue paper and crêpe de chine. After Tamar had gone to bed, pretending to be asleep, her mother had cried for hours. And when Sadie got up for breakfast the next day her eyes were swollen and her hair unrolled, dangling pins and loose strands down the back of her neck. For a week or so after that Sadie moped and wept. But gradually her chin had come up again, she'd gone to have her hair done at the beauty shop and then she'd begun to scan the small adverts at the back of the papers. Tamar knew exactly what would happen next.

They were going to move again. Sadie was full of plans. Everything would get better in a new place, the people would be nicer, the rooms cleaner, there would be better jobs. When she was very young, Tamar had believed her. But she was thirteen now, old enough to know better. Every time Tamar moved, it seemed that she left a part of herself behind. And there was always some precious belonging, a doll, or a book, that couldn't be squeezed into the cases and had to be abandoned. This time it was her teddy bear, Angus. His tartan scarf was threadbare and his fur almost worn away where she'd sucked him for comfort when she was little. 'You're much too old for such things now Tamar,' Sadie had said throwing him back on the bed with the pile of cast-offs they were leaving behind. But when Sadie went downstairs to the toilet, Tamar picked him up, undid the belt of her dress and tucked him into the small of her back, re-fastening the belt round her and putting her coat on quickly. She could feel his head bumping up against her spine as she followed Sadie down towards the station.

This was the second move in a year, and each time the rooms had got smaller and shabbier. Tamar's mother rarely kept a job for long – they were all too demeaning. After all, Sadie Fell had once been private secretary to the Marquis of Bath. But that had been before Tamar was born, in the west country somewhere, before they'd begun to move further and further north. In the hatbox there was a photograph of Sadie taken when she was young. It was framed in brown leather with initials embossed on the cover.

Sadie had her head turned slightly to one side, her blonde hair crimped into waves and lit from above so that she looked just like Mary Pickford. Sadie always kept it on the dressing table, but sometimes when she was feeling depressed she turned it face down so that she didn't have to look at it. 'Don't get old,' she said to Tamar. 'Just don't!' Sadie's hair was darker now, and there were lines under her eyes. She spent a lot of time in front of the mirror massaging Yardley's vanishing cream into her face and neck with the firm, upward strokes recommended by the magazines. And on her 'down days', as she called them, she treated herself to a little glass of tonic, which, on very down days, sometimes stretched to several. Tamar had begun to notice the regular appearance of bottles in the rubbish, discreetly wrapped in newspaper parcels so that they wouldn't give themselves away.

As they walked down the street Tamar could see curtains twitching in the windows. Somewhere a door slammed. 'At least we won't have to live with such spiteful neighbours,' Sadie said. 'It was none of their business. Such insinuations!' She held her head higher and her back straighter in spite of the suitcases. It was something they taught young ladies at finishing school, Sadie had told Tamar. They made you walk up and down with a book on your head with a kind of gliding, flowing step so that the book stayed on the same level all the time. Tamar had tried it on the landing during the school holidays when everyone was out at work and Miss Simpson and her mother safely in the parlour for their afternoon snooze. But however carefully she straightened her neck and stuck her chin out, the book would never stay on her head.

Sadie was trying very hard to bring Tamar up to be a lady. Sadie had told her that the aristocracy was like a kind of club. They used all sorts of tricks and tests to separate members from non-members, a bit like a Mason's handshake, only more difficult. Take a name like Ralph, for instance. If you were One of Them you pronounced it Rafe; if you said it like everyone else, they would know you weren't. Similarly St John was Sinjun, and looking glasses must never be called mirrors – that was vulgar and the People-who-Mattered would find you out instantly. Sadie knew all about these things. She was One of Them, even though she didn't have any money now and had to live on her wits, as she put it.

Uncle Richard had not been One of Them, even though he was quite wealthy. He had grey hair and yellow leather driving gloves. He'd collected her mother on Tuesdays and Thursdays and driven her off in his Armstrong Siddeley. One day, about a month ago when Sadie was ill, he'd taken Tamar out instead. She remembered how excited she'd been. Putting on her best frock, though it was six months too small and straining at the buttons where her breasts were beginning to expand inside the ugly cotton liberty bodice she was forced to wear. The bulge made Tamar self-conscious, in spite of the cardigan she borrowed from her mother's drawer to hide it. She didn't like the way Uncle Richard looked at her when she got into the car, or the way his hand kept brushing her knee when he changed gear. When he stopped the car on top of the moor to admire the view, he draped his arm along the back of the seat.

Tamar could smell the tobacco on his jacket. She shrank against the door, keeping her eyes turned away.

'You can come a little closer, you know,' he said. 'I won't bite.'

'I'm all right, thank you,' Tamar said, looking straight ahead where the walls ran down the moor towards the grey stone farm buildings.

She sensed that he wasn't pleased, and shortly afterwards he got out of the car, walked round the back bumper and began to pee against the wheel of the car. She could see him in the wing mirror. She knew about such things, of course, but it was the first time she'd seen a man's organ and it shocked her. It was like the swollen, purple tongue that poked from the mouth of Miss Simpson's younger brother ('A late mistake,' she'd whispered to Sadie when they moved in) who was kept locked up in a room on the other side of the landing. During the day Tamar could hear him shuffling around, moaning to himself and sometimes he would rattle the door handle and Miss Simpson would come upstairs and tell him to be quiet. Something of the fear Tamar felt whenever she passed that locked door, had surged through her as she'd turned her horrified eyes away from the mirror. Uncle Richard must have known she could see, but he got back into the car, started up the engine and drove her back without a word.

'Did you have a nice time?' Sadie had asked when she came back. Sadie's eyes were closed and she looked hot and uncomfortable lying among the pillows.

'He tried to cuddle me,' Tamar said, beginning to cry.

Her mother's eyes had flown open. 'You didn't let him did you?'

'Of course not. It was horrid.'

It was just after that, all the trouble had started and Tamar had a guilty feeling that they were having to leave because she had somehow upset Uncle Richard.

Tamar was sorry to leave this town. She loved the soaring cathedral that dominated the roof line, the medieval streets where the houses bent over towards each other as if they were gossiping, the way the moors turned purple in summer, rising up behind the chimneys of the woollen mills. On the way to the station they crossed the bridge over the river and Tamar shivered when she remembered how she'd pushed Bertie McCaffery off and nearly killed him because he'd called her a bastard. That had been one of the worst things that had ever happened to her and even thinking about it still gave Tamar a pain in her stomach. But the bullying had stopped afterwards. The children had all left her alone and she'd been treated with wary respect. Even Sadie had said 'I didn't know you had it in you, Tamar,' in an admiring kind of tone. But it frightened her to know that she had such a powerful force inside her. Supposing he had died? It had made Tamar aware that there were moments in time when on the turn of a coin, a split second, your whole life could be turned upside down. It was only luck that had saved her and she mustn't ever let it happen again.

Now they were leaving all this behind, heading further north, following the track of the Great North Road which Tamar imagined running northwards forever until it ran out of land. How far they were going this time, Tamar couldn't guess and knew better than to ask. She wondered which side the coin would fall this time, or whether her luck had finally run out.

Anna lay in bed, listening to the strident cry of gulls nesting in a neighbour's chimney, and wished she was back in Bavaria. The light filtering into the room through the lace curtain was dim and grey. At Partenkirchen, even in winter, the sun striking off the snow-fields of the Zugspitze would fill the room with a bright glare, and in summer the warmth beat back from the pine boards like a stove. Every morning, winter or summer Anna had jumped out of bed when her mother called and pulled back the wooden shutters to look out at the mountains. But here, in this cold, ugly, northern town where everything smelled of salt, fish and coal dust, the streets outside were a meaningless jangle – hardly worth opening the curtains for. Anna missed the early-morning peace and quiet of the Alps where she could lie in bed, half awake, and listen to the distant metallic bell claps of the goats and cattle, the jingling of horse harness, the herd-boys' echoing calls. In the winter their voices were muffled by the silence of snow which absorbed every other sound like thick white blotting paper and filled the room with its strange blue light. Anna also missed the deep feather quilts and pillows that had wrapped her in a warm cocoon on cold winter nights. Here, the beds were made with sheets that twisted themselves up in the night and scratchy blankets that were continually letting in draughts. The only thing that was better in England was the plumbing – the luxury of having a proper bath and a flush toilet. At least she would never have to go into an earth closet again. She shuddered involuntarily as the memory flashed across her mind. The sound of a door slamming, the taunting voices of the children who had once been friends and neighbours, Klaus Becker spitting on the floor . . .

Anna found it difficult to think about what had happened to her in the days before they had left. It seemed unreal and distant now, as though it had happened to someone else. Outwardly Anna knew she appeared to be the same, but inwardly she was aware of a dislocation. There were two people in her head now with two separate lives, one German, one English. The hidden bruise belonged to the German self. It was an internal wound that bled every month, something that had begun the very evening they had arrived in England. Anna knew she could never tell anyone what had been done to her. But every monthly bleeding was a reminder and sometimes in the night she woke sobbing from a dream she couldn't remember. There were times when men looked at her in the street and she was immobilised with terror.

Downstairs in the kitchen a lazy contralto rose in an ascending scale. 'Swee-ee-eet Kate. So-o-o late. . .' Her mother had recently joined a madrigal society and practised the lines whenever she could. Outside, the early buses were already running on the coast road, taking people to work, and Anna could hear the different notes of vans and wagons and bicycle bells, even the occasional hollow clop and rattle of a horse-drawn vehicle. She longed fiercely for her father and wondered what he was doing at this moment. How had he felt when he came back from Freiburg and found them gone? It had shocked Anna to discover that her mother had left without telling either her husband or her mother in law what she'd intended to do. The evening they'd arrived, exhausted, at her English grandparents' front door after a terrible journey, Anna had listened with a mounting, vicious anger, to her mother telling them the story of their abrupt departure.

'Such awful things were happening, but they wouldn't hear of me bringing Anna back to England,' she said. 'Otto's brother lost his job at the University, and then his brother-in-law's shop was burned out in some kind of riot. I was terrified.'

Anna heard her mother telling them how she had seized the opportunity offered when her husband and mother-in-law went to visit relatives, and had thrown a few clothes and mementos into bags leaving a note on the kitchen table.

'It's fortunate that Anna's still under fourteen and could travel on my passport. Thank goodness I still had it.' Sitting in the armchair in her parents' sitting room in front of the fire, Mrs Weissmann sounded triumphant, and her eyes glowed as if she had won a marvellous victory. Anna seethed with rage. How could her mother have done such a terrible, cruel thing to Papa? It had gradually dawned on Anna that this wasn't just a holiday; they were going to be here for a long time and she hadn't been allowed to say goodbye.

Since then there had been letters, written in her father's stilted English. Mrs Weissmann didn't let Anna read them – only the last line which usually said, 'Kiss Anna for me and do not let her forget her Grossmutter.' It made Anna writhe with anger. How could she forget someone she loved so much, a person so unlike her English grandmother, Mrs Cotteslow. Grandfather Cotteslow, or Grandpa as she was expected to call him, wasn't too bad, but her grandmother was positively repulsive, and they both called her Anne. The first time it had happened she'd reminded them politely that her name was Anna, thinking that they'd made a mistake. But after the second time Granny Cotteslow had said, 'Oh but it isn't, my dear. You were christened Anne Clara; Anne after me and Clara after your German granny.' And she made Grandpa open the bureau and get out a birth certificate. There it was in front of her in decorative official German script – Anne Clara, born February 4th 1922 at St Bernard's Clinic, Partenkirchen to Barbara Weissmann nee Cotteslow and Otto Benjamin Weissmann, occupation Merchant Seaman.

'I don't care what I was christened,' Anna said, jumping up and throwing the certificate back into her grandmother's lap. 'My name is Anna and I'm not changing it for anyone!'

Since then Anna had begun a mutinous campaign of silence.

Whenever her grandparents called her Anne, she ignored them. Her grandmother was furious. 'I don't know why you let her get away with it, Barbara,' she would say to Anna's mother. 'If you'd behaved like that at her age . . .' And Mrs Weissmann would sigh and say 'I know, I know. But you have to make allowances, mother. Just leave her alone and she'll come round.' As Anna listened to them talking about her as if she wasn't there, she would have given anything for her father to walk into the room. She missed him dreadfully. Sometimes she was so homesick her stomach ached with it.

Mrs Weissmann put her head round the door. 'It's time to get up. We've got to go and look at schools today.'

Anna flung herself back against the pillows. 'Do we have to? Why can't we go back home? I hate it here!' Her voice sounded petulant even to herself. She hadn't meant the words to come out like that.

Her mother came into the room and sat down on the end of the bed. 'Please don't be difficult Anna.' She looked upset. 'I know it's hard for you. I know how close you and your father were. But some day you'll thank me for this.'

'Why can't we go back?'

Mrs Weissmann's face flushed. 'There are reasons. I can't tell you now. Let's just see how things go.' She put her hand on Anna's arm briefly as if to comfort her and then got up and went out of the room. A tantalising smell of bacon floated up from the kitchen through the open door. Reluctantly Anna pushed back the blankets and got out of bed. Her clothes lay on the chair in an untidy mound. Slowly she put them on, avoiding having to look at herself in the mirror, beginning the translation from German Anna to English Anne that would happen as soon as she went downstairs.

Sadie hurried Tamar onto the train before she could make sense of the destination boards, finding a compartment with only one other woman in it. The luggage, too heavy to lift onto the rack, was piled just inside the door to deter anyone else from entering. Sadie sighed as she sat down in the vacant window seat, eased off her gloves, pulled down the blind and lay back against the prickly velvet plush with her eyes closed. By the time the train had jerked and bumped its way out of the station and across the points onto the main line, Sadie was asleep. It was Sadie's way of coping with boredom. She had the knack of falling asleep instantly like an animal, cleverly turning her head to one side and propping it on her hand so that her jaw didn't sag open in an unladylike fashion.

The elderly woman opposite looked at Tamar with curious, conversational eyes. She had a silver-mounted bird's claw in the lapel of her camel coat. 'Going far, my dear?' she asked, offering a paper bag of sweets across the carriage.

Tamar took one politely. They were butterscotch. 'To Scotland, I think,' she said.

'Really? Do you have relatives there?'

Tamar shook her head, 'I'm an orphan.' She glanced quickly at the unconscious Sadie, but her mother's breathing maintained a steady rhythm.

'Really!' The woman leaned forward slightly, and her faded eyes glittered with interest.

Tamar ran her tongue over her dry lips and then said 'When I was a baby I was found floating in a lifeboat on the sea just out of Plymouth Sound and no one knew who I was. That's why I'm called Tamar. After the river.' It was one of her fantasies, one of the many tales she had constructed to fill the information gap when people asked where she came from and other awkward questions about her family that she didn't know how to answer. Tamar waited, watching the effects of her story on the woman opposite – it was very gratifying to be believed. The woman leaned forward as if waiting for more. 'I was in an orphanage,' Tamar went on recklessly, 'and now I'm being taken to Scotland to be adopted.'

'Well I never!' the woman said. She offered the paper bag again and Tamar took another butterscotch, popping the first into her mouth so as to preclude further communication. A hot needle, part excitement, part fear, was shooting up her spine making her sit up very straight. A voice inside her head was reciting, over and over to the rhythm of the carriage wheels, 'Tamar Fell will go to hell, and the Devil will come and cut out her tongue!' But it was partly true, she told herself. Having no father and no family history – certainly none that Sadie had ever wanted to impart – made one an orphan, or at least half an orphan. And she had often, when she was younger, wished that she could be adopted into a proper family with parents who didn't spend time climbing out of windows or scurrying down back alleys to avoid having to pay the rent.

The woman got out when the train stopped at the next station and Sadie woke up and straightened her hat. One of her cherry red gloves had fallen on the floor. 'I wasn't snoring was I?' she asked.

Tamar shook her head. Her back was beginning to ache with the effort of not being able to lean against the seat in case she squashed Angus. The journey seemed interminable. But eventually the train slowed again, running between the backs of houses in endless, identical rows, allotment plots, factories and pitheads with turning wheels and a mountainscape of black slag heaps. Then they trundled slowly across an iron bridge, very high above a broad river. Looking down through the trellised metal, Tamar could see cranes and dockyards, barges filled with coal, a tug manoeuvring a cargo ship in mid-river.

The station was bigger than Tamar had expected. They seemed to walk for miles across platforms and bridges before they reached the entrance. Sadie took a piece of paper out of the pocket of her tailored suit and showed it to the porter. 'You'll have to take the trolley bus,' he said. 'But it's a canny way!' Everyone talked with a strange accent, high and nasal, as if they were singing the words slightly out of tune.

'I thought we were going to Scotland?' Tamar said. She was sure she'd heard someone asking the conductor whether the train went straight through to Edinburgh..

'Don't be silly!' It was the same words and the same tone of voice that Sadie had once used when Tamar was eight or nine and had asked, as she unpacked her suitcase, 'Are we going to stay here for ever?' Tamar had never asked again.

Sadie was consulting the numbers above the trolley stop. 'I think this is the right one.' She put the cases down wearily and began to massage her arms. Sadie always got excited about going to a new town. Tamar could feel the little bursts of energy that emanated from her like electricity. In spite of the journey and the weight of the suitcases, Sadie held her head up, alert, looking around her with bright anticipating eyes. Tamar was weary of changing places. The emotional effort of getting to know people all over again, perhaps becoming fond of them, knowing that one day soon she'd move on and have to say goodbye. Her friend Dora had made Tamar promise to write, but she knew she wouldn't. What would be the point? They'd never see each other again. The crumpled piece of paper with her address on it had been left behind with the other rubbish at Miss Simpson's.

Tamar had never seen a trolley bus before. They were yellow, double decked, with a kind of gantry that unfolded from the roof and gripped an overhead cable. They were almost silent, apart from a faint whine as they approached and a sharp, pneumatic hiss when they stopped. Tamar amused herself watching the other people on the bus. Here in this town the faces were different. People were watchful, sharp-eyed, the lines more deeply cut. They smiled more rarely.

Heaton Street, when they reached it, was yet another street of dirty house-fronts, dull red bricks stained with the sooty rain from railways, coal mines, steel furnaces and even the chimneys of the houses themselves, puffing up grey columns of cheap sea coal or nutty slack. At the top of the street there were green fields, pegged out into housing plots with wooden posts and beyond them, across the road that led to the sea, the long, white outline of a cigarette factory and its landmark chimney. A damp, salty wind, smelling strongly of fish blew in from the direction of the docks, tainting the air with an acrid, sour odour that prickled the inside of Tamar's nose.

The doorbell rang for a long time before they heard the grating sound of bolts being drawn and the door was tugged open about six inches. A woman stood in the gap, dressed in a floral, crêpe de chine dress that was at least two sizes too big for her gaunt figure. She looked surprised to see them.

'Are you Mrs Kennedy?' Sadie asked. Tamar could hear doubt and anxiety in her voice. 'I wrote to you about a room.'

The door was opened fully and the woman smiled. 'Come on in, pet. Sorry it took so long, but we don't have much call for the front door. It's either the undertaker or the debt collector. Most people go round the back.' Mrs Kennedy's face was lean and bony, with sunken, black-shadowed eyes and a wide, thin mouth outlined in orange lipstick. Her hair was dyed crow black, pinned up in a strange sort of pleat at the front of her head and frizzed at the sides. Her husband had been lost at sea in the Great War, she told Sadie over a cup of tea, making him sound like a parcel that had been inadvertently dropped overboard. She and her son George slept downstairs and rented out the upstairs to lodgers.

The house had a characteristic smell of cigarettes, chip fat and gas. 'You have to watch the gas poker,' Lily explained, 'If's the tap not just right, it leaks.' The decor was immaculate. Lily's husband had decorated it before he disappeared. 'A proper job,' she said with grudging pride as she showed them upstairs, running her fingers down the shiny doors, varnished in dark brown and combed and swirled in an unconvincing imitation of wood grain. The rooms were papered with Victorian trellises of peonies and roses, whose vivid colours didn't quite match the brocade curtains. The effect was dark and ponderous. 'I'd've had all the woodwork cream if it'd been my choice,' Lily sighed. 'And some nice pieces of chintz for the curtains. But it'll last my lifetime out.' She looked gloomily up at the ceiling through a cloud of cigarette smoke.

The back bed-room upstairs was only large enough for a double bed, a dressing table and a huge Victorian triple wardrobe that looked as if the room had been built round it. 'God knows how they got it up here!' Sadie said when she saw it. She bent down to look under the bed for slut's wool, but the linoleum was immaculate. There was a towel horse in one corner next to a small washstand with bowl, bucket and jug and a peeling notice on the wall which read 'No Washing to be Dried in the Room'. Tamar knew that Sadie would ignore it, rinsing out her knickers, stockings and underarm dress-shields every night, as she always did before she went to bed, balancing them on the towel horse to dry.

Sadie had once explained that the further north you went, the cheaper it got, but it seemed that they could still only afford one room. Sadie kept a five pound note folded up in a silk-lined bead evening bag at the bottom of the hat box. She only broke into it for emergencies, replacing it as soon as she could. There had been a fuss at the station when Sadie handed it over for the tickets, and she had had to write her name and address on the back. It had seemed a great deal of money, but Tamar could see, when her mother unclipped her purse and took out enough to pay the rent in advance that there was only a pound note and a few shillings left in it. When Sadie had gone downstairs with Lily to tour the rest of the house, Tamar quickly removed Angus from her belt and tucked him under the pillow on her usual side of the bed before she followed them down. The back door opened into a little yard. On the right-hand side there was a latched door painted green that opened into the toilet, a damp, brick cubicle with rough walls covered in yellow distemper which, Tamar knew from experience, came off on your clothes unless you were very careful. But the floor was clean, the broad wooden seat was comfortable and there was a box of antiseptic-smelling toilet paper in a metal holder.

Next to it was the wash-house with a big copper in the corner over a fire grate, and several large brass taps to let the water in and out. There was a crate of bottled beer sitting in the shallow stone sink and on the lines overhead were the most enormous corsets Tamar had ever seen. They were miracles of engineering – immense ramparts of pink satin decorated by a complicated arrangement of eye holes and laces. A collection of metal rulers, which had been removed for the wash, were lined up in order of size on the scrubbing board.

In the other corner of the yard a gate opened into the alleyway that ran like a tunnel through the terrace between Lily's house and the next, leading to the back lane that separated the houses from the council allotments. 'Your bedroom won't be overlooked, pet.' Lily was telling Sadie. 'And it's very quiet. It's the best thing about this side of the street.'

Cooked tea was served at half past six; thin, limp ovals of ham from Liptons, each transparent slice fringed with yellow breadcrumbs. There were little mounds of mashed potato and boiled beetroot. One of the slices shot off Tamar's plate as she nervously tried to impale it on the fork and the white surface of the table turned dark red.

Lily noticed her embarrassment. 'It's only enamel, pet,' she said. 'It won't take any hurt.'

Tamar flushed with relief. She glanced through her lashes at the boy sitting at the end of the table. Tamar thought he was probably about four or five years older than herself, but he seemed very shy. When she'd gone to the toilet before tea, she'd seen him coming out of the washhouse bare to the waist, his braces hanging down from his trousers and a towel over his shoulder. He'd blushed bright red and avoided her eyes. Now he wore a clean shirt without a collar and sat at table saying nothing but 'please' and 'thank you'. Tamar couldn't help staring at him. His looks were strikingly foreign – what Sadie called 'a touch of the tar-brush'. He had dark olive skin, thick black hair and huge, serious brown eyes.

'That's whoar George,' Lily said, nodding to Tamar, and a dark flush began to surge up George's neck as everyone turned to look at him.

The other residents were also at the table. Ida Lawrence who had the big room at the front, and a Mr Hake who occupied the small room over the alleyway. Tamar had to clamp her lips together to stop herself from smiling when Lily said his name. Mr Hake looked exactly like a fish, with flat, pale cheeks and eyes that seemed to look at you separately from both sides of his face. It was an indoor kind of face, and he held his knife and fork awkwardly with pale, indoor hands. He said nothing at all during the meal, keeping his head down over his plate, shovelling food into his mouth faster than Tamar would have believed possible and then he excused himself hurriedly as soon as he'd finished eating.

'He's a queer one that,' Lily said when he'd gone. Her voice was hushed and confidential. 'He keeps locked suitcases under the bed and sneaks them out of the house when he thinks no one's about. Mrs Whale sees him. That woman never misses a thing.' Lily pushed her chair back and lit up a cigarette. 'He's supposed to work for the Prudential, but I think he's on the fiddle.'

Ida had a more dramatic theory. 'Maybe it's the body of his wife, poor soul, cut up in pieces like that man in the News of the World,' she said.

Sadie raised a sceptical eyebrow. 'Don't you think he might be a door to door salesman – brushes or encyclopaedias or something? It could be that he's just ashamed of what he does. Maybe the insurance is a lie. Don't you think, Mrs Lawrence?'

'Just call me Aunty Ida, pet,' she said, smiling at Tamar to include her in the invitation. 'Everybody does. I don't like Lawrence – never have. Me stage name was Ida Lavelle. I used to be a dancer at the Palais Royale – ostrich plumes on me bum and tassels on me tits. But then I got married to the theatre manager and a bad do that was. Turned up his toes a few years after and all he left me was his debts.'

Tamar could see Sadie wince at the vulgarity. But Ida took no notice. She was so enormously fat Tamar had to keep telling herself that it was rude to stare. There were great ledges of flesh under Ida's dress, where the skin spilled down in pleats over her elbows, her stomach, her knees. The corsets Tamar had seen in the wash-house could only belong to Ida. It was difficult for Tamar to imagine her ever having danced – naked was too gross even to contemplate.

Ida held out crooked fingers to Sadie across the table. 'Just you look at those,' she said, 'I've been a martyr to arthritis these last ten years.'

'But she can still play the organ,' Lily interrupted. 'She plays in the cinema for the matinees and sings every Saturday night in one of the pubs down on the fish quay. It's a fair treat to hear her.'

After Tamar had gone into the living room to sit politely beside the fire, while George read the newspaper, she heard Ida telling Sadie about the time she'd performed with the Fabulous Popplewell's at the Vaudeville and then she began singing an old music hall song in a strident, lilting voice.

'Once in the window of a ham and beef shop
Two little sausages sat.
One was a lady and the other was a gentleman
Sausages are like that . . .'

'Whisht.' Tamar heard Lily say with a giggle. 'Give over.'

To Tamar's surprise Sadie laughed too and said, 'Little pigs have big ears.' Tamar could imagine her making little miming movements towards the living room. George looked up when Ida began to sing and his eyes met Tamar's over the top of the paper. For the first time he smiled in a shy but friendly kind of way.

'So, where do you sleep then?' Tamar asked, hoping he wouldn't think it a cheeky question. She was curious because there only seemed to be three rooms downstairs – the kitchen, the living room and a door through into what Lily had said used to be the parlour but was now her own bedroom.

George didn't seem at all put out. He nodded his head towards a large wooden bureau against the wall.

Tamar was puzzled until he got up and opened the front and she could see that it had a mattress folded up inside so that it opened out into a bed when the door was pulled down.

'You sleep in here?' Tamar was incredulous. 'Don't you mind?'

George shrugged. 'Only when I'm tired out after a day's work and that lot' – he jerked his head towards the kitchen – 'are nattering away till all hours.' He had a very quiet voice and Tamar noticed that he went very red when he spoke.

But at least he had a bed all to himself, Tamar thought, as George lifted the newspaper up in front of his face again like a shield. Tamar hated having to sleep with her mother. When she was a small child it had been comforting to have Sadie's warm body to cuddle up to. Now touching the hot flesh through the satin nightdress repelled her, and the combined smells of stale perfume, face cream and human sweat made her feel nauseous. So, when her mother got into bed, Tamar made herself as thin as possible, clinging to the furthest edge of the bed's horizon, making a little furrow of sheets and blankets between her mother and herself. Occasionally in her sleep, Sadie would roll over towards her and throw an arm over Tamar's body and Tamar would freeze, desperately resisting the impulse to push her away. She longed, more than anything to have a new bed, one that only she had slept in, a single bed with a sprung mattress, that she wouldn't have to share with anyone.

That night as Tamar lay in bed waiting for Sadie to finish her beauty routine she found herself wondering how it was that her mother – such a terrible snob – had spent most of the evening chattering away in the kitchen to Lily and Ida as if they were old friends.

'Of course they're extremely vulgar,' Sadie said to Tamar as she brushed her hair out and put in the long, curved metal clamps that kept her waves in place overnight. 'But at least they're good hearted.' She patted the underside of her chin ten times with the back of her hand to keep it from sagging, eyeing herself anxiously in the mirror. Then she smiled and turned round on the stool. 'I think we're going to be all right here, don't you?'

Tamar didn't answer. She'd heard Sadie say it too many times before to feel any confidence in the truth of it. She was already curled up, half asleep, on the edge of the bed, one hand secretly clutching Angus under the pillow for comfort. How long would it be this time before they had to move again? Tamar felt as if she would like to cry herself to sleep. 'Don't be such a baby,' she told herself. 'You're a big girl now.'

CHAPTER THREE

The next morning Sadie was up early. Tamar watched from the bed as she put on her suit with the tailored jacket and matching hat and her only pair of silk stockings – so precious she had to put them on wearing cotton gloves – ready to go up to Pergavie's department store in town. It was Ida who'd put Sadie on to it the night before, telling her that the senior saleswoman in the fur and gown department had run off to be married – and her nearly forty if she was a day – leaving them all up the Swanee River without a paddle. That was how Ida had described it. So Sadie was going to see the store manager.

She was back just before mid-day with a triumphant smile on her face. 'I told him I'd been a model in London before I got married,' she told Lily. 'And that I'd worked with furs in Harvey Nicholls.' People always believed what Sadie told them. She kicked off her suede shoes under the table and lit a cigarette. 'They gave me a little test, asking me to identify all the different coats. The floor supervisor was absolutely *dying* for me to get one wrong!' But Sadie had got the job, selling fur coats and evening dresses on commission.

Fur coats were Sadie's hobby. She spent hours looking at them in shop windows, in stores, fingering the pelts, sometimes even trying them on. She knew all the different skins – ocelot, sable, musquash, mink and persian lamb and knew how the pelts were matched together in patterns to create particular effects. She dreamed of owning one. Years and years ago, one of the Uncles had actually given Sadie a silver fox stole. It was made from two fox pelts, complete with paws, joined at the nose by a chain so that the bodies of the foxes and their silvery tails hung down at the front. Tamar had been fascinated by it as a small child and had often asked to stroke the stiff, cured faces with their staring glass eyes. Now she was older she felt repelled by it. How could Sadie possibly bear to wear two dead animals round her neck?

There was other news too. On her way back from town, Sadie had enrolled Tamar at the Queen Alexandra School for girls. 'You start first thing on Monday,' Sadie said. 'But I'm afraid you'll have to go on your own. I have to be at work by eight fifteen.'

Tamar shrugged. This was nothing new. She couldn't remember the last time Sadie had ever taken her to school. Then she was struck with an awful thought. 'What can I wear?' The uniform was bound to be different. Everyone would know she was a new girl. They would all be looking at her. Sadie hadn't even thought about it. 'You'll just have to wear your old things, I suppose. I can't afford anything new at the moment. The gymslips look the same, so it'll just be the cardigan and the hat thank goodness.'

Tamar felt desolate. Another new school. Another class of curious, hostile children. Without a proper uniform she would stick out like a sore thumb. How was she to cope? Her legs trembled just thinking about it.

In the afternoon Sadie took Tamar on the trolley bus down to the coast at Tynemouth to walk along the Grand Parade and look at the winter sea. 'It reminds me of Cornwall,' Sadie said, gazing out across the empty sands as the waves curled and crashed towards them. And then she dabbed her eyes and pretended that the wind made them water. Tamar imagined that her mother was thinking about James Fell, who existed only as a faded black and white photograph on the table beside the bed. There was also a curling, brown snap of him arm-in-arm with Sadie, tucked into the dressing table mirror. There was so little evidence of her father that Tamar sometimes doubted that he had ever existed. He seemed as unreal and far away as the smiling man in the signed photograph of Leslie Howard that Sadie kept on the window sill.

'I've always missed the sea,' Sadie said with another sigh.

It seemed a good time to ask her a question. 'Where does my name come from?' Tamar asked. 'Was I called after the river where we used to live?'

'Goodness no!' Sadie said. 'It's a Quaker name. Your father

was a Friend.'

'I never knew that. What are Quakers?'

Sadie immediately began to look vague. She was incredibly hazy about anything to do with religion. 'They go to meetings where nobody says anything and they're not allowed to wear fancy clothes. That's all I know, Tamar, so don't ask me anything else. Your father and I didn't talk much about things like that.'

It was too cold to stay long at the beach and the little seafront café was closed. Sadie shrugged. 'By the time we get home it'll be time for tea anyway,' she said. Sadie meant afternoon tea, Tamar knew. But when Lily said it, she meant dinner. Tamar found it hard to get used to the fact that in the north you had dinner at lunch time and the meal that should have been dinner was called tea. But at least the food was better at Lily's than it had been in their previous lodgings. Tamar still had vivid memories of a kind of minced slurry poured over grey potatoes that had been served up as Shepherd's Pie at Miss Simpson's, and a white spongy mass that Sadie had refused to eat because she said it was the inside of a cow's stomach. Just thinking about it made Tamar want to heave.

'D'you want to come rent collecting, pet?' Anna's grandfather put his head round the kitchen door. 'I'm going down the quay. I thought you might like to see the Wooden Dolly.'

Anna was sitting at the kitchen table finishing a sketch. She raised her head and nodded. 'I could do with some fresh air.' She didn't mind her grandfather so much now that she was beginning to know him better. He'd taken to calling her 'pet' or 'hinny' which avoided having to use her name without offending anyone. She put her sketch book away, pulled on her coat and joined him in the street. Arthur Cotteslow was a burly man – five feet eleven tall with muscular shoulders and a well-developed stomach that made him, even at seventy, a formidable man. He wore a Harris tweed overcoat, belted round the middle and a brown trilby hat to cover an unruly shock of steel grey hair. He had a double crown, he told Anna, and so his hair grew in two different directions. She thought he looked like a mobster in an American film, except that when he spoke his voice was soft and slightly musical. He smoked a pipe, which kept going out and needing to be relit. He tamped the tobacco down into the bowl of the pipe with his thumb and the nail was yellowed and cracked with frequent use. Grandma tried to ration his intake of tobacco, which she said was bad for his health. But Anna had noticed that he kept two different pouches in separate pockets, one to smoke and one to show his wife. Whenever Grandma asked how much he'd smoked that day, he would produce one of them, which always contained the same amount and say 'There you are! Still half full.' And she would be satisfied. It amused Anna, especially when he winked at her behind her grandmother's back as if they were co-conspirators and whispered 'Anything for a quiet life, eh pet?'

They took the trolley bus from the coast road to the town centre and walked down the Bank. Anna's grandfather owned two of the old houses at the lower end of Grey Street and she waited on the pavement while he knocked on the door and went in to collect the rent from the tenants and write it all down in his little red notebook. When he came out again they walked on past the ship's chandlers, down to the Western Quay and then along the Gut. Mr Cotteslow pointed out the moorings in the centre of the river where the whaling ships tied up when they came in. It was low tide and the water had trailing slicks of oil and coal, floating spars, rope, cans and bottles, brown froth from the tannery and the white under-bellies of dead fish thrown from the boats. The stench of it was intense. Even though she held her nose, it scorched Anna's throat and eyes. On the opposite side of the river, across the mud left by the draining tide, coal debris from the colliers loading at the staithes made black loops. Distant figures, with buckets and sacks, bent and straightened along the tide lines.

'Coal pickers,' Mr Cotteslow said, sucking his pipe. 'That's Jarrow over there – the Jarrow Slacks. They walked all the way to London asking for work. Silly buggers.'

The old fish quays were cobbled and narrow. The boats had sunk with the water level and only the masts and the glass windows of the steering decks were visible above the quayside. Anna had to step over hawsers looped around the stanchions and avoid piles of nets and floats and wooden fish boxes on the cobbles. Above their heads, the gulls shrieked and swooped on broad, muscular wings.

'How'd you get on with the schools yesterday?' Mr Cotteslow asked.

'All right, I think,' Anna stopped to look at a gull on a bollard, to admire it's yellow feet and the perfect feathers of it wings. 'I didn't like the Hollies though – the girl's were all so stuck up.'

'Mind it's a good school, pet. Your Mam thought they'd help you catch up on what you'd lost, changing places, like. Costs a bit, but I was willing to pay. 'He walked on a few paces. 'So is it St Aidan's then?'

Anna shook her head firmly. There had been something repellent about the convent atmosphere – a feeling of repression in the artificial quietness of its corridors. The nuns in black with their huge starched hats had looked like a fleet of black ships in full sail rather than human beings and Anna hadn't liked the sour odour that emanated from Mother Superior's habit, or the martyred, bleeding Christ on the wall behind her head. It had made Anna shudder. How could anyone worship suffering like that?

'Looks like Queen Alex's then.' Mr Cotteslow grunted. 'It's a pity you can't get straight into the High School where your Mam went, but if you work hard you should get through the entrance exam next year.'

Along the side of the quay the herring women stood at their trestles, the herring barrels stacked ten high behind them, wearing old coats tightly buttoned and scarves wrapped round their heads. Some of them seemed very young. Their hands, faces and clothes were spattered with fish scales, slime and clotted blood and the reek of it brought Anna's breakfast up into her throat. They worked so fast she could hardly see their hands move. One of the girls had lively, cheeky eyes. She called out something incomprehensible as Anna walked past and all the women laughed. Anna flushed with embarrassment, but stopped to watch in admiration as the girl picked a fish from the box on her left, flashed the knife along its belly and threw it into another box on her right. She was already picking up another before the guts of the first had had time to reach the bottom of the bucket. The woman next to her had the short, deformed nose Anna had been told came from syphilis.

'Don't you look down on them,' Mr Cotteslow said sharply as Anna made a face. 'They're marine aristocrats descended from the first folk that sailed the fishing cobles out of the Tyne. Your own great grandfather was one of them. He was a sea captain, very successful. Bit of a painter too. So that's maybe where you get it from.'

Anna seized her opportunity. 'Grandpa, if I go to Queen Alex's and you don't have to pay any fees, will you pay for me to go to art college later?'

He stopped to re-light his pipe, squinting at the bowl and shielding the flame with his hand. 'That depends, hinny,' he said, flicking the dead match away. 'It depends on the kind of college you want. Your Mam's keen for you to be a teacher – get yourself a profession. It'll stand you in good stead. No harm in being an art teacher though.'

'I don't really want to teach. I want to paint.'

'There you go! Whoever heard of a woman painter?'

Anna's spirits sank. His tone was jocular, but his words hit a nerve. He was right. She had no names to give him; no examples to follow. All the great painters had been men. The paintings she saw in books were all by men. There was the occasional little watercolour or drawing by a woman. There must be some! Anna thought. She couldn't be the first woman to put brush to paper, but where could she find out?

Her grandfather was already striding off ahead. 'Come and I'll show you the Wooden Dolly,' he called over his shoulder. He led her down to the end of the Quay, where the carved figure of an old woman with a fish creel on her back, had been so hacked and chipped as to be scarcely recognisable.

'Sailors believe it's good luck to go to sea with a splinter of wood from her,' Mr Cotteslow explained. 'If you carry one, you can't drown.'

'Is it because she's holy?'

Mr Cotteslow shook his head. 'Not that I've ever heard. Pagan more like. Sailors are superstitious buggers.'

Anna dug a small splinter of wood from the edge of the woman's sleeve with her thumb nail. It was already partly detached and came away easily. She put the slim spike of wood in her coat pocket like a talisman and fingered it as they walked back, forming silent words inside her head – a kind of unspoken request from one female to another.

On Monday morning Sadie had already gone when Tamar came down to breakfast. Ida was sitting at the table over a cup of tea and Lily was cooking scrambled eggs on toast. She put a heaped plate in front of Tamar, who found it hard to swallow anything. Her stomach was trying to turn itself inside out with dread.

'Get your coat on pet,' Ida said, as Tamar abandoned the struggle to cram it down. She was already on her feet pulling on an enormous black cape with a rabbit fur collar. 'I'll walk up with you on my way to the shops.'

'I'll be all right. Really.' Tamar said. But Ida just shook her head and picked up her gloves and her shopping bag.

Outside the wind was cold and the air was bitter with the soot of recently lit fires. 'You'll soon find somebody to walk up with,' Ida said, looking around at the groups of girls talking and giggling on their way to school. They were all wearing grey gymslips like Tamar's, but their gabardines were navy blue. Some of the girls turned and stared. It was difficult to walk with Ida. She was so heavy and crippled with arthritis that she waddled and lurched from side to side, wheezing audibly with every step, the black wool cape flapping up in the breeze like the feathers of a gigantic bird. Tamar heard some of the girls sniggering as they passed and she felt embarrassed. Supposing they thought Ida was her mother? And then she felt guilty about being ashamed of Ida when she was being so kind.

The school was a raw, new building on the coast road. Ida explained that it had been named for the Queen Dowager. 'We used to call her the Rose of Denmark. She was married to old King Edward, but he died when I was at school. There was a terrible to do and we all had to wear black crepe armbands.' There was a picture of Alexandra in the entrance hall. She seemed quite young – thin and rather disdainful, wearing a massive diamond-fringe tiara which looked too heavy for her slender neck, and she had long, elegant fingers which rested delicately in the lap of her white lace dress. Ida went with Tamar as far as the headmistress's door and then she turned to go, patting her arm as she left. 'Good luck pet. Just do your best and you'll be all right.' And then Ida disappeared into the mass of girls filling the corridor.

~~~~~~~~~~~~~~~~~~

Anna was up very early, even before her grandfather. She lit the gas under the kettle and warmed her cold fingers at the flame. Propped against the tea caddy was an envelope addressed to 'The headmistress, Queen Alexandra's School for Girls'.

Last night, Anna had watched her mother filling in the form, printing; 'Anne Clara Weissmann' in the space provided.

'Why can't you put Anna?' she'd asked. 'You're not going to let them call me Anne too are you?'

'It's the name on your birth certificate,' Mrs Weissmann had said, making a helpless gesture with her hand. 'You wouldn't want me to tell lies would you? Not on an official form.'

Anna looked at the envelope. She had two choices. She could accept what was on the certificate – the name of a grandmother she had little affection for, but which was her legal name. Or she could fight for the name that had been hers since she was a baby – a name that was so part of her identity that to lose it was to lose herself. Anna remembered how enchanted she had been when her father had showed her that her name was the same written backwards – the two halves of it a reflection of each other. 'It's a palindrome,' he'd explained.

The kettle had begun to boil. Feeling sick with nerves, Anna lifted the envelope and held the sealed flap over the spout. As the steam soaked the paper, it began to curl open. Quickly, but delicately, Anna peeled the flap back and eased the form and its accompanying letter out of the envelope. Her mother's fountain pen was in the handbag that hung behind the door. Anna studied the words for a moment. Her mother wrote her a's with a small
~~~~~~~~~~~~~~~~~~

loop where they were joined to the next letter and it was simple to form an 'a' around the 'e', creating Anna out of Anne. She did the same in the letter. Her heart was beating very fast as she returned her mother's pen to the bag and then refolded the form and pushed it back into the envelope. But when she came to stick the flap down again the glue had been steamed away and it was impossible to re-seal.

Anna's hands shook for a moment until she remembered the paper paste she kept in her painting cupboard upstairs. She slipped the envelope into her dressing gown pocket just as she heard footsteps in the bedroom above. Quickly she poured the water onto the tea, leaving it to brew beside the stove as she ran lightly up the stairs to her room. If her mother offered to come to school with her this morning, she must make sure that she came no further than the gate. The truth would come to light one day, but for now she would be able to keep her name.

Tamar stood outside the headmistress's door, reading the label and trying to summon up the courage to knock. An older girl with a monitor's badge stopped beside her.

'Do you want to see Miss Fenwick?'

Tamar nodded.

'Then you'd better hurry up, it's nearly time for assembly.' She reached across and rapped on the door and a deep, crisp voice inside said, 'Come in.'

'Go on,' the girl said. 'She won't bite.'

Miss Fenwick had grey hair, cropped short like a man and she was wearing a long black velvet jacket with sagging pockets and a grey ankle-length skirt with three little pleats at each side. She was standing beside the desk looking down at a piece of paper with Tamar's name on it. It was the only writing big enough for Tamar to read upside down.

'You seem to have attended a large number of different schools,' she said, looking up with an expression on her face that made Tamar feel as if she had committed a criminal offence.

'We've moved around quite a lot,' Tamar said defensively.

'Ma'am,' Miss Fenwick said severely. 'You must call me ma'am when you speak to me. And you should call your class teachers Mr or Miss whatever their respective names happen to be. Can you remember that?'

'Yes ma'am.'

'Good. Now read this aloud.' She handed Tamar a book, indicating the verse at the top of the page.

Tamar's heart lifted. It was from The Forsaken Merman, a poem she had read so often that she knew it by heart. She began immediately.

'Children dear, was it yesterday
(Call yet once) that she went away?
Once she sat with you and me,
On a red gold throne in the heart of the sea,
And the youngest sat on her knee.'

But she'd hardly got to the part where the Merking is calling *'come away children, come away down,'* when Miss Fenwick put up a hand for her to stop, cheating Tamar of the pathos of the last lines, where she could really let her romantic imagination go. Its stark beauty was something she often dwelt on. What kind of woman would abandon her children, leaving *'lonely forever the Kings of the Sea'?*

'I think that will be enough.' Miss Fenwick said. There was a twitch at the corner of her mouth as if she was going to smile. 'I've decided to put you into 3B and see how you get on. You may find you have a lot of catching up to do in some subjects.' A bell rang, loudly, in the hall outside and she nodded dismissal.

After assembly, Tamar followed one of the monitors upstairs and along corridors that smelled of hot metal boiler pipes, chalk dust and too many human bodies in a small space – a smell Tamar remembered being the same from every school she'd ever been to. 3B was on the first floor overlooking the new housing plot and the coast road. The monitor knocked on the door and waited until a clear voice called 'Come in!' Thirty two pairs of eyes turned towards Tamar as they entered the room. 'Excuse me Miss Wilson,' the monitor said. She gave her Miss Fenwick's note and went out again quickly, leaving Tamar standing awkwardly in front of the class.

The noise level rose as soon as the door closed behind her. 'Be quiet!' Miss Wilson shouted. She had a loud voice for someone so small and so young. She had pretty fair hair, slightly curly, clipped untidily back into a pleat and was wearing a hand-knitted lilac angora jumper with pearl buttons on the shoulder. She smiled at Tamar. 'There's a vacant desk at the front beside the door,' she said, pointing. 'You'd better sit there for the moment.' Tamar felt hot and conspicuous. In her last school that seat had been the Order Mark desk, kept free for girls who misbehaved, so they could sit under the eye of the teacher.

She didn't dare look at any of the other girls. She kept her head down towards the floor and slipped into the empty desk as quickly as she could. The rest of the lesson was a blur. They were all reading Dickens – Great Expectations – taking it in turns to read aloud. Tamar tried to shut out the agonising sound of voices stumbling over unfamiliar syntax, mis-pronouncing words or even leaving them out altogether. There were occasional cries of 'This don't make sense Miss!' How did Miss Wilson put up with it? Tamar concentrated on the piece of paper she'd been given. 'I want you to write a page about yourself,' Miss Wilson had said. 'Your family, the house you live in . . . You could tell me a little about where you lived before you moved here if you like.'

What could she write? It was hard. Much harder than Dickens. 'My name is Tamar Fell,' she began. 'I live with my mother in a rented room in Heaton Street.' Was that what Miss Wilson wanted? She certainly couldn't tell her about having to leave Miss Simpson's without paying the rent. There were other adventures that couldn't be written about too. Like the time Sadie had taken her into a fashionable club in Bath – signing herself in the book as the Honourable Mrs James Fell, and they'd had a sumptuous tea with three kinds of sandwiches and chocolate ices and cream horns. The teacups were so thin they were difficult to hold and they had silver bands around the edge. And there were tiny silver teaspoons and sugar lumps in a silver bowl with little silver tongs. Then Sadie had taken Tamar to the powder room and slipped down the back stairs without paying. Tamar could still remember how frightened she'd been, certain that the doorman was going to put out his hand and shout 'Stop thief!' as they walked through the revolving doors. It had worried her so much that when they got to the bus stop she'd been sick all over her new shoes. Sadie had been quite cross. Tamar looked up at Miss Wilson's delicate face, flushed with exasperation and knew that it would be impossible to write about such things.

When the lesson came to an end, the girls all gathered around Tamar's desk.

'So who are you then?' one of them asked. She was called Elsie and had matted ginger hair and impetigo scabs at the corner of her mouth.

'Stuck up southern bitch. That's who she is,' one of the other girls replied, and they all laughed.

'Tamar!' Elsie said with a sniff. 'What sort of name's that?'

Tamar was used to this form of attack, and now she had a new line of defence. 'It's a Quaker name.'

'Swallowed a dictionary have you?' they taunted her. 'What's that then?'

'The Society of Friends. They have services where they all sit round and nobody says anything.'

'Bleedin' pagan witch,' Elsie said to the others, giggling. 'You'd better watch or she'll put a curse on you.'

And they all fell about laughing, cut short abruptly as the next teacher swept into the room and the entire class clattered into their proper places, standing respectfully silent.

~~~~~~~~~~~~~~~~~

During the second lesson, as Tamar was struggling with a maths problem she barely understood, the classroom door opened and the monitor came in followed by a tall, awkward girl with penetrating hazel eyes and heavy masses of chocolate brown hair in a long plait down her back. There was a whispered conversation and Tamar heard the girl say, 'I'm sorry I'm late. Miss Fenwick made me do a test.' Then the teacher's finger pointed to the empty space beside Tamar in the desk at the front. The new girl smiled as she slid into the seat, glancing sideways at Tamar through thick, brown lashes. Her eyes were friendly and there
~~~~~~~~~~~~~~~~~

was a kind of sadness at the back of them that attracted Tamar instantly.

As soon as the lesson ended, the other girls gathered round the desk shouting 'So who are you then?' just as they'd done to Tamar. But the girl didn't seem to be intimidated.

'Anna Weissmann,' she said. Her voice was pitched in a deep confident alto.

Elsie said, 'I bet your middle name's piss.'

Anna put her books down on the desk, looked very coolly back and said, 'I expect your middle name's shit, and I bet you eat it too.'

Elsie's eyes were wide with respect. 'So, where d'you come from then?'

'We were living in Germany, in the Alps, but then we had to leave.' There was a flicker of something in Anna's eyes that Tamar couldn't interpret.

'Can you talk Boche then?' Elsie asked.

Anna nodded.

'Go on then. Say something.'

They all watched, rapt, as Anna began to recite a few sentences in guttural syllables.

At break, Tamar took Anna down to the cloakroom. She seemed rather nervous – dragging Tamar quickly out into the playground before she'd finished washing her hands.

'Tell me about yourself,' she demanded when they were outside. Tamar was silent for a moment, wondering where to begin, which part of herself Anna would want to know about. 'What does your father do?' Anna persisted.

It was the question Tamar had been dreading. Anna seemed quite nice, but if she told her the truth it would soon be all over the classroom that Tamar didn't have a father and then the gossiping would start. It was never any use to say that he had died. People looked at Sadie and they always thought the worst. She could hear the voices in her head already chanting 'Tamar Fell's a bastard! Tamar Fell's a bastard!'

Tamar took a deep breath. 'My father isn't here. He works abroad a lot.' Tamar Fell will go to hell . . . 'Somewhere in India I think. He doesn't come home very often.'

'Oh.'

Tamar waited for questions, but none came.

'I had to leave mine behind in Germany,' Anna said. Her brown eyes were very grave. 'We're living with my grandparents. What about you?'

Tamar told her. 'I don't have any other relatives – at least I don't think so. None Sadie's ever mentioned anyway. We live in a lodging house.'

'That sounds fun. My parents used to run a guest house back in Bavaria. You'll have to invite me back one day after school.'

This was something Tamar hadn't thought about. If Anna came back to Lily Kennedy's she'd quickly find out that Tamar had lied. But it was too late to think of that now.

Anna's grandparents lived in one of the big, semi-detached houses on the coast road. After school they walked home together and Anna invited Tamar inside. The house had an intimidating atmosphere – there was an affluent depth to the carpets, a rich polish on the furniture, odours of lavender and cigars and the kind of silence that made Tamar feel she should walk on tiptoe. They had a rosewood grand piano in the dining room and a cupboard full of crystal glasses. The chairs and tables in the living room were covered with embroidered antimacassars and lace doilies, and there were bookcases full of decorated board covers with titles like *Maisie's Choice, Hilda's Secret, Dora's Dilemma*. 'They were my mother's when she was a girl,' Anna explained. 'They're all deadly boring.'

The sitting room was kept only for visitors, but Anna turned the key quietly and sneaked in to show Tamar the painting on the wall. It was a seascape in an ornate gilt frame; two sailing ships and a smaller boat being driven before a storm. The sky was black behind the creaming waves and there were shreds of torn sail and broken spars in the ship's rigging. 'That was painted by my great-grandfather,' Anna told Tamar. 'He was a sea captain, but he really wanted to be an artist. He used to paint pictures when he came home on leave.' She touched the frame reverently. 'I can stand in front of this for hours.'

Up in her own room Anna showed Tamar some of the drawings she'd done herself – the kitchen windowsill with daffodils in a milk jug, a group of fishing boats tied up at the quayside, a rough sketch of her mother. 'I've got all my pocket money saved up for paper and paint. You've no idea how expensive it is to get the proper things.' She folded the drawings away again and then turned to Tamar as if she was going to tell her something really important. 'You won't breathe a word to anyone at school, will you?'

Tamar promised.

Anna still hesitated for a moment before she said, 'I want to go to art college, the Slade in London if I'm good enough.' Anna looked at Tamar as if she expected her to argue, or laugh.

'If you can draw like that, I bet you can go anywhere,' Tamar said admiringly. 'I wish I was good at something.'

Anna tied the strings of the folder and slid it back beside the wardrobe. 'My grandfather thinks it's silly for a girl to want to be a painter.'

'What about your Mum?'

'She calls it a "nice little hobby" and talks about me being a teacher.' Anna tossed her hair back. 'But I'll get there somehow. I've got to!'

Anna's mother was a full-bodied, dark-haired woman whose flesh hung loosely from her large-boned frame. Her upper lip was dark with fine down and she moved lazily as if lifting her limbs underwater. She smiled at Tamar rather vaguely, offering tea and homemade biscuits. Anna's grandfather, Mr Cotteslow, was down at the allotment, she said, when Anna asked where he was. 'He grows all our vegetables,' Mrs Weissmann explained to Tamar, 'And he wins prizes every year at the flower show.'

She gave Anna a tray with a teacup and a plate of biscuits on it, and Tamar was taken up to be introduced to Anna's grandmother – a frail presence in the front bedroom. She was tucked up in a big armchair with her feet on a stool. Anna put the tray on a swivelling table beside her. The hands that reached out to grasp the cup had large, liver-brown spots on the skin and there was a smell in the room like an un-emptied chamber pot. When Tamar said 'How do you do?' politely, Mrs Cotteslow smiled weakly and said, 'It'll be so nice for Anne to have a friend,' in a fading, breathy kind of voice.

'She's supposed to have a bad heart,' Anna said when they got outside again. 'But I think she just puts it on to get out of doing things. She's been an invalid for years.' Anna didn't sound very sympathetic.

'Don't you like your grandmother?'

'Not much. I know I should but I just can't help it.'

'Why did she call you Anne?'

'I was hoping you hadn't noticed. It's the name I was christened when I was born, but I've always been called Anna. You won't tell anyone will you?'

Tamar shook her head. It was nice to know that Anna too had secrets. 'Anne's a plain name,' she said. 'You don't look like an Anne.'

Anna smiled. 'I don't feel like an Anne.' She grasped Tamar's arm in a friendly, companionable way. 'Come on Tamar, I'm going to show you the garden.'

~~~~~~~~~~~~~~~~~~

On Saturday morning when Tamar got out of bed and looked out of the window, snow had covered the allotments, humping itself over the vegetable plots, turning cabbages into round white balls and topping the brussel sprouts with white berets, tilted at a rakish angle. The snow made her feel restless and she wandered round the house trying to think what she could do and where she could go. 'You're as jumpy as a flea in a blanket,' Ida said, with a laugh. 'You don't know what to do with yourself, do you pet!' She heaved herself out of the armchair and folded up the paper she'd been reading. 'Tell you what. You can come down with me to the Palace. D'you like going to the pictures?'

'I love it.' Sadie sometimes took Tamar to the matinee when she wasn't working and occasionally to the early evening show for a special treat. But only when she had money in her purse. Tamar blushed. 'I'm afraid I can't come with you Ida – I haven't any money and Sadie's at work.'

'Will you listen to the bairn?' Ida said to Lily who'd just come in from the kitchen. 'You don't need money, pet – you can come into the organ well with me.'
~~~~~~~~~~~~~~~~~~

The snow on the street was already being reduced to a dirty slippery slush and outside the cinema, a man in an usher's uniform was sweeping the pavement clean with a stiff brush. He put his finger up to his hat when he saw Ida and she stopped to say hello. 'Mr Timms in yet, Freddy?'

'He came in this morning, but I haven't seen him.'

'Who's Mr Timms?' Tamar asked.

'Curiosity killed the cat.' Ida said firmly. And then added. 'He's the manager, pet. I should have his permission to take you in.' But the girl in the ticket booth hadn't seen him either. Ida shrugged and smiled at Tamar. 'What the eye doesn't see! You just come with me and it'll be all right.' Tamar followed Ida down the back stairs, beneath the stage, along a passage narrowed by organ pipes and then through a door no larger than a cupboard, onto the organ itself. Ida was only just able to squeeze herself through and was red-faced and sweating with the effort of heaving herself up onto the seat.

'Now you sit quiet and keep your feet out of the way of the pedals,' she said as Tamar climbed up beside her. 'And don't touch anything.'

So Tamar sat with her hands folded and her feet tucked up, watching Ida pull out the stops and power a massive, deafening chord with her fingers and feet that reverberated round the pit and made Tamar's ears ache. There was a slight creak under the seat as the electric motor whirred into action and then they rode up from the dimness of the pit into the pink light of the cinema on a vibrating swell of music. There was a scatter of clapping from the stalls as Ida launched into one medley after another of 'Songs from the Shows'. Lilac Time, the Desert Song, Showboat – stretching her swollen, misshapen fingers over the keys through her entire repertoire, while her feet tapped out the rhythm on the pedals underneath with a series of hollow, wooden claps.

Tamar amused herself by looking at the double keyboard, wondering how on earth Ida could play them both at once as well as the foot pedals. And then there were the rows and rows of black and white stops with odd names like Diapason, Octave and Cherubini, and above them an ornate curve of pink, yellow, blue and green keys with numbers on them. Then, at a secret signal, Ida nodded to someone in the mirror and the organ began to sink back down as the first black and white images flickered overhead.

When they'd squeezed back through the door into the passage, Ida jerked her head to one side mysteriously and said, 'I think I'll just have a little look up here,' and turned to the left towards the fire exit. There was an opening on the right and another set of steps going down to a store room. Tamar peered past Ida and could see a man sprawled across the bottom step with his head in a pool of vomit. Ida sighed and said, 'The bloomin' idiot.' She sounded both cross and sad.

'Is he ill?' Tamar asked.

'No pet. Haven't you ever seen a man the worse for drink?'

Tamar shook her head. When Sadie was drunk she tended to cry a lot and then went to bed to sleep it off.

'Give me a hand to get him out of the way,' Ida said. She bent, wheezing, and grasped him by the shoulders. She didn't seem to mind the stinking mess he was lying in. Tamar got hold of his feet and together they dragged and pushed him through the store-room door, turning him onto his side and covering him up with an old rug. Ida propped the door open with a can of paint.

'He can sleep it off in there,' she said. Her chest was heaving with the effort and there were dewy beads of sweat across her upper lip.

'Why does he get like that?' Tamar asked. 'It's disgusting.' She wiped the side of her shoe carefully on a mop head that lay on the floor beside the door. She had to stop herself gagging on the stench.

'He's got money troubles,' Ida explained between breaths, 'and his wife just up and left him. Every now and then he goes on the binge. Me own husband was the same. The answer was always at the bottom of the bottle,' Ida said, shaking her head at Tamar. 'You mind you get yourself a good man, pet.' She was beginning to get her breath back. 'Go for a kind man. Kindness lasts. I always went for handsome bastards.'

At the top of the steps Ida paused again. 'At least you've never known anythin' of that, have you pet?'

Tamar didn't know what she meant.

'Never had your father come home drunk and clip you round the ears just for bein' there. Never had the Means Test man pokin' round in all your private things.'

'What's the Means Test?' Tamar knew only that people lived in fear of it – including Sadie.

'It's when you haven't got any money and you can't work. Before the panel give you anythin' they come round to your house to see if you've got anythin' to sell. We used to hide things under the floorboards and in an old cupboard behind the chest of drawers.' She smiled grimly. 'You'd be standin' there without the price of a loaf of bread, three weeks rent owin' and the bairn cryin' in the cot and they'd say "why don't you go and sell the sofa?" I had an old settle that belonged my Gran – all the stuffin' comin' out of it.'

'So what did you do?'

'What can you do, pet? I put it out on the street and a man gave me a shillin' for it.'

Tamar wondered with a shiver of fear what would happen if Sadie ever ran out of money. They didn't have any furniture, or anything else much to sell. Only the five pound note folded up at the bottom of the hat box. At least she was nearly grown up – almost old enough to leave school and start earning money. Tamar was curious to know what Ida's children were doing now. She was sure they had never been mentioned before. 'What happened to your children, Ida?' she asked. And then knew it was the wrong thing, because Ida's face changed and she stopped and leant against the organ pipes as if she'd been winded.

'You're a sharp one, you are,' Ida said. 'You never miss a thing.' She sighed. 'I had a bairn once. But he got sick and we couldn't afford the doctor. Toffee-nosed old sod he was. So I took Billy up to the chemist, Mr Storah, and he gave me some stuff to stop the diarrhoea. But it didn't. So then we got the doctor and it was too late. Three days after, the doctor comes wantin' his money. I was walkin' the floor with the milk goin' septic in me breasts and puttin' cold cloths on to ease it and when he tried to hand me the bill I fair went for him. Threw the washbowl across the room, water n'all.'

'I'm sorry Ida,' Tamar said. 'Really sorry.' She had wondered why Ida took such an interest in her, but now Tamar thought she knew.

Ida shook her head and sighed again – a long, lugubrious breath that made her flesh tremble. 'It was a long time ago, pet. But you mind, you get yourself an education and get out of here. You don't want to end up like me . . . Or your Mam.' She patted Tamar's shoulder. 'Come and I'll take you up to the projection box. Robby Wills won't mind and you can see the film from there.'

Mr Wills was a short, rather fussy, middle aged man in white overalls. He seemed quite happy to let Tamar stay and watch while he loaded reels of film as big as bicycle wheels onto the projector, oiled and cleaned the track and the gate, polished the lens and set it all going again with a rhythmic, ratchetty clicking, regular as a clock.

'Never, never touch the light,' he told Tamar, showing her the glass filament inside the projector. 'One flick with a duster on a hot bulb and – Bang! Flash! The bugger'll explode. Got glass in me eye once.'

Ida sat in the other corner and chatted to Robby while the film ran. They were talking about the manager. Tamar could hear Robby saying 'I don't know why you do it for him, pet.'

Ida sighed. 'There's no one else, that's for sure.'

'You should tell them. It's a cryin' shame the way he carries on.'

'No Robby. Times is hard and he's been good to me. I wouldn't put him out of a job. He'll do that himself soon enough any ways.'

'You're soft, Ida. Too bloody soft.'

'And you'd be one to know Robby Wills, wouldn't you!'

Most of the crowds had gone by the time Tamar and Ida came out, and people were trickling away down the slushy pavements towards the trolley stops. The light was fading and the flickering street lamps glowed blue and yellow where the gas mantles were just beginning to ignite. As Tamar waited for Ida to collect her money from the office, she noticed a girl standing on the pavement a few feet away, with an older woman. They were also patiently waiting for something or someone. What drew Tamar's eyes were the girl's clothes; she was wearing the most beautiful camel wool coat with a fur collar and a little fur hat over her bright red hair. The woman beside her was not so well dressed – her coat a little too short and tight and the material was thinner and cheaper. Tamar had lived with Sadie long enough to know the price and worth of other people's clothes. The girl turned, as if aware of being looked at. She had a pale oval face beneath the dark fur and very large, rather anxious, eyes. They stared at each other for a moment and then the girl smiled. Tamar smiled back. She looked nice.

A big black car drew up at the kerb and the woman with her said, 'Come on Holly. Stop day dreaming. We'll be late and your mother'll kill me.' She opened the door and the girl stepped inside.

'Did you see that,' Ida said behind Tamar's shoulder as the car pulled away. 'A chauffeur driven Bentley. You don't see many o' those round here!'

'Do you know who she is?'

Ida shook her head. 'With a car like that she's got to live up Jesmond Dene, or maybe Tynemouth. I know one thing. She's too good for the likes of us.'

Anna spent the afternoon writing a very difficult letter. It was a great relief to be able to pour out all her homesickness and feelings of grief and longing to her father. *'Mum won't let me read the letters you send to her,'* Anna wrote. *'She just reads bits out. Do you get any of my messages? I wish so much that I could come back home. You don't know how much I hate living with Grandma and Grandpa Cotteslow.'* Anna paused. Her head was full of questions she didn't know how to ask. She knew her mother had brought her to England because of the political unrest in Germany, but she was sure it wasn't the whole story. Her parents hadn't been getting on, but had their relationship been so bad that her mother could leave without even saying goodbye? And then there were other things. Was she really half Jewish? Anna thought for several minutes before she tried to put her confusion down on paper.

'*Someone told me that the children at school were . . .*' She paused again and then put a line through it. What words could she use to describe what had been done to her. It was impossible. She couldn't even say the words, let alone write them.

What had happened to her in the playground was something she tried not to think about, because whenever it came into her mind she experienced the same feelings of sickness and panic that she had felt then. Most of the time she was successful in suppressing the memory, but sometimes . . . Yesterday, on her way home, she had come round the corner of the street to find a group of men from the shipyard walking down the pavement towards her, coming off shift. For a moment she had been frozen to the ground, unable to move and then, instinctively, with no more control over her reaction than a wild animal, she had turned and run the other way, run and run until she was breathless and dizzy, aware that people were looking at her but unable to stop.

She picked up her pen to begin the sentence again. '*Were people at school unkind to me because we are Jewish? Is that true? Surely not. Please write to me. I really miss you. Kiss Grossmutter for me and tell her that I miss her too. I don't even have a photograph.*'

Anna didn't know how to send a letter to Germany, but she was sure the post office would be able to help her. She wrote 'Herr Otto Weissmann' on the envelope and printed the address very clearly underneath. The woman behind the counter took Anna's envelope without a query and the postage was much less than she'd feared. She could pay for it easily out of her pocket money. 'How long will it take?' she asked.

'About a week, maybe two with things the way they are at the moment,' the woman said. Anna's heart sank. She was going to have to wait a long time for a reply. Maybe as long as a month.

The woman saw Anna's face. 'If it's something urgent, you could always send a cable.'

'A cable?'

'It's a kind of international telegram. Quite expensive though.'

Anna shook her head. The letter would do, but it was nice to know that if she ever needed to get hold of her father quickly she could.

On Saturday night Sadie and Lily went up to the pub on the coast road where there was music and a bit of dancing. Tamar could hear them laughing and giggling – Lily singing her theme song – 'You know I'm always looking on the bright side of life!' – as she came down the street, knocking into the dustbins and Sadie shushing her loudly as they came back up the echoing side-alley to the back door. It was very late, but Sadie didn't come to bed.

The room Tamar shared with her mother was directly over the kitchen and she could hear the clink of glasses on the table. She could also hear almost everything they said to each other filtered through floor boards and linoleum. They were discussing the King's private life.

'What a cheek that Simpson woman has, thinkin' she can be Queen of England!' Lily said, 'She'll have another think comin'.'

Sadie was less censorious. 'But she's got such style, Lily. Such beautiful clothes!'

'She's an American floozy! Ought to have had a couple of bairns. That'd steady her.'

'Be truthful Lily. Put yourself in her shoes. If the King proposed to you, would you refuse?'

'Don't be daft!' Lily said. Tamar could hear the tap running and knew she was putting her cigarette out in the sink. 'Anyway, old Queen Mary's more than a match for Wallis Simpson. She'll never get past her.'

The conversation became more personal. Tamar heard Lily confessing that her husband had not been George's father. How she'd been brought up on a farm near Darlington, the eldest of ten children, and been sent away to go into service when she was only thirteen. Just put on a train at the station, she said, with her nightdress and an apron in a basket, wearing her Sunday clothes. 'Totally ignorant,' she said, 'And my word it was hard work. Scrubbin' and scourin' and heavin' coal up and down stairs all day. One half day off and tuppence a week. Not the sort of thing you'd want to be doin' with.'

She'd begun to notice a man watching her in chapel on Sundays. 'The people I worked for were very strict,' she said, 'Every Sunday mornin' we were made to go down to the Mission and sit through hellfire sermons as if we were magdalenes! It was enough to terrify the life out of you.' But there was this man who would smile at her as she came out and after a couple of weeks he spoke to her and asked her if she'd walk out with him on her afternoon off. He was first mate on a whaling ship, six months of the year away, but he brought home good money. 'So, when he popped the question, I thought, Lilian hinny, here's your chance for a bit of comfort. So I gave notice and we got married and came here to live with his Mam.'

She'd expected to have children pretty well straight away – 'As you did when you didn't know any better,' she told Sadie confidentially. But none had appeared. 'He said it was my fault. I was no good in bed. So, next time he went away, I thought I'd get a second opinion. And that's how I got George – named after my husband mind. He'd been gone nearly three month when I fell, but neither him nor his Mam ever said a word. Laugh! That pregnancy would have been in the record books.'

Tamar thought about George sleeping in the deskbed in the living room, probably listening to their conversation just as she was and wondered how he felt about it.

Lily's voice rattled on. 'And then his ship went missin' in the war and I was left here lookin' after the old body. But she went off with the Chinese flu a couple of years after that and I got the place to myself and started takin' lodgers. It's been a good livin'.'

'And didn't you ever want to get married again?' Tamar could hear her mother ask.

'What! When I've my own place and can come and go and spend my money as I like? Never in a month of Sundays!'

Then Tamar heard Sadie talking. 'My husband died shortly after we were married – I was only just pregnant,' and she heard Lily reply 'Jesus wept! And he never saw the bairn at all?' Then Sadie talked about a house called Ruthen, somewhere in Cornwall, with twenty bedrooms and a tennis court, and about Sadie's own father who'd lost a lot of money in an investment scandal and then been killed in a shooting accident. Tamar had heard some of this before in little snippets, but never the story told from beginning to end like this. She sat up in bed and leaned over towards the floor, listening intently. 'When James and I got married,' Sadie was saying, 'my mother threw me out and told me not to come back.' Tamar heard the click of a cigarette lighter. 'James wasn't good enough. He didn't have a proper job. She said he was a fortune hunter, though God knows there wasn't any fortune by then. And then he died.' There was a pause and Lily said something Tamar couldn't make out. A glass clinked. 'It's all been so hard . . . so bloody hard.' There was a hitch in Sadie's voice as she spoke.

A few minutes later Tamar heard Sadie feeling her way unsteadily up the steep stairs and then stumbling into the bedroom without putting on the light. She pretended to be asleep while her mother clumsily pulled off her clothes and fumbled herself into her nightdress and climbed onto the other side of the lumpy flock mattress. And then Tamar had to listen to Sadie crying herself to sleep.

Tamar wished she could ask Sadie more about the father she'd never known. Not just what he looked like and the kind of family he came from, but what kind of person he was. Sadie had once let slip that he'd been a conscientious objector in the last year of the war. Did that mean he'd been timid and afraid like her? She knew that her lack of confidence exasperated Sadie. 'Oh Tamar!' She would say, often, 'Why can't you be more like me?' Tamar spent long hours when Sadie was at work, staring at herself in the triple dressing table mirror. The straight mousy hair cut into a neat bob; eyes the colour of the north sea on a clear day; the definite, rather determined sort of mouth and narrow face. So unlike Sadie's soft, blonde prettiness. Tamar would peer at her father's indistinct face in the photograph, holding it up beside her own reflection, trying to trace a likeness. She longed to be more like Sadie – pretty, confident girls had no trouble finding friends. She imagined herself the centre of an admiring circle – all wanting to know her, clamouring to sit beside her in class.

But perhaps she took after her father. It would be nice to feel that. As Tamar lay there, sleepless, listening to Sadie hiccuping into her pillow, she wished that she knew more about him and his family. He must have had parents, perhaps even brothers and sisters. Why didn't any of them keep in touch? She thought of Anna with grandparents and cousins and aunts and uncles. Sadie had said that her own family had disowned her, but what about the Fells? Surely they wouldn't disown her too? For the first time Tamar wondered if Sadie was telling her the whole truth. Were there other reasons why she hadn't kept in touch with either her family or his?

CHAPTER FOUR

Anna woke early. It was more than three weeks since she'd posted the letter to her father and she was beginning to despair of a reply. Every morning she got up at seven, dressed and sat at the window, waiting for the postman to come up the street. She could time it exactly right to be down the stairs and waiting behind the front door as the letters dropped through onto the mat. But so far there had been nothing and she'd begun to wonder whether her own letter had gone astray.

As Anna plaited her hair, she could hear the postman going from house to house. The pavements were slushy where a light fall of overnight snow had settled and then melted almost immediately. His feet made a distinctive sound as he sloshed up and down the garden paths of the neighbouring houses, punctuated by the creaking of gate hinges and the clicking of latches. Anna counted the opened gates and then set off downstairs to collect the post. But her heart jumped when she saw her grandfather in the hallway. He too had heard the postman coming up the path.

'It's all right, grandpa,' Anna cried. 'I'll get it.' She plunged down the bottom steps two at a time and just managed to forestall him before he bent to pick up the four letters lying on the mat. She scooped them up, noticing with a rush of adrenaline that one of them had a German stamp and that her own name, not her mother's, was on the envelope. Still with her back to her grandfather, Anna slid the letter under her school jumper, holding it in place with her arm. Then she turned, flushed with the effort and handed him the other three.

'Bye, you're eager pet,' he said with a laugh. 'Anyone'd think you were lookin' for a valentine.' He winked and Anna blushed.

It seemed to take him an age to peer at the remaining letters and then turn to move back into the kitchen. Anna ran upstairs into the bedroom. Her hands shook as she tore open the envelope and took out the single folded sheet of paper. Two photographs slid out as she did so and her father's face stared back at her, smiling and familiar, from the surface of the dressing table where they had fallen. She sat down on the edge of the bed to read what he had written. It was the first time Anna had ever had to decipher her father's formal German script and the letter seemed stilted and hesitant and somehow unlike the man she knew and loved.

My dearest Anna, he had written. *You have no idea how much happiness your letter gave me. I was afraid I might never hear from you again. Grossmutter has your letter in the pocket of her apron and she reads it every day – over and over.*

The house is very empty without you and there aren't any visitors to fill it at this time of year. There's a lot of snow here and we don't go very far. The station's been closed for three weeks so I don't know how long it will take this letter to reach you. Grossmutter hasn't been out of the house for fear of falling in the street, so I do all the shopping now. She is far from well. How we're going to manage in the spring when the visitors return, I don't know.

You asked me to talk to your friends, but I haven't seen Fraulein Bateman and Fraulein Beatham since you left and the house is locked and the shutters over the windows, so perhaps they too have gone back to England.

How I wish you'd told me that the children at school were being unpleasant to you. Did you tell Mutter? Is that why she took you away so suddenly? It has grieved me deeply, so I will try to answer your questions as fully as I can. It's true that the family name is Jewish. My father and namesake, Otto Weissmann died when you were very young, so I suppose you would not have known. You look very like him, which is unfortunate when things are as they are now. Your grandfather left the Jewish community when he married a gentile wife and was cut off by his family. He moved to Partenkirchen and we were brought up in the Lutheran church. Both your uncle Joe and myself married non Jewish wives, but it seems that such a thinning of the blood and being adopted into the Christian faith means nothing. The crime of having Jewish blood can't be ignored unless only an eighth part runs in your veins. And there are those who are unwilling to tolerate even such a small contamination.

As far as I know, our family has been always been German, but now we have to register like foreigners, and wear a yellow band on our arms to show our Jewish origins. The hatred our fellow countrymen seem to feel for us is hard to get used to and we are constantly looking over our shoulders – so much so that there is a new phrase for it; 'der Deutsch blick'. In Freiburg some drunken youths put a stone through Uncle Joe's window and tried to set fire to the shop. Fortunately it was put out in time and although some of the stock was damaged, Uncle Joe's workshop and tools were saved. It was very unpleasant but everything's quiet now and it's business as usual again. We are all hoping that this state of affairs will not last and that things will be restored to sanity again soon.

I can't write anymore now. I must cut wood for the stove and feed the horses before it gets dark. We still have the foal you'll be glad to hear. I'm enclosing some photographs for you. One of myself and your grandparents standing outside the house, taken just after I joined the Navy, and one of myself with you when you were a baby. My dear Anna. How I miss you. But soon you will be old enough to visit us by yourself. Will you come? Grossmutter sends loving kisses.

Your sad Papa.

PS Cousin Maya says she's very envious of you and that she would like to visit you in England one day.

Anna kissed his signature and then folded the letter up again and tucked it into the pocket of her gymslip. A single tear slid down her cheek and dropped into her lap. As she dried her eyes on the cuff of her blouse she comforted herself with her father's words of invitation. It was something that hadn't occurred to her before and the simplicity of it made her breathless with excitement. If he didn't come to her, she could go to him. All the pocket money she saved to buy art materials could perhaps be used for a train fare. Anna wondered how much it would cost and how long it would take her to save that much.

Tamar's life had begun to settle into a comfortable routine. Lily cooked her breakfast after Sadie went off to work, then Tamar put on her old winter coat and dragged herself reluctantly up the road to school. Queen Alexandra's compared quite favourably with some of the schools that Tamar had endured. English was her favourite subject. It was the only class where her imagination was regarded as an asset. Miss Wilson never told her off for day dreaming, or marked her fictional experiments down for being improbable. To Tamar's great relief she'd been released from the oral mangling of Great Expectations on Mondays and Wednesdays.

'You're such a fast reader,' Miss Wilson said, 'You can have those lessons for silent reading.'

Tamar had finished the book by the end of the first week and was now devouring Oliver Twist. Miss Wilson was also giving her extra work, essays and occasional grammar exercises. But although Tamar thrived under this encouragement, it also attracted the derision of a whole group of girls in the class. When the teachers praised Tamar's immaculate pronunciation, and her command of written English, there were hate faces, poking tongues and whispers of 'stuck-up bitch' at the back of the class which she tried to ignore.

The girls punished her relentlessly for being different. Never before in her life had she been accused of being 'Posh', but here – because of the way she spoke and the fact that her mother sold fur coats in Pergavie's, she found herself – with Anna – at the top of a well-defined social hierarchy. On the next rung down were the girls whose fathers worked in the shipyards as skilled labour, and they considered themselves a cut above girls like Elsie, whose mother worked in Haggey's rope factory. But even Elsie was a whole social scale above those whose mothers gutted herring down on the fish-quays. These were the lowest of the low according to the other girls, and they were constantly teased for being snotty-nosed or having fish scales in their hair and humiliated by a repeated chant of 'Phew. Phew. Stinky Pooh! – I'm not sittin' next to you!'

Tamar's endurance was sometimes tested to the limit, but she kept her fists curled tight in her pockets, remembering Bertie McAffery. She mustn't let that extraordinary rage take hold of her again. Where had it come from? 'Sticks and stones,' she kept saying to herself through gritted teeth. Sadie was right. The girls couldn't keep it up forever. And in any case her tormentors would be soon be old enough to leave school altogether. Most of the girls in her class were nearly fourteen and in their last year of compulsory schooling. Elsie was already talking about the money she could be making in the Sunlight soap factory and counting the days off until her birthday.

And at least Tamar now had an ally in Anna. The hostility of the other girls had thrown them together, so without ever choosing to do so, they spent a lot of time in each other's company. In the playground or out in the street their classmates ignored them both. Once or twice Tamar and Anna tried to approach little groups of girls in a friendly way, but they always turned their backs and walked off.

'They don't want to know us at all,' Anna sighed, leaning against the wall, looking across the yard.

'It's just because we're different,' Tamar said. 'They've all grown up together.'

'I find it really strange to think I might have been one of them,' Anna said. 'If my mother had stayed here instead of going off to Germany I might have spent the last thirteen years here.'

'I can't imagine ever being in one place for that long,' Tamar said sadly. 'People ask me where I come from and I can't give them an answer. I don't belong anywhere.'

'Yes you do,' Anna said. 'Everyone belongs somewhere. What about Heaton Street?'

'It's just a lodging house,' Tamar said.

'Why won't you invite me there?' Anna asked.

Tamar hesitated. She'd seen Anna's comfortable home and felt sure that she would look down her nose at the run-down terrace and the rented room that smelled of gas and chip fat. And then there was the matter of the white lie Tamar had told about her father. If Anna came she would be certain to find out.

'It's not fair,' Anna went on. 'I invited you to my house.'

'I'm not allowed to have guests,' Tamar said, hoping that it was true. Friends had never been permitted at Miss Simpson's, on the grounds that they might jump on the furniture or make a noise on the stairs. Tamar counted on it being the same at Lily's.

~~~~~~~~~~~~~~~~~~

After school, Anna let herself into the house quietly. If her mother heard her come in she would immediately give her a list of jobs to do or errands to be run. Anna closed the front door, removed her shoes and tiptoed upstairs. It was important to get an hour's drawing practice before the light faded. The winter nights were short and cold. In her unheated room Anna took out her sketch book and pencils and the book that Miss Bateman had given her and began one of the exercises in perspective. It was a painting by Vermeer and the trick was to find the Golden Mean and then work out how each of the elements of the portrait had been arranged along the angles of sight to focus the eye in just the right place.

Anna had just begun to measure the planes and rule in the lines when her mother opened the door and came in carrying a cup and saucer. 'I thought you might like some tea.' Mrs Weissmann set the cup down on the dressing table. She seemed nervous and fidgety. 'It's cold up here. Why don't you work in the kitchen? It would be much warmer.'

'It's peaceful here,' Anna said. She could also have added that it was more private, but she didn't. She realised that she had instinctively put her hand over the paper when her mother entered the room.

Mrs Weissmann was in no hurry to leave. She sat down in the Lloyd Loom chair opposite the bed. 'I wanted to talk to you,' she said, looking distinctly uncomfortable. 'I don't know whether you've noticed . . .' she hesitated, biting her lip and filling Anna with irritation. What on earth was the matter with her? Then Mrs Weissmann took a deep breath and began again. 'It's very hard for me to say this Anna, but I think you ought to know that I'm having another baby.'

'You're what?' Anna felt as if a bucket of icy water had been thrown over her.

'I know it must be a shock to you. It was to me. I'm nearly forty.' She paused as if expecting Anna to say something and then
~~~~~~~~~~~~~~~~~~

went on. 'But you must see now why we had to leave? It wasn't safe to have a baby there. They were talking about preventing people with Jewish blood having children. It didn't matter that I was English. People used to spit at me in the street.' She paused again and then said, 'They took away Mrs Goldblum's child. Do you remember?'

Anna shook her head.

'The couple who had the little farm up on the alm – the ones who sold your father the horse? They never had any children and everyone assumed they couldn't. But one day, when she was just a bit older than me, Mrs Goldblum had a baby – a little boy. They were so thrilled. But it was an idiot – spastic I think. It used to dribble and make strange noises. But it didn't matter to the Goldblums, they doted on the baby. And then one day – you must have been about ten or eleven by then – some officials came and said that the child had to go into an institution. They took the little boy away from them and they never saw him again. Mrs Goldblum was almost demented. She never really recovered.' Anna's mother looked down at her hands, twisting her wedding ring round on her finger. 'So you see why I had to get out? Believe me, leaving was one of the hardest decisions I've ever had to make.'

Anna's feelings must have been written on her face because her mother sighed and said, 'Promise me you'll try to understand. Please, Anna?' She touched her arm briefly as if to comfort her and then went out of the room.

Anna felt stunned. How could her mother be having a baby?

She was so old. It was disgusting. But as she thought about it, several things began to make sense. She'd been too miserable to notice her mother's tiredness and swollen ankles. The amount of weight she was putting on. The visits to the doctor. As she thought about it, Anna realised that there was one question she hadn't asked. Did her father know about the baby? There had been nothing in his letter to suggest that he did.

Suddenly Anna couldn't bear to be in the house. She put on her shoes, grabbed her coat and beret and ran out onto the street.

Tamar was curled up in the eiderdown writing an essay. It felt cosy and comfortable. She could look out of the window at the dusk shrouding the allotment huts and listen to the sounds of Lily cooking tea in the kitchen underneath and feel almost at home. It was Tamar's greatest worry now that Sadie would decide she didn't like it here and move on. Tamar was beginning to enjoy living at Lily Kennedy's. Ida was usually there when Tamar came home from school, with the kettle boiling on the gas for a cup of tea. Then, if Tamar didn't have any homework, they would sit comfortably on the settee in the living room and listen to the wireless, or talk about Ida's music hall days until George and Sadie came home and Lily served up the evening meal. Sadie was often tired and fractious when she came in. Pergavie's was a trial; the customers were awkward, the floor manageress was a cow and her feet hurt. It sometimes took several glasses of Lily's gin before Sadie began to 'turn sunny-side out' as Ida put it. George, on the other hand, generally came home in a good humour because he'd just finished his apprentice-ship and been given his Union card.

'What's the Union?' Tamar had asked.

Lily laughed. 'The Union's like a religion round here, pet. If you don't belong, you don't work.'

'You pay so much a week out of your wages and they look after you,' George explained. 'In the big strike a few years back, people round here would've starved without them.'

Tamar found George fascinating. It wasn't just his foreign looks, it was his silence. He was very, very quiet – not the quietness of shyness, she was shy herself – but a deep and impenetrable reserve. George hardly spoke at all – letting his mother do the talking. Tamar had no idea what kind of person he was. When he came in from the shipyard he would go straight out the back and strip off at the sink to wash himself down before putting on a clean shirt and pullover to eat his tea. He had a bottle of brown ale with it every night from the crate Lily kept in the wash-house and he rarely said anything during the meal. Afterwards he disappeared into the living room with the daily papers while the women talked in the kitchen.

'George is too soft-hearted,' Lily had said dismissively the night before. 'He'll never get anywhere.' She told a story about a previous New Year's Eve when everyone had gathered in the square to hear the Town Hall clock chime midnight. George had been approached by a woman with a small child in her arms who claimed to have had her purse stolen in the crush. 'Can you lend me the fare home, hinny?' she'd said. 'I'll get it back to you, honest.' George had given her half a crown and his address. 'The great lummock,' Lily said. 'It's the oldest trick in the book. Fancy bein' taken in by that.' 'The bairn was crying.' was all George would say. But the money had never come back.

Tamar heard George's steps in the back yard, the scraping of his boots and then his voice talking to Lily. But, a few moments later, instead of his usual routine, she heard a strange and wonderful sound coming up from the living room. She put away her exercise book, combed her hair extra carefully and rubbed her cheeks to put some colour into them before she went downstairs.

On the living room table was a brand new wind-up gramophone and a stack of records in brown paper sleeves. George was standing beside the table in his overalls with a broad smile on his face.

'My overtime money,' he said, gesturing towards the gramophone as Tamar came through the door.

'What's the music?' Tamar asked.

'Opera. Benjamino Gigli.'

'An awful racket, pet! That's what it is.' Lily was standing in the kitchen doorway with a pained expression on her face. 'But you're goin' to have to get used to it if you live here. He likes his classical music does whoar George.' She sniffed and then added, 'I don't know where he gets that from,' as though it was a hereditary disease.

George smiled at Tamar as Lily went back into the kitchen. 'This is called Pagliacci. It's about a clown whose woman goes off with someone else. He sings this when he's getting dressed up to carry on with the show.'

'It's beautiful.' Tamar was entranced. 'I've never been able to listen to music much. Just films and radio and things like that. Sadie likes dance band music. But I've never heard anything like this before.'

'Neither had I until a couple of years ago. We had a lodger

who played the violin in the orchestra down at the Grand Hotel. I used to sit on the stairs just to listen to him practising. It was wonderful!'

'I bet Lily didn't think so.'

George grinned. 'Anyway, when the Carl Rosa Company came to Newcastle he got permission from a mate of his for us to go and stand in the pit. I'd never seen anything like it in my life. I went every night. Pagliacci, Rosencavalier, Rigoletto – I saw the lot.'

Tamar had never heard George talk so much before – his enthusiasm for the music seemed to evaporate his shyness.

Lily put her head around the door, nodding towards Tamar. 'I've got a visitor for you pet.' She opened the door wide to reveal Anna standing there, red-cheeked as if she'd been running. Her eyes were bright and swollen and Tamar suspected that she'd been crying.

'You go on in pet and I'll make us all a cup of tea,' Lily said.

'I hope you don't mind,' Anna said apologetically. 'I just needed to get out of the house.'

There was a moment's silence before Tamar recovered herself enough to introduce Anna to George, who was blushing the deepest shade of red.

'I love the music,' Anna said. 'I could hear it as I was coming up the path.' She lifted one of the wax discs from the table. 'Have you got any Wagner? My father used to play that on Sundays, very loud. He liked Tannhauser but my mother wouldn't let him play it during the week because she said it annoyed the guests.'

'I've got a list of records that I'm saving up for,' George said, taking a crumpled piece of paper out of his pocket.

Tamar was conscious of a pain in her chest as she watched them poring over it, wishing that she could share their interest. George seemed to be noticing Anna in a way he had never noticed her.

Tamar was hoping that Anna would leave before Sadie got back from work, but she seemed perfectly at home in Heaton Street. Far from turning up her nose, as Tamar had feared, she curled up on the sofa and looked around approvingly. 'I like your house,' she said. 'It's cosy. More friendly than mine.'

Sadie arrived home at half past six and flung herself down in the chair close to the fire, holding her hands out to the flames. 'So you're Anna,' she said, smiling. 'I've heard a great deal about you from Tamar.'

'I'm very pleased to meet you,' Anna said. She was staring at Sadie in the fascinated kind of way that people did when they met her for the first time.

'Your father's still in Germany, Tamar said. You must miss him a lot.'

'I do. But I'm hoping to go and visit him sometime soon – perhaps in the summer holidays, if I can save up enough money.'

This was the conversation that Tamar had been dreading. She listened to its progress with a feeling of hopeless inevitability.

'When is your husband coming back from India?' Anna asked innocently.

Sadie's eyebrows shot up. 'Who told you that?' she said sharply, looking across at Tamar. 'I'm afraid it isn't true. I'm a widow. My husband died before Tamar was born.'

Tamar's face was hot with shame. She could feel herself going bright red. Anna gave her a strange look but nothing more was said until it was time for her to go. Outside on the step Anna said, 'Why did you tell me that lie about your father?'

Tamar squirmed. 'I didn't want you to think that I was illegitimate.'

'Why on earth would I do that?'

'People sometimes do when you say you haven't a father. Promise me you won't say anything at school?' She hesitated a moment and then said, 'I've never said anything about your name really being Anne!'

'That's blackmail.'

'No it isn't. It's a bargain. You keep my secrets and I'll keep yours.'

'All right. It's a bargain. But you've got to promise not to lie to me anymore. If we're going to be friends we have to tell each other the truth. Agreed?'

Tamar nodded.

'Come and stay with me on Friday night,' Anna said. 'Will you? You can help me find out how to get back to Germany to see my father.'

When Tamar came in, Lily was in the kitchen setting the table. She turned and smiled. 'She's a canny girl that friend of yours. You tell her she can come any time!' Lily put down the cutlery and came closer, lowering her voice. 'Her grandpa, that old Mr Cotteslow,' she said, 'He comes in the Corner House up on the coast road on Saturday nights, all smarmy and hoity toity. But he's a dark horse, I can tell you. Got a woman down in Shields that he sees. One of the women on the quay. But don't you go tellin' that to your friend mind.'

Tamar went straight upstairs and climbed onto the bed to read her book. A few moments later she heard Sadie coming upstairs. Sadie came into the bedroom and sat on the bed, fidgeted for a moment or two and then said, 'I know how much you hate being teased, but you really shouldn't tell lies.'

Tamar felt too ashamed to say anything. She kept her head down, focussing on the page.

'I do understand, you know,' Sadie said. 'Better than you think. I used to get teased at school too.'

'Did you?' Tamar lifted her head. She couldn't imagine that anyone would want to tease Sadie. 'What about?'

'Oh, lots of things.' Sadie's face had become vague again. 'My parents, my clothes . . . being ambitious. I wanted to leave Cornwall and see the world.' She smiled ruefully. 'I used to dream about being in films. I was very pretty when I was seventeen or eighteen. But then I met your father.' She reached out her hand and stroked Tamar's hair. 'You're very like him you know, especially when you look at me like that. You've got his eyes.'

Tamar didn't know what to say.

'If people ever accuse you of being a bastard, tell them you're a love child. It's not a bad thing to be.'

~~~~~~~~~~~~~~~~~~

After school on Friday, Tamar and Anna went straight to the railway station. 'How much would it cost to buy a ticket to Germany?' Anna asked the man behind the glass in the ticket office.

He laughed. 'Thinkin' of runnin' away, pet?'
~~~~~~~~~~~~~~~~~~

Anna shook her head. She looked angry. 'I'm going to visit my father.'

'Sorry, pet. I thought you were havin' me on. We don't have much call for tickets to foreign parts.' He smiled and took down a big almanac with broken binding from the shelf, opened it and thumbed through the shabby pages. 'If you went by train you'd have to go to London and then get the boat train and change at Ostend or Paris.' He pronounced it 'Paree' and then paused as if struck by a sudden thought. 'But did you know about the ferries? You could get a boat from Shields to Hamburg. That's in Germany. I can't tell you how much it would cost, but it'd be a canny lot.' He scratched his head. 'Have you got a passport, pet?'

Anna shook her head slowly. Tamar could tell by the expression on her face that she hadn't thought of that.

'Well, you'll need one of them and a visa to get to Germany.'

'How do I get a passport?'

'Sorry, you'll have to ask your mother, pet. I haven't got one meself.'

'I thought it was going to be so simple,' Anna said as they walked slowly back up the hill. 'But I'd never get my mother to agree to let me go.'

'Perhaps you could write to your father and ask him,' Tamar said. She felt a sudden pang of envy. At least Anna had a father.

Anna seemed dispirited. 'I will. But it looks as if I'm going to have to save much more money than I'd thought.'

As they rounded the corner of the coast road where little alleyways opened down the backs of the terraced houses a man stepped out in front of them. They stopped and Tamar heard Anna gasp. He had his coat open and Tamar could see that the flies of his trousers were undone and his penis, stiff and purple, protruded like a swollen tongue. Anna screamed and the sound, echoing from the walls of the alleys, seemed to startle him. He pulled his overcoat round him and shuffled off down the alleyway.

'Come on Anna,' Tamar tugged at her sleeve, but she was rooted to the spot, shaking, her face white and tears beginning to pour down her cheeks. 'It's only a flasher,' Tamar said, swallowing her own fear and disgust. 'You get them all the time round here.

Lily warned me.'

Anna began to take great gasps of air as if coming up from under water. She shook off Tamar's arm and wiped her sleeve across her face. She seemed angry. 'Of course I know it's just a flasher! Don't be silly. That's not why I'm upset. Do you think I'd be frightened of a stupid, sad old man?'

Tamar said nothing, but she didn't believe her.

Anna's mother made an elaborate performance out of making Tamar welcome. There were clean linen sheets on the bed and a fluffy towel laid out on the chair. 'Do take a bath if you would like to,' she said as she showed Tamar where everything was. Tamar blushed, feeling obscurely patronised. Had Anna told her mother about the lodgings with the outside toilet and no bathroom? Mrs Weissmann's gracious offer made Tamar feel poor and dirty. She said 'No thank you,' in a firm voice, feeling sure that it was the polite thing to do. But the thought of having a bath in a real bath, with hot water, all to herself, made her long to accept. Tamar fantasised about bathrooms. Every Saturday evening she went with Sadie to the swimming pool on Saville Road and paid for a bath cubicle. In between, she had to make do with 'sponge downs' standing in a metal basin in the washhouse, filled with a kettle of hot water.

Despite Anna's daunting mother, Tamar enjoyed sleeping in Anna's room. Apart from the luxury of an indoor toilet, it was very companionable to lie in the darkness and talk after the light was switched off.

'It must have been beautiful in Germany,' Tamar said, looking at the picture on Anna's wall – mountains, lakes and tiny wooden houses like cuckoo clocks, just visible in the faint glow of the street lamps.

'I miss it,' Anna said wistfully. 'I get really homesick.' She paused as though thinking about something and then asked, 'Did you know my mother's having a baby?'

Tamar didn't. 'You don't sound very pleased. Don't you want to have a brother or sister?' Tamar had often thought how nice it would have been to have a sibling.

'It isn't that. I suppose it's because she didn't tell me.' There was another pause. 'I wish I had a mother like yours. You and Sadie seem to be really good friends.'

'I suppose so. Don't you get on with yours?'

'I used to. But since we came to England, she's changed and I can't talk to her any more. She doesn't understand me and I don't understand her. Why didn't she tell me about the baby when we first came to England? If she'd said we had to come here because of that, I'd have understood. But nobody told me anything.'

There was a brief silence and then Anna went on, 'I worry sometimes that my mother doesn't intend us to go back.' She sounded upset.

Down in the hallway a clock was chiming the half hour, and outside the wind was blowing someone's garden gate to and fro, banging it against the latch. Tamar listened to the night sounds and wondered what to say. But when Anna spoke again it was on a totally different subject. 'We're going to be fourteen soon. We'll be old enough to leave school. Almost everybody else in the class is leaving. Do you know what you're going to do?'

Tamar shook her head. 'I'd quite like to stay on at school. But they might not let me. What about you?'

'Mum wants me to take the entrance exams and go to the High School. They're going to pay for me to have extra lessons. Mum wants me to be a teacher, but what I really want is to go to art college and paint.' Anna propped herself on one elbow and turned to face Tamar. 'Isn't there anything you really want Tamar? Something you burn for secretly?'

Tamar watched the play of light from the street across the ceiling, thinking about what Anna had said before she answered. Anna's ambitions were so concrete; her own desires so vague. Last week in English, Miss Wilson had given her a poem to analyse. It was called 'A Prayer for my Daughter' and somehow it seemed to spell out everything that she most longed for in life. When she came to the lines where the poet wished his daughter rooted like a green laurel 'in one dear, perpetual place,' it was as though he'd written it just for her. That was what she yearned for. But a real home, a family, and a place where she belonged seemed as much a fairy tale as the afternoon matinee at the cinema, and if she told Anna that that was her dearest wish, Tamar wasn't sure she'd understand. 'I don't have anything you could really call an ambition,' Tamar said slowly. 'I just want to be happy and not have to worry about money.' It sounded rather lame.

Anna said nothing and Tamar could feel her contempt. Although she couldn't confess it to Anna, this lack of ambition worried Tamar too, making her feel like a rudderless boat swinging around on every tide. She'd never been in the habit of looking into the future – it was a scary place, full of disruption and disappointment. She dreaded what it might bring. But now Anna's words made her realise that she was going to have to think about it quite soon. She knew that Sadie couldn't afford to send her to the High School, but if she worked hard at Queen Alex's was it possible that she too could go to college? Was there something worth having ahead of her? 'I just want to be happy,' she said again before she went to sleep.

CHAPTER FIVE

At the end of the month, to Tamar's great disappointment, Ida left to take a ground floor room in the centre of town. She said she couldn't make the stairs any more, but Tamar could still come and see her at the cinema any Saturday she wanted. Tamar promised that she would. Ida's room was taken by Mr Coles, a draughtsman at Parsons whose wife had run off with a naval rating. This had obviously been a considerable blow to his pride. 'A rating!' he said often, 'Not even an officer!'

It soon became a joke. As he left the table after tea to go to his room, Sadie would mime 'A rating!' behind his back with an exaggerated expression of horror and she and Lily would collapse with laughter over the kitchen table.

The following week Mr Hake went as mysteriously as he'd lived – giving a week's rent in lieu of notice. He took the suitcases with him, leaving no forwarding address and when Tamar peeped inside, his room looked as if no-one had ever lived there. Lily put an advert in the paper shop window and the room was quickly taken by a civil servant called Miss Francis who worked for the Customs and Excise and smelled strongly of Yardley's Lavender Water which she sprinkled liberally on her clothes. She'd been living with her mother in Wallsend and told anyone who would listen how devotedly she'd nursed her until she died. Tamar heard the whole saga of the bed sores ('Big enough to put a pudding bowl in!') and the sodden sheets ('Sometimes half a dozen a day! I don't know how I managed.') several times over. Miss Francis had consoled herself with the thought that she would be comfortably off after her mother's death. But then, after the funeral, Miss Francis had discovered that the house and all the money had been left to her brother who lived in Hartlepool and was married to a fancy woman who wouldn't do a hands turn when it came to looking after her mother in law.

'He always was the favourite, though I don't know what he ever did to deserve it,' Miss Francis said. She was very bitter when she talked, and the atmosphere in the living room became rather uncomfortable. The only thing her mother had given her, before she died, was a beautiful square-cut antique emerald ring with diamonds round it, which Sadie said was probably worth as much as the house, only Miss Francis didn't appreciate it, not being the kind of person to wear jewellery. 'If only it had been something a little more discreet,' Miss Francis complained.

'You could always sell it,' Sadie said.

'Oh, I could never do that.' Miss Francis' mouth quivered with distress. It was as though Sadie had suggested something sacrilegious. 'It's all I have left of Mother.'

Tamar heard Sadie mutter 'Hypocrite!' under her breath.

Miss Francis stayed in her room most of the time reading books which she sometimes lent to Tamar. They were a curious mixture – cheap romances in brown paper covers, classics like Dickens and Austen, as well as modern novelists such as Rebecca West and Rosamund Lehmann. Tamar devoured them all. Lily teased her about being a bookworm, but it irritated Sadie, who had become quite sarcastic.

'It's about time you got rid of all those romantic illusions,' she would say every time she saw Tamar engrossed in another novel. 'You've got to toughen up if you want to survive.'

This attitude puzzled Tamar. Miss Francis, on the other hand, was impressed. 'My goodness, you're a fast reader!' she said as Tamar returned yet another book. 'Why ever don't you join the library yourself?'

'I didn't know I could,' Tamar said. She'd been under the impression that only adults could join.

'Anyone can,' Miss Francis said with a sniff. 'Fancy not knowing that!' So, on the following evening after school, Miss Francis met Tamar on the steps of the Carnegie Library and arranged for her to become a member.

The library was a revelation. Most evenings Tamar went there straight from school and did her homework at one of the long tables. It was more comfortable than trying to do it in the bedroom, or in the kitchen with Lily's wireless going full blast. Tamar loved the quietness of the big room with its high windows and roman columns, the smell of book-bindings, the rustle of paper. To be surrounded by so many books was utter bliss. When Tamar opened a book she was lost, the world around faded into fantasy and only the story was real. She fought with the characters, wept with them, stood on station platforms, climbed mountains, travelled to Australia and back, up dark rivers in Africa – sometimes she was so lost, she had to be retrieved and evicted when the library closed.

'You really like being here, don't you,' one of the women said as she waited for Tamar to collect her things.

'I love books,' Tamar said. 'I couldn't live without them.'

'Maybe you should think about being a librarian when you leave school,' the woman said. 'Have you thought about it?'

'How do you get to be a librarian?'

'You have to get your school certificate and then you can get taken on as a junior trainee. Or you can go to college and get qualifications. I started straight from the high school. Ask your mother to bring you in to see the head librarian, if you're really interested.'

George sometimes walked home with her. He too was keeping late hours, working a lot of overtime at the Yard in order to meet government targets on new ships ordered by the Navy. They all seemed to be named after Kings and Queens, Dukes and Duchesses, Cities and Counties. 'We can't lay the keels quick enough,' George said. 'If I work this much overtime, I'll be as rich as Croesus.'

'What's it all for?' Tamar asked. 'Why do they want so many ships?'

George shrugged and took a long drag on his pipe before he answered. 'The navy don't tell us what's up,' he said gruffly, 'but the rumour going round the yard is that there's going to be a war. What with Hitler in Germany and that Franco bloke in Spain. They're getting too big for their boots.'

The following evening Tamar heard Lily and Sadie talking in the kitchen about the possibility of war.

'Of course, nothing's going to happen,' Sadie said. 'It's all just alarmism.'

'I don't know, hinny,' Lily said slowly. 'Them lads at the yard know a thing or two we don't. It doesn't bear thinkin' about. Jesus wept! All those bonny lads!'

Tamar wondered how Anna would be affected if there was war with Germany. It would be very uncomfortable, having relatives who were supposed to be your enemies. Tamar no longer thought of Anna as German – she spoke English perfectly without an accent, but the first time she'd brought Anna to the house, she'd asked George afterwards what he thought of her and he'd said laconically 'She's all right. For a Boche.' And then he'd added 'But you'd never know to hear her talk.'

George was different with Anna around – more self-conscious. Tamar noticed that he scrubbed himself extra hard in the wash house and put a collar on his shirt if she was there when he came home. And his eyes followed her all round the room. There was something about Anna that made people look at her – not rudely, but in an admiring kind of way. Perhaps, Tamar speculated, it was her height, but there were other tall girls in the school who didn't merit another glance. Nor was she beautiful – more handsome really, with her big dark eyes, the long curved nose and her glossy, chestnut hair. There was something about Anna, a presence, that drew people to her, even though Anna was often quite rude to them. For there was also something spiky and dangerous about Anna. From being the sunniest person in the world she could turn suddenly, her eyes flaring with anger and lash out with her tongue – aiming unerringly for her victim's weakest point. She'd taken up smoking – not the Woodbine fives that Elsie and her friends smoked whenever they could get them, but long continental cigarettes in a black holder like women Tamar had seen in films. As she couldn't smoke at home, or at school she practised in the street. 'You shouldn't smoke in the street,' Tamar told her. 'Only tarts do that. Sadie said!'

'Then people will just have to think I'm a tart,' Anna said calmly.

But Tamar knew they wouldn't.

Anna spent as much time as she could at Heaton Street. She was glad to get out of a house increasingly taken over by the approaching 'happy event' – at least that's what Grandma Cotteslow called it. Anna had other names for the imminent arrival. Her mother was enormous now – unable to get out of a chair without assistance and the expected baby was openly talked about; a bassinet made ready in her mother's room, the layette neatly folded on the chest of drawers. 'Aren't you excited?' Anna's mother asked occasionally, without getting an answer. She wasn't entirely happy at the amount of time Anna was spending with Tamar. 'The girl's all right,' Mrs Weissmann said, 'Quite a sweet little thing. But the mother! Your grandfather's told me all about her. Something of a fast piece from what I hear – not the kind of woman I'd want to have anything to do with. And I'm not sure I want you mixing with her either.'

But Anna didn't reply. She was seeing less of Tamar anyway.

In the first weeks of the new year her mother had arranged for her to have private lessons in English Literature and History from an old school friend. Unlike Anna's mother, Mrs Davidson had gone on to become a teacher before she married. She had a husband who taught chemistry at the boys' grammar school and two dull, rather stolid looking children. Three evenings a week Anna took the bus straight after school to sit in Mrs Davidson's dining room making endless notes. Her hobby was embroidery and while Anna worked she would sit at the table pricking coloured thread in and out of a piece of linen. Doilies and tablecloths adorned every possible surface and the furniture was obscured by cushions and seat covers and antimacassars, the walls hung with embroidered dogs with ribbon bows, samplers and bouquets of improbable flowers. It was all so fussy and sentimental Anna tried not to look.

Occasionally Mr Davidson was at home when Anna went for her lesson. He was a ginger haired, serious man usually hidden behind a newspaper, but the papers he read were quite unlike the ones at home. Not Reveille or the Mirror or the Shields Gazette, but the New York Herald Tribune, Manchester Guardian and the Times.

One evening, when he was absent, the Herald Tribune was

folded on the table and, as Anna sat down, a sub-title caught her eye at the top of one of the columns. *Nazis say No to Degenerate Art.* Anna picked it up. 'Do you mind if I read this?' she asked Mrs Davidson.

'No, no. Take it home with you if you want. It's yesterdays. I've just finished the crossword.'

Anna put it in her bag.

Back in her own room, she read the article thoroughly. It seemed that a number of artists' work had been purged from German museums and art galleries under pressure from a group called the National Socialist Society for German Culture. The paintings and sculptures of artists considered to be degenerate or corrupt, were to be exhibited around Germany under the title *Entartete Kunst* and Anna was shocked by the list of names. It included Wassily Kandinsky, Marc Chagall, Paul Klee, Max Ernst, names that Miss Bateman had taught her to believe were the future of European art, however strange and incomprehensible their work. It seemed to be part of a general campaign. Jewish students and teachers were also to be excluded from German universities in an attempt to rid the cultural life of the country from what the article called 'Bolshevik' influences. *'Jewish artists,'* the article went on, *'will no longer be able to study at the major academies or have their work hung in national museums and galleries.'*

It occurred to Anna reluctantly that if her mother hadn't brought her to England, her chances of studying art in Germany would have been lost and it would probably have meant an end to her hopes of being admitted to the Slade. But what really worried Anna was a small paragraph further down the column which mentioned that the Reich Chancellor had sent troops to somewhere they referred to as 'the Rhineland' in preparation for possible conflict. *'The clouds of war hang over Europe and countries who should be allies are consumed with hatred and violence. A German spokesman said, "We cannot stand forever as a second class nation. We will defend ourselves against the creeping corruption of Bolshevism."'* If there was a war in Europe, what would happen to her family then?

The baby was born at the end of April while Anna was at

school. In the morning, her mother was sitting drinking tea in the kitchen quite normally, but before Anna left she said, 'I think you might have a little brother or sister by tonight. I've just sent your grandpa for the midwife.'

Anna felt a pang of anxiety. She knew that women died in childbirth. Was her mother going to be all right? 'Do you want me to stay at home?' she asked.

'Goodness no! You'll be better out of the way. You go to school and don't worry about it. Everything will be fine.'

When Anna came home with Tamar it was all over. A large grey-haired woman with big red hands and a dark moustache was sitting in the kitchen having a cup of tea. From her uniform and the black bag on the table beside her, Anna presumed she was the midwife.

'It's a boy!' Grandma Cotteslow said. 'Looks just like his Grandpa.'

'Can I see him?' Anna found that she was quite excited, in spite of herself.

'You can go up,' the midwife said in a strong Scottish accent, 'but don't disturb your mother if she's sleeping. She's had a hard time.'

They crept up the stairs and Anna opened the bedroom door carefully. The curtains were drawn and the room was dim. There was a strong smell of antiseptic. Anna's mother was lying on her side facing the door and she opened her eyes when they came in.

'Hello,' she said. 'Come and meet your little brother.'

The baby was in a wicker bassinet beside the bed. He looked red and crumpled.

'He's really big,' Tamar said. 'I thought newborn babies were supposed to be tiny.'

'Eight pounds, eleven ounces,' Mrs Weissmann said. She sounded very weary.

He was snuffling and moving his hands and mouth in a way that reminded Anna of the newborn puppies at Elke's house in Partenkirchen. She put her hand in to touch him and was surprised when his tiny fingers closed tightly around her own. It gave her a strange feeling in her chest.

'I'm going to call him Arthur Frank, after your Grandpa.'
'Aren't you going to call him after Dad?'
Mrs Weissmann shook her head. 'This isn't the right time to give a child a German name, Anna.'
'Have you told Dad?'
'Of course. Your grandpa's gone down to send him a cable.'
Anna felt relieved.
The midwife bustled in. 'Come along now girls and leave your mother to get some rest. His royal highness will wake her soon enough.'

At the end of May, George invited Tamar down to the docks to see one of the ships launched. 'You can bring that friend of yours, if you like,' he added casually. But Tamar wasn't deceived. George liked Anna, she could tell. So on a wet Saturday morning with an unseasonably cold east wind Tamar and Anna went down to the shipyard, walking through the poorer dockside streets where the houses stood back to back, looking like scale models underneath the tower cranes. As they got nearer Tamar could see the huge bow of the battleship moored at the end of the street growing steadily taller until it was three times higher than the chimney pots and she had to tilt her neck back to see the tops of the funnels. At the dock gates there were groups of children in grotesque clothes, shredded and blackened – an assortment of cut – down adult garments. One boy had a pair of over-large clogs tied to his feet with strips of rag, but most of them were barefoot. Some were pulling bogies made out of fish boxes and old pram wheels. They held out their hands as the girls passed and shouted 'Gimme, gimme, gimme!' in a rather half-hearted way.
Tamar had heard George talk about the gangs of children who survived by picking up lumps of coal dropped by the coal wagons, collecting bottles and jam jars for the paint shops, but it was the first time she'd seen it for herself. There were fewer of them now that the docks were in full production again, but George had told her how, a few years earlier, there had been queues of men outside the gates every morning waiting to see how many would be wanted. So many would be taken – the strongest and

fittest – and the others would be turned away, some of them skilled men with families to support.

Tamar and Anna gave their names at the gate and were allowed onto the quay to stand, damp and shivering, behind a rope and listen to the Lord Mayor's wife 'Name this ship "Newcastle",' her thin voice tossed away by the wind as the bottle shattered against the bow. Then the huge metal shell went clanging and grinding its way down the slipway into the oily water of the Tyne, where it was yanked back on a tidal wave by snaking chains, rocking uncertainly on its tether while the band on the quayside played Rule Britannia.

Afterwards they went with George to Lyons. The café was warm and steamy and reeked with the wet dog smell of damp overcoats. It felt very cosy. They ordered tea and toasted buns. George got out his cigarettes and Anna took one eagerly, holding it over the match George offered, dragging hard to draw the smoke deep into her lungs. 'I'm depressed,' she said. 'Everything at home's babies now. You can't get near the fire for drying nappies and you can't get a night's sleep for him crying.'

'I thought he was quite cute,' Tamar said.

'But then, you don't have to live with him!' Anna pulled a face.

'Just because your nose has been pushed out of joint,' Tamar said. 'You're really hard on your mother.'

'Ha'way, man,' George said, sensing the beginnings of a quarrel. 'Let's go to the pictures. They've got a Fred Astaire on at the Palace that'll cheer us all up!'

In the darkness of the cinema it was easy to leave the ordinary and mundane behind. Tamar loved it's warm, womb-like security.

The screen was like a window out onto a distant, glamorous world far out of her reach. She looked up from her seat in the stalls and watched the images dancing over their heads through the spiralling cigarette smoke, and wondered if Robby was in the projection box. Tamar felt rather guilty that she hadn't been to see Ida for weeks. There was no sign of her this afternoon. The Newsreel had already begun when they took their seats. After the home news, mainly about the new King walking in the grounds of the palace with his plump wife and the little princesses, there were less comforting images. A short feature on a nun who'd led a group of orphaned children through the mountains of Spain to escape civil war, and then to Germany where a stout man with a moustache was being driven swiftly in an open car between rows and rows of troops, his arm bent in a formal salute. A parade of tanks rumbled through streets lined with even more soldiers. Tamar felt Anna stiffen in the seat beside her, but nothing was said.

Afterwards Tamar excused herself and slipped up the back stairs to the projection box. Robby was there, rewinding the spools to replace in their canisters. 'Is Ida here?' Tamar asked.

'Why no, pet,' Robby said. 'She was given her cards a couple of weeks ago. Seems the new management don't want organ music any more. Not modern enough for them.'

'That's dreadful.' Tamar said. 'Do you know what she's doing?'

'Oh, she's gettin' by. She's a survivor is our Ida.' He paused to place one of the large reels in a leather bound box. 'Why don't you go down to Dean Street, pet? She'd love to see you. Had a real soft spot for you, did Ida.'

'I will.' Tamar promised, already feeling guilty about her neglect. 'I will.'

~~~~~~~~~~~~~~~~~

When she got back from the cinema, Anna went straight up to her room. The family were all in the kitchen, but no one asked her where she'd been or whether she'd enjoyed herself. They scarcely noticed that she'd come in. The focus was all on little Frankie now. Anna remembered Tamar's taunt about having her nose put out of joint. She shouldn't feel so rejected, it was stupid.

Upstairs, Anna took out her writing case and the pen she'd been given for Christmas. *Dear Papa,* she wrote and then paused. She still felt disturbed and upset. The pictures she had seen on the newsreel had filled her with fear. The rows and rows of soldiers wearing the same uniform as Willi Becker; the Nazi salute she had seen people using in the street. But there was a great deal that puzzled her. Why did being partly Jewish matter so much?
~~~~~~~~~~~~~~~~~

It was only a religion after all? She had once asked that question of Miss Bateman. 'The Jews were God's chosen people,' she had explained, 'but they murdered his only son and now they must be punished.' But how could that excuse so much hatred? Anna still had a triangular scar on her thigh where Klaus's belt buckle had bitten into her flesh. She could scarcely bear to think what he had done to her. Perhaps that was why seeing those pictures had affected her so deeply.

Anna went on with her letter. *'I keep worrying about you and Grossmutter – there are newspaper articles and newsreels about what's happening in Germany that frighten me. To be singled out because of a religion – to be even related to someone with that religion – is something I can't understand.*

Mum's told you about the baby – we call him Frankie and he's very noisy and demanding. Grossmutter would love him – she used to talk so often about you and Uncle Joe when you were little. Please persuade her to come here – life is awful without you both – I miss you so much and it doesn't look as if I'm going to be able to visit you, since I don't have a passport or enough money. When I talked to Mum about it, she said it isn't safe for me to go back to Germany and that they might not let me out again. So please will you try to come?'

Anna realised as she wrote that tears were running down her face and dripping onto her blouse. Would he come? Would he even get the letter?

That night, as she lay on the bed reading a book, Tamar overheard another conversation in the kitchen. Downstairs a voice very like the English teacher at school was saying '. . . her results have been exceptional, given the circumstances . . .' Sadie's reply was inaudible but then the clear pitch of Miss Wilson could be heard again saying, 'I'd urge you to let her stay on. If it's a question of money, there are scholarships to the teacher's college. Of course I can't guarantee she'd get one, but it's worth trying for. She has the ability – no question about that.'

Tamar's ribs tightened as she realised that they were talking about her. She lay very still to try and decode every word filtering through the linoleum.

'Waste of time educatin' girls,' Lily Kennedy said. 'They just go off and get married.'

'Not all of them,' Miss Wilson retorted.

'Sorry, no offence pet.'

Tamar tried to think whether she'd like to be a teacher – standing in front of a class, the butt of rough humour and outright hostility. She thought about the neat propriety she'd observed in a succession of Miss Wilsons, the prettiest of them flaunting little coloured chips on their engagement fingers before floating off to marry doctors, vicars or other teachers, and lead lives of flawless respectability. Could she ever be like that? No, Tamar thought. I'd hate it. I enjoy being at school, but I don't want to spend my life there. The thought of being a librarian was more attractive; to work with books, to have an unlimited amount of them to read . . . It was a dream. Tamar realised that for the first time she knew, clearly, absolutely, what she wanted to do. So much of her life had been spent surviving, avoiding, adapting, there had been little time to think of the future and how it might shape itself around her. Until Anna had brought up the subject, Tamar hadn't thought beyond the next move or the next set of lodgings. She'd been waiting for a suitable moment to talk to Sadie about how she might become a librarian, and whether it would be possible for her to stay on at school, but now it seemed unlikely that she would be allowed to find out. Under the floor her mother was saying, 'Pergavie's have told me they would take her on as a trainee. It's good money.'

Tamar closed her eyes and clenched her fists. Just as she had glimpsed a future that might offer her something she wanted, the door was to be closed, while Anna, who hated English and didn't want to teach, was going to have the chance to stay on at school and go to college. It was terribly unfair.

Three streets away, Anna slept soundly through the early part of the night but was woken just before dawn by a series of small staccato cries that she knew would soon escalate into a crescendo of hunger as little Frankie began another round of eating and sleeping. His appetite was insatiable. It seemed to Anna that every time she saw her mother now, she was sitting in the nursing chair by the kitchen fire with Frankie chomping at her breast. And her mother seemed to get thinner and paler as the baby sucked and sucked and grew fatter and fatter.

Everyone cooed over him except her and it made Anna feel guilty and unhappy. Was it simply that she was jealous of him?

'You're unnatural,' Grandma Cotteslow had said, cooing down at the squirming white bundle in her arms. 'Isn't he a beautiful little diddum diddum dumpling then?' Grandma Cotteslow, who seemed to have made a remarkable recovery since Frankie was born, wanted to send his photograph to the Bonny Baby section of the Shields Gazette.

When Frankie was in the pram out in the garden Anna would go and look at him, swathed in bonnets and mittens and propped against a frilly cotton pillow. Sometimes he would be asleep, his face blanked into unconsciousness, but sometimes he would be awake and staring up at her with a blue, impersonal gaze that seemed both to acknowledge her existence and dismiss it as irrelevant all at the same time. But however often Anna looked, there was never any repeat of that contraction of the heart she had experienced when she saw him for the first time. In fact, she felt no emotional connection to him at all.

Anna heard her mother get out of bed in the room next door, stumble over to the cot and pick Frankie up, making soothing, shushing noises as she carried him back to her own bed. Soon there was silence, broken only by the wind buffeting the window. Looking out as the sky lightened, Anna could see the clouds and the chimney smoke blowing across the rooftops in strange ragged patterns. It had been stormy during the night and the early light in the sky was mixed with the light from still-glowing street lamps to create a greeny-yellow sheen on the wet slates.

Restless and tired of tossing between the sheets, Anna put on a jumper and a thick corduroy skirt and let herself out of the house as quietly as possible so as not to disturb anyone. She got her bicycle out of the shed and pedalled hard against the wind, bending her head forward over the handlebars, down to the promenade.

The sea was level with the road, surging and heaving itself

through the railings onto the cobbles as the slack tide turned to ebb. Every now and then the wind would whip up the top of the swell into an arc of spray and hurl it across onto the front of the buildings opposite. In Cullercoats Bay, the fishing boats bucked and pitched on their long lines. Two of them had broken loose and smashed against the quay, washing to and fro in a litter of splintered wood entangled with nets and floats.

Anna parked her bicycle against a lamp-post on the upper level and got out her sketch pad. Sitting on the steps leading down to the sea-front, curving her arm around the pad to protect it from the wind, she rapidly pencilled in the curve of the bay, the cast-iron bollards, the grey, swollen masses of water and the parabolas of spray. Racing home as fast as she could, Anna made herself a mug of strong tea and went out again to the garden shed she had been allowed to use to paint in since Frankie was born. She lit the paraffin stove, put a large sheet of watercolour paper on the table in front of the window and began to select brushes, swirl them in water, mix the paint and then, drawing a deep breath, run the brushes over the absorbent paper in sweeping, liquid movements. As the curves and counter-curves began to balance each other, intersected by the straight lines of railing and bollard, Anna felt her cold fingers tremble with pleasure. Nothing really mattered except being able to do this.

Anna remembered how Miss Bateman had once taken her to Nürnberg to see the Dürers in the city museum. She had looked for a long time at the woodcuts of the Apocalypse and the drawings – not a change of line or a careless thought anywhere to be seen. Then Anna had been taken to see one of his altar pieces – the Seven Sorrows of the Virgin. She could still remember how she had felt when she studied the sheer weight of detail, the subtlety and luminosity of colour, and the balance of the composition which Miss Bateman had demonstrated by drawing imaginary lines across the canvas following an arm here, a fold of drapery there. She had shown Anna how all the lines converged on the focal point of the painting as the eye was drawn in towards it. Anna had been aware of a leaping pulse under her breast, the hairs lifting on her skin – a feeling she had never experienced before. Looking at paintings in books wasn't the same.

And then Miss Bateman had told her how Dürer's father had been a Hungarian goldsmith with eighteen children and too poor to send his sons to study painting. Albrecht and his brother Albert had flicked a coin to see which one of them was to go to the Academy in Nürnberg first, while the other supported him by working in the mines. Albrecht Dürer won. When he finished his studies and came home to tell his brother that now it was his turn to study and be supported, Albert had mutely held out his ruined, broken fingers and with tears coursing down his cheeks told Albrecht that he could no longer paint. The mines had crippled his hands.

I wouldn't have let it happen to me, Anna thought. If I'd lost the toss I would have gone somehow. Surely if he'd really cared enough about wanting to paint he wouldn't have submitted so meekly? Sometimes it occurred to Anna to wonder whether Albrecht might not have cheated in order to win the chance. It was something she might have done herself. Looking down at her paint-stained fingers as she held them over the paraffin heater to warm, Anna made herself a promise. 'Nothing must ever get in the way of this,' she said out loud. 'I'm not going to let anyone stop me.'

CHAPTER SIX

When Tamar told Anna that Sadie had written to the school telling them that she would be leaving at the end of term to start work at Pergavie's, Anna was incensed. 'Just refuse to go,' she said. 'She can't make you. You heard what Miss Wilson said about scholarships and things. There's bound to be a way.'

'But it would all be such a terrible fuss.' Tamar bit her lip. Her heart almost burst when she thought of what she would have to go through to defy Sadie. With Tamar earning as well, Sadie said she was counting on what she called 'a little more elastic' in the budget and some relief from all the years of struggle.

'You don't know what Sadie's like when she decides something,' Tamar said. 'And I'm not like you. I hate arguments and people being cross with me.'

'Oh God, Tamar! You're such a weakling. You'll end up like Elsie, drudging in a factory, with a drunken husband and a family of bairns you can't afford to feed! It's such a waste! But if you won't stand up for yourself, I wash my hands of you.'

Anna flounced out, banging the back door hard and Tamar felt miserable and ashamed of not being able to live up to her expectations. Anna's words stayed in her mind all night as she lay awake listening to Sadie snoring rhythmically on the other side of the bed.

In the morning Tamar had made a decision. She ate her breakfast with Mr Coles – Miss Francis and Sadie having already gone to work – and left earlier than usual. At school she tapped nervously on the headmistress's door. Miss Fenwick was sitting at her desk marking a pile of books. When Tamar came in she pushed her glasses up on top of her head and sat back in the chair.

'It's Tamar Fell, isn't it?'

'Yes, Ma'am.'

'Well?' she prompted, looking at Tamar expectantly.

It was much more difficult to begin than Tamar had thought when she rehearsed the interview in her mind. Everything came out in a rush of words. 'I would really like to stay on at school, but my mother says there's no money and she wants me to work in the shop.'

'Sit down,' Miss Fenwick said gently.

Tamar sat.

'Miss Wilson's already spoken to me about you. Your English results are good, very good indeed. Have you any idea what you want to do when you leave school? Not shop work evidently.'

She gave a wry smile.

'I'd like to be a librarian.'

Miss Fenwick looked at Tamar for several moments. 'You wouldn't like to be a teacher?'

Tamar shook her head. 'I don't think I'm brave enough to stand up in front of a class. But I love books.'

Miss Fenwick nodded.

'Are there any scholarships or things like that, so I could stay on without my mother having to pay?'

'There are scholarships for the high school, Tamar, and charities to cover the cost of your uniform. In two years time you would probably stand a very good chance of getting one, but you'd need to do a lot of extra work in maths – your result was very poor.' Miss Fenwick paused and sighed. 'We'd be very happy for you to stay on here and coach you for your school certificate, but your mother would have to keep you until you were sixteen. Could you persuade her to do that do you think?'

'I don't know,' Tamar's heart was thudding with disappointment. 'I'll have to ask her.'

'I'm sorry I can't be more helpful,' Miss Fenwick said. 'We hate to lose a good pupil, but as you can appreciate here, there are many, many students who have to leave because of financial hardship. Tell your mother to come and see me if you think it would make a difference.'

The hopelessness Tamar felt must have shown on her face because Miss Fenwick immediately said, 'Don't despair.' She rose to usher Tamar out and put a hand briefly on her shoulder. 'You'll find that there are a number of very good organisations that offer the chance to study in the evenings. If you are really determined, you'll succeed in the end.'

Tamar dreaded having to tackle Sadie. After school she went home with Anna. Frankie was outside in the pram sleeping under a sunshade. He seemed to have doubled in size since the last time she'd seen him.

'Does he make you feel anything?' Anna asked, as Tamar gazed into the pram.

She shook her head. 'He's the fattest baby I've ever seen. But I suppose he is quite sweet. Most animals are when they're small.'

Anna nodded. 'It's a relief to find someone else who doesn't rave about him.'

'Why do you dislike him so much?'

'I don't dislike him, I just think babies are boring.'

'Maybe you'll find him more interesting when he gets older.'

'I hope so. He's my brother!'

Mrs Weissmann and Mrs Cotteslow were in the kitchen.

'Was there any post for me?' Anna asked.

'No second post at all today.' Mrs Weissmann said. 'Were you expecting a letter from your father?'

Anna nodded.

'I thought you might be. He hasn't written to me either – not since Frankie was born. It's very worrying.'

'It's the first time she's even mentioned being worried about him,' Anna told Tamar after her mother had left the room. 'All this talk of war. It's horrible.'

'Wouldn't it be nice if you could see into the future,' Tamar said, gazing out of the window into the garden, where Mr Cotteslow was pruning roses.

'I tell you what,' Anna said, smiling, 'we could ask my grandmother. She reads tea leaves, don't you Grandma?' She raised her voice as she turned to Mrs Cotteslow who was sitting at the table knitting what looked like a baby's jacket.

Mrs Cotteslow gave a thin smile. 'My sister had the second sight. She was a spook.'

'What's a spook?' Tamar asked.

'People who belong to the Spiritualist Church up at Wallsend, pet. Not that I'd have anything to do with it. Some of the riff raff that used to go to that church! But she did teach me to read the leaves.'

Anna poured out the tea and they drank it, leaving the grounds in the bottom of the cups. Anna passed them to her grandmother – 'Mine first! If there's anything horrible I want to know now.'

'Remember your manners, Anne. It's always visitors first.' Mrs Cotteslow swirled the grounds around two or three times and then turned Tamar's cup upside down in the saucer. She picked it up and peered at the little flakes of tea patterned around the white porcelain. 'There's a cross here,' she said. 'Can you see? That means trouble of some kind. And there's a winding road – so you're going to go on a journey. And then there's a clover leaf. That means you'll get what you wish for.'

'Now mine! Now mine!' Anna pushed her cup towards Mrs Cotteslow who repeated the procedure. But when she looked inside Anna's cup, she put it down again quickly. 'I can't read that,' she said. 'It's all just a jumble.' She got up as if to put the cup in the sink, but Anna snatched it out of her hand. She gazed into the bottom of it and then held it out for Tamar to see. 'What would you say it looked like?'

'There's a cross.'

'And . . ?' Anna face was totally drained of colour.

'It looks like a skull,' Tamar said reluctantly.

Mrs Cotteslow was upset. 'It's the death sign. I should never have agreed to do it for you. If I'd thought . . .'

'You should have had more sense mother,' Mrs Weissmann came through the door and swept the crockery off the table. 'It's all superstitious nonsense. Old wives tales.' She sounded really angry. 'Don't you take any notice of it. Either of you.'

Tamar didn't talk to her mother that night. Sadie came home from the shop in a really bad mood. She had a bottle of gin in her bag which she put on the table after tea and Tamar knew that she and Lily would be there for the rest of the evening.

George had bought a new record, the first movement of Mozart's *Eine Kleine Nacht Musik* and as Mr Coles and Miss Francis were in their rooms, he wound up the gramophone and put it on. Tamar and George went out into the front garden and stood under the window to listen to the music drifting out into the street. George lit his pipe and Tamar rested her back against the warm brick wall. It seemed wrong to be indoors on such a fine summer evening. 'If I had the bus fare I'd go down to the sea front,' Tamar said.

'I could loan you a push bike,' George said.

Tamar shook her head. 'I've never learnt to ride.'

George was incredulous. 'Everyone can ride a bike, man!'

'Not me. Sadie never had enough money to buy me one.'

'Your Mam's had a tough time bringing you up on her own. It can't have been easy.'

'I suppose not. But we've always managed.'

'She's a real trouper, your mam.'

The record came to an end and they could hear the needle scratching as it circled the empty grooves around the label, but George didn't go in immediately. 'The Carl Rosa's coming again in September,' he said. 'Would you and your friend like to come with me do you think?'

Tamar was surprised. 'I'd love to. I'll ask Anna for you, shall I?'

George nodded and said, 'Good, that's settled then.' He turned to go back indoors, but Tamar could see the blush spreading up the back of his neck above his collar.

It was days before Tamar was able to talk to Sadie. In the end she went down to Pergavie's and waited for her to come out of the shop after work.

Pergavie's was a large, old-fashioned department store that had been there almost a hundred years, rambling up through three or four floors, spreading out along the other houses in the street as it grew. The shop front was polished mahogany with big, engraved glass doors. Inside, on the rare occasions that Sadie had taken her in, there were huge mahogany counters and glass fronted shelves. It was very dark and claustrophobic. Tamar wondered what it would be like to work there. Seeing it somehow made her more determined to stand her ground.

As she waited on the pavement the red-haired girl that Tamar had seen at the cinema came out of the front door. She was wearing the same coat and hat, but this time she was accompanied by a woman with a petulant face wearing a fur coat. As they passed Tamar, the girl turned as if she felt Tamar's eyes on her and smiled. 'It's almost as if she remembers me, the way I remember her,' Tamar thought. 'Or maybe I just look like someone she knows.' Tamar smiled back and lifted her hand impulsively in a half wave and to her surprise the girl returned it, raising her brown leather glove slightly, with a shy glance towards her.

'Don't dawdle, Holly,' the woman with her said impatiently. 'We mustn't keep Johnson waiting.'

Tamar watched as they climbed into the Bentley and were driven away.

A uniformed doorman began locking the doors as if he'd just been waiting for them to leave and soon a stream of chattering girls came out of the side entrance, followed by a few older women, all neatly dressed in navy and then, almost last, Sadie, looking more like a customer than one of the assistants. She had changed into an outfit Tamar hadn't seen before – a cream skirt and black jacket with a little black and white hat to match.

'Hello, Tamar,' she said. 'This is a surprise.'

'I wanted to talk to you. There isn't a chance at home – there's always too many people.'

Sadie sighed, almost as if she guessed what was coming. 'Let's go to Lyons. We can have a cup of tea.' She glanced at her watch. 'I'm meeting someone at seven, so I mustn't be too late.'

When the Nippy had brought their tea and an iced bun, Sadie said. 'So, what's all this about? It isn't anything to do with school is it?'

Tamar nodded. She swallowed the crumbs in her mouth and said, 'I was hoping I could be a librarian, but I'd have to stay on at school for another two years. Please can I? Please?' She paused. 'I've never asked for anything before.'

Sadie looked stricken. The knuckles gripping her cup were white. 'Tamar darling, if I could, I would. But it isn't as simple as you think. Have you any idea how much I earn? And how much it costs to feed and clothe us both?'

'It's not fair,' Tamar exclaimed. She was trying hard not to cry. 'You got an education – your parents sent you to finishing school, but you won't even let me stay on to get my exams!'

Sadie gave her a strange look. 'That was different,' she said quietly. Her voice was flat.

'I could get a Saturday job if that would help and work in the school holidays?'

Sadie seemed upset. 'It's more complicated than that Tamar.' She paused and then went on, reluctantly, 'I borrowed some money when we came here. I was relying on someone and they let me down, so now I have to pay it back. If you're not earning anything, I can't.' There was a catch in her voice. 'I've scrimped and pinched for fourteen years and I just can't do it anymore. I'm only thirty three Tamar – I want to have the chance to live a little before it's too late.'

Tamar thought of all the glass bottles in the rubbish bin, the clothes on Sadie's back and swallowed hard. She felt angry, it was like a seething, writhing mass inside her. When she looked at her mother she felt an intense, burning hatred. 'It's not fair!' she said again.

'It isn't,' Sadie said. A tear was working its way down her cheek, leaving a dark trail in her face powder. 'But sometimes that's how life is.' She stood up. Her voice was shaking. 'You're the most precious thing in my life, Tamar. If I could give you the moon, I would.' Sadie picked up her bag and gloves and walked out.

'Are you finished pet?' the Nippy said at Tamar's elbow.

'Yes.' Tamar let the girl take her cold tea away. Such bitterness was welling up inside her and such sadness she felt unable to move. She pushed the plate towards the girl with its half eaten bun and realised that her hand was trembling.

~~~~~~~~~~~~~~~~~~

When Anna came in from her lesson and was taking off her coat in the hall, her mother came out of the sitting room to intercept her before she went upstairs to her room. Mrs Weissmann was holding a piece of paper in her hand.

'Anna, I'm terribly sorry – this came today.'

Anna took the letter held out to her.

'I'm afraid your grandmother's dead.'
~~~~~~~~~~~~~~~~~~

'Grossmutter?' To Anna's mortification, her first feeling was one of relief. Ever since Grandma Cotteslow's prediction she had been suffering an irrational fear that the death sign in her tea cup meant that her father was going to die. But her relief was fleeting. She was immediately overwhelmed with guilt and sadness. 'How did it happen? Has she been ill?'

'I'm sorry. Your father found her in the chair beside the stove. The doctor said it was a heart attack. It's all in the letter.'

Anna read her father's fluent, but slightly uncomfortable English. *'I had to fetch a doctor from Leinz because old Brünner would not come. The funeral is tomorrow. It has been very difficult to find anywhere to bury her since the Pastor refused, but Joe's friends have found a plot in Freiburg. There is much more I could tell, but cannot put in a letter.*

Hug Anna for me. I know how much she loved her grandmother. In her last letter she wrote that she has thoughts of coming back here, but tell her she must not. It will be a surprise to you, but I have decided when all this is over, to sell the Gasthof and get a visa to come to England. How long that will take me, I do not know. Things are far from easy here at the moment. But I will try to come as quickly as possible. It is difficult to do things when my heart is so heavy. How I long to see you both again – and my little son.

Will you send me a photograph of the three of you?

My love always,

Otto'

Then Anna's mother's arms were around her, hugging her close. She smelt of stale baby milk and Frankie, but it didn't seem to matter.

'I'm so confused,' Anna sobbed. 'Why can't everything be like it used to be?'

'It'll all work out in the end,' her mother said, rubbing Anna's shoulders as if she was a child, and Anna wished that she could believe her.

~~~~~~~~~~~~~~~~~~

On their last day of school together, Anna came to tea at Lily's and brought her autograph book with her. 'I got it for my birthday. You've got to put something in it for me, Tamar. Everyone
~~~~~~~~~~~~~~~~~~

else has.'

Tamar turned the pages. It was about a quarter full and all the things that Tamar could think of were already in it. "Paddle your own Canoe", "Into each life some rain must fall", "Roses are red, violets are blue, If you won't tell on me, I won't tell on you". The art teacher had drawn a cartoon of Anna, paintbrush in hand, jumping up and down with rage in front of an easel, above the neatly printed caption "Mr Collins predicts a bright future for Miss Weissmann." How could Tamar possibly follow that?

She gave Anna her own reluctantly, because it was old and grimy and turned over at the corners, the cover slightly loose on the stitching. Anna immediately began to do a sketch with rapid strokes of the pencil, finishing off with a big scrawled signature in her dark, bold, handwriting and three exaggerated kisses in one corner 'to my best friend'. Tamar was still sucking her pen. 'I'm not very good at this. I can never think what to put.' She felt miserable and inadequate.

Lily turned round from the pan she was stirring and winked at her. 'What you want is a limerick, pet. Somethin' a bit naughty like "Said Mabel to Gable, I will if you're able." I know a few of those. Or you could make up your own, somethin' like, "There was a young lass from Bavaria . . ."' Lily paused to think of a rhyme, but was stumped.

Tamar felt herself blushing. She looked at Anna, at the expression of distaste moving across her face and knew that she couldn't possibly write anything like that. Sadie was sitting there saying nothing, looking at Tamar through a haze of cigarette smoke.

'You can keep it till tomorrow,' Anna said, smiling again. 'It'll give you time to think of something.'

Upstairs, before she went out, Sadie pulled the hat box down from the top of the wardrobe. There was a small, leather-bound book in the bottom of it with 'Poems by Charles Carter' stamped in gold letters on the cover. Sadie opened it at the fly leaf and handed it to Tamar. 'Years ago, when I was about your age, someone wrote this for me. Would it do for your friend, do you think?'

On the marbled end papers a verse was written out in a shaky, thin script.

'This is my heart's desire,
That you should have all fair,
A soft breeze to blow upon your rest,
And the sun to shine upon your hair.'

Underneath the same hand had written 'For the lovely Sadie, with compliments, Charles Carter.'

'It's beautiful.' Tamar could feel herself flushing with pleasure. This kind of thoughtfulness from Sadie was unexpected. 'Did you really know a famous poet?'

Sadie nodded. 'He was very old,' she said. 'I'll tell you about it one day.' Then she put her arms around Tamar and gave her a hug. Tamar hugged her back. It was impossible to be angry with Sadie for long. After all, it wasn't Sadie's fault they didn't have any money.

Later that night, before she went to bed, Tamar copied the poem out and wrote "To Anna, from your friend Tamar" in the right hand corner. She felt she should have put kisses underneath as Anna had done for her, but there wasn't really room at the bottom of the page.

Sadie had left the hat box on the dressing table stool and, when Tamar took off the lid to replace the book of poems, an envelope caught her eye. Sadie kept all her private papers in this box – photographs, letters and certificates – and it was usually kept on top of the wardrobe, out of reach, tightly buckled with a leather strap. Tamar had rarely ever had the opportunity to look inside, and now she couldn't resist the temptation to delve into its forbidden interior. The envelope that had drawn her eye was long and cream-coloured – quite different to most of the square white or blue envelopes Sadie kept tied in bundles. Tamar lifted it out. It was addressed to Miss S.R. Tomlinson, which Tamar knew had been Sadie's maiden name, but it had been sent to Miss Simpson's lodging house, so it was obviously recent. Intrigued, but feeling very guilty, Tamar peeked inside and saw an embossed letter head. Poultenay Hall, Winterings, North Yorkshire. The writing paper was the same stiff cream vellum as the envelope. Who would write to Sadie from an address like that? And why call her by her maiden name?

With trembling fingers, Tamar gave in to her curiousity, drew out the letter, unfolded its single page and began to read. *'Dear Miss Tomlinson,'* it began. The script was elegant but rather tremulous as if the writer was very old. *'I think you have taken a great liberty in writing to James at this address. I have not, of course, passed the letter on to him. We do not wish to see the child, or have any involvement in her upbringing – as I made perfectly clear at the time. I am enclosing a sum of money for your relocation expenses and must warn you that any further communications will be placed in the hands of my solicitor. This is the very last time I shall send you anything. You are a very foolish woman and must live with the consequences of your behaviour.'* It was signed *'Mrs Emily Fell'*.

What could it mean? The possibilities whirled inside Tamar's brain. Who was this woman and why had she written such a horrid letter to Sadie? And who was James? The thought of who he might be and all the repercussions of that made Tamar's head swim. She could feel the whole fabric of her life and her identity collapsing around her. Better to slip the letter back in the envelope and bury it at the bottom of the box. But the words, and the suspicion they conveyed, couldn't be put back in the envelope as easily as the letter. She could never ask Sadie about its contents. If she did she would have to confess that she'd been prying into Sadie's private things and that was impossible. But the thought of not being able to know, of having this terrible doubt inside her indefinitely was very bitter.

'I wish I'd never opened it,' Tamar whispered to herself. 'They say eavesdroppers never hear anything good about themselves. Reading other people's letters is just as bad.' Outside the window the waning moon was leaning over the allotments like a collapsed balloon in a summer sky still bright with the sun's reflected light. Everything looked peaceful and ordinary, but Tamar had the strangest feeling – a sensation of being on the threshold of something. It was the same feeling she had sometimes when trying to get hold of a dream – you were aware that it was there, but unable to call it up into memory. Now, some sort of knowledge, or awareness, was within the range of her consciousness, if only she could grasp it.

PART II

DREAMS AND AMBITIONS

1938 – 39

'Take, if you must, this little bag of dreams;
Unloose the cord, and they will wrap you round.'

W.B. Yeats, *Fergus and the Druid*

CHAPTER SEVEN

'I hate it,' Anna said. Tamar had rarely seen her so passionate. 'All the girls have done Latin and they treat me like an idiot because I haven't. Nobody takes art seriously – it's just for dumbos.' Anna had begun her second year at Tynemouth High School in September and was finding it harder than she'd anticipated. The school curriculum was slanted towards academic training, she explained to Tamar, and art was taught more as a recreation than a proper subject. To make things worse, the art mistress's taste inclined naturally towards the Victorian narrative school or the romantics – both anathema to Anna. 'I'm so sick of being told to paint like Leighton, Reynolds and Romney. And as for art history, I think she cribbed the essay titles from a book.' Anna put on her most sarcastic voice. 'The first one was "Why Rembrandt liked to paint the Poor People of Amsterdam", and last week it was even more stupid – "The Master's touch that put the thought behind the smile". What I really want to learn about is their technique. I can't bear to sit through such utter rubbish. If it goes on like this, I'm going to skip the lessons and study by myself.'

'Won't you get into trouble?'

Anna shrugged. 'I don't care. If I do then maybe they'll take me seriously.'

'It's so unfair. I'd give anything to be where you are.' Working at Pergavie's was quite pleasant, but the thought of standing behind a counter for the rest of her life, like Miss Timms, made Tamar feel giddy with horror.

'It's your own fault. You should have fought for it when you had the chance,' Anna said. 'You've got to learn not to be so passive Tamar. Not just sit back and let things happen to you.'

'I can't ignore everyone else to get what I want like you. I can't help it – it's just the way I am.'

'Are you accusing me of being selfish?' Anna's voice was sharp.

'No. Not really. I admire your dedication – I really do, but sometimes you're . . . ' Tamar tried to think of a tactful way of putting it, 'extremely single-minded.' Anna's eyebrows flew up and Tamar rushed on. 'It makes you seem hard and uncaring. Though I know you're not, but sometimes there doesn't seem to be room in your life for anyone else.'

But Anna was offended. 'You're just jealous!' she said. 'Because I'm still at school and you're not.' And she picked up her sketch book and went home.

Maybe she's right, Tamar thought miserably as she watched Anna slamming the garden gate back on its latch. Maybe I am a little bit envious. Anna has everything, and she doesn't appreciate it – a proper home, a room of her own, enough money, and the courage to stand up for what she wants, however much of a fuss she causes.

'Sometimes I think I admire Anna more than I like her,' Tamar said to George later as they walked down to the chip shop to get the Saturday night supper. 'She's so intense and I don't always know what she wants from me. She asks my opinion and when I give it she goes off in a huff. We seem to spend all our time arguing these days.'

'She's trouble, that one,' George said. 'But bonny.' He sighed. 'A right bobby dazzler.'

'George! You fancy her. I've caught you out.'

His skin darkened with embarrassment. 'Ha'way man!'

'You do! I've seen the way you look at her.'

'Don't be daft! And don't you dare say anything neither.'

As Tamar undressed for bed, she wondered what it would be like to be loved by George. Although Tamar had been attracted to him when she first arrived in Heaton Street, she'd been living at Lily's for more than two years now and he'd become a kind of honorary older brother. She turned the thought over in her mind as she unbuttoned her satin cami-knickers. At Christmas he'd kissed her under the mistletoe and his mouth had felt strange against her cheek – hot and powerful and she could feel his whiskers because he'd come straight from the Yard and hadn't shaved. What would it be like to be touched by George, to lie in bed beside him? It was very disturbing to feel her nipples hardening against the satin as she thought about it.

So far she hadn't met anyone who attracted her. A few months ago a moist-handed, Brylcreemed new recruit from the gents' wear department had taken her to see a colour film at the Palace. Tamar had been more interested in what was on the screen than the boy, but had found it difficult to concentrate on the gigantic red Sequoia trees which were supposed to be thousands of years old when Sam was trying to get inside her clothes in the most determined way. She'd sat, rigid, as he fumbled with her blouse and rubbed her leg through the folds of her skirt, knowing that he'd paid for her ticket and expected something in return and not wanting to hurt his feelings. Sam had seemed quite likeable and jokey in the shop but at such close quarters she'd been repelled by him – his damp skin, and the personal smell that breathed from his body in the warmth of the rear stalls. Tamar sighed, and wondered whether she would ever fall in love with anyone.

~~~~~~~~~~~~~~~~~

The following week, on the day of the art class, instead of returning to school after lunch, Anna took the tram up to Newcastle, to the Art Gallery and sat in front of the paintings trying to copy them into her notebook. Amazed that her absence from the class went undetected, Anna did it again and then again.

The second time she was there she noticed a man watching her. One of the curators, she presumed. The third week he came and stood right behind her and she instinctively put her hand over the page, fearing that what she was doing was forbidden. She half turned and asked, 'It is allowed, isn't it?'

'Oh, yes,' he said, in a cultured voice. 'It's quite all right.' He held out his hand. 'May I see?'

Reluctantly Anna passed him the book and watched, hot with embarrassment, as he turned the pages slowly, holding them first close to his eyes and then further away, squinting slightly. And then there were more questions – who had taught her – what was
~~~~~~~~~~~~~~~~~

she doing. Anna explained as best she could, finding it difficult to be anything but truthful under his direct, interrogating gaze.

'I'd like you to see someone,' he said at last. 'And show him a selection of your work.' He wrote a name and address on the back of a visiting card and gave it to Anna. 'I'll write him a letter and ask him to see you.'

When she got out into the street, Anna looked at what he'd written. Professor R. Drew, Principal, King Edward VII School of Art.

Robert Drew was not at all the kind of person Anna had imagined. He was small and bird-like, with a slightly feminine softness about his face and his movements. There was paint ingrained in his finger nails and round the cuticles, and he was wearing an old fisherman's sweater similarly smeared. A pair of tortoiseshell spectacles hung on what looked like picture cord around his neck. The desk in his office was hidden underneath shaggy piles of books and papers stacked haphazardly across its surface. He put Anna's portfolio down on top of the uneven stacks so that it sloped dangerously and Anna had to hold one corner level to stop her drawings sliding off onto the floor.

One after another he took out the sheets of paper and held them up to the light, squinting at them over his glasses. He said nothing until he had put the last one back in the folder and dropped his spectacles back around his neck.

'How old are you?'

'Sixteen.'

He looked down at the folder again. 'I won't lie to you. You certainly have a gift. What you do with it is something else again. Do you have the capacity for hard work and dedication? Or are you going to be content to paint tourist pictures and pretty little watercolours as a hobby? Is that what you want?'

Anna shook her head vigorously. 'I want to go to the Slade.'

He raised his eyebrows. 'Why the Slade?'

'I've been told it's the best.'

He smiled with a wry slant of the mouth. 'Not necessarily. I studied there myself. It depends what you're interested in. Looking at your work I'd say you'd have no trouble getting in. But what about the fees? It isn't cheap.'

Anna had once hoped that her grandfather might pay for her, but since the birth of little Frankie the subject had never been mentioned. When she'd tried to broach it, Mr Cotteslow had seemed surprised. 'I thought you'd grown out of that,' he said, as if it was some kind of childish dream. And then he'd added; 'Your mother's right, you know. Teaching's the thing to do. A nice secure future for you, hinny.'

So now Anna said cautiously, 'I was hoping that there might be some kind of scholarship.'

'There are. But you aren't good enough for that yet.' He looked out of the window thoughtfully. 'I think you should come here and study full time for a while, if your parents will allow it, and I'll write to my old professor at the Slade and see what's possible.'

'Thank you,' Anna said. 'You don't know what it means to me.'

He smiled at her again, the same wry, rather sad tilt of the lips. 'Oh, but I do,' he said. 'I do.'

Robert Drew kept his word. The letter arrived the following morning. Anna watched her mother open the envelope and read through the two pages of script. When she'd finished Mrs Weissmann laid it down on the kitchen table and looked at Anna. 'Well,' she said. Her tone wasn't encouraging. 'He obviously thinks very highly of your work. . .'

'But you're not going to let me are you?'

'Don't jump to conclusions. Just hear me out, Anna. You know how I feel about you abandoning your education for painting. It's such a risk. Supposing you don't have enough talent? There's security in teaching. Regular money, and you'll never lack for a job.'

'But I'd hate it! I know I would. At least if I study painting, if I'm no good at it, I can always teach art as a last resort.'

'It's such a lot of money for your grandfather to find, Anna. And with a war coming. You've got another year until your school certificate, and then it would be at least a year at King Edward's before going on heaven knows where to study. We'd have to keep you for another five years. It's such a long time!'

‘Professor Drew says there are scholarships to the Slade in London if I’m good enough. But if you don’t let me go to the college I’ll never be good enough to get one!’

‘I’ll have to talk it over with your grandfather,’ Mrs Weissmann said wearily. ‘I hate having to constantly ask him for money, but I don’t want to spoil your chances.’ She paused and then asked, with difficulty. ‘Why are you always so angry with me Anna? Why do you treat me as if I’m your enemy?’

Anna couldn’t look at her.

‘It’s as if you blame me for everything that’s happened. I’d hoped as you got older you’d begin to understand. You’ve seen the newsreels.’

Anna felt hot with shame. ‘I’m sorry,’ she murmured. ‘I don’t hate you.’

‘I’m glad about that.’ Mrs Weissmann came and put her arms round Anna and gave her a hug. Then she held her at arm’s length and looked at her regretfully. ‘I wish we could get on better,’ she said. ‘But it’s probably impossible. I never got on with my mother at all when I was your age.’

She turned to go and Anna, full of anxiety, couldn’t prevent herself from asking again, ‘You will let me go to King Edward’s, won’t you?’

Mrs Weissmann sighed. ‘I’ll talk to your grandfather. That’s all I can do.’

After her mother had left the room Anna put on her coat to go out into the shed. She felt disturbed and sad. She thought about what Tamar had said about being selfish. Was it so wrong to want to be the best, to try to realise your dreams? After all she wasn’t harming anyone by it. ‘If I’d been a boy,’ Anna said out loud. ‘There wouldn’t have been all these arguments.’ Why was it always the women that had to make choices? Who had decreed that they were supposed to be pliable, to consider others and put them first? It was easy enough for Tamar – there wasn’t anything she really wanted to do. Anna thought about her mother’s dilemma. How would she have acted in her place? ‘I’m not going to let it happen to me,’ Anna told herself. ‘I’m not going to get married and I’m never going to have children!’

'Will you look at that!' Miss Timms said. On the pavement outside the shop, a man was standing with a sandwich board, brandishing a newspaper and shouting something they couldn't hear through the plate glass windows. As he turned to pace back in the opposite direction, they saw the words 'Hitler invades Czechoslovakia' chalked on the board. Miss Timms was biting her lips, then, almost furtively she took her purse out of her pocket and gave Tamar sixpence.

'If you go to the cloakroom, you can nip outside and down the alley for a minute and get me a paper, pet,' she said in a low, breathless voice. 'And if anyone sees you, mind, you're just steppin' out for a breath of air.'

Tamar complied and a few moments later was in possession of the evening news. It was true. The Germans had broken their word and overrun a part of the country called the Sudetenland. But as Tamar quickly scanned the columns it seemed that there would be no war. The British government had given a pledge. Germany was simply expanding into old territory; providing they went no further, there would be no retaliation. It was a reprieve. Tamar knew she should be comforted, but felt only apprehension as she turned to go back into the shop.

Tamar had been made to start in haberdashery, among the handkerchiefs and stockings and scarves and gloves and silk corsages. Miss Timms, who ran the counter, was a tall, rather indistinct woman with greying hair and a soft, pale face cobwebbed with fine lines. She had a rather distracted air about her, but, in contrast to her dithery manner, her blouse was luminously white, her worn, frumpy shoe leather buffed to a mirror finish and not a single hair escaped the crimped waves neatly pinned to her head. On Tamar's first day she had showed her how to use the pneumatic machine; how to put the bill and the customer's payment in a metal canister, push it up the tube and watch it whizz up through the ceiling all the way to accounts and then back again with the change and a receipt. At first Tamar had been both fascinated and terrified by it. But soon she was using it as casually as everyone else.

'I'll say this about you pet,' Miss Timms had said at the end of the first day. 'You pick things up quick.' Tamar had flushed with pleasure. There was more to haberdashery than she'd imagined. She had to learn how to measure a lady's hand for size, know which colours went with which, and understand the differing properties of lisle and silk and cotton. Miss Timms was pleasant to work for, explaining everything with great patience and an air of martyred resignation. She'd had a 'disappointment' in the Great War she told Tamar, and still wore a rather depressing looking engagement ring in seed pearls and garnets. 'If only I'd chosen differently,' she would sigh. 'Pearls for tears, red stones for blood.'

Despite her lapses into superstition, Miss Timms was an ardent Christian Scientist and whenever there was a lull at the counter, she lectured Tamar about the power of the mind to keep the body healthy. Illness was just an illusion, she told Tamar, who wondered how Miss Timms expected to be taken seriously, when she herself had a permanent snivel – an odd little sniff and swallow, followed by a discreet dab at the end of her nose with a scrap of white she kept tucked up her dark sleeve. And then there was her back, which, she complained, 'postitively *creaked*' when she bent down to the bottom drawers. But it was only a question of mind control. 'I am striving for perfection,' she said, at least once a day, 'but I haven't got it licked yet.' She brought leaflets for Tamar to read. One was entitled 'A Healthy Mind in a Healthy body,' and warned of the dangers of eating the dead flesh of other animals. *"The decomposition of this carrion in the stomach, poisons the bloodstream and causes a chemical imbalance which pollutes the purity of our God-given body. Meat eaters are more likely to sweat profusely, have foul smelling breath and suffer an excess of those negative energies that lead human beings into sin – anger, intolerance and unwholesome thoughts."*

It was also Tamar's job to go down in the lift to the stores to collect orders from Charlie who walked with a pronounced limp and had a thin high voice, like a girl.

'Why does he talk like that?' Tamar had asked after her first visit and Miss Timms had lowered her voice confidentially as if imparting a great secret.

'He had his privates shot off in the Great War, pet. Such a pity. He's neither fish nor fowl now poor man and his wife went off with a stoker at the gas works.'

Some of the other girls teased him, in a casual, unthinking kind of way that Tamar thought was unnecessarily cruel. Only last week one of them had marched up and down the corridor singing "Charlie is me darlin', me darlin', me darlin'" in a very provocative voice, while the others giggled outside the door. Tamar found that there weren't many of the girls she could really like. There were a lot of other young trainees at Pergavie's and some of them lived above the shop in dormitories with an elderly woman as matron. They were supposed to live in for the first year, but Tamar was allowed to be at home because of Sadie. Tamar was always conscious of Sadie watching her in the canteen.

'You should make more effort to fit in,' Sadie said repeatedly. 'Chat to the girls more. Go out with them sometimes. What's wrong with you?'

But Tamar felt she had no connection to these girls with their hand-knitted twin sets and carefully waved hair, their talk of boys and film stars, the life-histories and dilemmas of relatives she didn't know.

Sadie was currently walking out with Reg from the accounts department. They went to the cinema on half day closing, and on Sundays he would take her out tea dancing. Reg was a widower with two grown-up children who lived in a three bedroom semi on one of the new estates near Billy Mill. 'You play it right,' Lily kept saying, 'And you'll be properly set up. Your time of life you need a bit of comfort.' Reg wore Fair Isle pullovers and smoked a pipe. He called Tamar 'the Little Lady', and treated her with the kind of fatherly concern she'd come to dread. But, apparently, according to Sadie, he had 'strong moral principles'. Tamar heard her telling Lily in her most sarcastic voice, that he didn't believe in fun, except within the sanctity of marriage.

The other girls on the shop floor gossiped when they thought Tamar wasn't listening. But she heard enough in hints and whispers, to know what was being said.

'Reg is too good for her.'

'Lady Muck. Just looking for a Sugar Daddy.'

'She'd better hurry up then, before her looks go. Those sort of fluffy women are all blown over by forty.'

'She'll never stick it anyway. He's too bleedin' ordinary for her.'

'Don't worry. First time he sees her drunk that'll be it.'

'Finds her with someone else more like. She's got more fish than Reg to fry.'

And so on.

Tamar was conscious that her perception of her mother had been subtly altered. She couldn't decide whether her new, more critical attitude towards Sadie was a result of the letter she'd read, or simply because, working at Pergavie's, she'd begun to see her mother as a separate person, and look at her with the eyes of other people. What she saw was a soft, pretty woman, always stylishly dressed in clothes that never looked as cheap as Tamar knew they were. She could assume an air of helplessness and bewilderment that had everybody rushing to offer assistance as though she was a child. Tamar thought it was pathetic and deceitful. She could tell that Sadie was bored with Reg. There'd been a mysterious bank holiday visit to Scarborough and a night in a bed and breakfast that Reg wasn't supposed to know about. Sadie was also tired of working at Pergavie's. Tamar recognised the signs. There was an aura of recklessness about Sadie these days and there were incidents that filled Tamar with shame. Once when Sadie was doing a window display while they were being cleaned by a very young boy, she took out a pair of gent's lock-knit underpants (size extra large) and did unspeakable things with them until he became so embarrassed he fell off the ladder and cracked the glass.

A few weeks ago she'd borrowed a silk cocktail dress for a clandestine date with a merchant shipping captain, smuggling it out under her uniform. Everything would have been all right, except that someone had dropped cigarette ash on the sleeve putting a spray of tiny black-edged holes in the cream fabric, so she'd been unable to put it back. There was all hell let loose when the dress was discovered missing. There were veiled hints dropped in Tamar's presence and she was sure the supervisor suspected Sadie.

'She sails a bit close to the wind, does your mother,' Miss Timms told Tamar confidentially. 'She only keeps her job because Mr Pergavie has a soft spot for her.'

Tamar wondered what would happen when his indulgence ran

out or she provoked him once too often. The spell wouldn't last forever. Would Sadie move on again? She'd already lasted longer at Pergavie's than she'd ever managed anywhere else. But perhaps that was because she really did love modelling the coats for rich customers, running her fingers across the expensive pelts and saying 'I do think the darker mink has the edge over the musquash when it comes to style, don't you?' And then the customer would try it on – in a larger size. But when the woman looked in the mirror she wouldn't see herself, she'd see Sadie's slim, blonde figure looking helpless and alluring over the deep fur collar, like Garbo in the pictures, and they always bought the most expensive coats.

Sadie laughed at them, with her feet up on the furniture in the staff room and a forbidden cigarette in her red-tipped fingers. 'She looked like a gorilla in it – positively dreadful darling.' And she would drawl the words out to imitate the false-posh Tyneside intonations of the wealthy ship-owners' wives who came into the shop, adding viciously 'Money doesn't buy you class,' implying that she had it and they didn't.

As Tamar turned to go back into the store, Charlie came out of the back door trundling a barrow load of boxes for delivery. She waved the paper towards him. 'Hitler's invaded Czechoslavakia.'

'It's no surprise to me,' Charlie squeaked in his strange falsetto. 'Should have finished the Boche off properly last time. And then lettin' them re-arm!' He took the paper from her to have a closer look. 'It's you lot I feel sorry for.'

'Surely it won't come to that?'

'Just you wait and see.' Charlie stabbed the headline with a misshapen finger. 'Churchill's the only one who's got it right and nobody'll bloody listen to him. We'll have the Boche marching their jackboots up Northumberland Street before anyone'll believe it.'

'They won't come here, will they?'

'You go and take a look at the north sea, hinny.' He pointed down the street towards the docks. 'That's Germany over there and there's only the British Navy between us and them. But they'll not get me this time.' He lowered his voice and beckoned Tamar nearer. 'I kept me pistol, mind. I'll take a few down before they get me.'

Feeling shaken by Charlie's words Tamar stood for a few moments looking at the familiar street. It seemed so peaceful and ordinary. Tamar found it impossible to imagine tanks rumbling over the cobbles; storm troopers marching down the street, or even what it might feel like to live under a code of fear.

Back in haberdashery, Tamar gave Miss Timms the newspaper and watched her read it surreptitiously under the counter. Suddenly Miss Timms pushed it away underneath the wrapping paper. 'Stand up straight, Tamar, we're about to have a royal visit.'

The red-haired girl Tamar had seen before was coming across the shop floor towards them. She was wearing different clothes – a fitted green coat with a velvet collar and a little velvet hat, but she looked just as expensive and elegant.

'Who is she?' Tamar asked.

Miss Timms looked horrified at such ignorance. 'That's Mr Pergavie's daughter!' And then she whispered out of the corner of her mouth, trying to smile at the same time 'So mind you be extra nice.'

'Hello,' the girl said. She hesitated for a moment and then said, 'I'd like to see some handkerchiefs, please.'

Miss Timms nodded curtly to Tamar, who brought out a drawer of their best Swiss lawn squares, arranged in neat rows, some trimmed with lace, some delicately embroidered, and laid it on the counter.

The girl fingered them, glancing at Tamar with a puzzled expression on her face. 'Haven't I seen you somewhere before?' she asked.

'At the cinema in Shields and then once outside in the street when I was waiting for my mother.'

'Oh.' She seemed disconcerted. 'You don't talk like a shop girl. Have you always worked here?'

Tamar tried not to be offended. She nodded. 'Since I left school.'

'I wish I could leave school.' Holly sighed. 'My parents insisted I go to some dreadful ladies college in Morpeth. It's so tedious. We learn how to fold napkins and arrange flowers and where to put a bishop if you have him for dinner. I can't wait to leave.' She sighed again and then asked. 'What's your name?'

'Tamar. Tamar Fell.'

'That's unusual. Almost as odd as mine.'

'It's a Quaker name. What's yours?'

'Holly.' She pulled a face. 'People always ask if I was born at Christmas. But I wasn't. I don't know where they got it from.'

'There's a girl called Holly in a book I've just been reading,' Tamar said. 'Maybe your mother liked John Galsworthy. Have you ever read any of his books?'

Holly shook her head. 'I don't think my mother ever reads anything. Are you sure it was my name?'

'Positive. She has a twin brother called Jolyon. Everyone calls them Holly and Jolly.'

The girl began to laugh and then clapped a gloved hand over her mouth as though laughing was impolite. She picked up three of the lace-edged handkerchiefs. 'I'll take these please. And could you book them down to Mummy's account?' She addressed the question to Tamar, but it was Miss Timms who answered.

'Of course, Miss Pergavie.' Her voice was full of syrup. 'Is there anything else we can do for you?'

'No. That's all, thank you.' She took the tissue wrapped package from Tamar and turned to go. 'I expect I'll see you again.' She raised one gloved hand in a farewell wave.

'Well!' Miss Timms said. 'You were a bit forward weren't you? Talking to her like that. Asking her personal questions!'

'Was it wrong?' Tamar was startled. 'I've always wondered who she was. She gets picked up from the cinema in a chauffeur driven Bentley.'

'Spoiled rotten, that one,' Miss Timms said with a sniff. 'Not allowed to go a step without a chaperone. A bonny girl mind, don't get me wrong. There's no side to her. But she's never known the want of anything since the day she was born. I remember her da bringing her into the shop when she was just a toddler – so proud of her he was.'

Tamar wondered what it would be like to be Holly Pergavie, but such wealth and security was unimaginable.

On the way up to the canteen for her tea break, Tamar told Sadie about Holly's visit.

'Don't imagine the Pergavie's are the real thing,' Sadie said. 'Working class posh, that's all. His father had a corner shop down on the quayside and then married the daughter of a big ship's chandlery. Her father set them up in this store. And Holly's mother once worked in the shop like you. That's how he met her. So don't you go thinking Holly Pergavie's any better than you, because she isn't!'

Anna was waiting for Tamar when she came out of the shop at half past six, looking particularly vivid in a blue and red dress, with a red beret pulled down over her thick wedge of newly-cropped hair. It seemed that their quarrel had been forgotten and Tamar was grateful.

'I've bought you a present,' Anna said, pushing forward a package in brown paper.

Tamar was embarrassed. 'You shouldn't have spent your money. You need to save it all up for art college.'

'Don't be silly, it sounds ungrateful. Open it.'

Under the wrapping was a small, blue-bound book with gold lettering – A Golden Treasury of Verse.

'I saw this in the shop,' Anna said, 'and I remembered that beautiful poem you put in my autograph book. I'm not much of a one for poetry, but there are some lovely things in it.' She snatched the book back and flicked quickly through the thin, gold-edged pages. 'Here,' she said, turning it back towards Tamar, 'Read this. Isn't it the most beautiful thing? "Pity me not because the light of day, at close of day no longer walks the sky." It should be sad, but it isn't. Sort of defiant.'

Tamar was overwhelmed by her thoughtfulness. She felt instantly guilty because she'd accused Anna of never thinking of other people. 'Thank you Anna,' she said awkwardly. 'You couldn't have given me anything I'd like more.' She would have liked to hug her, but hesitated, unsure how such a spontaneous gesture of affection would be received, and then it was too late.

'Where's Sadie?' Anna asked as they walked up from the trolley stop. A cool evening breeze was blowing in from the sea. The pavements were crowded now with men coming home from work and women struggling back up the hill with tired children and bags of shopping.

'She's meeting someone. I think they're going to the pictures.'

'Come and stay the night with me. We'll make a cake and buy some lemonade and lie awake and talk all night. . .' Anna paused, in danger of being drowned out by a loud, stuttering, unfamiliar sound. They both stopped, looking round for the cause of it. A large black and chrome motor-bike and side-car was moving slowly and rather jerkily up the street towards them in the dusk, mounted by a dark-haired man in overalls wearing goggles. He juddered to a halt beside them, grinned and pushed the goggles up on top of his head.

'George,' Anna shrieked. 'You nearly frightened the life out of us. Wherever did you get that?'

George patted the tank. 'BSA. Latest model. You like it?'

'I'll say.' Anna's eyes admired it all.

Tamar couldn't think of anything to say except 'It must have cost the earth. How did you do it?'

'This is courtesy of old Adolf. All my overtime building ships to sink the Boche. Come on you two, jump on and we'll go for a spin.'

Anna swung her leg over the leather seat behind George, carelessly gripping his jacket and Tamar climbed awkwardly into the side-car – a wooden box, bolted onto the bike frame. The seat was hard and desperately uncomfortable.

'Hold on,' George shouted and the engine kicked as he let out the gear lever on the handlebars, sending them roaring and shuddering up the terrace towards the coast road watched by every curious window in the street. They parked on the sea front and walked down to the promenade.

'Isn't this great?' George said, leaning against the railing. He seemed so happy and relaxed, Tamar wondered if he'd been drinking.

'I've got coal specks in my eyes and my face is numb,' Anna said, feeling her chin with her fingers.

Tamar was rubbing her ears, where the evening wind coming off the sea had chilled them. It was almost dark and the street lamps made rippling circles of light on the wet sand as the tide ebbed. For some reason the sound of the waves hushing themselves to and fro on the beach made Tamar feel sad and reflective. Ever since this afternoon there'd been an anxious hollow just below her ribs. 'I wonder where we'll all be next year?' she asked.

'If there's a war, I'll be joining up,' George said.

'What'll your mother say?' Tamar had heard Lily telling Sadie about the uncle and two brothers she'd lost in the 1914 war, not to mention her husband. Lily was always going on about how thankful she was that George had such an important job in the shipyard. If there was a war, he wouldn't have to fight.

'She can't stop me.' George's face was set. 'It's a dead end here. I want to get out, move on, see a bit of the world. If there isn't a war, I'm going anyway. They say there's good jobs in Australia or South Africa. I'm a skilled fitter – someone'll take me.'

Anna was silent.

'Penny for them?' Tamar asked.

'I was thinking about my father. If there's a war . . . I can't bear it.'

'You'll be all right,' George said. 'Bein' one of them like.'

Anna said nothing, but Tamar saw her face twist into an expression of contempt.

'George is so stupid,' Anna said as they were getting ready for bed.

'Why? What did he do?'

'It's what he said. About me being German.'

'Oh. Things will get complicated won't they?'

'Everybody's going to take sides. Which side am I going to be on? I can hardly fight myself.'

'You could always be neutral. Sadie said my father was a conscientious objector in the Great War.'

'Why do you never talk about your father?'

'I don't know much about him. He died before I was born.'

'We're both orphans of a sort.' Anna sighed. 'God, I miss mine. You've no idea how much. He would have let me go to art college.'

'How's it going?'

'They told me this afternoon that I can go to King Edward's two days a week as a compromise so long as it doesn't interfere with my school certificate and I can go to the life classes in the evening. But not to draw the men mind! As if I was some kind of innocent.' Anna gave a strange, harsh laugh.

'Would you want to? I'd be too embarrassed to look!'

'It's only bodies, Tamar. If I'm going to be a painter, I've got to be able to draw men and women. You've got to be able to be objective whether you find them attractive or not.'

'Do you find George attractive?' Tamar said after a short pause.

'Why are you asking me that?'

'Because I think he's a bit sweet on you.'

Anna laughed again. 'I don't like men.'

'Why? What's wrong with them?'

'You wouldn't understand. You're such a baby Tamar.'

'I am not!'

'Yes you are. You don't know anything about sex.'

'Don't be silly Anna. I know the facts of life.'

'Do you? So what do you think your mother gets up to with all these men she sees, then?'

Tamar was stung into a retort. She felt the red mist rising behind her eyes. 'Much the same as your grandfather does with that snotty herring woman down on the quay!'

'Who told you that?'

'Lily. She says everyone knows. He's been carrying on with her for ages.'

'You shouldn't say things like that about my grandfather.'

'Then don't be horrid about Sadie!'

There was a silence and Tamar wondered if Anna was mortally offended, but after a few moments Anna spoke again as if their angry exchange had never taken place. Her mind had wandered off onto another subject.

'Do you ever see anything of Ida these days?' she asked.

'Not for ages.' Tamar, relieved that Anna was still speaking to her, was struck by a pang of guilt. 'She isn't at the cinema anymore.' It sounded weak, like an excuse.

'I can't understand you Tamar. She was so good to you and

such a character.'

Tamar shook her head in the dark. 'All my life people have been coming and going. At first I used to get upset when we went to a new place and I had to leave them behind, so I tried not to care so much about them. It was easier.'

'What about me?' Anna asked. 'Don't you care about me?'

'What a strange thing to ask.' Tamar was startled. 'Of course I do. We're best friends. You're the first proper friend I've ever had!'

'Good,' Anna said. 'Because that's how I feel about you too.' And to Tamar's surprise, she leant across and kissed her on the cheek.

CHAPTER EIGHT

The gas mask notices arrived in May. At Pergavie's, everyone was allowed to have time off work to go down to the Sacred Heart school to get them fitted. The mask stank of rubber and left a line of dark grey powder round Tamar's face when she put it on. It made a strange, rasping noise when she tried to breathe and felt airless and claustrophobic. The ugly contraption somehow made the idea of war more real. She was glad to take it off and put it back in the box. 'I hope I never have to wear this,' she said to the woman on the desk as she signed for it.

'It's purely precautionary,' the woman assured her. 'There's no cause for alarm.'

As Tamar walked back into the shop, Charlie was trundling in with some new deliveries. He nodded at the leather box over her shoulder. 'I pity you, hinny if it's anythin' like the last war.'

'What was it like?' Tamar asked.

'Don't ask hinny. But you make sure you get your mask on in time . . .' Charlie made a gesture with the edge of his hand across his throat. 'You don't want to get a lungful of that stuff.'

The following morning when Tamar collected the mail from the door mat there was another letter addressed to Miss S.R. Tomlinson that had Tamar's stomach somersaulting under her ribs. The envelope was the same stiff cream paper as the one in the hat box, but this time it was square and it was edged with black. The address was written in a thick black italic script. Tamar gave it to Sadie at the breakfast table and watched as she ripped the envelope open, scanned the contents briefly and then laughed. 'Well,' she said. 'The old bitch's gone at last, thank god.'

Tamar summoned up the courage to ask. 'Who's died?' But Sadie said 'No one you know,' in a way that precluded any further questions. Then she walked into the living room and threw the letter on the fire standing for a moment to watch it flare up and burn. 'I hope she's enjoying similar privileges,' Sadie said.

Nothing more was said but as they walked down to the shop through the familiar brick alleyways, misty with the smoke of newly lit fires, Tamar noticed Sadie looking gloomily around her. 'It's like living in a zoo,' she said. 'People peering at you from every window from behind the curtains.'

'I like it,' Tamar said. 'Particularly in the evening when the house lights are on. I like imagining the lives of the people in them.'

'There's nothing worth imagining!' Sadie sniffed with contempt. 'I'm tired of these northern towns, everyone's so small minded. What would you say to London, Tamar? Do you think we should give it a try?'

Tamar said nothing. She was stricken with a terrible fear and, when they reached the post box on the corner beside the newspaper shop, as if to confirm it, Sadie took a letter out of her pocket. Although she had her thumb over the name as she put it in the box, Tamar could see that it was addressed to London SW1.

Before he opened the shop, Mr Pergavie called all the staff up to the canteen to give a talk on safety. He stood at the front, facing them, clutching his gas mask in one hand. 'You must take it with you everywhere,' he said earnestly, holding it up. Tamar could see the sweat shining on his bald forehead. 'Keep it on the shelf under the till; bring it to the canteen for lunch; you must even take it with you to the cloakroom. Be prepared! The Germans could strike without warning at any time.'

Tamar found it difficult to understand why everyone had begun to talk about war as inevitable when it was supposed to be less likely. Hitler and Chamberlain had agreed peace, and now Hitler was negotiating some kind of pact with Russia. True he'd occupied Austria and Czechoslovakia, but why would he want to invade England?

Mr Pergavie was taking no chances. The windows were all to be taped up to prevent them shattering in a blast and the basement storage area was to be turned into an air raid shelter, with sandbags and camp beds. 'When you hear the sirens,' he said.

'You must stop what you are doing straight away and escort the customers downstairs.'

'But, Mr Pergavie, what if they don't want to go?' It was Miss Sinclair from the Fur and Gown department. Her face was furrowed by the thought of having to coerce wealthy, capricious women into a dark and rather dusty basement in their best clothes.

'You must insist,' he said. 'Safety is our paramount objective.' He thumped his gas mask on the top of the table enthusiastically. 'Pergavie's must take the lead in showing we care for the people we serve.'

Downstairs, as they tidied their gas mask cases under the till, one of the cheeky new juniors asked, 'So what about the power of the mind over this, Miss Timms?' She was biting her lips to stop herself laughing. 'D'you reckon it would be a match for Hitler?' Some of the younger girls began to snigger and then they all burst out laughing.

Miss Timms flushed and looked down without answering. Later she whispered confidentially to Tamar that Pergavie's weren't getting the class of girl now that they used to. 'They all go into the factories, you know. It's much better money.'

Tamar had seen the recruiting films at the cinema. The girls all seemed to be immensely happy in dungarees and headscarves, lifting bits of metal on and off lathes that squirted a constant emulsion of grease and steel filings. To Tamar it looked messy, noisy and repetitive, but the hourly pay was half as much again as she was getting at Pergavie's. Yesterday, as she walked home she'd met Elsie coming out of Lyons, looking very smart in a camel coat.

'You're not still working in that stuffy old shop are you?' Elsie had asked, giving a derisive glance at Tamar's uniform. 'You want to get yourself a decent job like me. Earn yourself some money.' She swung the hem of the camel coat provocatively and laughed.

All the girls at Pergavie's had at least one friend who worked in the munitions' factory, and in the canteen they discussed its pros and cons. Apparently the atmosphere was very democratic – they could listen to music while they worked, wear trousers and there was a union for grievances. 'Don't you fancy it?' they asked Tamar, but she always shook her head. Factory work didn't appeal at all.

That evening Tamar and Sadie came home from the shop to find a huge mound of earth in the back garden and piles of bricks and sheets of corrugated iron stacked in the alley. Lily was standing outside looking at it. 'They're diggin' us an Anderson shelter, so we can hide from the bombs. Have you ever heard anythin' so stupid in all your life? Who's goin' to bother to drop bombs on us here?'

'It seems such a dreadful waste of money,' Sadie said. 'One of the officers told me at the club last night that all this war-mongering is just a big bluff, like a game of poker. They'll all back down at the last moment.'

George, sitting at the kitchen table eating his tea, raised his eyes to heaven but he said nothing.

Tamar took her coat from the hook behind the door. 'All this talk of war's depressing me,' she said. 'I'm going down to the Palace to see Jeanette McDonald.'

'Not again pet!' Lily exclaimed. 'How many times have you seen it now?'

'Twice,' Tamar said. 'I'd go every night if I could afford it. It's wonderful!' The music haunted her, floating through her mind during the day as she folded handkerchiefs and sorted drawers of silk flowers. Every evening when she passed the cinema on her way home she would linger for a few moments at the open door, hoping to catch a few strains of Naughty Marietta distantly over the clicking of the machine at the ticket office. Sometimes, Tamar dreamed as she walked past that some theatre producer would come into the shop to buy a present for his wife – gloves, or a scarf perhaps – and see Tamar as she opened boxes and peeled back tissue paper and laid them on the counter in front of him. 'Have you ever thought of going on the stage?' He would say. And give her his card. 'Come and see me at the stage door. I've got a part that just might suit you!' And then she would be waltzing across the boards with the juvenile male lead, perfectly synchronised, her skirt swirling about her silk-stockinged legs . . .

'It's only operetta!' George said scathingly, interrupting her idyll. 'One day I'm goin' to get to Covent Garden – that's the place. What I'd give for a seat in the gods!'

'You won't be seeing the Ring Cycle there for a while,' Sadie murmured. 'The Fuhrer's very fond of it, I believe.'

'Well, I won't hold it against Wagner,' George said heroically. 'Anyone who can write music like that can't be all bad.'

There was a long queue outside the Palace, despite the fact that the film was into its second week. Obviously other people were as captivated by it as Tamar. By the time she got to the ticket booth the only seats left were in the circle and Tamar had to dig deep into her purse to find the extra money. It would mean not having any pudding in the canteen tomorrow and praying that she wouldn't need to buy another pair of stockings until the end of the week. As she climbed the carpeted staircase to the circle, Tamar noticed that the door to the projection box was slightly ajar and she could see Robby inside unpacking a canister of film. 'Hello, hinny,' he called as she passed.

Tamar put her head round the door. 'How's Ida,' she asked, raising her voice above the hiss of the newsreel through the projector.

'Poorly.' Robby looked solemn. 'She's not been right all winter. Fair pulled down she is. My wife takes her a bit of something now and then, but there's not much else a body can do.'

Tamar felt guilty. 'I ought to go and see her really. It's just – what with work and everything . . .'

'She'd love to see you pet. Not many people get down there these days and you know how she likes a bit of a crack.'

After the film was over, as Tamar joined the press of people queuing to get out through the foyer, she saw Holly Pergavie again, coming down the stairs from the Grand Circle. She was wearing the same coat and hat, this time accompanied by her mother and a middle aged man in uniform. As they passed Tamar, Holly looked in her direction and Tamar smiled expecting an answering smile of recognition, but although she was sure that Holly had seen her, the girl's face remained determinedly blank. Tamar felt as if she'd been slapped. As she glared at the averted head an angry retort leapt into her mind. 'Sadie's right, you're a snob. But I'm not going to be a shop girl forever, Holly Pergavie!' How she wished that she could have said it out loud.

George was waiting outside the cinema when Tamar came out, still burning with the injustice of it.

'I've been down to the Union,' he said. 'Thought I'd just walk up with you.'

It was nice of him, Tamar thought. She hated the walk back on her own after dark.

George pulled a folded piece of paper out of his pocket. 'They were giving these out. Do you still think of going for a librarian?'

Tamar was startled. 'I don't know. I'd like to do something – I don't want to work in a shop all my life.' Holly's rebuff had made Tamar realise that secretly she still cherished hopes for the future, though she had no clear idea of how she was going to fulfil them. The leaflet George had given her was for the Workers Education Association and it advertised evening classes and a programme of lectures. Tamar studied the programme as she walked. 'There's one on Sunday about the Bronte's. I'd quite like to go to that.' She'd already made up her mind to visit Ida, but perhaps she could do that as well. 'You won't tell anyone at home will you?' She couldn't put it into words but she was afraid that if she made it public they would laugh at her or that something else would happen to get in the way of her ambitions.

On Sunday afternoon Tamar dressed carefully. She'd been paying into a club at the shop ever since she started work and that, combined with her staff discount, had made it possible to afford a beautiful spring suit in French navy and a pin-tucked blouse with a swiss lawn collar. Sadie had helped her to choose it, and now she stood watching her daughter from the doorway, with her eyes narrowed.

'You'll never be a beauty,' she said critically. 'But if you dress properly you'll always be elegant.'

'I'd rather be beautiful. It's much easier to get what you want.'

Sadie shook her head. 'Beauty's a trap. You're better off without it. At least *then* you know that people want you for yourself.'

She took a long drag on her cigarette. 'God, you look grown up in that suit. It makes me feel old.'

Tamar hadn't told Sadie or Lily about going to the lecture, only that she was visiting Ida. As Tamar went out through the kitchen, Lily caught her and pushed a paper bag into her hand. 'There's some home-made shortbread for you to take. You don't want to go empty handed, hinny. And you tell Ida we're all thinkin' about her.' It was impossible to refuse. Here people always took something with them when they went to someone's house. Tamar crammed the shortbread into her handbag and hoped it would survive.

Tamar was surprised to see how many people had packed themselves into the hall. One or two of them weren't dressed like workers at all, though the majority had an air of Sunday best about them, like herself, she thought. Middle aged women in shabby tweed suits with voluminous leather bags and scuffed shoes predominated. One of them had brought her knitting. There were a smaller number of men in cloth caps and raincoats whose faces, either pale or weathered reflected lives spent in factories or shipyards. There were also quite a few younger people, some of them clutching notebooks and Tamar realised that, if she was serious about learning, she should have brought one too.

The speaker, a rather nondescript woman about Sadie's age, was introduced as a romantic novelist called Ellen Flynn, though the name meant nothing to Tamar. But from her first words Tamar was captivated. 'Currer, Acton and Ellis Bell?' she asked the audience. 'Can anyone tell me who those three gentlemen were?' Not a hand was raised. 'Then I'll tell you. They were the pen names that Charlotte, Anne and Emily Bronte used when their work was first published. And do you know why? Because it was considered scandalous for a respectable woman to publish anything.' She then launched into an account of the Brontes' tragic lives that had half the audience weeping.

'It's sadder than Little Women,' the woman beside Tamar said, dabbing her eyes. 'I come every week,' she went on. 'It's grand!'

Ida's lodgings were on one of the narrow streets leading down to the quayside. Her landlady was outside, holy-stoning the step when Tamar arrived. 'Don't smudge me whitenin'!' She scolded, shuffling to one side to let her through.

'How is Ida?' Tamar asked. She was careful to step right in the middle.

'Not too clever, between you and me, hinny. Keeps us awake half the night coughin' and she doesn't eat enough to feed a spuggy! Not that she gets any thinner, mind.'

Ida had the back room with a big window out onto the yard that flooded the room with sunlight. The brass bedstead was pushed into a corner and Ida was lying on it propped up with a mountain of pillows. Her eyes lightened the moment Tamar stepped into the room. 'Oh pet,' she said. Her voice was hoarse and her breath wheezed in and out. 'You shouldn't have come.' She offered her cheek to kiss and Tamar brushed her lips over the clammy skin trying not to inhale the suffocating odours of sour flesh, eucalyptus and some kind of sickly perfume presumably meant to cover up the pervading smell of decay.

'Lily's sent you some of her shortbread.' Tamar put the paper bag down on the bedside table among the medicine bottles, tea cups and magazines, hoping that it hadn't been reduced to crumbs during its long journey. 'And I brought you these.' She put a bunch of anemones she'd bought from the stall outside the crematorium on the bedspread where Ida could see them. A smudge of dark pollen stained the counterpane. Tamar thought how clean and fresh they looked against the grubby linen.

'You shouldn't have spent your money, pet,' Ida wheezed. She looked as if she might cry. 'You're too good to me.'

Tamar felt embarrassed and guilty. If only Ida knew how little she really wanted to be here; how much she was repelled by the squalor and the smell of sickness. 'How are you?' she asked.

'I've been better,' Ida said. But the effort of talking made her begin to cough.

Tamar had never seen anyone cough like that. She was appalled. It was a cavernous, rasping bark that convulsed Ida's enormous body with paroxysms. The bed jangled against the wall and her face went dark purple as she struggled to get her breath, coughing and coughing until it seemed that the entire contents of her body must have been brought up into her throat. Suddenly

Ida leaned over the side of the bed and spat a column of green and yellow slime into a chamber pot under the bed. Then she lay back exhausted, wiping her face with a piece of rag, while sweat ran down her cheeks and onto the pillow.

'Sorry about that pet,' she whispered. 'It's disgustin'.' She stopped to gasp for breath again.

'Don't try to talk. It's all right Ida.' Tamar swallowed down the bile that had risen into her mouth. 'It upsets me to see you like this. Can't anything be done?'

Ida shook her head. When she spoke she had to stop every three or four words to reach for breath. 'Emphysema. The doctor says. . . . How's your mam?'

Tamar made herself smile. 'About as usual. Optimistic as ever. George sends his regards. He's working so much overtime he's hardly home at all except to eat and sleep.'

'He's a canny lad . . . And you?'

'I'm still at Pergavie's. Miss Timms is supposed to be retiring at the end of the year and they're going to let me manage her counter.'

Ida nodded. 'And your friend? The German girl?' The whisper was almost inaudible.

'Anna's at art college now. She's painting Lily, when she can get her to sit still long enough.' Tamar paused. 'We all miss you at the cinema.'

Ida nodded again and tried to smile. She had her eyes closed.

'I'm sorry. I've tired you out. I'd better go.'

Ida opened her eyes again. 'Father O'Malley's comin' in to say mass for me. . . You're a good bairn, Tamar. . . You never laughed at me like most of them.' She was ratching around under her pillow as she spoke, looking for something. She took out a purse, opened it and then beckoned for Tamar to come closer. 'Here you are pet,' she pressed a pound note into her hand. 'That's for you to buy yourself something nice with. . . Treat yourself on me.'

'Ida, I couldn't!' Tamar was appalled. She tried to push the money back into her hand, but Ida waved her away.

'I'll be hurt if you don't. . . Now you take it. I've got a bit put by for a rainy day . . . So don't go thinkin' I'm on me uppers. . . 'Cos I'm not. It'll do me good to think of you enjoyin' yourself.'

'Oh, Ida!' Tears had begun to slide down Tamar's face.

'Go on with you,' Ida whispered. She was wheezing badly again. 'You get on out before the priest comes . . . And give my love to everybody at Heaton Street . . . Mind you do.'

Tamar kissed her, this time more warmly. Ida had her eyes closed, the cloth pressed to her mouth. As Tamar closed the door she heard her begin to cough again.

The landlady was in the hall polishing the brass door knocker when Tamar went out. 'Will she be all right?' Tamar asked.

'Who's to say, hinny.' The woman shrugged. 'We're lookin' after her as best we can.'

On Monday Anna's mother was waiting for her at the bus stop when she got off the Tynemouth bus after school. She had Frankie in the pram for his afternoon stroll.

'We've been down to the park and I thought we could walk back with you,' Mrs Weissmann said. There was something about her manner that made Anna think she had an ulterior motive, but her mother said nothing more until they crossed the street.

'The enumerators are coming to see us next week,' she said.

'What on earth are they?'

'They're visiting everyone to register them for identity cards and war rations – that kind of thing.'

'Oh. Is that a problem?'

Mrs Weissmann was quiet for a moment and then she said, 'I'm frightened, Anna. The same thing happened in Germany. I never told you, but the day before we left, while you were at school, a Nazi official came to the house asking questions about where we came from, your father's relatives – that kind of thing. There was some kind of register. And so I've decided that I'm going to change my name and Frankie's by deed poll. Just a little alteration. From now on it's going to be spelt Wiseman.'

Anna stopped. 'Why?'

'If there's a war, it might be better. Someone put this through the door today.' Mrs Weissmann pulled a crumpled piece of paper out of her pocket and gave it to Anna. It was a sheet of cheap writing paper with misspelt words scrawled unevenly along the lines in ragged capitals. "TRAYTER. GO BACK WERE YOU CUM FROM." 'It's not the first. I thought I'd left all that behind in Germany, but people in the shops comment on my name and make nasty remarks behind my back. I can still remember what it was like in the last war – all that anti-German feeling – and I don't want to go through the same thing again. Wiseman sounds English enough not to attract any attention.'

'Well, I'm not changing mine! That would be like . . . A betrayal. I think it's hateful.'

'But I'm only doing it for your sake, and Frankie's. Anna – don't you think it would be safer if you changed yours as well? Anne Wiseman. It sounds rather nice. Promise me you'll think about it?'

Anna was too angry to speak. She had tried so hard to keep her first name and now she was being asked to change her second name as well.

When she got home she went straight upstairs to her room and took out the photograph of her father. What would he say if he knew? Would he ever come to England? A couple of weeks ago a train load of Jewish children had arrived in Newcastle from Germany as refugees. If they could get out, why couldn't he?

It was time for Frankie's bath. Anna could hear her mother turning taps and then his protesting shrieks as she lowered him into the water. Anna tiptoed downstairs and turned the key in the parlour door. It was very quiet in there and musty – she could smell the moth balls her grandmother kept under the settee to protect the carpets. She looked automatically at her great grandfather's painting of ships at sea. Her gaze was more critical these days – her trained eye saw all its faults of perspective, line and colour, but it was still beautiful in a rough, untutored way. He had had such talent. If only the opportunities had been there in those days. What might he have done?

'Well, at least I'm not going to waste my chances,' Anna told herself. 'And I'm certainly not going to change my name.' She opened the bureau drawer and took out her birth certificate. No one was going to take away her name or her identity, whatever her mother told the enumerators when they came. Upstairs again,

Anna took out her calligraphy pen and some black ink. It was the matter of a few seconds to round the 'e' of Anne and turn it into Anna. The loop of the 'e' seemed quite natural once Anna had gracefully drawn it down into the tail of the 'a'. She did the same for the 'a' in Weissmann, altering all the other 'a's as well so that the registrar's handwriting was consistent. Anna held it up and looked carefully at the certificate. It was a brilliant forgery. Now, if she ever had to produce it, no one would know that she hadn't been born Anna Weissmann. And she would keep the certificate herself, so that no one could ever take her name away.

As May gave way to one of the warmest Junes anyone could remember, no one talked of anything but war at Pergavie's, or at Heaton Street. A big anti-aircraft gun emplacement had been built on the coast road near the school and in the evenings as they ate one of Lily's enormous high teas they could hear the thud thud thud of practice firing. It made Tamar shudder. The town was full of servicemen. Sadie had given Reg up as 'a bad job' and she and Lily were having the time of their lives with naval officers that a much more worldly Tamar suspected had wives elsewhere. An increasing number of mornings Sadie wasn't fit to work after coming in from pubs and clubs in the early hours of the morning. Tamar hated having to go to the floor manageress and say, 'I'm sorry Miss Sinclair, my mother's sick again,' and see her hard, unbelieving eyes and know what she was thinking.

'Gallivanting, if you ask me!' Tamar heard her say to the senior saleswoman as she left the department. 'She'll do it once too often, just you wait.' It was only a matter of time now before they were as tired of her as Sadie was of them.

But the crisis came quicker than Tamar had anticipated. On the Tuesday after Tamar's visit to Ida, Sadie received another letter – blue Basildon Bond this time – written in a neat small hand, and with a London postmark. This is it, Tamar thought as she picked it up off the mat. Sadie's going to try to drag me off to London. But when she gave the letter to her mother, Sadie didn't seem at all eager to have it. She put it quickly in her pocket without opening the envelope. And later, when Tamar went to the toilet, there were shreds of blue paper stained with ink floating in the pan. All day at the shop Sadie seemed her usual bright, sarcastic self, but it was no surprise to Tamar when she and Lily went up to the pub after tea, returning long after Tamar was asleep. Sadie, she knew, was drowning some kind of sorrow. The following morning the cup of tea Tamar put on Sadie's bedside table skinned over and became cold and the huddled shape under the eiderdown failed to respond to her shaking and nagging.

'I'm afraid my mother's sick again,' Tamar told the floor manageress. She felt humiliated by the lie and the look of cold distaste that spread slowly over Miss Sinclair's face.

'Tell her not to bother to come in again,' she said. 'If you go up to the office before you go home, they'll give you her cards.' Her face settled into an expression of virtuous martyrdom, the look of someone who has done something unpleasant but necessary.

Anxiety ate into Tamar all day. How would Sadie manage without any money coming in? Tamar was earning almost enough now to keep herself, but not enough to keep Sadie as well. Tamar made several mistakes with customers, giving one woman gloves the wrong colour, telling another the wrong price, which earned her a ticking off from Miss Timms. 'I don't know what's the matter with you today, Tamar. Left your brains at home did you?'

When she went up to the office at six o'clock the girl at the desk had Sadie's cards already waiting for her. 'Mr Pergavie wants to see you before you go,' she said.

Tamar was terrified. She'd never been into his office – hardly anyone ever did, except people who'd done something terrible, and then a whisper would go round the floor that 'so-and-so had been *sent for*'. She knocked on the frosted glass, hardly able to breathe for nerves, and heard his deep voice shout 'Come in!'

He was standing beside a ledger desk turning over the pages of a big account book. When Tamar entered he turned round and smiled at her. 'Shut the door,' he said.

His room had the same thick red carpet as the shop floors and the furniture was the same old, polished mahogany. There was a big desk near the window with a red leather top, brass angled lamp, a telephone, a wooden stand for pens and a huge green leather blotter. Tamar stared at it all, concentrating on the objects in front of her in an attempt to control the uncertain state of her stomach. Small details seemed to jump out at her; the tuft of curly, grizzled hair sprouting from Mr Pergavie's left ear as he turned towards her; the crooked little finger on the soft white hand he held out to her.

'It's Tamar isn't it? Tamar Fell? Unusual name. Pretty.'

Tamar put her own hand in his and it was warmly shaken. Having braced herself for an angry encounter, perhaps the loss of her own job, she felt dizzy with the unexpected kindness of his tone.

'I just wanted to say how sorry I was that your mother's health has become too poor for her to continue with us.' He walked back to the desk and picked up a brown envelope from the corner of it. 'Would you give her this as a token of our appreciation for her services?'

Tamar took the envelope, felt its thickness and the surprise must have registered on her face.

'Your mother has been a valued employee and her commission rates have not, perhaps, been as generous as they should have been.' He coughed slightly, glancing across at Tamar with eyes that didn't quite meet hers. 'This represents a little "adjustment", shall we say?' He patted Tamar's arm, his smooth face betraying nothing.

'Thank you very much,' Tamar managed to say. 'It's very kind of you.' She had to stand for a few moments leaning against the door jamb after she'd closed the door behind her. Her cheeks were flushed and she felt hot all over as if she had a temperature.

Sadie was getting ready to go out when Tamar got home.

'What did the old cow say?' she asked. She was carefully rimming her mouth with a new lipstick called Pink with a Wink, rolling her lips together to spread the colour evenly.

'You're not to bother to go back,' Tamar said, putting the envelopes down on the dressing table. 'Your cards are in there and the other's a present from Mr Pergavie.'

Sadie snatched it up, tearing the paper open with her finger nails to look inside. 'Stingy old goat. Still, it's better than nothing.'

'What are you going to do now?' Tamar asked.

'How should I know.' Sadie was dabbing loose powder over her cheeks with a piece of dirty cotton wool. There were spots of powder on her blouse. 'Something'll come along.' Her voice was lazy and Tamar knew she'd been drinking during the afternoon.

Suddenly she wanted to grab her mother by the shoulders and shake her. How were they to manage? How would they live, pay the rent? The strength of her own anger surprised Tamar. The whole of her childhood she'd relied on Sadie, assumed somehow that everything would always be all right. Now she knew how fragile that sense of security had been. How close to the edge they'd always lived.

Sensing something of this, subliminally aware of Tamar's sudden blaze of hostility, Sadie stood up and turned round. 'It'll be all right. You'll see. We've always managed, haven't we?' She put her arm clumsily round Tamar's shoulders for a brief, rare hug and then picked up her bag from the dressing table and went downstairs.

After she'd gone, Tamar went down to the kitchen and tried to explain to Lily Kennedy what had happened. 'I can probably find the money for the rent. But I won't be able to afford to pay for the meals.'

'You're not to worry, pet,' Lily said. She was frying sausages with a cigarette in one hand. 'I'll see your mam right. We've had some good times, her and me.' She winked at Tamar. 'Women like us've got to stick together.'

CHAPTER NINE

'Gee gee!' Frankie said, pointing a sticky finger at the drawing on the wall.

'It's a horse!' Anna corrected. Why did they have to teach him nonsense words he would later have to unlearn? It was like expecting him to learn two languages. But when she thought about it, Anna realised that she hadn't found the process particularly painful herself. She'd learned both English and German before she was five.

'Gee gee!' Frankie repeated, grinning as if it was a game he wanted her to play. Really, Anna thought, he was quite sweet when he smiled. She put him down again and watched him toddle shakily along the floor to clutch at his mother's skirts as she stood in front of Anna's work. Anna watched her mother's face intently for any expression of approval, but could detect only a kind of puzzled inspection, abandoned as soon as she felt Frankie's groping hands at her knees. She picked him up, smiling as if with relief, and moved along the wall to glance at the next painting.

Feeling vaguely disappointed and rejected, though aware that there was no real reason why she should, Anna turned to look around her at the crowded gallery. This was the annual exhibition for students of the School of Fine Art and, although Anna was not yet a full time student and much younger than the rest, her work had been included. The piece that they'd selected was not one of the paintings she'd spent so much time and effort over in class, but the big, almost abstract, watercolour sketch of the sea front she'd done at home on a stormy morning more than a year ago.

Anna had taken it into class when it was her turn to be subjected to what the students called the 'monthly crit' – an ordeal where every aspect of technique and composition would be mauled by tutors and fellow students. Anna had seen several people's work destroyed by this ruthless examination and she had stiffened herself for the same treatment. But to her surprise, the watercolour had met with approval. 'It's the best thing you've ever done,' her tutor had said, pursing his eyes up to look at it over his glasses. 'Now perhaps you can see why we make you do all those tedious exercises you complain about – so that you can paint spontaneously without having to think about technique.' John Cornell was one of the youngest of her teachers. He was a graduate of the Nottingham School of Art, rather than one of the London academies, but he had considerable glamour having just spent a year painting in France and Italy.

On the wall the watercolour bothered Anna because it was so much less worked over than any of the other paintings. It didn't seem to fit into any of the traditions followed so assiduously by her fellow students. When she looked at their work, Anna could see the influence of the Impressionists – so revered by her tutor – drawings that looked back all the way to the Renaissance, as well as the occasional self-conscious excursion into surrealism. Her own, semi-abstract scrawl in sepia tones seemed limp and unformed hung beside this more sophisticated work.

A balding middle-aged man carrying a raincoat and a crumpled felt hat had paused about three feet away from her to look at it. He stood for a long time before he turned to Anna and said – almost as if he knew what she'd been thinking – 'How refreshing it is not to find pastiche in a student's work.'

'Thank you!' It was not what Anna had expected him to say.

'Is this yours?' The man's English was good, but very heavily accented. He put his face close to the frame as if examining the surface of the painting. Then he said 'Whose work are you studying?'

'Monet, Renoir . . .'

'Picture postcard painting!' he said abruptly. 'You should be looking at Cezanne, Matisse, Picasso. Abstraction is the future, not representation. The camera's made representation obsolete. Do you ever work with colour?'

'Sometimes. I don't really know how to use it yet – the possibilities are so infinite.' Anna made a gesture of hopelessness. 'So I thought I'd better get to grips with form before I start exploring it.'

The man nodded as if he agreed with her.

'Have you thought of studying in London?'

'I'm hoping to get into the Slade.' When Anna said it, baldly like that, it sounded presumptuous, almost criminal, an utterly impossible ambition for someone like herself.

'Why the Slade?' He looked down at her with a quizzical expression in his eyes and Anna remembered that Robert Drew had once asked the same question. As though he read what was in her mind he went on – 'It's not what it was, since Professor Tonks retired. Why not the Royal Academy?'

Anna felt unable to reply. She had no idea why she wanted to go to the Slade, except that Miss Bateman had talked about it incessantly and it had somehow come to represent for her the ultimate goal – the only place worth going to. She knew hardly anything about the Royal Academy – stuffy and boring – Miss Bateman had said.

The man was looking carefully at the corner of the canvas where Anna had boldly signed her name. 'Anna Weissmann. That's a German name is it not?'

She nodded.

'How long have you been here?' he asked in German.

It was a long time since Anna had spoken the language and she realised with some sadness that she had to concentrate quite hard to understand what he was saying. 'Three years. Too long,' she said. 'All I can think about is going back.'

He shook his head. 'For those of us of Jewish extraction there is nowhere to study art in Germany at present. Maybe in the future, but not now.'

Anna was reeling. Was it so obvious that she was Jewish?

'I came here five years ago,' he went on, 'because I was suddenly not allowed to teach. You must learn all you can, Anna. Perhaps one day we will be able to go home.'

When he'd moved on, John Cornell came rushing up to Anna and said 'You were lucky! What did he say?'

'Who was he?'

'That's Walter Suzmann. Didn't you know? He's working on a commission down at the shipyard. I was amazed to see him here. You'd think a student exhibition would be the last thing he'd want to see on his day off.'

~~~~~~~~~~~~~~~~~

At the other end of the room, Tamar was day-dreaming. She was a princess – foreign royalty. Russian probably. She was wearing a long black sable coat fringed with fur tails that Sadie had once described to her, with a huge shawl collar that rose seductively to her cheekbones. And there was a hat, a huge brim of black felt, swathed in thread net and decorated with ostrich feathers that tickled her face. Everyone's eyes were on her. People asked in whispers 'Who *is* that woman?'

Then a voice at her elbow asked 'Do you know anything about painting?'

Tamar opened her eyes. She was just Tamar in her best navy two piece and a coat that had once belonged to Sadie, standing in a corner with her gas mask slung over her shoulder, looking at a portrait of a woman chopped up into zig-zag pieces like stained glass, painted in green and tomato red. Next to her a dark-haired, olive-skinned boy with thickly lashed eyes was peering at the label underneath and writing something down in a notebook.

'I don't know anything about art. Do you?' he asked again, turning a serious face towards Tamar.

His unusually deep voice startled her and she realised that he was much older than he looked. She shook her head. 'Nothing at all. But my friend does – she's got a painting on the wall in the corner over there.'

He looked relieved. 'That's great.' He smiled at Tamar and as he did so she was conscious of a strange sensation, as though the room rocked slightly. She could feel herself flushing as he said, 'You wouldn't like to introduce me, would you? I've been asked to cover this for the local paper. It's my first proper assignment, so it's got to be good.' He held his hand out. 'My name's Edward Antonelli. I'm a cub reporter for the Star. How about you?'
~~~~~~~~~~~~~~~~~

Tamar told him her name and put her hand into his warm, firm grip. She could feel herself blushing again as his eyes probed her face unselfconsciously.

'My family have an ice cream business. They've got a parlour at the Spanish City and several vans. Maybe you've noticed them?'

When he told her, Tamar remembered seeing 'Antonelli's' on the awnings above the ice-cream barrows down at the beach.

'I used to work for them in the summer holidays,' Edward said. 'We all had to. I was expected to go into the business when I left school.'

'Were your parents upset when you didn't?'

'My Dad was a bit. But my Mum's English, and she persuaded him that there was only enough work for my brothers in the firm, so I could go and do what I liked.'

'How did you get onto the Star?'

'I won a "Young Reporter" competition when I was still at school. It was a piece about the derelict old Music Hall. We used to break in through a window at the back and smoke fags in the dressing rooms. Some of them still had signed photos pinned up on the walls and dog ends of greasepaint in the drawers. I wrote about the ghosts of Marie Lloyd, Maud Allen and Bertie Flynn still wandering about backstage – pretty far-fetched, but someone must have liked it. So when I left school my English teacher wrote to the editor and he offered me a job.'

Tamar was impressed, but Edward laughed. 'I spent the first year making tea in the office, nipping round to the off-licence at lunchtime for the boss's brown ale, and covering the results at the greyhound track. The boss said he was trying to 'kick the Pulitzer out of me' – at least that's how he put it!' What Edward really wanted to write, he told her, were thrillers and detective stories like Dashiell Hammett. There was a new writer too, called Graham Greene, whose work Edward admired.

'I'll lend you a couple of his books if you like. I could bring them round one evening after work!'

'Thanks!' Tamar said, only half believing that he would, but she told him her address anyway. Then, reluctantly, she took him over to introduce him to Anna. She couldn't explain why, except that for some reason, she wanted to keep Edward to herself. Was she afraid that he might be attracted to her best friend rather than herself? But Anna was deep in conversation with another man Tamar thought might be her tutor. She seemed distracted and almost irritated by Edward's naive questions. They were standing in front of a small abstract of squares and lines. Tamar was taut with vicarious embarrassment as Edward asked 'But what does it mean?'

'It doesn't mean anything! That's the whole point.' Anna was sharper than usual. 'The idea is to abstract cultural and anthropomorphic references so that the painting's entire *meaning*,' she stressed the word sarcastically, 'is contained within itself.'

It was almost a relief when Edward moved away to talk to someone else.

'You weren't very nice to him,' Tamar accused.

'Sorry. Did you want me to be?'

'He said he'd lend me some books, but I don't suppose he'll remember.'

'Bet he does,' Anna said. 'He looked quite taken.' There was an edge to her voice that Tamar didn't quite understand, and a flash of disapproval in her eyes. What was wrong with Anna these days; what had happened to make her so restless and edgy?

Edward was in Tamar's thoughts all day and she was certain that she would never see him again. But he arrived the following evening bringing the newspaper with him, ostensibly to show Tamar the review he'd written. 'It's only two column inches,' he said ruefully, 'the editor cut most of it. But it's a start.'

He'd also brought Brighton Rock and Tamar hadn't the heart to tell him that she'd already read it. The corner shop was now lending out books at 2d a time and if you couldn't afford to buy them it was a good way of reading the newest books which were sometimes slow to get into the library.

Tamar introduced Edward to Lily and then to Sadie.

'Gosh,' he said, as she shook Sadie's hand, 'I would never have guessed you were Tamar's mother! You look more like sisters!' And then his face coloured and he said 'Oh I'm sorry! I hope I wasn't rude?'

Sadie was smiling in an odd kind of way. 'Not at all. I take it as a compliment.'

She and Lily were going out dancing and Sadie was wearing the stolen cream silk dress. Now she no longer worked at Pergavie's she said she didn't care who saw her in it. Tamar noticed, almost bitchily, that it had got rather tight at the seams.

When they'd gone, Edward asked Tamar if she'd like to go for a walk. It was a warm, midsummer evening – muggy and slightly thundery and they took the tram down to the sea front and stood on the promenade watching the fog bank roll in across the North sea.

'I can't get over your mother,' Edward said. 'She doesn't look old enough to have a grown-up daughter.'

It gave Tamar a pain in her stomach to hear him talk so admiringly about Sadie. When he'd looked at her in that way it had made Tamar feel dowdy and plain. She always felt gauche in company beside Sadie anyway, but this was different – more painful.

'I can see where you get your looks from though,' Edward went on, smiling at her now in a way that lifted her heart.

'Do you fancy going to the pictures on Friday?' he asked as he delivered Tamar back to the gate. 'There's a new Clark Gable at the Palace and the latest Thin Man at the Metropole. Do you like Myrna Loy?'

A strange, new sensation ran down Tamar's spine, and when she tried to reply her lips felt as if they were made of wood. She was smiling like an idiot. 'Yes, thank you,' she managed to say. 'I'd like that very much.'

George was in the living room reading the paper. He looked over the top of it as Tamar came in. 'You'd better watch those Eye-tie lads,' he said. 'Charm the birds off the trees and more besides!'

'Shut up, George,' Tamar said. She picked up a cushion and threw it at him, crushing the newspaper against his chest. 'I've got a date with him on Friday!'

But any hopes Tamar had of an evening alone with Edward were dashed when they got to the ticket office at the Metropole and there were Anna and George standing in the queue.

'This is a nice surprise,' Anna said unconvincingly, 'We can all go in together.' To Tamar's annoyance, she and George immediately gave up their places and moved to the back to stand with Tamar and Edward. George winked at Tamar as he passed and she managed to kick him hard on the shins.

They all sat together in the back row and watched a rather dull B feature about a spiritless young widow with a child who got a job as a comparative shopper in New York. Tamar had no idea what a comparative shopper was or why one would be needed and found it hard to concentrate with Edward so close she could feel the warmth of his body. Sometimes he put his mouth very close to her ear to make little ironic comments and during the newsreel, despite the presence of Anna and George in the next seats, Edward managed to hold Tamar's hand under the armrest, squeezing her fingers tight as if to deliver some secret message.

Afterwards, they walked home to save the tram fare, parting at the top of the road so that George could escort Anna up the coast road, while Edward walked Tamar back to Heaton Street. Outside the back door, Tamar felt shy and awkward. 'Thank you for a nice evening,' she said. It sounded very prim and far too formal, but Edward didn't seem to notice.

'I liked your friends,' he said. 'Perhaps we could all go out again sometime.'

Tamar felt the tight band of anxiety that constricted her chest relax. It had been all right.

'Can I call round again?' he asked and when Tamar nodded, he bent forward to take her hand. He kissed her lightly, first on the cheek, and then, rather experimentally on the lips – a soft warm caress that was almost too brief and elusive.

'Goodnight,' he said, and he tipped his hat in a kind of Cagney parody as he went back down the alleyway.

'Goodnight.' Tamar laughed, hearing her voice echo round the tunnel before she went indoors determined to be in bed before George came back so that he wouldn't have the opportunity to tease her.

~~~~~~~~~~~~~~~~~~

As Anna walked into the kitchen for breakfast on Monday
~~~~~~~~~~~~~~~~~~

morning, some kind of discussion was going on that concerned her father. For a moment she wondered if there'd been a letter, but there was nothing on the table but a brown, rather official looking envelope with a government stamp on it. Nothing to justify the paleness of her mother's face or the fact that she had obviously been crying.

'I told you how it would be when you married him,' Anna's grandfather was saying, jabbing his finger in the air across the table. 'I knew no good would come of it. We saw what they were like in the last war. Bloodthirsty lot, the Huns.'

It was more than Anna could bear. 'That's my father you're talking about,' she shouted. 'My gentle, peace-loving Dad. He hated war! How can you talk about him like that?'

'Anna!' Her mother stood up.

Mr Cotteslow banged his hand down on the table. 'You give her too much rope, Barbara. You'd never have been allowed to speak to me like that at her age!'

'I think you'd better apologise to your grandfather, Anna.'

'I'd rather die!' She slammed the door to and ran upstairs to throw herself on the bed. How could they think of her father as a bloodthirsty war-monger? He was the most gentle person she could ever imagine. He'd had two ships torpedoed from under him in the last war and always said that nothing would induce him to take part in another.

Anna heard her bedroom door open and guessed that it was her mother. Mrs Weissman sat down on the edge of the bed. 'You shouldn't have been so rude to your grandfather, Anna. You know we're dependent on him for everything. You should be grateful that he pays your school fees, buys the clothes on your back. We couldn't manage without him . . .' her voice tailed off as if she couldn't quite believe in what she was saying.

Anna sat up and turned round. 'Has Grandpa always felt like that about Dad?'

Mrs Weissmann nodded. 'You don't know what it was like at the end of the war. Everyone hated the Germans. Almost everybody knew someone who'd been killed. So when I fell in love with your father . . . it was difficult. You've got to understand that your grandfather fought in the last war, and then I came home with one of the people he'd been fighting. And then when we went to live in Germany – they didn't want me to go. I'm their only child, Anna.'

'I didn't know any of this. You never said.'

Anna's mother sighed. 'Well, it's all water under the bridge now.' She turned to go back downstairs. 'But I think you'd better apologise when you come down.'

She went out of the room, leaving the door open but Anna stayed on the bed. Deep inside, under her anger, was a great mass of anxiety. Neither she nor her mother had had a letter since her father had written to say he was going to get a visa to come to England. What had happened to him? Were letters going astray? Or was he simply too busy to write. The worry of it and the deep need to see her father gnawed at Anna like permanent stomach ache. She was beginning to be afraid that she would never see him again, although she could never say that to her mother. Whenever her father's name was mentioned Anna could see her own fears reflected in her mother's eyes.

'Your breakfast's ready, Anna,' Mrs Weissmann called up the stairs.

Anna swung her legs over the edge of the bed. She was hungry, but if she went down she was going to have to apologise for something she didn't feel sorry for in the least. But what would happen if she didn't? Was this the price she was going to have to pay for a place at the Slade? Being nice to someone who hated every drop of German blood in her veins? Was this what it was going to be like if there was a war? Her mother called again, but Anna stayed sitting on the edge of the bed. She would be late for school, but she found herself unable to care.

When Anna eventually went downstairs the kitchen was empty. She quickly ate a bowl of cornflakes and threw the congealed egg and slice of fried bread her mother had left to keep warm under the grill, into the bin. Then she put on her coat, collected her satchel and set off towards the bus stop. But when she reached the coast road she changed her mind and took the narrow cinder path that went up to the allotments. She could see her grandfather's tweed cap above the poles where the runner beans were beginning to wave ambitious green tendrils. He was walking along the row pinching out side shoots with his thumb and forefinger. Anna took a deep breath. She had, after all, vowed that nothing, absolutely nothing would be allowed to get in the way of her dream.

He caught sight of her as she turned the corner of the row but he didn't say anything, simply gave her a straight look. 'I'm sorry,' she said with as much grace as she could muster. 'I know it was rude, but I couldn't bear to hear you talking about my father like that.'

He grunted. 'I suppose I should be glad you stick up for your Da. But it's time you grew up and thought about things as they are. What's he doing leaving the lot of you to live on my charity, eh? Not a cent your mother's seen for nearly two years. Wouldn't surprise me if he'd done a runner. Taken up with another woman. If he'd come over with you I'd have held my tongue between my teeth and given him a welcome. We've always been civil. But he's dodged all his responsibilities – said he was coming and then never put in an appearance. Never sent any money or let your mother know what was what.'

'You are so unfair!' Anna couldn't help herself. 'Don't you think he'd come if he could? He might be dead for all we know – or . . . or in some dreadful labour camp.' Anna stopped shouting to gasp for breath. 'Why do you hate him so much?'

'I don't hate him. It's what the German's did that I hate. It was a living hell! And don't forget your dad wore a German uniform last time. And now they're going to do it all over again.'

Anna was very still, her stomach had turned to ice. 'Don't forget I'm German too,' she said as she turned quickly and ran down the bean rows and out of the allotment gate.

It was too late. She had surely lost her chances now. He would never pay for her to go to the Slade or any other art college. Anna stopped to let the stitch in her side fade away. Her mind was whirling. The fees for the current year at King Edwards were already paid, but she couldn't count on him paying next year's. So she had only until the end of the school year to learn enough to earn herself a scholarship to the Slade. I'm on my own, Anna thought. It's up to me now.

Tamar came back from the shop exhausted. The store manager had asked for volunteers to stay behind and tape up the windows. There was only a small amount of overtime, but since Sadie had lost her job Tamar felt she had to earn as much as possible. The rent was still being paid, though she didn't know where Sadie found the money. Tamar wondered just how much the bonus from Mr Pergavie had been and how long it would last.

Anna was in the kitchen, packing up her sketch pad and pencils. She seemed very subdued. 'Lily's gone down to Shields. Your tea's on the stove.' She indicated two plates, one turned up over the other, balanced on a pan of bubbling water. 'Do you fancy going to the pictures tonight? Just the two of us? Rebecca's on at the Albion.'

'Sorry.' Tamar shook her head regretfully and sat down at the table, aware that every muscle in her body ached from all the unaccustomed bending and stretching. 'I'm so tired I can hardly move one foot in front of the other. Can we go another night?'

Anna looked disappointed. 'It's not often I get you to myself these days. Tell you what, why don't you come to Warkworth Castle with me on Sunday. George said he'd take us on the bike. We can take a picnic. The forecast's brilliant.'

'I'm sorry Anna I can't come then either! I've promised to go to Edward's for lunch, to meet his parents.'

'Right!' Anna slung her bag across her shoulder and walked to the door. 'You talk about me being selfish. What about you? I wouldn't dump my friends just because I was seeing someone!'

'But I'm not dumping anyone!' Tamar was bewildered by the ferocity of her tone.

'Yes you are! You never have time for me these days. Either your head's in a book or you're out gallivanting round town with these spivvy Italian types.'

'Edward isn't a spiv! Why are you in such a mood?'

Anna tossed her head. 'It's difficult being friends with you, Tamar. You're so cool and collected. You don't give much!'

'I'm sorry.' Tamar didn't know what else to say. 'I'm really fond of you Anna. Really. You're my best friend. What more do you want from me?'

'I don't know.' Anna shrugged. She came back to the table and sat down again. For a moment Tamar thought she was going to cry. 'There's a . .' she paused to search for the right word and then went on 'a distance about you that drives me crazy. I never know what you're thinking or feeling. It's infuriating.' She lit a cigarette and held it between her fingers, looking at Tamar through the spiral of smoke.

'I can't wear my heart on my sleeve like you.' Tamar felt angry. Anna didn't know what it was like to be surrounded by people all the time. The only privacy she had was inside her head.

'One day something will get through to you,' Anna said. 'Somewhere in that imaginary world you live in. You're going to feel things so much it'll be like they're being burnt into your skin.'

'That's a horrible thing to say!'

'Don't take any notice of me,' Anna said. She stood up and went towards the door. 'I'm just upset about something at the moment. I'll get over it.'

'Nothing you can tell your friends? Or am I too cold and distant to confide in?'

Anna put her arms round Tamar and hugged her. 'Oh, I'm sorry. Really sorry I said that. It's just . . . Everything's a mess. And I can't talk about it. Even to you. I'll just have to wait and see how it all comes out.'

It was almost a quarrel. Afterwards Tamar felt uneasy when she thought about it. And puzzled. Why did Anna say such things? But what hurt most was the knowledge that there was a kernel of truth in her accusations. Tamar knew she seemed cool to other people. Sadie had once said that she was inscrutable, which meant the same thing really. But it couldn't be helped. She had feelings – powerful feelings – she just wasn't good at showing them. And always in her memory was that terrible occasion when they'd burst out in spite of her and she'd pushed Bertie McAffery off the bridge.

The Antonellis were Catholics. On a sideboard in one corner of the crowded living room was a little table with a crucifix, candles and a small plaster sculpture of the Virgin Mary. Edward had been horrified when he heard that Tamar had never been to church in her life.

'Well, possibly when I was christened. But definitely not since then. I'm an aetheist.'

'How can you say there isn't a God when you don't know anything about it?'

Tamar had to think hard. 'Maybe it would be better to say I'm an agnostic. It's not something I've thought about much.'

'Then you ought to.'

Edward took her to morning mass in a borrowed headscarf and they sat at the back. The inside of the cathedral was very beautiful, with old stained glass that filtered the sunlight onto the altar. Tamar thought it all very theatrical; the coloured robes of the priests moving to and fro in the sanctuary, a man robed in white and gold who chanted and mimed, while in the background a bell tinkled and a censer hanging from the roof swung to and fro with clouds of scented smoke. But the service itself was incomprehensible. Tamar understood not a word of it and she was in a constant state of terror because she didn't know when she was supposed to stand up, kneel, sit down or speak.

After mass, Edward took her home to meet his family. Tamar had spent Ida's money on a new yellow linen dress with navy blue piping and navy suede shoes with little buttons on the side. She wanted to look her best for the occasion, but as soon as she got inside the door she realised that it was too smart.

They went in through the kitchen, which was full of steam from the big, catering-size pans boiling on the stove. Mrs Antonelli's hair was drooping out of the roughly pinned roll on the top of her head. Damp strands clung to her broad, pillowy face. She had her sleeves rolled up and was wearing an enormous flowered overall. She didn't shake hands – she hugged.

'All Edward's friends are welcome,' she said in response to Tamar's stilted attempts at a 'how nice of you to invite me' speech. 'The place is like Peggy Murphy's Fair!' she went on, cheerfully, 'But you take us as you find us.' And she dashed back to rescue something that was boiling over.

In the living room two boys of about eight or nine were playing on the floor with a train set and Edward's sisters were setting the table, quarrelling about who was to sit where.

'Bertie and Tony aren't going to be here,' Edward said. 'So that's two less. And Tamar'll sit next to me at the end.'

In the parlour Edward's older brother Tom was listening to the wireless and Mr Antonelli was asleep in an armchair with the paper over his face.

Tamar was amazed by the casualness of the family. Mr Antonelli sat at table in his shirt sleeves, his wife in her overalls, and the children bickered constantly, passing things haphazardly around the table with lots of elbowing and whispering. Tamar was aware of Edward's sisters staring at her and giggling quietly when she wasn't looking.

'Behave yourselves, you two,' Mrs Antonelli kept saying, in such a lazy way that it was obvious she didn't expect to be obeyed.

The food was extraordinary. Tamar had never eaten an Italian meal before. There was a large bowl filled with something called spaghetti swimming in tomato, topped with grated cheese, then some kind of meat dish, again with tomato and a plate of sliced sausage that Tamar didn't like because it was too chewy and spicy. The bread was circular, like a crisp pancake and you were supposed to tear a piece off to mop up the gravy from the plate – something Sadie had always forbidden as the height of bad manners. Tamar dripped some of the tomato sauce onto her new dress and Mrs Antonelli insisted that she be taken to the kitchen straight away to be mopped down with water and bicarbonate of soda, just as if she was one of the children.

Anna was still in a difficult mood when they went to the cinema on Tuesday. Going out in a foursome was becoming a habit. Where once Tamar and Anna had gone out together, with George as an occasional third, now Edward joined them and inevitably they were becoming two couples – Tamar and Edward

– George and Anna. This worried Tamar because she knew how fond George was of Anna and couldn't forget how bitterly Anna had once said 'I don't like men!' She thought it was irresponsible of Anna to let it happen if she wasn't serious about George, but it was difficult to think what else could be done. They were all friends; they went out together and since Tamar and Edward were a couple, Anna and George inevitably became one too.

Tonight Anna was in a skittish mood and more sarcastic and provocative than even Tamar was used to. George had bought a new trilby hat and overcoat from the fifty shilling tailor's. 'Doesn't he look smart,' Lily had said when he put it on. 'Done up like a dog's dinner!'

Anna didn't agree. 'I think you look silly in it,' she said as they walked down to the Palace.

'Well, I don't,' Tamar said in his defence, though privately she did think it was a bit overdone. George was short and stocky and the hat made him look even more so, but she couldn't let his feelings be trampled on without some protest.

'Bet it would look better on me,' Anna said. She whipped the hat off George's head, despite his attempts to snatch it back, and put it on her own. She buttoned her jacket, put a cigarette between her lips and her fingers in her lapels and swaggered down the pavement. Tamar was startled, almost shocked at the difference the hat made. This was a new Anna – absurd, affected, androgynous, but oddly attractive. Tamar found it unsettling.

'Your friend's mad,' Edward said. 'Why does she do such crazy things?'

Just then a blast of wind, funnelling up from the river, caught the hat and whirled it off Anna's head, bowling it along the pavement in front of them. They all chased after it, down the street towards the quayside, reaching the waterfront just in time to see it landing on the surface of the river like a large brown gull.

'Thank you very much,' George said emphatically.

'If you were a real gentleman you'd swim out and rescue it,' Anna said.

'I'd have to be daft or desperate!' George said. 'What did you have to do that for? That hat cost me three and six!'

Anna put her arm in Tamar's and pulled her away. 'Come on

Tamar, it's not going to be much fun if they're going to be cross with us all evening.'

Tamar was puzzled to find herself included. 'What's got into you Anna,' she asked as they walked back up towards the cinema. 'Why are you so hard on poor George?'

'You have to give them a hard time every now and then or they take you for granted. You're much too easy on Edward.'

But Tamar found Edward very easy to get on with. He talked to her about books and told her all sorts of things she'd never really thought about before – history, politics. He tried to get her to understand what was happening in Europe. Talked about the Spanish civil war. Tamar had only been dimly aware that there had been a war in Spain. She was ashamed of her ignorance and eager to learn. She'd begun to buy a newspaper on the way to work, so that she would be able to discuss it with him.

Tamar could talk to Edward about anything but religion. That was one thing they couldn't agree on and their conversations always resulted in stalemate. 'If you prove to me that God really does exist, then I'll believe,' Tamar would say.

'So, prove to me God doesn't exist,' Edward said.

'How can you prove a myth isn't true?' Tamar argued. 'They're like fairy tales, they exist only in people's imaginations and you can't prove them either way.'

'But the very fact that you can't disprove the existence of God, proves that he must exist.'

'But that's terrible logic! It's like saying there's a . . . a ghost in the corner of the room, and that just because you can't prove it isn't – it must be true!'

Tamar hated arguing, it made her feel wobbly and uncertain. It was almost the same kind of feeling she had when Edward took her home after the film and led her round the corner into the alleyway to say goodnight. There, out of sight of the street, he kissed her and held her against the wall. Tamar had never wanted anything so much. His touch made her shiver, and when he kissed her open mouth, caressing the inside surfaces with his tongue, her whole body burned. When he put his hand inside her coat and stroked her breasts, lightly pressing her nipples through the cotton and satin of her clothes, it made her legs tremble and her stomach ache.

'I wish we had somewhere to go,' he said regretfully. 'More than anything, I'd like to take your clothes off and look at you. Really look at you. You feel so beautiful in the dark.'

Anna lay awake all night and cried. She cried for her father and she cried because she didn't know what was happening to her. Why had she been so horrible to Tamar, whom she loved more than anything? Why had she been so beastly to George? There was no one she could talk to about it. Did other girls have these confused feelings? She tried to reason it through. George was very easy to be with. He didn't talk much, didn't try to paw her around and he liked a lot of the things that she did, music and – surprisingly – paintings. A few weeks ago he'd told her about a group of miners who painted and had exhibitions and took her up to Ashington to see their work. George had a quietness about him and a stillness that made Anna feel balanced and secure when she was with him. She liked that. But when he held her hand she wanted to shrink away. And then she felt sad, because he was a nice man and genuinely cared for her. What was she to do? The only solution was to stop going out with them. But then she would hardly ever see Tamar at all and the thought of that was insupportable.

Over the next few weeks Tamar was aware that Sadie was watching her anxiously. Occasionally she asked questions such as 'You are happy with him aren't you?' And once when Tamar had gone to bed early, she woke up in the night and saw Sadie sitting on the dressing table stool, smoking a cigarette and looking at her with a sad, serious expression on her face. 'Don't tie yourself down too young, Tamar. Don't do what I did,' she said. 'Promise me!'

Being in love was strange and terrifying. If Tamar didn't see Edward it produced a feeling that was indistinguishable from fear and just as unpleasant. When she did see him, a kind of voltage ran through her, speeding everything up, making her different – talkative, energetic, willing to dare anything. Tamar had never felt so vulnerable. If Edward was quiet and preoccupied during the evening she thought she'd offended him; if he wasn't waiting for her when he said he'd be, she was convinced she'd never see him again. Her whole emotional being was dangling from the strings he held in his hand and it made her feel sick and anxious. That's why it had hurt so much when Anna accused her of not having feelings. Sometimes she had too many. In the middle of the night, it would occur to her that it would be less emotionally confusing not to see him at all. But the following day, standing in the cinema queue with her arm tucked securely in his, she felt that without him, her whole world would end.

CHAPTER TEN

Sadie was unhappy. Tamar noted all the little signs she'd grown to recognise when Sadie was having 'a fit of the glooms' as she referred to it when in a lighter mood. First of all Sadie became reluctant to get out of bed in the morning – sometimes she would still be in it when Tamar came home from work. Then there was the way she sighed when she looked at herself in the mirror, tugging her hair this way and that, dabbing her make up on with grim ferocity. The following week she didn't even bother to do that and her hair remained unbrushed and her clothes unwashed, day after day. The mirror was shrouded with an old silk petticoat. 'I may be a wreck,' she said aggressively when Tamar complained. 'But at least I don't have to look at it.'

Several evenings when Tamar came home from work she found Sadie sitting on the floor of the bedroom in her dressing gown with the contents of the hatbox spread over the carpet. Photographs, letters. The mementos of Tamar's childhood – a tiny pink kid slipper wrapped in tissue paper, her first tooth and a lock of her baby hair tucked into a velvet box that had once contained a child's silver bracelet.

Sadie's descent into depression was somehow linked in Tamar's mind to an incident a couple of months earlier, just after Sadie had lost her job. Tamar had been sent home from the shop after lunch with a stomach cramp, and as she limped across the yard, longing to climb into bed with a hot water bottle, a cup of tea and a couple of aspirins, she was curious to hear strange noises from the wash house. Peering cautiously through the steamed-up window, Tamar was startled to see Mrs Whale from across the street bending over Sadie in the big metal bath tub. Sadie appeared to be drunk, weeping and talking in a loud, but rather indistinct voice. The sight of it made Tamar shiver with disgust.

In the kitchen Lily, wearing the waterproof laundry apron she kept for wash-day, was boiling a glass syringe and a length of rubber tubing in the big potato pan. She jumped when she saw Tamar and then put her finger to her lips and tipped her head in the direction of the door. Tamar said nothing and went through into the living room to lie down on the sofa. There was a lot of shouting from the direction of the wash house. After a while Tamar heard the door open and she retreated to the hallway, knowing instinctively that she wasn't meant to witness any of this. Sitting on the stairs, she peered through the crack in the door jamb and saw Mrs Whale and Lily dragging a semi-conscious Sadie between them, her feet trailing on the floor behind as they supported her by the shoulders, encouraging her forward. 'Only a bit more, pet, then you can lie down,' Mrs Whale kept saying.

Instead of coming upstairs, they went straight through to the front room where Lily usually slept. As they paused to coax Sadie through the doorway, Tamar noticed a slim trickle of blood down the back of Sadie's leg. Through the open door Tamar heard the creaking of bed springs and then the metallic rattle of an enamel bucket and the sound of vomiting. Then Sadie's slurred voice, loud and bitter. 'Fancy! Getting caught again at my age!' The angry words broke up into a kind of sobbing laugh.

Lily came through to the kitchen on her own. 'I'm just going to make us a nice strong cup of tea,' she said as Tamar came through to join her.

'Is Sadie all right?' she asked.

'Your Mam's not well, so I'm going to keep her in my bed for tonight. But don't you worry about her. She'll be as right as rain tomorrow!' And that was all that was ever said. Sadie had stayed in bed for days, pale and quiet. The incident was never explained and Tamar knew that she must never ask what had happened.

Since then, there'd been a sudden increase in the assorted glass bottles that cluttered the dressing table and the bedside cabinet, overflowing onto the floor, until at last someone – Tamar or Lily – took them down to the bin. Tamar tried not to worry. Sadie had been like this before. Once in Yorkshire she'd stayed in bed crying and drinking for a week after one of the 'uncles' had left.

But then one day she'd suddenly got up and gone out to buy herself a new hat, got a job as a receptionist in a hotel and everything had been all right. 'When you're at rock bottom,' Sadie had said, 'the only thing to do is to pick yourself up and start again.' But as the days went past there was no sign of Sadie doing that this time. Only Lily didn't seem concerned. 'It'll blow over,' she said. 'Don't you worry about your Mam. She's a born survivor.'

~~~~~~~~~~~~~~~~~

The college was closed for the summer and – aware of how little time was left – Anna spent most of her days painting in the shed. She was working on a portrait of Lily Kennedy, sitting upright in the kitchen chair as she always did, her hair in its strange black roll on top of her head, thin and determined looking, her bony hands on the table, a cigarette smouldering in a saucer beside her. Anna was finding it difficult to achieve the right level of abstraction. To suggest Lily's distinctive physical form as well as her character and yet make her part of the complicated scheme of lines and blocks of colour laid down on the canvas. One line in particular was proving difficult to get right. Anna traced it with her brush – down the cupboard then through Lily's shoulder and arm and across the edge of the table. It was important that Lily's arm intersected it in just the right place and that her head should fill the right amount of space in the block of colour made by the cupboard. She had had to move the cupboard slightly to the left to improve the composition and elongate Lily's head.

Pinned up on the wall around the shed were the preparatory drawings Anna had done over the past few months – Lily would never sit still long enough to pose. So there were sketches of the cupboard, the white enamel sink, pages of Lily's hands in different positions, her head from a variety of angles, her neck and shoulders, sketches of her clothes in different materials and designs – Anna still hadn't completely decided on the patterning of Lily's blouse. And then there were the bigger, working sketches of the whole before it was transferred to the canvas. Anna intended the portfolio to form the basis of her application to the Slade.

As Anna turned away from the easel to rinse her brush, she
~~~~~~~~~~~~~~~~~

glanced out of the window and saw a man standing at the gate looking up at the house. There was something about him that made her put down her brush and walk down the path towards him. He was a strange little man – short and almost folded over – wearing an odd-looking long dark wool coat and big-brimmed hat in spite of the August heat. Something white protruded from underneath his waistcoat as though he had forgotten to tuck his shirt tails in.

He watched Anna walk towards him and when she stopped a few yards away he said 'Fraulein Weissmann?'

'Ja!' Anna answered automatically in German and the man responded in the same language.

'Won't you come in?' Anna asked, wondering at the same time whether her grandparents would welcome him. It seemed unlikely.

'Thank you, but no,' the man said politely, and Anna was relieved.

'I have a message for you from Switzerland,' he said, and took a letter out of his pocket. It had no postmark or stamp and the envelope was crumpled and grubby. As Anna looked at it, the man touched the brim of his hat with his hand and said "Wiedersehen. Shalom' very quietly as he walked off.

Anna was torn between wanting desperately to open the letter and an equally strong desire to run after him and ask who he was, where he had come from, and did he know anything about her father? She tore open the envelope quickly leaving smudges of paint across the paper and then felt a surge of disappointment like heartburn rise into her throat. It was not her father's handwriting. Turning it over she read her cousin Maya's signature on the back. Anna ran straight out of the gate, but the man was out of sight. She continued running until she reached the corner of the coast road, but there was no one in any direction wearing a black coat and hat. It was as though he had vanished into the air.

Anna read Maya's letter as she walked slowly back to the house. There was no date and no way of knowing how long the letter had taken to reach her.

My dear Anna,

I don't know if you will ever get this letter. I'm sending it with someone who's going to Spain and he says he will try to pass it on to someone going to England. I'm in Switzerland now – in Berne, and we're being well looked after by a family here.

They took my father away to a labour camp in Sachsenhausen two months ago while I was staying with friends. (There must be no names, we're told, for sometimes the letters are taken and read and I don't want to bring trouble to anyone.) A neighbour wrote to me and told me not to come back, because if I did they would take me as well. I talked about it with my friend – she's expecting a baby and she was very afraid of what might happen. So she and her husband and two of their brothers decided to walk into Switzerland over the mountain passes and they persuaded me to come with them.

One of the older men, who was a guide, said that he would take us. We had to go at night when there was sufficient moonlight. It was very cold and my feet were bleeding inside the boots – so cold that one of my toe-nails has dropped off since we got here. But by daylight we were over the border and the guide left us to find our own way down into the valleys. The people in the first village we came to gave us milk and bread and didn't know what to do with us. But we got a ride on a carrier's cart into Berne and asked at the Synagogue and now we're officially registered as refugees. There are five of us and we're hoping to get passports and then go to Spain and either to America or to England. There's an organisation here that can arrange it.

I don't know what's happened to your father – I haven't seen Uncle Otto since Grossmutter's funeral.'

Anna stopped. Her heart thumped in her chest. With an increased sense of foreboding she returned to Maya's letter.

'Many people are being sent to the labour camps now. We are very thankful to have been spared that – but I worry about my father and feel guilty that while he's suffering I'm free. I pray that this may be over very soon. I would like to get to England and if I do I will try to find you. Do you remember that once you wrote to me and said wouldn't it be nice if I could come on a visit – you talked of all the fun we could have together? Who could have foretold this?

Your loving cousin

Maya.

Anna stood quite still on the path, as if she had been turned to stone. Suddenly everything seemed unimportant – her dreams of becoming a painter, her anxieties about George, the quarrel with her grandfather, worrying about whether she had done well enough in her school certificate. They all faded into insignificance beside the dreadful possibilities that Maya's letter had called into being. All Anna's fears had been confirmed. Uncle Joe had been taken to a labour camp, so it seemed very likely that her father had been taken too. It explained why she hadn't heard from him, and why he had never arrived in England. Anna felt that she would almost break with the pain. What must he be suffering? Like Maya, she felt guilty that she was free and he was not. Just for that moment, Anna would have given anything that she had – would even have forfeited the right to paint, if it could have brought her father there to stand in front of her, well and whole, to take her in his arms and give her one of his big, bone-breaking hugs. She could smell the mingled odours of tobacco and pine resin that came from his clothes, hear his infectious laugh.

Her mother had come to the door of the house. 'Is anything the matter Anna? You look awful.'

Anna said nothing. She held out the letter and watched her mother stretch out a reluctant hand to take it, an expression of dread already on her face.

Tamar's seventeenth birthday fell on a Saturday and they planned a big picnic tea at the beach, all of them together, followed by a visit to the Spanish City. 'After all,' Lily Kennedy said, recounting rumours that the beaches were being fenced off with barbed wire, 'Who knows when we might get a chance like this again.'

It was a fine clear afternoon. The tide had gone out, leaving the sand sculpted by the retreating waves into semi-circular shapes like fish scales, highlighted by the long angle of the sun, low in the sky behind them. Through the clean sand, runnels of water made a last minute dash towards the distant surf, skirting round the big cubes of concrete with embedded metal spikes that had recently been placed at intervals along the beach. At the far end, near the cliffs, long coils of wire stretched out towards them like skeins of unravelled wool. A group of men in uniform were pegging them out with steel stakes and the quiet afternoon was punctuated by the bat, bat, bat of their mallets.

George and Edward went along to have a look. 'It's the Royal Engineers,' Edward said when they came back. 'We asked what was happening but apparently they aren't allowed to tell us.'

They began making sandcastles with a bent metal bucket they'd found half submerged in the sand. It had a multi-coloured picture of a fairground on it, very scratched – some child's lost possession that he would cry for when he got home. They were talking about Chamberlain's ultimatum and whether or not Hitler would be faced down.

Anna listened to them with a miserable and preoccupied expression. 'I can't bear it if there's a war,' she said. 'Everyone talks as if the German people are devils, but they're not. They're just people like us.'

She and Tamar had collected shells and pebbles in a towel and were decorating the sand turrets with windows and battlements of stone and mother of pearl. Lily sat, smoking a cigarette, on a sand bench George had mounded up for her, covering it with a rug. The picnic tea lay unopened in a tartan holdall beside her.

'I can't think what's keepin' Sadie,' Lily said for the third time.

Edward heard her and lifted his head. 'All the trams are in chaos. There was an accident. Someone got knocked down.'

Tamar felt a tremor of apprehension that immobilised her fingers as she was about to place a shell above the castle door.

'What tram accident?' She looked up at Edward.

'I don't know any details. I expect it'll be in tomorrow's paper.'

Tamar continued to worry about Sadie as the afternoon cooled into early evening and the picnic tea was reluctantly opened and eaten without her.

'You don't think something could have happened to Sadie, do you?' she asked.

'She's probably met a boyfriend and gone off for a drink.' Anna said. 'You know what she's like!'

'Sadie promised!' Tamar said, angry in spite of herself. And then the terrible thought that had occurred to her when Edward spoke, began to settle in her mind. 'You don't suppose . . . .?'

'Not in a million years, hinny!' Lily said, lighting another cigarette.

'You're getting worked up over nothing,' Anna said. 'You know how unreliable Sadie is.'

'I'm sorry.' Anna was right. Tamar tried to think how long it was since Sadie had actually been there to celebrate her birthday. Usually it was a card and a small present (if Sadie had remembered in time) propped up against her breakfast plate after Sadie had gone to work. Once or twice there had been extravagant treats – a visit to a circus with one of the Uncles, once – very magical – a ballet matinee at the Bristol Hippodrome. Less pleasant, the memory of that terrible tea in Bath when they had left without paying.

The evening was quite cool as they walked back up Heaton Street from the tram stop and Tamar felt tired and flat, worn out with apprehension and disappointment. As they came up to the gate, there was a policeman standing at the front door. It was as though a cold hand had seized her heart and crushed it so that it couldn't beat. There was something in the man's eyes that told Tamar exactly what he was going to say before he opened his mouth to speak to Lily. Tamar was conscious of Edward holding her arm and Lily exclaiming 'Jesus wept!'

'She just stepped off the pavement right in front of the Tynemouth tram as it was coming up to the stop.' The policeman said. 'The driver didn't have a chance. Poor bloke, he did his best. He was in a right state.'

'Where's my mother?' Tamar demanded, realising afterwards how rude it sounded. She wondered why there was so much concern for the tram driver when it was Sadie who'd been hurt. Then a terrible thought almost paralysed her. Had Sadie been killed?

'She's been taken to the Infirmary, pet.'

Tamar felt her face go hot with relief.

Tamar had passed the Infirmary many times, but she'd never been inside. It was a big, Victorian building with fluted columns holding up a portico over a flight of stone steps – more like a museum than a hospital. The casualty department was round the side, through double swing doors level with the street and marked 'Ambulances only'. Inside, there were brightly lit corridors of painted brick and grey linoleum, with snaking lines of pipework stretching for miles and miles through the roots of the building as far ahead as Tamar could see and opening off at intervals on either side. There was a strong smell of Jeyes Fluid.

Edward knew what to do. Covering accidents was one of the things he had to do for the paper. He steered Tamar to the admissions office and commandeered the attention of the harassed nurse manning the desk and a constantly ringing telephone.

'How can I help?' she said at last. 'It's been utter madness here all day.'

'Sadie Fell.' It was all Tamar could say. 'She's my mother.'

The nurse's brisk face softened. 'I remember. She was brought in a couple of hours ago. She's in theatre at the moment.'

'Theatre?' Surreal images formed in Tamar's mind.

'She's having an operation. Afterwards . . .' the nurse put on her glasses and checked a ledger in front of her. 'They'll be taking her up to Princess Victoria Ward.' She took her glasses off and glanced at Edward before looking back at Tamar. 'She'll be a while. Do you want to wait up there, or go and have a cup of tea? I expect Dr Fletcher will want a word.'

It was a long way up to the ward. They sat on hard chairs in the corridor, looking at a notice that said 'Visitors 2-3, Saturdays and Sundays, 7-8 weekdays'. The wait seemed endless, punctuated by the quick, firm tread of nurses' feet clad in sensible brogues. Tamar looked at the different colours of the uniforms as they passed; and wondered what the differences were between navy or pale blue stripe, pink or green. They all seemed to wear identical white aprons over their dresses and the same starched white triangles on their heads.

While she sat there gripping Edward's hand, a policeman arrived and asked strange questions such as 'Was your mother depressed at the time of the accident?' And then, 'Could she have been drinking, pet?' He wrote Tamar's stupefied answers down in a notebook. 'The people waiting at the stop said she just seemed to tumble off the pavement in front of the tram,' he explained. 'Maybe she just tripped. I'm very sorry pet.' He took Tamar's details and went away.

When the lift door eventually clanged and a stretcher was wheeled out into the corridor by two green clad porters, Tamar leapt up towards them and was aware of Edward holding her elbows as if to restrain her. As the stretcher passed Tamar found that she couldn't tell whether the sleeping form mounded under blankets was Sadie or not.

A man in a white coat wearing brown suede shoes came along the corridor carrying a manilla folder. There was dried blood on his sleeve. 'Are you the next of kin?' he asked, looking at Edward.

'I'm her daughter,' Tamar said. Her mouth was dry.

'She's had a pretty bad time,' the doctor said. 'We've had to take off the leg and she's lost a lot of blood. Had a bit of a thump on the head as well. It's going to be touch and go, I'm afraid.' He nodded to them both and went on through the double doors into the ward.

After he'd left, a young nurse put her head outside. 'I've got your mother settled,' she said. 'I know it's not supposed to be visiting, but sister's gone for her tea. Would you like to see her for a minute?'

Tamar nodded, on her feet immediately, with Edward still holding her arm.

'I'm afraid I can only let one of you in at a time.'

Edward sat down again. 'I'll wait for you,' he said. 'Don't worry about me.'

They'd put Sadie in a bed about half way down the ward. There were curtains drawn around it. Sadie was laid on her back, her head bandaged and a black rubber tube in her mouth. A glass bottle half full of blood hung upside down on a stand and was dripping slowly down a tube in her arm.

'We usually put the ones that need observing next to Sister's office,' the girl explained. 'But there's someone already in that bed who can't be moved.' She spoke very softly as if Sadie might hear her.

The bedclothes were draped over a metal frame. The nurse

folded the covers back at the end so that she could look inside. 'It's for the amputation,' she explained. 'Did Dr Fletcher tell you about that?'

Tamar nodded. She found it difficult to imagine what Sadie was going to do with only one leg.

'What about your Dad. Is he coming?'

'I haven't got a father,' Tamar was surprised by how bleak it sounded. 'There's just Sadie and me.'

'Oh. I'm sorry. I thought . . . Is that your boyfriend out there?'

Tamar nodded again.

Somewhere a bell rang. The nurse turned to dash off. 'I'll leave you here for a few minutes. It won't hurt. There should be someone with her. I'll be back in two shakes.' And she was gone.

It was impossible to recognise the small, white face between the bandages and the top edge of the sheet as Sadie. Tamar would have liked to touch her, to stroke her face, but she was afraid of hurting her. There was a graze on Sadie's cheek and a bluish area on the temple beside her eye like the beginning of a bruise. Her breath sounded very strange as it whistled in and out of the tube. She looked young and vulnerable. It made Tamar feel instinctively protective towards her mother. She thought how rarely they'd been separated. She could actually count the number of nights that she and Sadie had been apart – more in the recent past, but when she was little, hardly any. Tamar remembered ruefully how she'd been given a seaside holiday when she was about six or seven – some charity connected with the school – a whole group of children in a stark boarding house with two stern elderly women keeping them corralled like unruly sheep. That first night, cold and miserable, she had cried and cried for Sadie and would not be consoled either then or the next day. They had tried to coax her to eat, but the food had stuck in her throat and brought processions of tears pouring from her eyes and down her cheeks until the neck of her jersey was soaked. Tamar could still remember how bereft she had felt without her mother. The following day she'd been taken home in disgrace, light-headed with happiness, flinging herself round Sadie's legs the moment she saw her on the station platform. Sadie hadn't seemed at all pleased to see her.

'What am I going to do with you?' she'd said, giving Tamar's arm an angry shake. 'It was supposed to be a treat.' And then she'd sighed and taken Tamar back to their lodgings to spend the summer playing happily with the landlady's dog in the back garden.

Tamar took Sadie's limp hand and held it in her own. It felt cold.

The curtains rattled and a small woman in a dark blue uniform with a pert lace cap on top of her tightly coiled hair, bustled into the cubicle. Tamar guessed instantly that this was the ward sister.

'What are you doing here?' she asked peremptorily. 'Visiting time finished at three o'clock.'

'This is my mother. I was told I could sit with her for a while.'

'Who told you that?' Her voice was abrasive. 'Visitors are strictly not allowed except at specific times. It disrupts the routine of the ward and disturbs the patients' rest.'

There was something about the woman's manner that got under Tamar's skin. She could feel herself growing warm, her muscles tautening and the dangerous mist beginning to gather in her head. 'Why can't I sit with her? She's very ill – the nurse said she ought to have someone.'

Sister gazed at Tamar as if she couldn't believe what she had heard.

'Haven't you listened to what I've just said. It's against the rules.'

'But it's not against the law is it? To want to stay with your mother when she's ill?' Tamar was sure that everyone in the ward could hear what was going on, but she was past caring. 'I'm not leaving her. I'll sit here quietly and I won't get in anyone's way.'

There was a very audible cheer from the other side of the ward.

'I've never heard such cheek in all my life. This is my ward and I'm asking you to leave it. If you don't then I shall have no alternative but to send for Matron.'

Tamar said nothing, but remained quietly where she was. The sister turned on her heel and left the cubicle with a swishing of curtain rings and crackling of starched linen. Tamar could hear the staccato tap tap of her heels all the way up the ward.

A few moments later a disembodied grey head appeared through a fold in the curtains. 'That's right pet, you tell her! It's like a bloomin' prison in here. Once, I've seen my Tommy since I got in here, only once, cause he works shifts and he can't make the hours. Why can't he come in other times? I said to the Fuhrer – that's what we call her like – I said to her, "why can't he come in? He's not botherin' anyone." Nancy over there now,' the head nodded back over her shoulder, 'she's good on her pins and she sneaks down to the laundry and her old man comes in the back door and they have a bit of a crack and a cuddle, but I'm not so nimble. You don't let her bully you.'

There was the sound of feet tapping up the corridor again and the head disappeared. The curtains opened and the sister came in again accompanied by a slim, grey haired woman in a dark green dress without an apron. She had a slender cone of white pinned to her neatly waved hair. The badge pinned to her lapel told Tamar that she was Assistant Matron Holmes.

'Now,' she began in a calm, quiet voice, looking first at Sadie and then at Tamar. 'What's the problem?'

'I'd like to stay with my mother for a while,' Tamar said. 'Sadie doesn't have anyone else. I can't leave her on her own when she's so ill.' She tried to speak firmly, but somehow it was more difficult to be angry, to stand her ground against this mild and gentle woman.

The assistant matron went to the foot of the bed and began to look at Sadie's charts. 'Are you her only family?' she asked.

Tamar nodded. 'There's just the two of us.' She was aware of sounding pathetic. The surge of anger that had given her the courage to challenge the ward sister was receding rapidly.

The assistant matron looked towards the sister and said, 'She seems a sensible girl, sister Ferguson. Couldn't we make an exception in view of the circumstances?'

It was said in the most silky tone, but Tamar could see that sister's face was red with indignation. The assistant matron ignored her and carried on talking to Tamar.

'We don't normally allow relatives in after hours except for the most seriously ill patients. I must have your word that if your mother requires any medical procedures and a nurse or a doctor asks you to leave, that you'll go without a fuss?'

Tamar nodded again. 'If I can just sit with her for a while, I won't get in the way I promise.'

'Thank you sister,' the matron said nodding to her, and the two women went out of the cubicle.

Tamar sat down. She legs were trembling and she felt physically sick, just as she'd felt when she pushed Bertie McAffery off the bridge.

Every now and then the nurse came back, held Sadie's wrist to take her pulse, wrote it down on a chart above the bed, looked inside the frame and left. The third time she did this she said, 'I think you'd better stay the night, if you can manage it. She really shouldn't be left and there's not enough of us to sit with her.'

'Will I be allowed?' Tamar asked.

The nurse smiled. 'The Fuhrer's gone off duty. Night Sister won't care, and it's Sister James on tomorrow – you won't have any trouble with her. She's a lamb! You go and say goodbye to your boyfriend and I'll make you a cup of tea.'

Edward was still sitting patiently on the chair outside and Anna was sitting beside him. They both stood up as Tamar came out of the ward. 'What's happening?' Anna asked. 'You seem to be causing quite a fuss.'

'They didn't want me to stay with Sadie. It's not visiting hours.' Tamar looked at the notice on the door. 'According to that, I'm not supposed to be here until tomorrow night. I looked at her, lying in that bed, so ill and alone and I just couldn't bear to leave her. If it was me lying there, she wouldn't leave me, I'm sure.'

'It's barbaric,' Edward said. 'I once had to go up to the children's ward for the paper and there's all these cots of babies crying for their mothers. You'd think they'd realise.'

'Anyway, Matron says I can stay for the time being, if I'm quiet. The nurse says someone should be with Sadie all the time.'

'How is she?' Anna asked

'Very ill. Unconscious. I don't know enough to know just how ill she is, but I'm afraid.'

Edward put his arm around her. 'I'll stay here. You shouldn't be on your own.'

'There's no need. I'll be all right.'

'You'll need someone to walk you home.'

'The nurse thinks I should stay all night.'

'I'll stay as long as I can. Someone should be here for you.'

'We'll both be here,' Anna said.

Tamar gave up. She leant her head against Edward's shoulder, feeling the comforting warmth of his body through the fabric of his jacket. Anna turned away and began to stare out of the window in a purposeful kind of way.

'Don't be so stubborn and independent.' Edward said, with his mouth against her hair. 'Let somebody do something for you for a change.'

When Tamar came back into the ward there was tea and a slice of toast waiting for her in the kitchen.

'I expect it was quite a shock,' the nurse said.

'I've never been in a hospital before. It's all so strange.'

'I suppose it must be.' The girl looked at her watch. 'I'd better go. Ten patients to wash before supper.' And she was gone again.

They brought Tamar a more comfortable chair so she could doze beside the bed and a bell for her to ring if there was any change. After that there was nothing to do but sit and listen to Sadie's whistling intake of breath and the sounds of activity on the other side of the curtain. The clash and clang of trolleys; someone groaning; the occasional shout of 'Nurse! Nurse!'

Night Sister arrived at ten o'clock. She was much younger than Tamar had expected, tall and slim in her navy blue dress. She wore her frilled cap at a jaunty angle on the back of her head. 'You'd better make yourself scarce for half an hour while the doctor comes to look at her,' she said. 'Pop up to the kitchen and the runner will make you a cup of cocoa.'

The runner was a young girl not much older than Tamar, loading an enormous metal trolley with cups and saucers and jugs of boiling milk. 'It's the Ovaltine round,' she said, pulling a face. 'Sometimes I think I'm just a glorified waitress. I'd be better paid at the Corner House.'

'Can I help?'

The girl shook her head. 'Sister would kill me. You just sit there and have your drink until old Letcher-Fletcher's gone.'

About two o'clock Sadie became restless, her breathing louder, making a dreadful rasping sound as it was sucked in and out. When Night Sister came she flashed her torch at the chart and held Sadie's wrist for a long time, looking at her watch.

'It's not good, I'm afraid,' she said, frowning down at the chart.

The doctor came again at three o'clock, but left after a few moments. He had a murmured conversation with the nurse, but didn't speak to Tamar at all.

Gradually a faint, grey light seeped between the curtains and there were restless sounds from the beds on either side, as those who'd been able to sleep began to wake up. Trolleys clanged in the corridor and rumbled down the ward. Water was poured. A peremptory voice said 'Come along Mrs Bishop. Rise and shine! Time for a wash and brush up.'

A plump figure in the dark blue of a sister's uniform bustled into the cubicle. Her starched apron rasped against her legs as she walked. 'I'm Sister James,' she said. 'I gather you've been here all night.' She was a comfortable middle aged woman with iron grey hair. She had squeaky black shoes that bulged slightly at the sides where her feet had swollen. After nodding to Tamar she proceeded to check Sadie's pulse and look at her charts. She touched Sadie's forehead and listened to her harsh breathing for what seemed a long time before she turned and said 'Are you sure you feel up to staying with your mother?'

'Yes,' Tamar said firmly.

She looked sternly at Tamar for a few moments and then nodded again. 'I'll see that you get some breakfast.'

Beside the bed, Tamar held her mother's unresponsive hand and listened to her breathing. It was quieter now, but erratic – sometimes Tamar found herself holding her own breath, waiting for Sadie to take hers and realised that unconsciously she had synchronised their rhythms. Tamar was dimly aware of Sister coming to stand at the foot of the bed and then silently leaving again. It happened several times.

She could never afterwards pinpoint the exact moment when Sadie ceased to breathe. It was so imperceptible. She knew only when Sister took her by the arm and said 'I'm so very sorry.' She took out the tube and the drip and folded Sadie's arms across her chest. Then she turned to Tamar. 'Would you like to say goodbye to your mother?' she asked.

Tamar nodded. She had absolutely no idea what she was expected to do. She looked for what seemed a long time at the still, pale figure on the bed, but the face on the pillow was no longer Sadie's. The skin had gone slack and slipped away from the bones as if it no longer fitted. The bruising around her eye had become a dark brown stain and her mouth gaped open with a faint crusting of blood at the corner. Tamar remembered how Sadie had always fastidiously propped her chin with her hand in the train so that her mouth would stay shut when she slept. The memory of it gripped Tamar like a cramp, knotting her stomach with pain. She looked down at her mother, but Sadie's face was deserted – like a discarded dress, left in the corner of the room, shapeless without its wearer. Tamar leant over and put her lips to Sadie's cool cheek before Sister pulled the sheet up across her face.

'Would you like to come along to the office and sign for your mother's things?' The starched triangle at the back of the Sister James' head quivered interrogatively.

Tamar nodded again, dropping her gaze to the wooden bedside cabinet with its white plaque. Number Twenty Seven. She knew she would remember every detail of this for the rest of her life. Bed number twenty seven with its shrouded figure, so very lately her mother; blue cotton curtains on metal rings; grey linoleum that squeaked under her shoes.

Tamar followed Sister up the ward to her office, cluttered with paperwork – as untidy as the ward was immaculate. Sister sighed as she plumped herself down on an old velvet cushion in the desk chair. The runner had hinted wickedly to Tamar that she suffered piles. She slipped off her starched cuffs and stacked them on the corner of the desk like paper cones before pulling a form towards her on the blotting pad.

She read out a list, pathetically short, before giving it to Tamar to check, while she unlocked a drawer and took out the leather handbag and a small box containing a gold cross and two rings. Tamar signed.

'What will you do?' Sister asked, more kindly than before. 'Do you have family?'

Tamar noticed that she had tired lines round her eyes and puckers at the corner of her mouth as if she'd spent a lifetime trying not to smile.

'I don't know.' It sounded more despairing than Tamar intended. 'I'm seventeen, so I suppose I'll be called up for war-work or something.'

Sister nodded. She re-locked the drawer and tucked the keys into her pocket. 'I feel very sorry for you young girls. War takes away your youth, spoils your chances.'

Tamar wondered whether she was speaking from experience.

'I was a VAD in 1916,' she said, as though reading Tamar's thoughts. 'Believe me, I know.'

'Maybe it won't happen,' Tamar said, without much conviction.

The sister shook her head. 'If you fancy nursing, come and see us here. You could do worse.'

'Thank you.' Tamar hoped she sounded suitably polite. Even the smell of the place made her feel ill. It was the first time she'd ever been in a hospital and she never wanted to enter one again.

As she walked along the silent corridor on the top floor, clutching Sadie's handbag as well as her own and a brown paper parcel with Sadie's clothes inside, Tamar could see smoke rising from the chimneys of the streets and streets of houses that stretched all the way to the distant sea. In each of those houses someone would be cooking Sunday lunch, the papers spread over the parlour carpet in front of once-a-week fires. In each of them families would be gathering. Tamar had never, in her entire life, felt so totally alone, so completely abandoned. Whatever Sadie's shortcomings as a mother, she'd always been there. Now Sadie was gone. Muddled thoughts of funerals – how was she to organise one and how would she pay for it? – kept running through her mind as she walked.

Just inside the main door, a huddled figure was dozing on the leatherette bench. Anna raised her head as Tamar came down the stairs and then heaved herself off the seat and came across the hall, her face heavy with lack of sleep. 'Edward had to go back to the paper,' she said. 'The government declared war on Germany this morning.'

The grief in Anna's voice was almost more than Tamar could bear. But she still couldn't cry, even when Anna wrapped her arms around her, rocking her to and fro like a child, and saying, 'Oh, Tamar!' over and over and over. All she could think of was 'Whatever are we going to do now?'

PART III

PHONEY WAR

'I have spread my dreams under your feet;
Tread softly, because you tread on my dreams.'

W.B. Yeats
He Wishes for the Cloths of Heaven

CHAPTER ELEVEN

Sadie was buried in the cemetery behind the cigarette factory on one of the most brilliantly sunny September days anyone could remember. Ida's landlady sent a message saying how sad Ida was to hear about Sadie, but that she was too ill to come to the funeral. Only nine people stood round the grave with Tamar; Lily, George, Edward and Anna, three people from Pergavie's and a tall woman in a fur coat whose face was shrouded in black veiling. She had arrived in a large dark-green morris, spattered with mud as if it had been driven a long distance. As she walked down the path towards them, Tamar wondered whether she'd come in response to the notice that Edward had insisted should be put in the papers. Sadie might have family, he argued, who were still alive and should be notified of her death. So Tamar had let him put a notice in The Times. Whoever the woman was, she spoke to no one and stood apart from the group to watch Sadie's cheap plywood coffin lowered into the ground. By the time Tamar emerged from her distress sufficiently to take notice of anything, she was already being assisted into the back seat of the car by a uniformed driver. Tamar was too stupefied by grief to regret this, but afterwards she castigated herself for letting the woman leave before she could find out who she was.

Tamar was surprised to find that a church service was not obligatory and a short committal ceremony beside the grave was all that was necessary. Lily, who'd been brought up as a Methodist, got the local minister to take the service. Tamar found him straightforward and sincere and was relieved that she could understand everything he said. When Tamar bent to place her small bunch of red roses on the coffin lid, he prayed for her and her mother as if he and God were the best of friends.

'Dear Jesus,' he began, 'Who knows the secrets of our hearts and minds and who opens his arms wide to all sinners, please receive the soul of our departed sister with compassion, and surround her daughter, her friends and her family with your boundless love in their moment of grief. Give us your divine understanding of the incomprehensible and the strength to endure in times of trouble.'

The simple, plainly spoken words seemed perfectly appropriate and Tamar found them comforting, but this choice had been the subject of her first real quarrel with Edward. He was horrified that Tamar could contemplate putting her mother to rest without the benefit of a church blessing. And he wasn't talking just about the Anglican church. Did Tamar know for sure that her mother hadn't been baptised a Catholic? If there was the slightest doubt, then Tamar should have a proper requiem mass said for her.

'But why?' Tamar asked. 'Sadie never stepped inside a church in her life, why should she have to do it now she's dead?'

'Because otherwise she'll spend eternity in Purgatory.' Edward described it as a kind of unpleasant limbo for all those who had set out without the right kind of ticket for the journey.

'So why don't the prayers of a Methodist minister count?'

'Because as Catholics we don't recognise the dissenters. They're heretics.'

'What a stuffy thing to say! Especially as my father was a Quaker. What kind of religion is it that condemns people to no-man's land just because they didn't have the right kind of mumbo-jumbo whispered over them when they died? That's not religion – that's superstition!'

Edward looked hurt and angry.

Standing at the graveside with a restless and uneasy Edward beside her, Tamar felt guilty. Supposing he was right and Sadie was caught in a cold, dark void between heaven and hell, floating, eternally lost, just because she wasn't prepared to give the priest a couple of shillings for a mass? How could anybody know what happened after death? It consoled Tamar to hear the Methodist minister describe a God who was all seeing, all knowing, understanding and endlessly forgiving. 'If there is a God,' Tamar thought, 'then that's the kind of God I would want to believe in.' He would know what was inside Sadie's head, understand her motives and know that she always tried her best in difficult circumstances. He would forgive her for failing to get it right sometimes and admit her to the heavenly club, where no doubt she would have to work her way up from the bottom.

'She'll give those stuffy old Archangels a thing or two to think about,' Lily said, as they walked away from the grave. 'Cause a bit of a stir up there, your mother will.'

To pay for even such a simple funeral, Tamar had to sell every item of jewellery Sadie had, including the wedding ring she'd kept in her purse.

'They're only things after all, pet,' Lily had said. 'Thcy aren't goin' to bring her back.'

Anna went with Tamar to the pawnbroker down on the quayside and held her arm protectively while he sorted through the pathetic heap of objects in Sadie's jewel case. It was worse than Tamar had feared. The chunky gold bracelet Sadie had been given by one of the uncles, proved to be plated after Mr Bernstein had scratched it with a nail file, and the pretty diamond and ruby earrings that were supposed to have belonged to Sadie's grandmother were only paste. The rest of it was weighed on a small brass scale and a number of crumpled pound notes were counted into Tamar's hand. It was just enough.

There was nothing else. All Sadie's important possessions were kept in the old leather hat box on top of the wardrobe. After the funeral tea was over and everyone had gone, Tamar went up to the room and lifted it down, dreading what she would find. There were bundles of what looked like love letters, whose faded addresses charted the progress of Tamar's entire childhood. She put them aside, unable to throw them away, but knowing that she would never be able to read through Sadie's private tragedies. There were several long envelopes with the name of a solicitor embossed on the back and Tamar knew that she should look at these, if only to try to make sense of all the unanswered questions, but she was too exhausted by grief to undertake the task. 'One day,' she told herself. 'One day, when it doesn't hurt so much, I'll sort through it all.'

It took all her strength to lift the certificates from the brown envelope that contained them. There were only two. If Sadie had been married, she'd kept no record of it. Her birth certificate was there; Sarah Rosemary Tomlinson, born at 3 Headland Cottages in Looe, Cornwall. Her parents were listed as Rosie Libby and a man called Harland Tomlinson whose occupation was given as a fisherman. Had Sadie's stories of her childhood been a lie? A fisherman's cottage in Looe didn't exactly match up to the description of a house with twenty bedrooms and a tennis court. Did Ruthen ever exist or had Sadie invented it?

The other birth certificate was her own. Tamar unfolded it with unsteady fingers, steeling herself for what she thought it might tell her. But no. She was the legitimate daughter of Sadie Fell nee Tomlinson and James Fell, gentleman. They'd been living in Plymouth at the time. Her mother's age was given as nineteen. Tamar hadn't realised that Sadie had been so young – only a couple of years older than she was now. Sadly she added Sadie's death certificate to the envelope.

And then there were the photographs. Most of them she'd never seen before. There was a sepia studio portrait of a large, good-natured looking woman sitting in a chair with her arms folded self-consciously, and a young girl standing behind her with a restless, 'I haven't got time for this' expression on her face. There was a Penzance photographer's stamp on the back. Something in the girl's face made Tamar think it might be Sadie, so perhaps the other woman was Sadie's mother – the grandmother Tamar had never known. There were two or three faded snaps of the man on the dressing table, one of them taken with Sadie on a tennis court wearing a white dress and carrying a racquet. There were others of people Tamar didn't know with cryptic comments scrawled on the back. 'Lynmouth 1920'. 'Pam and Robert at Exeter.' Tamar's baby photographs were there too, wrapped in tissue paper, and a succession of studio poses Sadie had commissioned fitfully, when she could afford it. Tamar put them carefully in her underwear drawer. The best of them, the framed portrait of Sadie in her twenties, beautifully lit to make her look like a film star, she kept to put on the bedside table, tucking her father's snapshot into the corner of the frame.

At the bottom of the box, under the letters, was a little multi-coloured glass animal – cheap and badly moulded. It was too big to be a dog and too long-necked to be a horse. Tamar remembered, with vivid, painful recall, the day she'd bought it for Sadie as a birthday present. She'd seen it on the corner of a market stall, refracting the light in great splodges of red and blue and green. When she'd picked it up there were bubbles inside where air had been trapped in the mould and she'd imagined it on the window sill of their room, thought how much pleasure Sadie would have looking at the bright colours. It was only when Sadie was unwrapping the tissue paper that Tamar had known how wrong it was, how tasteless and tawdry. Sadie's face had briefly registered dismay and then quickly assumed an expression of tactful gratitude. 'How sweet,' she'd said, with unusual kindness. 'You shouldn't have spent your money.' And then she'd burst into tears.

Tamar could still feel those caustic emotions, the excitement and anticipation of the eight year old child, wanting to please her mother and the guilt and bewilderment afterwards because she'd somehow made Sadie cry. And now here was the terrible glass object, which to her knowledge and her secret shame, Sadie had never, ever displayed – here it was, carefully put away among her most treasured possessions. A tear slid down Tamar's face and splashed onto the varnished surface as she placed it on the dressing table beside Sadie's silver hairbrush, the crystal ring dish and the Chinese pot-pourri bowl with its swirling dragons and cracked lid.

Lily had suggested that she move into the small back room over the alleyway, which was empty again, so that she could let Tamar and Sadie's room as a double. The rent Lily had asked for was much lower than Miss Francis had been paying, and Tamar was conscious that Lily was doing her a favour. She gave her the pick of Sadie's wardrobe, including the long silver-fox stole that had both fascinated and repelled her as a child.

Lily was delighted. 'Are you sure you want to give this away, pet?' She swung the pelts over her shoulder and ran her fingers gently down the soft fur. 'It must be worth a bit, you know.'

'You were very good to Sadie. She'd be glad to know you had it.' Tamar reassured her.

Lily put her arm around Tamar briefly. She smelled of cigarette smoke and cheap face powder. 'Your Mam and me came from different sides of the street, if you know what I mean, but she was my best friend, and you can't put a price on friendship.' She squeezed Tamar's shoulders and let her go. Tamar could see that her eyes were swimming with tears. 'You're to count this as your home from now on, hinny,' she said as she gathered up the bundle of clothes. 'That room's yours and you can do as you please.'

It seemed odd walking down to the Palace without Tamar or Edward, and Anna felt nervous and rather exposed being with George on her own. She knew that he expected things of her, things she couldn't give. When they got to the door of the cinema, the lights were out and a notice pasted on the billboard said 'Closed for the war'.

'They can't do that, can they?' Anna asked.

'They're frightened of air raids,' George said. 'But they can't keep it up. People've got to do something.' He sighed. 'Anyway, perhaps it's just as well. I'm not in the mood tonight.'

'Nor me. I keep thinking about Tamar. She must be going through hell.' Although it was Tamar's bereavement they talked about, Anna knew that it wasn't the main thing in her thoughts or in George's. Her letter from the Slade had arrived that morning, offering her an interview with a view to considering her for an entrance scholarship. Earlier, before they went out, she'd shown it to George and he'd said. 'Right. Good. If that's what you want.' And he'd seemed pleased for her. But since then he'd hardly spoken about it.

They walked down to the sea front and stood for a while looking at the waves curling through the barbed wire. Then they bought fish and chips and walked home. When they reached the house George took her in his arms and kissed her with unexpected force, as though determined to provoke some response from her. But as always when he kissed her, she felt nothing at all. It was as though that part of her was completely detached. And if he tried to stroke her breasts or fumbled with the buttons of her blouse she was overcome by revulsion. Her skin shrank from his touch and she had to physically prevent herself from shuddering. Usually George would accept that she didn't want physical contact – in his opinion this was how good girls behaved. But Anna knew her unresponsiveness bothered him. 'You don't have to be that good,' he would joke sometimes. 'A bit of a cuddle wouldn't hurt.' Then they'd smoke a cigarette together, talk.

Tonight George made a scene. 'I need to know where I stand, Anna,' he said. 'Are we seeing each other or are we not? You're happy enough for me to pay you into the pictures, but you don't want to know me after. What's wrong with me? Is it all this London business?'

Anna had dreaded the moment George would start to push her into some kind of declaration about their relationship. He never said he loved her, though Anna knew he did. He talked sometimes about 'caring' for her, being fond of her. 'You matter to me more than anything,' he would say in a self conscious kind of way.

It was impossible to formulate the words without hurting him. 'George you know what I dream of doing; you know if I want to be a painter I can't afford to get involved with anyone.'

'You mean you care more for a few tubes of coloured oil than you do for people?'

'No. I'm not saying that.' How could she explain to George if he didn't understand. 'It's really difficult. Why can't we just be friends?'

'Look Anna, I'm a man, not a ... a ... Greek marble or something! I'm human, I've got feelings. But I can't wait forever. If you don't want me, tell me.'

'George.' Anna felt miserable. 'If I was going to get involved with a man, it would be you, believe me. I'm really fond of you. Fonder than anyone else. But don't base your life round me. Please. I don't want to hurt you. There are things I have to do. All I know is that painting matters to me more than anything.'

'Right then!' George's face was set. He put his hands in his pockets. 'At least I know where I am now. I'm glad you've put me straight.'

~~~~~~~~~~~~~~~~~~
~~~~~~~~~~~~~~~~~~

On her first night in the small back room Tamar woke at 3 am and lay awake in the single bed aching with misery. All her childhood she'd longed for a room of her own – but not like this. The bed was cold and hard. There was no Sadie snoring or mumbling in her sleep on the other side – she would never have to dig her elbow in Sadie's back again. The darkness was so black, so complete, Tamar felt she might suffocate.

Reaching out, she felt for the bedside lamp and switched it on. The light from the bulb inside its blue fringed shade was relentless, creating crude shadows on the walls and ceiling. Tears leaked from the corners of Tamar's eyes and trickled down her temples as she thought about Sadie. Raising her head to look at the photograph on the dressing table, Tamar remembered the book of poetry that had belonged to her. Sliding her feet out of bed she picked it up from the shelf. It was comforting to touch something that Sadie had touched, to hold a piece of Sadie's life in her hands. Tamar opened the cover and read the inscription again. When she'd mentioned Charles Carter to Edward he'd said dismissively that he was *fin de siecle* – a Victorian left-over – of no real value in the history of twentieth century literature.

Tamar turned the flimsy, gold-edged pages. She would never know the story of Sadie's friendship with the poet now. The pages were printed in a very small, ornate type face that was not easy to read and the poems had strange titles such as 'For Jocasta Out Walking', 'The Black Virgin of Funchal', 'Idomineo in Venice'. Here and there a line or a word, caught Tamar's attention as she read and then one poem in particular, because it seemed to put into words everything she felt about Sadie and Sadie's death.

Now that your restless spirit
has passed across that final sea
blown by other winds
than swell the sails of life,
there is none here that can console
none that can ease your absence
or fill for me the vacant space
left by your departing form.
There is only the silence in my soul

your voice once filled
and all the pain of your going
before I could cry 'Stay!'

It comforted Tamar a little to imagine Sadie sailing on a celestial ocean, in some bright zone of peace and comfort.

There was a light tap on her door and then it opened a crack. It was George, half dressed in shirt and trousers. 'I heard you up and I thought you might like a cuppa.' He came in with a mug of tea. 'And I brought the last of the biscuits.' He took a couple of Lily's homemade ginger snaps out of his pocket and put them on the bedside table. 'Mam says there won't be any more 'till the end of the war.'

George sat down on the edge of the bed.

'How was the film?'

'The cinema was closed, so we just walked down to the beach. Anna was in a funny mood again. She's got her letter for the college in London.'

'That's good! I hope she gets in.'

'I don't.'

'Whatever for?'

'If she goes to London, do you really think she'll look at me when she comes back? *If* she comes back?'

'I'm sorry George.'

'She's just using me, man. And I can't stand it.'

Tamar sighed. 'I used to think that Anna was totally selfish and didn't care about anyone but herself. But since Sadie died, she's been so good . . .' Tamar felt tears begin to prick behind her eyelids again.

'She cares more for painting than she does for me, that's certain.'

'Love and friendship can only go so far George. In the end everyone's on their own. There's no way Anna would give up going to the Slade just because you or I needed her. And there's no way Edward would stop being a Catholic just because I don't believe in it. We've all got our own lives, and we've all just got to get through them as best we can.'

~~~~~~~~~~~~~~~~~~
~~~~~~~~~~~~~~~~~~

Anna's senior high school term had begun two days after the outbreak of war but Anna's attendance lasted exactly a week. The letter from the Slade had eroded what little motivation she had. Why waste time on studies that in a year's time would be useless? But she was also aware that she was gambling everything she had on her Slade entrance, and had not allowed herself any second choices. The following Monday she stood in the kitchen watching her mother ironing the damp sheets she'd just taken off the line and tried to explain why she wasn't going back to school.

'I hate it. I'm not even good at it – I only just managed to scrape my school certificate. There's no way I'd get any further – it would be a waste of everyone's time.'

'Then what are you going to do?' Anna's mother asked. She looked tired and Anna thought she had lost weight.

'I know Grandpa won't pay for me to go to King Edward's full time, but if he'll keep me, I'm going to study on my own until I'm old enough for the Slade. Another year. Do you think he'll do that?'

'It's possible Anna. I'll talk to him when he gets back. He's gone off to volunteer as an air raid warden. I told him he was probably too old, but apparently not.' She sighed deeply and went on with the ironing.

Anna was surprised. She had expected more argument. Her mother had been so determined that Anna should continue at the High School and go on to take her teaching certificate. Now she could see her mother acknowledging defeat. Somehow since Maya's letter and the outbreak of war, Mrs Wiseman – as she now wanted to be known – had changed her priorities.

She looked up again. 'Well, I can't see that it matters so much now,' she said as if she knew what Anna was thinking. 'We'll probably all be dragged into some kind of war work. I remember what it was like last time, all the men went away and women had to do the jobs – one of my friend's mothers was a crane driver down on the docks.'

'I hope I won't have to do anything like that.'

'You won't get a choice, Anna. But I hope I'm wrong.' She picked up a crumpled sheet from the basket. 'Just hold the end of this will you.' Anna took the corners and held them tightly while they shook, stretched and folded the sheet between them in a practised rhythm. The simple domestic action seemed comforting and companionable. 'Perhaps it'll all be over soon. I just wish I knew what had happened to your father. He could be in a prison camp, or in hiding, or maybe he got across the border somewhere like Maya and is trying to find his way back to England.'

Anna knew she had only added in the last possibility for personal comfort. She knew, as did her mother, that if he was able to, he would have got a letter to them somehow. They both stood silently for a moment contemplating their own fears.

'When it's over,' Anna said. 'Will you go back?'

Mrs Wiseman shook her head. 'I know it's not what you want to hear, Anna, but no. I wasn't happy there. This is where I belong. But I won't stop you, if you want to go. You're old enough now.'

'When the war's over, I'm going back to find Dad.'

Anna's mother put a hand on her daughter's shoulder and squeezed it. 'Let's just hope it's over soon.'

A week after Sadie's funeral, George came home late from his shift at the yard smelling of beer. He had the cheerful, reckless, rather expansive air about him that meant he'd had a few drinks down at the Union on the way home.

George put his bait can in the sink and before Lily could chase him out to the wash house so she could serve up his tea which was keeping warm on the stove, he said, 'I've joined up.'

Lily had her back to him, turning the gas up under the pan. Tamar was sitting at the table and she saw Lily's hand freeze on the knob of the cooker and her face turn deathly white. 'Jesus wept,' she said – hardly audible, holding on to the front of the cooker as if it was the only thing preventing her from falling to the floor. 'Jesus wept!'

'Sit down Lily,' Tamar took her by the arm and lowered her into a chair.

'Why? Why? You daft bugger!' Lily was looking up at George

who was no longer smiling. 'Holy Elijah and all the Saints! Why did you have to go and do that? You haven't got the sense you were born with!' Then she began to weep and put her face down on her arms sobbing violently. Tamar stroked her shoulders.

Tamar followed George out of the back door as he crossed the yard to the wash house. 'You could have broken it more gently,' she said accusingly. 'You know how she feels.'

'There was no other way to put it,' George said. 'And I had to have four pints before I could even do that.' He paused at the doorway and half turned. 'I'm not in the Navy, tell her. I've had enough of ships. I've joined the Royal Engineers.'

As Tamar turned to go back indoors a terrible thought struck her. If George had joined up, did that mean that Edward would too?

CHAPTER TWELVE

The train window was stuck. It wouldn't move at all, however hard Anna pulled or pushed. 'I wouldn't do that dear,' one of the passengers said. 'We don't want any draughts do we?'

Anna gave the window another futile, rebellious tug. She wondered how she was going to manage all the way to London in a small, hot compartment – every seat filled with sweating, squirming humanity. The elderly lady who'd spoken was wearing a thick wool coat that smelled of moth balls and she was sucking mint imperials. Opposite, a heavy man with bulging stomach and quivering jowls was smoking Turkish cigarettes which he half stubbed out in the ashtray below the window, leaving the dog ends to smoulder repulsively. A young couple sat giggling and whispering on the end of the seat and on the other side were two soldiers who'd tried to engage Anna in conversation with offers of cigarettes. When she declined they turned their attention to the young couple opposite and soon began a raucous debate. One of the soldiers smelled of beer and he kept breaking into snatches of a popular song 'I'm a regular guy. You'll be all right with me . . .' glancing sideways at Anna and winking. How was she to endure another three hours in this stifling, noisy carriage? Anna looked at her precious folder, squashed dangerously on the rack between suitcases, gas masks, kit bags, folded coats and what looked like a picnic hamper and wondered whether that too would survive the journey.

Getting up, she went out into the corridor, slid down the window in the carriage door and put her head out into the smoky slip-stream, holding her hat on with one hand. Sultry heat lay thick under autumnal trees; a heron stood motionless beside a stagnant pond, like a garden ornament; and there were people harvesting in the fields who made the train's passing an excuse to rest their backs for a moment. Anna waved. It looked very paintable in the thundery light. The horses and carts laden with sheaves, a child holding a horse's bridle, the small shocks of corn dotting the field, the matchstick people wielding pitchforks. It had the quality of a design; but before Anna could take her sketch book out of her bag it was gone. Now they were running along a derelict canal with rows of rotting barges moored amid bulrushes and pond weed.

'What am I going to do if they won't have me?' Anna kept asking herself. For it seemed impossible that the Slade would think her good enough, and even more impossible that they might grant her a scholarship. There were very few of these, and her tutor had warned her that the entrance scholarships usually went to men. Even the wording on the form seemed to ignore the possibility that the applicant might be female. '*He* must send written notice of his intention . . . *he* may also be required to attend for interview'. It was daunting. There were other scholarships specifically open to women, but they were only available once Anna was at the Slade. How was she to find the money for her keep? The fees alone were twenty eight guineas without rooms or food. She had saved about eighty pounds, but that wouldn't last long.

Anna was wearing her best dark green linen suit with a pale yellow picquet blouse and yellow beret with a tassel on the side. The hat had caused some anguish. Anna hated wearing them, but her mother had been so scandalised by the thought of Anna going to London without one, she had at last given in. 'Anyone would think that a hatless woman was a harlot,' Anna had said to Tamar as they browsed the racks at Pergavie's. Most of the hats were either too formal or too middle aged or simply ridiculous.

'You don't suit hats,' Tamar said as she looked at Anna's reflection in the mirror and Anna knew she was remembering the episode of George's trilby. 'At least not these ones.'

It was true Anna thought, gazing critically at her own image. She was tall, what was usually described as 'well made', with athletic limbs, an outdoor kind of face and short, thick hair that swung in a burnished bob that somehow seemed to be covering enough for her head without anything else. The beret was a compromise to satisfy her mother and because Anna wanted to make a good impression.

Anna hadn't been to London since the journey from Germany four or five years ago. When she got off the train at Kings Cross the station was even more noisy and crowded than she'd remembered. There were soldiers with unwieldy kit bags on every platform, and in the ticket hall there were large groups of forlorn looking children with gas masks being shepherded by harassed women in WVS uniforms. Everyone seemed to be shouting and pushing. Anna took out her instructions, carefully dictated by Robert Drew and went out into the street in search of a bus. The first thing Anna noticed was that every window in the street was criss-crossed with tape, and above the roof-tops huge silver barrage balloons were tethered, glinting in the sunlight as though they'd been inflated for a children's party. On the other side of the street a large notice read 'To the Air Raid Shelter' with an arrow pointing diagonally down. Anna shivered. Supposing there was an air raid while she was here? There'd been none at home yet even though they'd been warned to expect them. Her grandfather had fitted bunk beds in the Anderson shelter to make it more homely, but even in summer it felt clammy and big garden spiders continually wove shawls of web across the corners. So far the shelter had not been needed. Not a single bomb had been dropped anywhere and people were already calling it 'the phoney war'. Anna hoped that it would stay that way.

The Slade itself was not as imposing as she'd expected from the name. It was lost in the rambling Victorian sprawl of the buildings that formed University College. Inside, the staircases were dingy and in need of decoration. As she searched for the Principal's office, Anna stared anxiously at the groups of people wandering through corridors that smelt vaguely of turpentine. There were quite a few older individuals Anna imagined to be tutors, as well as others who looked like undergraduates. It was all very casual and hardly any of them were carrying gas masks. The men were in shirtsleeves with their jackets slung casually over their shoulders. A girl only a little older than Anna in dark blue slacks and a blouse was walking with another, dark, bespectacled girl in a bright chintzy dress and poppy red cardigan, talking animatedly as she walked, chopping at the air with her hands as if to demonstrate something. Neither of them were wearing hats. Next year, Anna thought with a shiver of excitement, next year that could be me.

Anna's first interview was with Miss Hayter, the tutor to women students – a thin, nervous woman in a brown suit and brogues who talked in a clipped, monotonous voice. 'Of course, even if I approve your application,' she said, 'you'll still have to see the Senior Tutor if you want to be considered for an entrance scholarship.' Her tone of voice was not hopeful. 'And you know, of course, that as a woman you have to start in the Antique rooms and wait for his approval before you move up into the Life Classes?'

'How long does that take?' Anna asked. Her spirits sank at the thought of spending even more time copying old masters.

'Months, sometimes years. You must expect at least two to three terms.'

As Anna turned to leave the office she added 'You know that we are moving to Oxford for the duration of the war? Will that make any difference to you?'

'I didn't know. But I would still want to study here.'

The woman nodded approvingly. 'We're in the process of moving now. When you next contact us we will be at the Ruskin School of Drawing in the Bodleian.'

Professor de Gris was a tall, big-stomached, balding man wearing a wrinkled three piece suit frayed at the cuffs, with stains on the waistcoat. His lank grey hair was long enough to have darkened his collar with grease, and his finger nails were broken and dirty. He put on a pair of glasses to look at Anna's portfolio – an old fashioned pair of rimless lenses on a chain tucked into his top pocket. He went through Anna's work very fast making occasional comments in a high pitched, rather affected voice. Anna's precious pencil studies of Lily were unceremoniously thrown to one side. Every now and then he would tap three times on a drawing with his index finger and say 'yes', before continuing with the catalogue of rejection.

Anna felt more and more depressed. When he'd finished he sniffed loudly and put his glasses back in his pocket. Anna thought she was going to burst into tears of shame and mortification as she gathered up her paltry little drawings and water colour sketches and crammed them back into her folder.

'Do you know the difference between good painting and bad painting?' he asked sharply.

Anna hesitated and then nodded.

'So who would you say was a bad painter?' he persisted.

Anna didn't know how to reply. 'I don't like Romney . . or Grey . . . or . . any of the Victorian narrative painters very much.'

'Why?' He glared at her.

Anna's legs shook. She was still standing – she had not been invited to sit down. 'I suppose . . . I suppose because . . . they lack honesty.'

He was still looking at her, as if to suggest that her answer was incomplete. Anna struggled on, trying to articulate a dimly perceived idea. 'They achieve their effects by means of tricks . . . and sentimentality . . . rather than the use of form or colour . . . But I don't really know . . .' She trailed off into silence.

He picked up two of her drawings from the desk. 'So if I asked you to tell me which of these is a good drawing and which is a bad drawing – could you tell me?'

Anna shook her head. She had been very pleased with both of them until she saw them in his hands.

'Frankly, my dear,' he said as he gave them back to her. 'You know nothing about painting. I suggest you go back to the north, find yourself a husband and have babies. But,' he held up his hand – 'if you still feel obstinately inclined to persist in your foolish notion in about a year's time, do get in touch with us again.' He nodded his head in a gesture of dismissal.

Anna picked up her portfolio and went out of the room on legs that felt almost too wobbly to carry her.

'Any luck?' The young man who was next in the waiting room looked up at her enquiringly. Anna shook her head and swung her hair across her cheek to hide the angry tears that were threatening to blind her. She went quickly out of the door and into the small garden opposite where she sat on a seat looking across the grass. Her eyes ached with the effort of trying not to cry. She pulled the beret from her head and tossed it into the metal bin beside the seat. After a moment she pushed the portfolio in on top of it. She felt utterly humiliated. When he had looked at her drawings in that scathing, dismissive way she had felt as if he was mauling her soul with his horrid, dirty hands. And how dared he question her motivation? All the life and joy had suddenly gone out of everything. Anna's stomach churned with anger and grief, as she went over every word of the interview in her mind, over and over. What had he meant by 'if you still feel inclined to persist in a year's time?' Did that mean there was a window of hope? Even so, where would she get the money? She had hoped so much for the chance of a scholarship.

Above the trees the barrage balloons dipped to and fro in a cumbersome dance as they were caught in a breeze imperceptible at ground level. There were three hours before Anna had to catch the train home. She walked in the park, cursing the gas mask strap that cut into her shoulder. Parts of the park were fenced off and Anna could see gun emplacements through the wire – their long green barrels protruding over the walls of sandbags. In another corner a huge generator and two big searchlights on wheeled trailers stood idle, guarded by three young men in uniform. It seemed incongruous to have these things placed next to couples lying in the grass enjoying the Indian summer sun. Children were playing – a ball was thrown for a dog, a child on a tricycle pedalled past accompanied by a tall middle aged woman in the grey and white uniform of a nanny.

Then there was a procession of prams – their scrolled handles and spoked wheels in a long line that made Anna's fingers twitch for a pencil in spite of her disappointment. It was like the first stirring of life after a presumed death. Why should I let some pompous, upper class, self-important man put me off? Anna thought. She set her lips in a determined line. 'Bugger him,' she said to herself. 'Bugger him.'

'We could get married next week, if I got a special licence,' Edward said, almost casually, as they were walking back from the cinema, which had stayed closed for a few days and then, when it became clear that life was going to continue, opened again shamefacedly.

Tamar's heart thumped and her mouth went dry. This wasn't how she'd imagined a proposal of marriage – this casual assumption that it had somehow already been decided. She'd been thinking about it quite a lot lately. Edward had followed George's example and although he wasn't in uniform yet, he'd volunteered for the press corps, hoping eventually to become a fully fledged war correspondent. Tamar struggled to feel glad that he wasn't going to be in direct combat but was unable to suppress her dread of losing him. Everyone was going away from her – Sadie, George . . . But Edward seemed perfectly happy with his decision. Like George, he viewed it all as a great adventure, a chance to get out into the world. Now he wanted Tamar to marry him before he left.

'The priest would give us a dispensation if you agreed to take instruction while I was away,' Edward persisted.

'I'm too young to marry yet, Edward,' Tamar said. She couldn't understand why her stomach tied itself into a knot whenever the word was mentioned. This was every girl's romantic dream wasn't it? She wished desperately that Sadie was here to advise her. Several of the girls at Pergavie's had married newly enlisted boyfriends and Tamar knew that everyone expected her to follow. 'It's not that I don't want to marry you,' she added quickly – seeing the expression on Edward's face, 'it's just that everything's so uncertain. It's not a good time.' Whenever she thought about marriage she felt frightened. Not just about the religious side of things. It was such a big thing to commit yourself to someone before your life had really begun. And they would be bound to have children straight away, because Catholics didn't believe in birth control. Tamar knew about that now.

When she was younger it had always puzzled her how Sadie had slept with all those men for so many years without getting pregnant. When she'd tentatively broached the subject with Lily Kennedy, Lily had said, 'Rubber Johnnies, pet,' and winked at her. 'You mind you don't go with anyone who doesn't have one,' and she'd winked again. Then, when Tamar had gone through Sadie's things after her death, she'd found a funny little round rubber cap in a box with a tube of cream and in the box a leaflet with the address of a clinic in Newcastle on it. Tamar had kept the address, though she really didn't know why. It was a pity that Edward didn't believe in such things. Tamar had got into the habit of looking in prams as she passed the shops – an assortment of babies, some sleeping, some crying, some staring up at her as if in possession of secret knowledge. None of them made her feel in the least maternal.

'Why won't you marry me? Don't you love me enough?' Edward's brown eyes were beseeching. How could she resist someone she loved so much?

'Oh, I do. I do. It's just . . . I need more time. It's such a big step.'

'But we can be engaged?'

'If you like.'

'You don't sound very enthusiastic.'

'I'm sorry. I didn't mean it to come out like that. It's so difficult to explain. There's so much to think about – it's not just how we feel about each other.' Tamar felt trapped and wretched. She did love Edward. She couldn't imagine sharing her life with anyone else. Yet his assumption that she was willing to adopt a religion she didn't believe in made her angry, though she couldn't say anything to him about it without provoking the kind of row she dreaded. Why should she have to become a Catholic in order to marry him? But even beyond her religious doubts there was another feeling – the same kind of feeling she'd had every time Sadie had moved, every time Sadie had said 'I think we're going to like it here, don't you think?' – a knowledge, or perhaps it was only a fear, that this wasn't permanent, that there was another kind of future just around the corner.

'Why don't you believe in God anyway?' Anna asked when Tamar told her about her dilemma the following afternoon. They were having tea in Lyons. 'Most people do, even if they're not religious.'

It was something Tamar had thought about quite a lot. When she was small she had certainly believed and could dimly remember someone, an elderly woman, making her kneel beside the bed and recite a prayer 'Now I lay me down to rest'. And she could remember being told that if she was a good girl and asked nicely, God would sometimes let her have the things that she prayed for. Now she tried to describe the process of disillusionment to Anna. 'When I was little I used to ask him for things – just little things, but always something that was really important to me. And they never came. So then I started to set him tests. I thought if God really existed and he was as powerful as everyone said he was, he would give me some kind of sign. Sadie used to call him 'the great magician in the sky'. But then when I was about ten I asked her if God was like Santa Claus and she said, 'probably' and I began to suspect that it was all just a fairy tale. When we did Darwin in science, well . . that just clinched it really.' Tamar paused and sighed. 'I wish I could believe. It would make things so much easier with Edward. But it's rather like wishing yourself in love when you're not. The feeling just isn't there.'

'Are you still going to marry him?'

Tamar nodded. 'Eventually. What about you and George?'

'I'm never going to get married. I've told him but I don't think he believes me.'

'Never's a big word. Do you really want to spend the whole of your life alone?'

Anna shook her head. 'That's the difficult question. I don't want to get married, but I don't want to give up the idea of being loved. Sometimes I dream about passion – the kind of love that would turn my life upside down and make everything else seem insignificant. Maybe if I meet someone who makes me feel like that, I'll marry them. I just don't know.'

Love and passion were very much on Tamar's mind as she walked home. Supposing she allowed herself to be swept away by the powerful physical temptations she felt when she was with Edward? Tamar knew in her mind that good girls didn't do things like that. Good girls said no – that was what Edward expected of her. He believed that sex was a sacrament. It was only right within marriage, he'd explained, and only then if you intended to have children. But the instinctive, emotional part of Tamar knew that it wasn't quite so simple. She wanted to make love with Edward more than anything in the world. Sometimes she felt almost ill with desire. It would be so easy just to let herself be carried away and she didn't think that Edward's carefully guarded virginity was entirely bullet proof either, despite his pious intentions. And what then? Supposing she conceived a child? To marry Edward just because she was carrying his baby would be wrong – as wrong as marrying him without being absolutely sure she was doing the right thing. Back in her room Tamar opened her lingerie drawer and retrieved the piece of paper she had found in Sadie's things, with the address of the clinic in Newcastle. Her hand trembled as she looked at it. Edward would think she was terribly wrong to even think of it. Sinful. But need she tell him? Wouldn't it be better to be prepared . . . Just in case? It was more instinct than logic that made Tamar decide to go there on her way home from work the next day and ask for contraception. She was after all engaged to be married, so she wouldn't have to lie. She knew what Sadie would have wanted her to do. Sadie's voice was in her head. 'Don't do what I did, Tamar. Don't tie yourself down so young.' And if she asked Lily's advice she knew that Lily would say 'Better safe than sorry, pet. What he doesn't know can't hurt him.' Already feeling guilty at the deceit that she was contemplating, Tamar put the address into her bag, and allowed herself a wry smile in the mirror.

Anna's letter from the Slade arrived on Tuesday morning and it told her what she had already guessed. Clutching it in her hand she went down to the college to see her tutor. The building was unusually quiet. There were one or two students in the entrance hall, but none of the usual bustle and clamour of a term-time morning. Where had they all gone? John Cornell was in his office moving a book case.

'If there's a bomb and the windows are blown in I don't want my books facing the blast. Some of these are irreplaceable.'

Anna helped him turn it round and push it towards the internal wall. His desk too, she noticed, had been moved away from its position under the window.

He dusted his hands with a piece of rag and asked, 'What can

I do for you?' Anna produced her letter. 'They've accepted me for next year, but I'll have to pay all my own fees.'

'Can you do that?'

Anna shrugged. 'I've got some money saved up – maybe enough for six months.'

'What about your relatives?'

'I can't even ask them to pay my tuition for the current year here. They're scandalised because I refused to go back to school and study to be a teacher. I could probably pay this term's fees out of my savings, but I don't know what I'm going to do for the rest of the year.'

'It would be tragic if you gave it up.' He thought for a while. 'We'd hoped you were going to come full time. If it makes any difference, I won't charge for the life classes in the evening – that's where you need to put in the most effort. But that doesn't help your main predicament – or the problem of where you get the money to go to the Slade afterwards. You should keep your savings.' He stopped as if something had just occurred to him and then he said, 'Why don't you go and see Walter Suzmann and ask his advice? He really seemed to like your work.'

John wrote an address on a piece of card and added a few words at the bottom. As he handed it to Anna he seemed to be struck by another thought. 'Have you considered some kind of war work? Even part time. Most of the factories are working round the clock. If you did a night shift, you'd still have time to paint during the day and it would solve your money worries.'

Anna shook her head firmly, but she didn't bore him with her reasons.

'Pity. That might have been a solution.' John turned to go back to his programme of re-organisation. 'Good luck with Walter, anyway.'

Anna picked her way carefully among hawsers and nets and stacked creels. Walter Suzmann's studio was in an old sail loft above a fisherman's lock-up in one of the dilapidated buildings that staggered along the quayside, where her grandfather had once taken her to see the Wooden Dolly. The stairs to the studio were littered with fish and chip papers, cigarette butts and pigeon droppings. There was an old pram on the landing, spattered with paint and the door had a broken panel as though someone had tried to kick it in.

There was no reply to Anna's knock, so she pushed the door gently and peered inside. Walter was under one of the huge windows in his shirt sleeves, glasses poised on the end of his nose, making sweeping strokes across a large canvas with a priming brush. He looked up, saw Anna and smiled. 'Come in, come in. Willkommen!' He seemed somehow younger than she remembered from the exhibition. She went towards him with the card that John Cornell had given her in her hand, the folder of drawings in the other.

'So,' he said after a while. 'Do you want to study with me? I don't know what I can teach you, but if you want to come here and watch me and work with me, perhaps there will be something I can give you.' He leafed through her drawings again. 'Your technique is good, except in the figure drawing and that is something you can learn. But you are not yet looking at things closely enough. That is the secret – to look at an object until it resembles no other object you have ever seen and then – only when it has become utterly unique – to paint it.'

The studio was warm – so warm Anna was sweating. A pot-bellied cast iron stove stood in the middle of the floor with a chimney that was wired up to the ceiling and which protruded through a crudely cut hole in the roof next to a skylight. There was a stain on the floor where rain regularly dripped through. A pile of drift wood and broken orange boxes beside the stove waited to be fed through the plate at the top which was currently covered by a soot encrusted kettle. There was a bed in the corner and an old drop leaf table covered in tubes of paint, opened and un-opened cans of food, bottles of beer, a couple of half burnt candles in saucers, a mouldy loaf of bread, bottles of turpentine, jars of brushes in assorted sizes – Walter's life and work all jumbled up together.

'Come any time in daylight,' Walter was saying. 'But there's no electricity and no facilities – only the public toilet on the quay – I warn you now.' Anna followed his eyes towards the bucket of water next to the stove and a bowl of unbelievably dirty water scummed over with grease on the table.

'It's all right,' Anna said. 'I'll manage.'

He was looking at her quizzically over his glasses and Anna thought how fine his eyes were. He smiled rather shyly and she smiled back.

~~~~~~~~~~~~~~~~~~

The day before Edward had to leave he and Tamar took the bus to Seahouses and walked along the coast to picnic among the dunes. It was a cool, blustery day and there was no one else on the beach. When Edward held her and kissed her Tamar kept thinking, perhaps this is the last time, perhaps I won't ever see him again. Something like panic rose inside her, constricting her chest, forcing her to hold him tighter and tighter. She could feel the strength of his desire for her in the pressure of his kiss, the way his teeth bit into her lips, the way his hands shook as he stroked her face, her covered breasts.

'Will you do something for me before I go?' Edward asked.

Tamar looked up into his irises, dilated almost black with wanting, and thought she knew what it was. Slowly, very slowly, with shaking fingers, she began to undo the buttons of her blouse and the tiny, slippery fastenings of the satin camisole beneath, and then she lay back in the sand and waited, aware of his ravenous eyes sweeping her skin.

It was cold in the late afternoon air and, when Edward ran his warm fingers down the side of her breast, hardly touching, it almost burnt her skin. She arched upwards, instinctively, towards his hand, but it was suddenly withdrawn.

'We shouldn't,' Edward said, pulling away from her. She sensed that he was slightly shocked at her forwardness. 'I couldn't do it without wanting to go all the way and that wouldn't be right.' His voice was gruff, his face swollen with emotion.

Tamar felt tears trickling out of her eyes and down the side of her face into her hair, where they chilled her scalp. She sat up, pulling her blouse together, letting her hair fall forward to hide her stupidity. 'Hold me,' she said. 'Please. Just hold me.'

He put his arms around her and began to kiss her wet cheeks,
~~~~~~~~~~~~~~~~~~

disturbed by her tears. 'I might never see you again,' Tamar said. 'And I just can't bear it.' She felt that she would like to tear her nails across his prudent, white face. 'Why do you have to be so good,' she cried. 'Why?'

Then his hot rough mouth was over hers and she could feel the hardness of his body through the fabric of his trousers as his desire for her re-kindled. She had never wanted anything as much as the touch of his hands on her breasts, the taut skin of her stomach, his fingers fluttering gently in the soft hairs between her legs. Thankful, desperately thankful that she had thought to prepare for this moment, Tamar gave herself up to erotic delight.

But it wasn't what she had expected. It didn't hurt as much as she had feared, as Edward pushed inside her, but just as she had begun to feel a kind of pleasurable anticipation as he moved to and fro, Edward experienced some kind of convulsion and his body relaxed on top of her, motionless. Tamar felt terrible. All her desire for him was still there, unsatisfied, though she had no idea what it was that was supposed to happen, and the space between her legs felt sore and raw.

Edward raised his head to look at her. 'We shouldn't have done that,' he said. 'I shall have to go to confession tomorrow morning before I leave.'

'You mean you have to tell the priest what we've just done?'

Edward nodded and then smiled. 'The trouble is I'm not at all contrite.' He kissed her again. 'Oh, Tamar, I love you so much. I should feel guilty, but I don't.' As he pulled on his trousers he looked very serious. 'I just hope that nothing's happened.' Edward blushed. 'You know what I mean.' He fastened his belt. 'If it does . . . You will tell me straight away, won't you? I could apply for special leave to get married.'

Tamar thought of telling him what she'd done, but her instincts told her that it wouldn't be well received. She simply nodded. The idea that their private act of togetherness would be discussed with some black robed priest made her feel sick.

When Tamar got home she took all her clothes off and for the first time, looked at herself naked in the mirror. Her skin felt soiled by unsatisfied desire and guilt – like a layer of dirt. She touched herself, her breasts, her stomach, her thighs, but it didn't feel as it had done when Edward touched her. This wasn't how it was supposed to be in the books she'd read. When she crouched over the wash basin and pulled out the little rubber cap, dousing herself with water as she'd been shown at the clinic, it felt unbearably sordid.

CHAPTER THIRTEEN

Anna was dreaming that she was back in Partenkirchen, in the playground, and the boys were coming towards her, closer and closer, and they were chanting something and there was a strange wailing sound she couldn't identify, or even tell whether it came from them or from herself. Someone had grasped her by the shoulder and was shaking her, but she couldn't move, couldn't run. There was no way she could get away. Convulsed with panic, Anna opened her eyes and saw her mother bending over her in her nightdress, hair down to her shoulders, very agitated. The wailing sound was still there.

'Wake up Anna! Wake up. It's an air raid – we've got to get down to the shelter!' Her mother was gone in an instant. Anna heard Frankie's protesting cry from the next room as he was lifted from his cot. She tried to shake off her dream as she heaved her sleep-heavy limbs over the edge of the bed, tugging a jumper over her pyjamas. She could hear her grandmother's voice raised in argument. 'I'm not going in there – I'll be all right. You go on. Just leave me.' The words were slurred as she tried to speak without her false teeth.

Anna went to help her mother coax the old woman out of bed, push slippers onto unwilling feet, thrust her limp arms into a dressing gown and then hurry her downstairs and out into the garden. Outside everything was utterly dark except for the search lights probing the sky. When the sirens stopped Anna could hear the drone of distant engines. German engines. Somewhere up there were planes, piloted by her own countrymen. Perhaps even boys she'd been to school with, or had passed in the street. The family who'd owned the bakery had a son who'd gone into the air force.

'Quickly Anna!' Mrs Wiseman's voice cut into her reverie. 'Get your grandmother into the shelter.'

Mrs Cotteslow was confused and disorientated and Anna had to half carry her down the rough steps. Inside the dank interior, her mother had lit a candle and was rocking a weeping Frankie to and fro. Anna could hear the thudding of the guns. Their percussion sent a tremor through the ground under her feet and rattled the door of the shelter.

'Where's grandpa?'

'He went down to see what was happening. When there's an air raid the wardens are all called out.'

After about half an hour the guns fell silent. Anna opened the door and slipped outside. Everything was quiet now, although the search lights were still criss-crossing themselves over her head. Down towards the river the sky was red with light as from some gigantic bonfire. Something was burning. She wondered if her grandfather was down there and if he was all right.

It was dawn before he came back, long after the all clear had sounded. Frankie and Mrs Cotteslow were asleep in their own beds again and Anna and her mother were having a cup of tea in the kitchen. He looked terrible – grey and drained. There was ash in his hair and on his uniform. Anna stood up to get another cup for him and top up the teapot from the kettle.

'They were bombing the shipyards,' he said as he hung his gas mask up behind the door. 'Not much damage there, but a direct hit in Dean Street. The gas mains caught fire and the wind blew it across into Grey Street.'

Anna saw her mother's face and the tea slopped into the saucer as her hand faltered. 'The houses?' Mrs Wiseman's voice was hardly audible.

He nodded wearily. His shoulders sagged as he sat down and took the cup that Anna pushed towards him. 'Couldn't see the damage – the police and the fire brigade had it all roped off. It'll have to wait till morning.'

~~~~~~~~~~~~~~~~~

There was hardly an inch to spare on the station platform as
~~~~~~~~~~~~~~~~~

Tamar pushed her way through the crowds of parents, wives, girl-friends and children, tripping over the kit bags and suitcases piled on the platform and getting separated from Edward a dozen times before they reached the train. His family had declined to come, preferring to say goodbye to him in the privacy of their own home, tactfully leaving it to Tamar to wave him off. When they reached the train door Tamar bumped into a woman in WRAC's uniform who looked vaguely familiar. When she turned round Tamar saw that it was Elsie.

'Hello Tamar,' she said, smiling. 'Who are you seeing off? Is this your boyfriend?

'I didn't know you'd joined up!'

'Yes. I couldn't stand the factory. It was good money but it makes you feel badly. This is going to be much more fun.' Her skin was tinged with yellow and her face was haggard and ill.

'She looks awful,' Tamar said to Edward after she'd turned away to lift her kit bag into the train.

'It's the chemicals in the gunpowder when they're packing the shells. I did an article about it, but the editor wouldn't run it. Said it was unpatriotic and would jeopardise recruitment.' Edward put his arms around her. 'Promise me you won't go into munitions, Tamar? I don't want you ruining your health.'

'I promise.' She buried her face in the rough fabric of his uniform jacket. 'You will come back, won't you?' The tears were held back so tightly they made her head ache.

'Of course I will.' He kissed her forehead and his lips felt very cold.

Tamar fumbled in her pocket and took out a creased envelope. 'I want you to have this,' she said. It contained the four-leafed clover that Sadie had brought back from one of her 'jaunts' two years ago. It pained her to part with it, but she wanted Edward to have something of hers. 'It's supposed to be lucky.'

'I didn't know you were superstitious, Tamar?'

'I'm not. At least I don't think so. But I'd feel better, knowing that you had it.' Edward smiled, and tucked the envelope back into her coat. 'You keep it, if it means something to you. I've got this.' He showed her the rosary he kept in his inside pocket. 'This is all I need.' He kissed her again. 'God will take care of me. And you.'

~~~~~~~~~~~~~~~~~~

When Tamar walked up the path Anna thought that she looked bereft.

'I've just said goodbye to Edward,' Tamar said. She was almost in tears.

Anna was in the shed, painting, but she put her brushes down and gave Tamar a long hug.

'What are you going to do now?' she asked.

'I don't know. Volunteer for some kind of war work maybe. I need to do something or I'll go mad. Edward says they're going to bring in conscription and if that happens I won't get any choice. I can't think of anything worse than a munitions factory – or an army barracks.' Tamar shuddered. 'And I'm probably not posh enough for the WRAF. George says they only take girls from the top drawer. But I wouldn't mind the Wrens.'

'I'm afraid I'm going to avoid it all for as long as possible. I don't care if I have to go to jail as a conscientious objector. I'm not going into the forces to fight my own people.' She thought of Elke Haagen, who'd betrayed her, and of Klaus and Willi Becker. No. Whatever hurt she had suffered from them, she could take no part in killing them.

'I'm sorry you didn't get your scholarship.'

Anna shrugged. 'Everything's changed anyway. Do you remember that elderly man who came to the college exhibition? Walter Suzmann?'

'I remember you talking about him.'

'I went down to his studio in Shields. He's going to give me some extra lessons and write to a friend of his. There's a kind of cooperative for writers and painters on the coast in a place called Seaham. If I can persuade my mother, I might go there for a while.'

'I'll miss you.'

'We can write. I'm glad you're not marrying Edward.'

'We're going to be married sometime – just not quite yet.'

'You'd better be sure.'

'How can anyone be sure? I do love him.'
~~~~~~~~~~~~~~~~~~

'But do you love him enough?'

'Just at this moment, I love him more than anyone in the world.'

There was a pause and then Anna asked, 'Did you know that Dean Street had been bombed?'

Tamar looked startled. 'No, I didn't realise there'd been any bombing. We heard the air raid warning but we thought it was just another false alarm. Lily wouldn't go into the shelter, so we sat in the kitchen. It hardly seemed real at all. Edward told me this morning that some houses had been hit down near the dockyards, but he didn't say where. With Edward going away, I haven't been able to think of anything else.'

'My grandfather told me. He went down there this morning. Apparently the lodging houses he owns were caught in the fire storm afterwards. Do you want to go down and have look?'

It was difficult to get close. Grey Street was piled with wreckage. A fire engine was still there and a couple of firemen stood playing a hose over a smoking house front. Only the shell remained – gaping windows and smouldering rubble.

Anna sighed. 'Well, there goes any hope of persuading my grandfather to pay for art college. My mother says she doesn't know how we're going to live. That was Grandpa's pension. Apparently there's still a house in Pearson Street but it's rented out to a family who've been there a long time and don't pay much.'

'Well, at least you've still got a roof over your own head,' Tamar said, rather tartly. A group of women were standing in the middle of the street weeping and comforting each other as they looked at the burned out ruins of their homes.

'I know,' Anna said. 'I should count myself lucky.'

The bomb had fallen in Dean Street, leaving a gigantic crater in the middle of the road, which had already partly filled with water. The houses on either side had vanished as if they had never been there at all.

'I'm sure that was Ida's house,' Tamar said. She looked stricken.

A man was pulling bits of wood from the rubble and loading them onto a hand cart.

'The people who lived here,' Tamar asked, tugging his sleeve to get his attention, 'Do you know what happened to them?'

He straightened up and tipped his cap back on his head. 'They're all dead, hinny. Did you know them?'

'I knew Ida. Ida Lawrence. She was lovely.'

'Aye, she was a character. Everyone knew Ida. But mind hinny, she wouldn't know what hit her. She couldn't get to the shelter, you see, hadn't been out of bed these three months, and Mrs Young stayed with her for company. Both of them blown to smithereens.' He saw Tamar's face. 'Oh, I'm sorry pet. But don't take on. She wouldn't have lasted more than a month or so anyways. It did her a kindness. Suffering something terrible she was.'

A week after Tamar waved Edward off from the station a letter arrived addressed to Private G. W. Kennedy in a brown envelope with a crown stamped in the top corner. Tamar knew that this must be George's call up. She said nothing to Lily and quietly put the letter on the mantlepiece beside the clock for George to open when he got back from the shipyard. She knew how much Lily was dreading him going.

That evening as Tamar walked up the street after work she could hear someone screaming and, as she got nearer to the house, she could see that all the neighbours were standing on the pavement. Lily was leaning out of the parlour window throwing clothes into the garden. One of George's shirts was draped over the privet hedge, a pair of his trousers over the rose bush. George stood at the gate, bewildered, as an empty suitcase flew past his head.

'I can't do anything with her, man,' he said to Tamar. 'She told me to get out and then locked all the doors.'

'She can't bear you to go away,' Tamar said. 'She's afraid you won't come back.'

'It's too late now,' George said. 'They've sent for me to Catterick. If I don't go I'll end up in the clink.'

'Poor body,' Mrs Whale said. 'She'll be to take to Morpeth if you don't do something.'

'I think I could climb in the bathroom window if you gave me a leg up,' Tamar said. It was a tight squeeze and the window sill inside was narrow. Tamar could only just get her feet on it, scattering tooth powder and soap and a bottle of TCP all over the floor as she climbed down. Then it was only a moment to unbolt the back door and let George in.

Lily was hysterical all evening and it took the combined ministrations of Tamar and Mrs Whale and half a bottle of gin to calm her enough so that she could be put to bed. George was disgusted. 'I was supposed to be going out for a drink with the lads tonight, but she's scuppered that good and proper. Fancy making a spectacle of herself like that. Everyone in the street could hear!'

'Haven't you got any sympathy for her?'

George flushed. 'I wish she wouldn't get in such a state. I'm a grown man and she still treats me like a lad.'

There was a pause and then Tamar asked, 'Have you told Anna that you're going?'

He shook his head. 'I haven't spoken to her since I told her I'd joined up.'

'Aren't you going to see her before you go?'

'If I thought she wanted to see me, I would. But she doesn't. Got her head full of other things.'

Tamar almost exploded with exasperation. 'You're both so obstinate and stupid! Why can't you just be friends?' She jumped up. 'I'm going to bed. Don't go tomorrow without waking me, will you?'

Later, lying in bed, she could hear the strains of Pagliacci floating up the stairs. George was playing the gramophone. She lifted her head off the pillow. If she listened carefully she could hear Gigli's voice lamenting the agonies of love.

~~~~~~~~~~~~~~~~~~

Anna was waiting on the corner of the coast road the following morning when George came up on his motor bike. He slowed and stopped, pushing his goggles up to the top of his head.

'Mrs Whale told me you were going. How's Lily?'

'OK this morning. She was past herself last night.'
~~~~~~~~~~~~~~~~~~

'I couldn't let you go without seeing you.'

'Hop on,' George jerked his head towards the pillion seat. His suitcase was in the side car. 'I'll take you down to Shields.'

He parked the bike on the quay and they wandered down to the studio. A fishing boat had just come in and the gulls were screaming over their heads. It was so noisy they could hardly hear each other speak. 'Where will they send you?' Anna asked.

He shrugged. 'Down south probably. Maybe London.'

'That would be good. You might finally get to Covent Garden.'

He smiled wryly. 'It doesn't seem such a good deal just at the moment. What about you? Tamar says you might go to Seaham.'

'I've got a year before I can go to the Slade, so I need to study quite hard.' She paused and then asked, 'Why are you so jealous of what I do?'

'I suppose because I know it's going to take you away from me and then I kick myself and think, what would a talented girl like that want with an ordinary bloke like me anyway? There's no logic to it Anna. It's just feelings and I can never get them straight.'

Anna nodded. 'Mine are so confused I don't know what I feel about anything anymore. All I know is, I have to paint – it doesn't matter if I'm not good enough in the end – I have to try.'

'When I was listening to Gigli last night, I thought, if I could sing like that bloke there's no way I'd be in a shipyard or joining the army. But I can't, so it's no use. But it is for you. You've got a gift and you've got to do something with it. I just wish,' he paused and Anna saw the pain flicker across his face, 'I just wish there was room in your life for me as well.'

She put her hand on his arm before she could stop herself. Why she didn't really know, a compassionate impulse perhaps? But as soon as she had done it she knew that the gesture was open to misinterpretation. 'You're a lovely, lovely man, George. Write to me will you? Promise? We mustn't lose touch.' She kissed him on the cheek and felt him flinch. As they moved apart he caught her hands. 'Don't play with me Anna. It means far too much.'

'Why can't we just be friends, George?'

'Because I want to marry you.'

'I can't see myself ever getting married. A husband would want me to have children and expect me to give up painting. If I ever married, my husband would have to accept that painting was my life.'

'But you will let me love you?'

'Everyone needs to be loved George.' Anna slipped her hands out of his and ran up the studio steps and through the door. As soon as she saw Walter standing at the window she burst into tears and he came and put his arms around her and allowed her to cry on his shoulder. His tweed jacket smelt of tobacco and carbolic soap and wood smoke. 'Is that your boyfriend?' he asked.

'No. Just a friend. He loves me but I can't love him back.'

'Ah. That is an impediment.'

Anna dried her tears on a tea towel. 'Why do men always want marriage? And commitment? I don't want to do without love and passion, but if I want to paint I have to be single minded. Does that sound selfish?'

'Not at all. I had a wife once. We were very badly suited. And then when I came to England she decided she would stay in Berlin and move in with another man. Since then I have found that it is much more restful to be by oneself.'

'Don't you ever get lonely?'

'It is better to be lonely than with the wrong person.'

Anna looked out of the window, but George had gone. 'I'm very fond of him,' she said.

Walter chuckled. 'That is such a damning phrase.' He picked up his brush again. 'Concentrate on art. Canvases are less troublesome than people.'

About a month after George's departure there was a solitary letter waiting for Tamar when she got home from Pergavie's after work with Anna. Now that Edward and George had gone and Anna was working in Walter's studio she often called at the shop to walk home with Tamar. It was like old times, when they were both at school.

The letter lay on the kitchen table with a note from Lily saying she'd gone up to the club and Tamar's tea was in the oven. Tamar picked it up with a quickening pulse anticipating Edward's handwriting, but it had a typewritten address. Disappointed, she looked at the solicitor's crest on the back of the envelope and hesitated.

'Go on,' Anna said. 'It looks important.'

Tamar opened it slowly. The letterhead was from a firm called Black and Mellor in North Shields. *Dear Madam*, it began. *As you may already know, our client Mrs Ida Lawrence of number 14, Dean Street, was reported missing presumed killed in a recent air raid. Due to the distressing paucity of mortal remains, it has been necessary for a coroner to determine the proof of Mrs Lawrence's demise but, subsequent to the inquest, a death certificate has now been issued. Under the terms of her will, made on the 16th March, 1939, you are her sole beneficiary. Until all bills have been paid and the will submitted for probate, it is not possible to give an exact figure for the residue of her estate but we do not anticipate it being less than three hundred pounds. If you could call at our office at your convenience, you may inspect the will and we will attempt to answer any queries you may have.*

'Goodness,' Anna said, reading over her shoulder. 'You're rich, Tamar.'

'I can hardly believe it. Why should Ida leave her money to me? I wasn't even that nice to her. I hardly ever used to see her after she moved out.'

'She was very fond of you,' Anna said. 'Anyone could see that. But I would never have thought she'd have money – not this much.'

Tamar thought about it. Three hundred pounds! It was enough to put a deposit down on a small house. Could she? But then she thought of the devastation she and Anna had witnessed. There was no security in bricks and mortar any more. But – and Tamar experienced a sudden lift of the heart at the realisation – perhaps she could achieve her dreams now, she could train for a profession once the war was over, if she put it in a savings bank. Bless you, Ida, she thought. This was her future, the future that had been denied. Tamar could hardly believe it.

Anna was looking at her with an odd expression on her face.

'Tamar, you wouldn't consider lending me some of it would you? Just for a couple of years, for my college fees? I'd pay you back just as soon as I was earning – I promise.'

Tamar was stricken. Here was her future security in the palm of her hand – the means to achieve her dreams and Anna was asking her for it. But then, immediately, she was flooded with guilt. How could she refuse to help her best friend whose own hopes had been so cruelly dashed. The same bomb that had brought her this good fortune had deprived Anna of hers.

Anna was watching her face. 'I'm sorry, Tamar,' she said quickly. 'Forget I ever asked. I shouldn't have said anything. It wouldn't be right. This is your money for your future. You're right, I'm selfish – I only think of myself.'

Tamar felt herself flushing crimson to think that her feelings had been so transparent. 'Anna, don't be silly, of course I can lend you something.'

Anna gave her a hug. 'I'm not going to take your money, so there. We've got to stand on our own feet now.'

'But it wouldn't be fair, that I can do what I want and you can't.'

'Tamar, you once told me that I had everything and you were right. I've got parents, grandparents and a home to go to. You've got none of these things. I couldn't take your money, even as a loan.' She picked up her folder and her coat. Anna's eyes were very bright. 'I'll see you tomorrow. We'll go to the cinema or something to celebrate your windfall.'

After the door had banged shut behind her, Tamar re-read the letter. There was less excitement now. What would Lily say when she told her? Would she put the rent up now that Tamar had Ida's money? And there was bound to be an atmosphere between her and Anna. Things would never be the same again.

~~~~~~~~~~~~~~~~~~

Anna lay awake for hours after she had gone to bed thinking about the future. She must have been mad to ask Tamar for money like that. Tactless, insensitive, selfish, avaricious. She felt herself flush with shame at the thought of what she had done.
~~~~~~~~~~~~~~~~~~

But she had got to find money somehow. Anna felt her dreams slipping away from her. It was like trying to walk in quicksand. Even her goals were shifting in front of her. The Slade was now in temporary and much reduced accommodation in Oxford and, since her interview with Professor de Gris, simply didn't seem as wonderful as she had imagined it would be. But they had accepted her and there were few alternatives. The Royal Academy was moving out of London – even King Edward's College was talking about evacuation to a country estate in Northumberland. All the younger tutors were expecting to be called up – some had already volunteered. The war had changed every perspective, made everything uncertain.

To make things even more complicated, since her grandfather's houses had been bombed it was no longer just a question of acquiring an education in art, but of scraping a living. What was she to do? Anna thought about what her mother had said about war work, that even women would be conscripted into men's jobs. Now that Grandpa's income had been so reduced, she could no longer expect him to keep her. There had been a terse conversation over dinner about 'cutting back', and her mother had talked about leaving Frankie with his grandparents two days a week to work in an office organising evacuees and the issue of ration books. No one had said anything to Anna, but she knew that she would be expected to 'do her bit' as her grandfather put it.

But what could she do that wouldn't interfere with painting? She held her hands up in front of her face in the darkness and felt her long muscular fingers, calloused from holding pencils and brushes, and she shivered. Not the armed forces, or a weapons factory, with its deadly machines. Not shells or any other agent of destruction. That was where they'd send her. But then she thought of a poster she'd seen a couple of days earlier on a bill board outside the labour exchange. She closed her eyes and willed herself to visualise the picture. It showed an airman falling to earth under a parachute and in the foreground a girl rather like herself folding silk and pushing it into a pack. Could she work in a parachute factory? And if what John Cornell had said about night shifts was correct, she might be able to go to Walter's during the day and then come home and have a few hours sleep before reporting for duty again.

With a pounding heart, Anna realised that if she worked, not only could she earn her keep, she might also be able to save enough money for her first year at the Slade. She found herself smiling in the dark at the thought that, in spite of war and family misfortune, the future might once more be under her control.

Several streets away Tamar was also awake. The scenes she'd witnessed in Dean Street kept recurring in her mind, however hard she tried to blot them out. War was a terrible thing. Until she'd seen that devastation it somehow hadn't occurred to her that what was happening so many hundreds of miles away in Europe could affect her life here so profoundly. She remembered what Charlie had said –- 'That's Germany just over the water there, pet . . . the Boche'll be marching their jackboots up Northumberland street before you know it.' Tamar had been unable to imagine it a few months ago, but now it seemed perfectly possible. And there were other things to think of. The memory of Elsie's yellow eyes and skin, her gaunt face, haunted Tamar. She was going to have to take some kind of step to prevent herself from sharing Elsie's fate. What should she do? The thought of leaving Lily's made Tamar feel sick with apprehension. She had been here for more than three years now and it was the nearest thing to home she had. How could she do anything that might mean she had to move again, just as she'd become settled? Then she thought about conscription – if *that* happened she would have no choice.

But if she volunteered for some kind of war job, what effect would it have on the career she dreamt of? Last week at the WEA she'd been told that she could study for her school certificate by correspondence course. Tamar had intended to send off for it straight away. Once she got her certificate, with Ida's money for her training, everything she'd dreamt of would be within her grasp. Tamar sighed. It was no use planning any kind of future while the world around was so uncertain. War had changed everyone's expectations. 'If a bomb fell here, I could be dead tomorrow,' Tamar thought. The bomb that killed Ida could just as easily have fallen on her and Lily sitting in the kitchen.

Lily had been very nice about Tamar's windfall, and had refused to take any more money from her for the room. 'You deserve a stroke of luck,' she'd said. 'You keep it hinny!' Tamar thought Lily must be struggling a little financially without George's wages coming in. The big double room was still not let and Mr Cole was mysteriously talking of moving to Wallsend. But Lily didn't seem bothered by money worries at all. She was still grieving for George. His photo had been turned to the wall and every last vestige of his clothes and belongings – including the gramophone – packed in boxes and stacked in the cupboard under the stairs. Tamar wondered how Lily would manage completely on her own, once they had all left.

Lily had become a different person since Sadie had died. She was going out less and less in the evenings and had stopped singing around the house. Every now and then she would stop what she was doing and say, 'Oh, I do miss your Mam!' And she would stand and sigh and look gloomily out of the window for a few moments before lighting another cigarette, blowing the smoke up towards her eyebrows out of the corners of her mouth before carrying on. Tamar knew how she felt. All the fun seemed to have gone out of things without Sadie and the house was quiet and empty. Tamar felt Sadie's absence like a bad stomach ache. Not for the first time in the past month she wondered what Sadie would have advised her to do now.

In some ways it was exciting – a whole new series of opportunities – but it would mean leaving behind everything familiar and dear. Tamar sighed again. This was war. There was no security anymore. She slipped her hand under the pillow where Edward's first letter lay, already tattered from re-reading. She knew it by heart now – *'My own darling Tamar,'* it began. *'How I miss you and long for you.'* Her first love letter. Now she longed for him to write again. Feared for his safety. If they sent him abroad . . . There was heavy fighting in France, which Edward was itching to be in the thick of.

Gradually, lying in the darkness, Tamar made up her mind. Not all her ambitions need be postponed. She would send off for the correspondence course as soon as she could. With Edward away she would have plenty of time to study through the long dark nights of the black out. Tomorrow she would go down to Black and Mellor and arrange to have her legacy put into a bank account to be used after the war. And she would lend Anna some of it – she would find a way to persuade her to accept. It was unfair that Anna shouldn't have her chances too. Then she would go down to the labour exchange and join the queue for recruitment.

At breakfast on Friday morning Tamar thought Lily was going to cry.

'Not you too, hinny. Not you too! You're only a bairn.'

Tamar felt awful. She hadn't expected Lily to be so upset. 'I'm sorry. But if I don't volunteer, they'll draft me into something I don't want to do. And at least if I get into the Wrens, I'll still be here for quite a while.' It was hard. Tamar put her arms around Lily's bony body and hugged her. 'I don't want to go away, but I don't think I've got a choice.'

Anna was waiting for her outside the labour exchange. 'Are you still going to do it?'

Tamar nodded. 'What about you?'

Anna inclined her head towards the poster on the wall and the happy looking girl in head scarf and overalls surrounded by billowing silk – 'That's me. Providing I can get in. If there aren't any vacancies I'm frightened they'll try to make me do something else.'

Once inside the door there were separate sections for the armed forces and the factories. Tamar stood in a line of girls under a stern looking poster that showed four young women in attractive uniforms gazing resolutely into the future, admonished by the words 'For your country's sake today – For your own sake tomorrow.'

The woman at the forces recruitment desk was wearing an expensive tweed suit and had her hair cropped fashionably short. She was very brusque, asking Tamar's name and age without looking up. When Tamar replied she lifted her head and said, 'I'm afraid the only service that accepts girls under eighteen is the land army.'

'Oh.' Tamar hadn't been aware of this.

'Do you know anything about animals?'

'Not really. But I like the country.'

'Then it will have to do. Have you any preferences for a placement? Not that we can guarantee one, of course.' She had an accent just like Sadie.

Tamar hesitated. She had no idea what to ask for and thought for one moment of shutting her eyes and sticking a pin in the map that hung on the wall behind the desk. There was a calendar hanging beside it with a picture that reminded her of the one on Anna's bedroom wall. Mountains and lakes and clear, blue sky. It looked peaceful and utterly beautiful. 'Is that England?' Tamar asked.

The woman turned her head. 'Yes. That's Cumberland. The Lake District.'

'Then that's where I'd like to be posted.' It seemed as reasonable a way to choose as any.

The woman seemed surprised. 'Good heavens! No one wants to go there; there's no night life and the weather isn't very good.' She frowned doubtfully. 'Do you really?'

Tamar nodded.

'You know of course that you won't get the same concessions as you would if you joined the WAAF's or the WRNS?'

Tamar didn't. 'What does that mean?'

'The armed services get subsidised travel for leave, and extra clothing allowances. In the land army you won't even be able to join the NAAFI. It seems unfair, but that's the way it is I'm afraid.'

The information meant very little to Tamar. She shrugged. 'I'd still like to join.'

'Well, we'll see what we can do. You'll have to have a medical of course, but it's usually a formality. If that's satisfactory you'll be hearing from us shortly.' The woman folded up the papers and dismissed Tamar with a twitch of the head.

CHAPTER FOURTEEN

It seemed strange going to work just when everyone else was going home. After changing into her stiff new overalls, Anna joined the stream of chattering women queueing up to push their cards into the punching machine and place them in the alphabetical rack. Anna shared her slot with a Watson, two Wilsons and a Warmley.

'Weissmann, that sounds like a German name.' A tall fair girl was peering over Anna's shoulder as she put her own card into the rack.

'Yes, it is.'

'I'm surprised they let you in here, then.'

'What do you mean?' Anna sounded more aggressive than she'd intended.

'There's no need to take offence! I only meant it as a joke. Only, you know – you could wreak havoc on the RAF, couldn't you?'

Anna ignored her and walked straight past into the packing room to report to the supervisor. There were two other new girls who had to be shown how to pack the chutes and as Anna stood waiting, the tall fair girl came in to join them.

'Tonight,' the supervisor said, 'you're only going to practise. You must concentrate very carefully. Remember, someone's life depends on what you do.'

After they'd put on their cotton gloves – to prevent their nails snagging the silk, the supervisor explained – she showed them how to spread the material on the packing table and fold it carefully into the canvas satchel so that when the release cord was pulled it would billow out in exactly the right way. There seemed to be an awful lot of material, but it was amazing how the silk folded into so small a space.

Anna, shown once, got it right first time and had to suffer the agonies of doing it again and again, only to have the supervisor pull it out for yet another practice run.

Around midnight Anna's eyelids began to droop in spite of the sleep she had attempted in the afternoon. She was glad when the canteen bell was rung and they all trooped upstairs for a hot meal. The women all seemed to know each other or be in friendly groups already and Anna found herself alone at the end of a table occupied by five other women of varying ages who laughed and chattered without addressing a single word to her for the whole of the meal. It felt odd, like the first day at school all over again, except that this time there was no Tamar. The tall fair girl was sitting at another table and Anna saw her point across and then whisper something to the girls she was with. The rest of the night was long, tedious and cold. How she was going to survive the boredom and the endless repetitions, Anna didn't know. She was tireder than she could have thought possible when it was time to push her card into the slot and wheel her cycle out of the factory gate. It was a grey miserable winter morning, with the wind coming north east across the sea from Norway.

Walter had the stove going full blast when she got to the studio. He had a bucket of coal he'd picked up off the beach and the sides of the stove were almost transparent with heat. He made Anna a mug of tea while she warmed her hands. 'I'm so tired,' she said. 'If you don't mind, I think I'll have a rest and work this afternoon.' She curled up on Walter's bed and was instantly asleep.

Walter woke her up at four with a mug of tea. 'I tried to wake you earlier, but you kept going back to sleep. You must have been exhausted.'

Anna could have cried with frustration. What had happened to her plan of working all night and having a few hours in the day to paint? There was only time to cycle home for some breakfast and a change of clothes and then back to the factory for her shift.

But the second night it was easier and on the third morning, she had enough energy to go to the station to wave Tamar off to the farm training school where she was being sent.

'I hope it's more interesting than what I'm doing – I'm just consoling myself with the thought of the pay packet at the end of the week.'

'I'm terrified,' Tamar said. Anna thought she looked pale and nervous as she leaned out of the carriage door. 'Supposing I'm no good at it? I've never had anything to do with animals in my life! I must have been mad to sign up for it.'

'Well, they can always send you back. Have you heard from Edward again?'

'Yes, he's at a training camp somewhere down south. He's not allowed to tell me directly, but I think it's near Dorchester because he keeps talking about Thomas Hardy. He says they might be allowed home for Easter.'

'I had a letter from George. He says they've found out he's a skilled worker and he's being transferred to another section once he's finished square bashing. Apparently it's very boring and he doesn't much like having to share a barracks. He's in a hut with twenty other blokes and they're rather a rough lot.'

'Poor George.'

The whistle blew and the guard began to wave his flag.

'Bye Tamar. Don't forget to write.'

'I won't. Bye Anna.' Tamar blew a kiss and waved as the train jerked away.

Soon Anna could glimpse only the red light of the guard's van disappearing through the steam and the smoke. God knows when I'll see her again, Anna thought. She felt unexpectedly bleak.

~~~~~~~~~~~~~~~~~~

Tamar settled herself in the carriage as the houses on either side of the track began to rush away from her with gathering speed. She was astonished to realise that this was the first time she'd been on a train since she'd come to Newcastle with her mother four years earlier. It seemed odd to be travelling without Sadie. She took her new watch carefully out of her pocket and noted the time. Last night the staff at Pergavie's had given her a leaving party in the canteen after the shop closed and Mr Per-
~~~~~~~~~~~~~~~~~~

gavie had presented her with this beautiful pocket watch, like a man's only more delicate. They'd engraved her name and the date on the inside of the case. 'We knew you wouldn't be able to wear a wrist watch,' Miss Timms had said. 'And we wanted to give you something useful that you could remember us by.' Tamar had been touched by their demonstrations of regret. Even Miss Sinclair had come to shake her hand and say that she hoped Tamar would call in when she came home on leave and 'let us know how you're doing'.

The letter Tamar had received instructed her to change at Carlisle station and take the Penrith train. She was relieved to find that Carlisle was only a small station and she simply had to cross from one side of the platform to the other to wait for her connection. There was a bitter northerly wind blowing through the station and Tamar turned her back to keep the smoke from blowing into her eyes. Facing south along the platform she could see across the concourse to where a red-haired girl was standing under the clock, gazing intently up at the departures board. She looked lost. Tamar watched her saying something to a porter and then saw him gesticulating in the direction of the platform. He stooped to pick up her case, which was large and, from the lop-sided way he was carrying it, quite heavy. He dumped it on the platform near to where Tamar was standing and the girl gave him a tip. There was something familiar about the tall figure with the pale, translucent skin and shy, rather frightened-looking face. The girl's eye caught Tamar's and for a moment they both stared at each other and then the girl smiled tentatively. It was Holly Pergavie.

'You don't know how good it is to see a familiar face.' She sounded breathless with relief.

'Are you going to Newton Rigg too?' There were several other girls on the platform and Tamar was sure they were all bound, like herself, for the land army training school.

Holly nodded. 'Please don't laugh at me, but this is the first time I've ever been away from home on my own.' Tamar moved closer to catch her words against the background clamour of guard's whistles, the clash of closing doors and an engine discharging steam on the other platform. 'I wish they hadn't taken down all the station name signs!' she was saying. 'I've already been on the wrong train twice. The first one was going to Preston and the second one didn't stop at Penrith, so now I have to go all the way back again!' She was laughing, but seemed also on the verge of tears.

At Penrith station they had to climb into the back of a Bedford lorry for the rest of the journey. Tamar was thankful that she'd put on sensible woollen stockings, not just because of the primitive wooden seating in the truck, but because the canvas top was open at the back and let in a cold and bitter wind. She wondered how Holly, whose long legs were elegantly encased in silk, was going to survive in her immaculate city clothes. The driver of the truck – a lance corporal, had already drawn attention to Holly's suitcase and matching leather dressing case when he loaded their luggage into the truck after them.

'Who's this swanky lot belong to then?'

'They're mine,' Holly said. She looked embarrassed. Some of the other girls started laughing.

'You're not going on a bleedin' cruise, you know,' one of them said. She was a big, raw-boned girl with peroxide hair. There were two girls with her, all with strange accents that Tamar couldn't place. As she listened to them making ribald comments to the driver and his companion, she hoped not to have to spend much time with them.

Through the canvas flaps Tamar could see stone walls and rough fields and beyond them, a craggy ridge capped with snow. She nudged Holly. 'Look. Mountains!'

'Bleedin' heck!' the blonde girl said, poking her head out. 'This is the back of beyond. I wish I'd joined the friggin' army.'

'They wouldn't have you, Margie,' one of the others said. 'That's why you're here.'

When they climbed out of the lorry, a woman with a clip board was waiting for them. Tamar and Holly gave her their names and she waved them towards a Nissen hut.

'Number three. Sort yourselves out. Tea's in the recreation block at six.'

'It doesn't look much like a farm,' Holly said looking at the rows of Nissen huts as she dragged her heavy case along the gravel path. When she'd packed it she obviously hadn't contemplated the possibility that she might have to carry it herself.

'It's a farm school,' Tamar said. 'So maybe they keep the animals somewhere else. I expect we'll find out tomorrow.' She paused for a moment to look up at the vast amphitheatre of sky encircled by hills and sniff the unfamiliar air. It smelled of wood-smoke and an earthy, animal smell that reminded her of the compost heap on the allotments. It was very quiet as if the whole landscape was listening.

There were twelve double bunks in the hut, most already occupied by earlier arrivals. Tamar was appalled to discover that the remaining empty beds were right next to Margie and her friends. There was a locker and a cupboard beside each pair of bunks which had to be shared, but they provided only limited space for clothes and possessions.

Tamar took the photograph of Edward out of her case and put it on the bedside locker. He looked incredibly handsome in his uniform with those large, dark eyes smiling at her from under the peak of his cap.

'Is that your boy friend?' Holly asked.

Tamar nodded. 'He's in the press corps.' She was conscious of Margie eavesdropping from the other bunks and it felt rather glamorous to have a fiancé in the forces. She turned back to deal with the rest of her belongings and was astonished as she looked at the cashmere jumpers and skirts that Holly was unpacking. How could anyone have so many expensive and totally unsuitable clothes? When she'd finished there wasn't a lot of room left for Tamar's own meagre wardrobe, but, she thought with a sigh, at least her clothes were clean and sensible. They tucked their suitcases under the bunk. Holly's dressing case with its silver initials sat at the back of the cupboard, blatantly out of place.

'I probably shouldn't have brought it,' Holly said, biting her lip. 'But I really didn't know . . . The letter said Sunday clothes and toiletries.' She looked suspiciously as if she might cry again.

'I'm sure you'll get a chance to wear some of them while we're here. Come on. We've got to go and collect our uniforms.'

The hut next to the canteen contained boxes and boxes of clothing in different sizes. There were corduroy trousers which looked a bit like jodhpurs, an aertex shirt and a thin looking jumper but no boots. 'Your shoes will have to do for the moment,' the woman said. She looked harassed. 'No overcoats either, but we should be getting them in the next couple of weeks.'

'Are we allowed to wear our own?' Tamar asked.

'I shouldn't think so,' the woman replied sarcastically. 'This is the land *army* after all!'

Tamar noticed that Holly went off to the shower block to change rather than take her clothes off in front of the other girls. Tamar knew how she felt, but was practised in undressing without revealing a great deal. The uniform was stiff and uncomfortable. She hoped it would be better once it had been worn in. Holly obviously thought the same. 'These trousers are so scratchy,' she said when she came back.

'They're not very warm either.' Tamar felt cold even in the Nissen hut. What would it be like outside? The clothes she'd just been issued seemed no more weather-proof than the ones she'd just taken off. 'I'm going to keep my woollen stockings on underneath, whatever we're told.'

'There's no heating in here,' Holly said. She looked thoroughly miserable. 'Have you noticed? It'll be freezing at night.'

Tamar looked at the two thin grey blankets folded on the bunk and thought of the down quilt on her bed at Lily's. An unfamiliar wave of something she vaguely recognised as home-sickness came over her. There were tears in Holly's eyes too. 'Come on,' Tamar said. 'We're here to fight a war, not have a holiday. Let's go and find the canteen. Things'll be better when we've had something to eat.'

Curled up in her bunk after tea, Tamar wriggled her cold toes inside two pairs of socks and began a letter to Edward. '*I'm writing this in bed because it's the only warm place. Spartan's not the word. And the smell! Apparently some of the girls from the previous intake have been spreading manure on the fields. They told us you get covered in cow muck and you just have to put up with it because there's only one clean uniform a week. Hopefully they'll have finished by the time we're let out. We've got two weeks of lectures and practical lessons on how to milk cows and harness a horse before they send us out onto the farms. It's not at all how I imagined. Just at the moment I'm not sure I've made the right decision at all. I wish I was at home.'* Tamar looked at what she'd just written. At tea, one of the girls had asked 'Where d'you come from?' And Tamar had unhesitatingly replied, 'North Shields'. How odd it was to have somewhere she could call home.

Anna, in the hall putting on her coat to go down to the studio, overheard her mother and her grandmother talking in the kitchen. Mrs Cotteslow's querulous voice was saying; 'Aren't you worried about the time she's spending with that man down at the quay? She's never home. And where's she sleeping? You ask her that!'

'It's all perfectly innocent mother. He's middle aged, older than me. You know how much Anna misses her father.'

Anna pulled a face. Was that how her mother saw her relationship with Walter? As a replacement father figure? She made it sound very neat, but Anna knew it wasn't exactly like that at all. There was an attraction between her and Walter, she could feel it. Something that was lacking between her and George. They could paint all day in silence and it felt perfectly natural, but then there would be that little flicker of electricity when their eyes met, or their hands touched accidentally as they reached for a brush or a tube of paint. She liked being with Walter. He allowed her space to be herself, and didn't demand anything of her.

'You're far too trusting, Barbara,' Mrs Cotteslow was saying. 'You don't want "you know what" to happen, do you?'

'For heaven's sake! She's only there during the day.'

'What's that got to do with it? Anything you can do at night you can do in the day! You don't want her following your example, do you?'

'There's no need to drag that up mother, after all these years.'

'She's there more time than she's here. People are talkin', you know. They'll say she's livin' over the brush. And with a German.'

'Don't be ridiculous mother!' There was a sharp silence. Then

Mrs Wiseman said, 'I trust my daughter. Anna's got other ambitions than romance.'

'We trusted you and look where that got us!'

Something inside Anna snapped. She had never hated her grandmother so much as she did at that moment. How could her mother put up with it? She walked into the kitchen. 'You can't trust Grandpa either, Gran. He's had a mistress down in Shields for years. Everyone knows that.' It was regretted as soon as said, but Anna knew it was too late.

'Go and wash your mouth out, our Anne, telling filthy lies like that!'

'No more filthy than the things you were saying about me and Walter.'

'Ungrateful girl. After all we've done for you . . .'

'I'm tired of being grateful Gran. As soon as I can get lodgings, I'm moving out.' She heard her mother begin to protest. 'Don't worry Mum. I'm not going far. I think Lily's got a spare room. At least these days I can pay my own way.'

The following afternoon after lunch, the land army trainees were all marched off to a shed where three very innocent looking cows had been lined up in the stalls for them to practise on.

'Now, just tuck yourself in,' the foreman said, sitting down on a three legged stool and putting the bucket between his feet. He laid his head against the cow's flank. Tamar noticed with a shudder of revulsion that it had manure and straw caked to its skin where it had been lying down in the stall. The foreman didn't seem to notice. 'Just take the teats in your fingers like this,' he rolled his first two fingers and thumb around the fleshy protuberances, 'and pull down and squeeze at the same time.' He pulled and squeezed and the milk sang into the bucket. 'Now it's your turn.' He stood up and handed the bucket to Margie.

'That's milk?' she said looking down into it. Tamar saw her face change colour. 'I'm never going to drink another bleedin' drop.' She sat on the stool trying not to touch the animal and gingerly put her fingers on its udder. She recoiled immediately.

'Uggh. They feel horrible.'

The foreman gave a groan of exasperation. 'This is a farm,' he said. 'Not bloody Butlins. You're all goin' to have to toughen up. Anyone that doesn't want to work with animals had better leave now.'

'You!' he said pointing at Tamar.

She said nothing but her mouth was set in a determined line. She sat down and grasped the teats in her fingers and pulled. Nothing happened.

'Not so hard! Gently.'

At the second go a small trickle of milk dripped into the bucket and as she persevered a steady stream began to pulse from her fingers. There were beads of sweat on her forehead. But there was something quite comforting about the cow's warm flank. She could hear its heart beating.

Only three girls managed to get any milk out of the cows and the foreman was scathing. 'Call yourselves land girls! There's not a ten year old child this side of the Pennines that isn't more useful on a farm than you lot.'

Before they could recover from the ordeal by cow, they were taken down to the stables where the foreman opened a door and the most enormous horse emerged and stood patiently, blinking at the light. Tamar had fed crusts to the coalman's horse in Heaton street, but she'd never seen one this big. 'This is old Dobbin here,' the foreman said, clapping him on the side of the neck. 'He's a Clydesdale and weighs over a ton. But he's as gentle as a babby so long as you treat him right. You're all going to have a go at putting his bridle on and then afterwards Joss will take you into the tack room and show you what to do with the harnesses.'

The knack was to make Dobbin lower his head so you could slip the bridle over his ears and then pop the bit between his enormous yellow teeth. Tamar had three goes, but every time she reached up with the bridle, he lifted his head beyond her reach and shook his mane contrarily, curling his lip and looking at her with a rather vindictive eye. 'He knows just what he's doing,' Tamar said as she gave the bridle to Holly. 'He's teasing me.'

But Holly didn't have any trouble at all. She talked to him and stroked his nose and he obediently put his head down to let her slip on the leather band and then he snaffled up the bit from the palm of her hand without needing to be coaxed at all.

'Have you done this before?' the foreman asked.

Holly shook her head. 'I used to ride the ponies on the beach when I was little. I always wanted a horse of my own, but I've never had one.'

'Well, aren't you the deprived child then!' Margie said. There was a spiteful edge to her voice. Holly flushed, but she said nothing.

'Don't let it get to you,' Tamar murmured as they walked back to the canteen. 'You were amazing with that horse.'

'I really like the country,' Holly said. 'And the animals. If only the human beings were as nice!'

~~~~~~~~~~~~~~~~~~

Anna decided not to lodge with Lily, but took a room in Nelson Street near the studio. It was small and ugly and there was an outside toilet, but she knew she would be spending very little time in it. A few hours to sleep in the afternoon. On her nights off she went home to the Cotteslows to be fed and pampered. Both her grandparents treated her like an unexploded bomb and Anna felt slightly guilty because she sensed that her outburst had made things much more difficult for her mother.

Anna found that she missed Tamar and George far more than she'd expected. There was no one to discuss things with, no one to go out with. But working at night meant that there were actually very few evenings left to fill. She had arranged her shifts so that she could still go to John Cornell's life drawing class on Wednesday evenings. It was the part of her studies that she found most difficult. The human form somehow resisted representation and as soon as she pencilled in the lines, the life went out of them.

One of the models, a woman in her forties, came regularly, sitting with peculiar patience throughout the two hour session, adjusting her pose when asked and somehow filling the room with an energy that animated Anna's pencil in a new way. Her name was Alicia and she had thin, muscular arms, and sinews
~~~~~~~~~~~~~~~~~~

that stood out like hawsers in her neck and wrists. Her breasts hung down limply and her soft stomach was a slight convexity between prominent hip bones that stretched the skin tight over her pelvis. She had white, heavy thighs and bony knees and feet.

But it was her face that fascinated Anna most. A strong, straight nose, high cheekbones and forehead framing deeply-set grey eyes fringed with thick, dark lashes. Her eyebrows were also thick, meeting in the middle. They should have overbalanced the face, making it top-heavy, but they didn't. It was a long face, with deep grooves running from the nose to the corners of the mouth, which was large and loose, putting her whole face in motion when she spoke or laughed. And the jaw bone was strong and angular, a perfect counterpoise for the straight, square cut of her cropped grey hair, curving from the jaw line up and back to the exact point where the spine entered the skull. Alicia's expression was bold, slightly sardonic. It was a 'what the hell are you staring at me like that for?' look. But sometimes when she caught Anna's eye in class, she would curl her lips into a faint smile and sometimes they would exchange a word or two in the corridor or on the stairs before they went in opposite directions in the street.

One evening after Alicia had dressed behind the screen and the class were packing up their pencils and folders, she paused as she passed Anna's easel to look at the drawing still pinned to it. 'Not bad,' she said with a little nod. 'Not bad at all.'

'Thanks!' Anna said, with as much sarcastic inflexion as she could.

Alicia grinned. 'I've been doing this for a long time. I know drawing when I see it. You've got talent. I hope you're not going to let it go to waste.'

Anna just smiled and shrugged, not knowing what to say.

'You ought to go and study in London. There's no one up here who can teach you anything.'

'I went for a scholarship at the Slade,' Anna said. 'They told me to go home and have babies instead!' She was surprised how angry she sounded.

Alicia helped Anna tie up her folder. 'Are you meeting someone, or have you time for a coffee before you go home?'

Alicia lived in a top floor flat two streets away from the college.

It was the most amazing room Anna had ever seen. Two grossly obese cats were stretched out in front of the gas fire and barely opened an eye as she tiptoed past them. The walls were covered in theatre posters – Gaslight, Uncle Vanya, Lady Windermere's Fan, several Shakespeare productions as well as more obscure plays Anna had never heard of. In between there were framed programmes, signed in faded ink. On every flat surface in the room were stacks of books and records, lamps of coloured glass, bronze women in flowing dresses, porcelain bowls filled with an assortment of gloves and keys and envelopes. There were books on the floor, armchairs whose innards had prolapsed onto the carpet, and a long leather settle with crocheted rugs thrown over to hide the holes.

Anna was looking at a picture of a tiger staring malevolently back at her with lantern eyes when Alicia came back with two mugs and a plate of biscuits. 'I was an actress,' she explained, nodding towards the wall of posters. 'But now I teach.' Alicia moved a cat aside with her foot in order to sit down beside the fire, motioning Anna to do the same.

'I hope you aren't going to be put off by one rejection,' she said. 'There are other places as good as the Slade – some would say better!'

Anna shook her head thoughtfully. 'They've offered me a fee-paying place next year. But they didn't offer me a scholarship. I suppose my hopes had been raised too high.'

Alicia nodded agreement. 'John Cornell's a good tutor, but he does tend to fall into the trap of having star pupils. There are drawbacks to being one of his favourites. And have you ever thought how it must feel to be one of the others? They get much less time and attention than you do.'

'I hadn't thought about it like that. It's just been so wonderful to find someone who was prepared to encourage me. My family don't. They just assume that wanting to paint is some kind of craze I'll grow out of. I have to fight every inch of the way. The idea that I might have the ability to do it is never considered. It's very unfair.'

'And if you have that special gift? What will you do? Because it's not enough to have talent. It'll be harder for you than it would be if you were a man. As a woman you'll have to abandon any notion of a conventional life with conventional relationships. Can you do that?'

Anna thought hard. 'I think so.'

'It's very difficult to marry and have a career, particularly in the arts.'

'I can't imagine myself ever marrying. The fact is that I'm not very comfortable with men. And *babies*!' Anna thought of Frankie with his sticky fingers and permanently runny nose, smelling of stale milk and wet nappies. 'Babies don't appeal to me at all! But I don't want to give up the idea of love and spend my life alone.'

Alicia laughed. 'I felt like that too! Fortunately there are other relationships.' She pointed to a woman's photograph on the mantelpiece – a pretty, slim woman in a cloche hat. 'I used to live with my friend Jo, until she died of cancer last year. We were in repertory together. Travelled everywhere. We were inseparable.'

'You must miss her,' Anna said politely.

'Do I!' Alicia sucked her lips together painfully. 'We met in the war driving ambulances in France. More than twenty years ago. We always counted ourselves the lucky ones – so many men died, there was no-one for the women to marry afterwards – haven't you ever wondered why there are so many spinsters? But we didn't need a man – we had each other.' She paused. 'I prefer women. Always have.' She looked across at Anna as if checking that she'd understood and stroked the cat now clambering slowly up into her lap. 'Is that how it is with you?'

Anna couldn't answer. The most appalling thought had just entered her mind and she felt paralysed by it.

Alicia was watching her face. 'It's not easy.' she said gently. 'There's always that first moment of realisation. That terrible revelation of what's inside you.'

Anna sat very still.

'I've seen you watching me in class,' Alicia went on. 'Watching me in that different way, like men do. It made me wonder.' She took the plate of biscuits off the cluttered table and offered them to Anna.

The quiet, domestic gesture broke Anna's trance. She stood up, knocking the biscuits out of Alicia's hand. She was shaking so much she could hardly speak. 'You horrible, perverted woman! How can you imagine I might be like you?'

Alicia's voice was very gentle. 'Then I'm sorry if I made a mistake. I invited you here because I thought you might be unhappy and I thought I might be able to help. I'm sorry.' She looked stricken.

Anna didn't reply. She grabbed her coat and her folder, and ran out of the door, down the stairs, banging the front door behind her. When she reached the tram stop she realised she was sobbing.

Walter was in the studio, lying on the bed reading by the light of a single candle fixed to the bed head in a pool of melted wax. He stood up as Anna flung herself into the room, putting his glasses down on the table so that he could hold out his arms to her. For what seemed like a long time they sat on the edge of the bed while Anna sobbed out her story against his shoulder. He stroked her hair and murmured comfort into her ear. In the warmth and security of his embrace Anna could feel herself growing calm again. She lifted her head and put her damp cheek against his. She felt his lips against her ear and then they slid across her face in a gentle caress, settling on her lips. Kissing him seemed natural and right, natural too to fold her body against his as they lay back on the pillows. His hands stroked her arms, her shoulders, her stomach and moved at last to her breasts. Anna knew that she wanted him to touch her there, but as his fingers began to circle her nipples she couldn't prevent herself stiffening with revulsion.

Walter stopped. He sat up. 'You don't like it, do you?'

Anna shook her head. 'I don't like any man touching me.' She felt the tears flooding into her eyes again. 'It isn't natural is it? I keep hoping it will go away – that next time it'll be different.'

Walter lit her a cigarette and handed it over. 'Is it because someone has hurt you in the past? Men can sometimes be clumsy.'

Anna hesitated. She had never spoken about it, never mentioned it to anyone. She pushed it as far down in her psyche as she could. But now, under Walter's gentle gaze, speaking her own native language, she somehow found the words. 'It's something that happened to me in Germany – some boys . . .' Anna almost broke under the stress of having to articulate something so painful. She turned her head away. 'And then he called me a filthy jew.'

Walter put his finger over her lips. 'You don't have to say any more. It happens. And I can see how you must feel. But you mustn't let it destroy the pleasures of love for you. Rape is a degradation of a woman, but the act of love is the most beautiful thing you can share with someone. They are not the same act.' Anna began to weep again and he stroked her hair. 'Don't let it destroy you – think of it as a physical assault like any other kind of beating. Then, when you find the right man, it will not be difficult to let him make love to you.'

'Alicia insinuated that I might be . . . like her.'

Walter threw back his head and laughed. 'The trouble is you are such a beautiful girl – both sexes will fall in love with you – you must be prepared for it.'

'I didn't even know there could be . . . that kind of thing!'

'What? Have you never heard of Sappho?'

'No. Who was she? Or is it a he?'

'How young and innocent you are! She was one of the greatest of the Greek poets – a woman who had lovers of both sexes.'

'A woman poet!' Anna sighed. 'And I've never heard of her.' She paused to take another drag at her cigarette and thought of something else. 'Have there been any great women painters in the past?'

Walter nodded. 'Perhaps not very great, but then there are so few. Who knows? If there had been more . . . In France there was Berthe Morisot – a good impressionist. She was married to Eugene Manet and had children, but she still managed to paint. In Italy there were several. You should go to the Uffizi in Florence if you want to see their work. There's an interesting painting there by a woman called Allegria Gentileschi. She began very young, was raped by the man who shared her studio, suffered torture in order to determine the truth of her accusation and afterwards devoted her life to art.' He paused, incredulous. 'Have you never heard of these women?'

'Never,' Anna said. 'I wish I had. It's hard to believe in yourself when you go to art galleries and stare at all those canvases painted by men. It's as though they're all saying "Women can't paint! Women can't paint!" On and on.'

'I forget that you are only a little provincial from Partenkirchen,' Walter teased.

'I know there are women painting now,' Anna protested. 'Laura Knight here in England – John Cornell told me about her. Then Georgia O'Keefe in America. And in Germany I know there's a woman called Kathë Kollwitz, but when I was there her work was banned and I never saw any of it. I don't know if she's even still alive.'

The smile had left Walter's face when Anna mentioned the name. 'I knew her,' he said quietly. 'We worked together for a while, but when I left she decided to stay in Germany and I haven't heard from her for some time.'

There was a pause and then Anna said. 'I haven't heard from my father for over a year. It's terrible not knowing what's happening to people you love.'

'Many jews have been put into camps or herded into ghettoes. It's hard to credit some of the stories that have come out. Like you, I still have friends and family in Germany. Half my heart is there. As is yours, I think?'

Anna nodded. 'It's like being two people. I was actually christened Anne after my English grandmother, but in Germany I was never called anything but Anna. I sometimes think there are two different people in my head – English Anne and German Anna, part Christian, part jew. I don't always know who I am.'

Walter put his hand on her head and stroked her sleek black hair. She could feel his strong fingers against her skull. He got up. 'Stay there!' He told her. 'Don't move. I want you just like that.'

Still in his shirt tails and socks he picked up a pencil and began to trace an outline on a big sketch pad, squinting hard in the candlelight as he stared first at her and then at the paper. 'I am going to paint you as you are. Then when you are in any doubt you can look at it and say "That is me, Anna Weissmann" and you will know!'

CHAPTER FIFTEEN

The turnip tops were white with the rime of overnight frost and the steel of the machete Tamar had to use to lop them off was so cold it took the skin off her hand. A bitter east wind scoured the furrows, finding every gap in their uniforms. 'It's a lazy wind,' the foreman said with a laugh in his voice. 'It goes through you rather than round.'

Tamar bent down again, her back screaming in protest. It was difficult to get used to the continual punishment of heavy physical work. As part of their training in animal husbandry and crop cultivation, they were to be sent out to the local farms to help whenever they were needed and for the last week they'd been given the job of pulling turnips out of frozen ground, chopping the leaves off and throwing them up into trailers.

Their uniforms were totally inadequate for the weather. It was three weeks now since their arrival and still only a few lucky people had been issued with greatcoats or wellington boots – there was no wet weather gear at all and only three pairs of socks each. 'One to wear, one to wash and one to darn,' the supervisor explained. They were of such poor wool that they were in holes within a week and Tamar's heels had blisters where the darns rubbed her tender skin.

Holly was suffering even more. She had blisters on both palms from the shaft of the fork, and her fingers had weeping sores. Every time they began to heal, the cold broke them open again. No amount of Zambuk seemed to do any good, though Holly coated her hands in the evil green slime every night before she went to bed. Tamar, trying to find a comfortable place on the hard mattress between the rough, unbleached linen sheets and thin grey military blankets, could hear Holly crying herself to sleep in the bottom bunk after the lights went out.

'The hostel's not too bad,' Tamar wrote to Anna that night. *'Though the food's pretty awful. We seem to live on a horrible kind of vegetable and barley stew with stale bread and marge. Occasionally they put a bit of scraggy meat in it. What I'd give now for one of Lily's fish suppers! The girls are quite fun – such a mixture of ages and backgrounds. One of them was a stripper in a club in Liverpool and she's quite colourful. You'd never think we'd get on, but we manage somehow. Most of them are good sports. On Saturday nights we're allowed to have a late pass. The others all went dancing at the Cameo in Carlisle. I didn't go – I thought about Edward and I just couldn't. Holly didn't feel like it either. So we had a hot bath – bliss! – and went to bed early with a book. Sleep is in short supply just now so a little extra is very welcome.'*

Tamar paused to re-read what she'd written. It wasn't entirely true that they all got on. Tamar had long since learnt the knack of keeping her head down and making herself invisible in order to fit in, but Holly had no idea how to be anything other than she was. She couldn't even disguise her facial expressions, registering horror and incomprehension in quick succession as she listened to some of the ribald conversations.

One of those crude exchanges was going on now between the girls in the next pair of bunks. 'He was hung like a horse,' Margie was saying. There was a lot of giggling 'So what did you do?' More giggling. Then an incredulous 'Go 'ed, Margie!' Creaking bed-springs and choking laughter. Margie said 'No, really!' and then something in a false whisper, most of which Tamar didn't catch, except the end phrase which was said more loudly as if intended for the ears of the girls in the surrounding bunks, '.... didn't even take my knickers off!' The boastful, exaggerated way she said it made Tamar doubt that she was telling the truth. Then another voice said, 'Look at Little Miss Christmas. She's red as a beetroot!' Tamar gripped her pen tightly as the girl intoned in a terrible mock-posh accent, 'So sorry if we're embarrassing yew.' And then Margie's voice said. 'For God's sake, have a fag.' Out of the corner of her eye, Tamar saw the other girl deliberately hold the cigarettes out towards Holly across the gap between the bunks and then pause theatrically. 'Oh, I forgot. Miss Good-as-

Gold-ilocks doesn't smoke!'

Tamar watched the colour fade out of Holly's face, the hurt, almost uncomprehending expression in her eyes, then she turned and ran out of the room. Tamar jumped down from the bunk to go after her. 'For god's sake haven't you anything better to do?' she shouted at the girls. 'Why don't you leave her alone!'

There was complete silence. Margie stared straight at Tamar. For a few moments the atmosphere was very tense, but then Margie shrugged and dropped her eyes.

Outside there was no sign of Holly. Where would she go? The shower block? No, Tamar thought. She'd head for the stables. It was very dark down in the yard, but the quarter moon gave just enough light to pick out the doors. Tamar could hear the occasional whinny, the creaking of a hayrick. The tack room door was half open and Holly was inside sitting on a stool weeping. Tamar pulled up another stool and went to sit beside her.

'I can't bear it,' she said. 'It's so hard, Tamar, so hard.'

'Is it just the teasing Holly, or the work?' Tamar put her arms around her thin shoulders. The girl was shaking with emotion.

'Everything. Oh, Tamar, I can't bear to fail. Everyone sort of expects me to. My parents said I'd never stick it out. The foreman's always shouting at me, and those girls in there hate me.'

'Don't be silly Holly. You're doing really well. You just have to ignore the girls – they tease anyone who's different. If they see that you mind they'll tease you even more.' Tamar paused and then went on. 'I used to get teased everywhere I went because I didn't have a father. They used to call me a bastard. You just have to shut your ears and keep your head down.'

'Do you know why I joined up?' Holly asked. 'It was because I felt so useless. And trapped. You've no idea what it was like at home. I've never, ever, been allowed to do anything for myself. I'm an only child you see – Mummy was quite old when I was born. My aunt died of TB when she was sixteen and Mummy was always afraid I would be the same. My nanny Greta stayed on and she looked after me – they never let me out of their sight.'

'They must have loved you a lot.'

'You've no idea what a burden it is to be loved so much, Tamar.'

'How did you persuade them to let you go?'

'It wasn't easy. I'd been asking them for ages. All the girls I was at school with were in the Red Cross or the Women's Auxiliary. And all I was doing was arranging flowers and taking Mummy tea in bed. I couldn't bear it. They wouldn't let me join the forces in case I got killed or injured and the Red Cross wasn't allowed because I might catch a disease, or see naked men or something like that. Honestly Tamar! But then . . .' She paused as if coming to something very difficult. She lowered her voice. 'I found Daddy in the office with another woman. I think someone who worked at the shop. I promised I wouldn't say anything to Mummy about it and I didn't. But next time I asked if I could do some kind of war work he said yes. He talked to a friend of his, who said, "Why not the land army?" I like gardening and animals and so I thought the land army would be fun. I didn't know it would be like this.' She started to weep again. 'I left home to try to make a life for myself. How can I go back and say I've failed?'

'You aren't going home,' Tamar said. 'You're going to stick it out. We both are. It's just the same for the rest of us you know. Look at Margie. She'd never seen a cow before in her life. She makes a joke out of it, but she's finding it just as hard as you are.'

'She's so horrid to me.'

'That's just her way of surviving. Come on Holly, you can't give up. Besides you're really good with the animals. Particularly the horses.'

'It's strange, isn't it? They do seem to like me.'

It was odd, Tamar conceded, that Holly, so gentle and diffident, could coax these great brutes to listen to her.

'Keep your head down, Holly,' Tamar said. 'Don't let yourself get drawn into it. Words don't matter. Just keep on being nice to them, whatever they say. Don't be a victim. Shame them!'

'I'm so glad you're here,' Holly said. She wiped her cheeks with the sleeve of her jumper. 'I don't know what I'd do without you. Do you think we might be able to get a placement together?'

'You used to look down on me when I worked in the shop,' Tamar said. She couldn't resist it. 'What was it you said? "I didn't know you were just a shop girl." And then next time we met you looked right through me.'

'I'm sorry,' Holly said simply. 'I know you better now.' She stood up awkwardly. 'It's hard to escape the way you were brought up, isn't it? But now we're all having to do it because of the war.'

Back in the dormitory, Tamar clenched her teeth and continued her letter to Anna. '*We get our placements at the end of the month and then a weekend of home leave. It'll be great to see you again. We can go out on the town together as we used to do and you can tell me all the latest gossip. Has Lily got over us all leaving yet? I write to her regularly but she never replies. I think it's because she's not all that good at putting pen to paper. I heard her once telling Sadie that she'd left school at twelve to go into service, so I don't suppose she got much education. Isn't it the weirdest coincidence meeting Holly Pergavie again? I'm afraid the others tease her dreadfully. But it's good to be with someone I know. You're not to be jealous,*' Tamar added and underlined it twice. '*You're still my best friend. Write to me. I like to think of you at home, quietly painting away. It makes me feel that at least one thing hasn't changed. That life goes on just the same somewhere.*'

After the episode of Alicia, Anna was consumed by a kind of fierce energy. She painted furiously, only stopping to eat or sleep or put in her shifts at the factory. With Walter's encouragement she had begun work on a large semi-abstract painting of the dockyard almost six feet by four. From the window of the studio she sketched battleships and fishing boats onto the big canvas, blocking out squares and rectangles of colour with the occasional tiny detail. Walter had finished her portrait – an oil sketch in dark, almost Dutch tones with a single splash of magenta and it now sat in her bedroom at home drying out before the final varnish. Anna didn't know quite what to make of it. The lines were bold and muscular – the effect uncompromising. It made her look resolute, but at the same time sad. The sadness in the eyes that Walter had painted bothered Anna whenever she looked at the canvas. Was that how she appeared to other people? When she looked at herself in the mirror she saw only anger, but Walter had seen grief. He was now working on a landscape – painting on the sea front, so Anna had the studio to herself most of the time.

One morning when she came off shift, Walter was waiting for her outside the factory, pushing the old pram he used to transport his easel and paintbrushes when he was working out of doors. 'I'm afraid I'm going to be leaving,' he said. 'I've been appointed an official war artist.'

'Congratulations.' Then a thought struck her. 'Does that mean you'll have to give up the studio?'

He nodded. 'I'm very sorry. But the rent's paid up to the end of the month and you could keep it on after that – it would save you having to rent lodgings if you could bear to live there.'

They were chattering in German as they always did and it didn't occur to Anna that it might seem odd to anyone else, until she noticed the tall fair girl who had once commented on her name. She was standing on the pavement watching them with a group of two or three other girls. Something in the way they were looking at her made Anna feel uneasy. She tugged Walter's sleeve. 'Let's go. It's cold standing here.'

'Have you thought about what you are going to do if they conscript you?' Walter said as they walked side by side towards the main road, Anna wheeling her cycle alongside the pram. 'There is talk of it.'

'I'm hoping that my job at the parachute factory will exempt me. I keep thinking, what if my father, or one of my cousins, was killed by a shell that I'd helped to make, or deliver.'

'It's always difficult for exiles. But you are Jewish . . . Don't you think that in joining the fight against the Nazis, you might actually be helping your own people?'

'Is that what you would do?'

'I'm much too old to fight. I'm simply going to record my own response to the reality of war. Somehow to do anything else would seem immoral. But if I was younger . . .'

Anna felt his words as a criticism of her own pacifist stance. But what else could she do? I can't fight, Anna thought. I can't be involved in killing people I once knew. She had no inclination for anything medical, so no point in joining the Red Cross and she was certainly not going into the land army. She shuddered when she thought of what Tamar was going through.

Tamar's letter was in Anna's pocket and she took it out to show Walter as they walked. '*I've never been so tired in my life.*' Tamar had written. '*Every bone aches. And the men do it so easily! I'm becoming very disillusioned with country life. I thought cows were such nice creatures – not a bit of it. They're all horns and teeth at one end and a great deal of muck at the other. And then there's the feet! They kick you while you're trying to milk them and stand on you at every opportunity. My legs are black and blue. Sadie was right – I'm too romantic.*' There was a gap in Tamar's untidy script where she had paused before continuing. '*I really miss Sadie. You've no idea how much. I know she was often unreliable and not everyone's idea of a good mother, but she was there. And I can't go on a train now without thinking about her. Trains will always mean Sadie.*'

The following morning there was thick ice on the inside of the windows and Tamar's breath condensed in a cloud whenever she breathed out. 'However are we going to survive without coats?' she said as she crawled into her trousers under the blankets. They had all adopted this manner of getting dressed. They even slept with their clothes under the pillow so that they were warm in the morning when they woke up.

'I don't expect anyone would notice if we wore extra clothes under our uniforms,' Holly said. She sounded much more cheerful this morning. She opened the cupboard door and took out a couple of jumpers. 'Here, Tamar, put this on.' She handed her a beautiful pale blue cashmere.

'I can't wear this,' Tamar said, fingering the expensive fabric. 'It'll be ruined. We're doing pigs today.'

'It doesn't matter,' Holly said. 'It's better to be warm.' She looked at the next bunk where Margie was shrugging her regulation uniform over the scanty petticoat which was the only kind of underclothing she seemed to possess. 'Would you like to borrow a jumper?' Holly asked.

There was a silence. Then Margie turned round. She looked

surprised. Then she smiled and said, 'If you've got one spare.'

Holly handed it to her without comment.

'Thanks pet,' Margie said.

When they all stood in line in the yard the foreman said, 'This week you're going to learn about pigs,' with the sardonic upward twitch at the corner of his mouth that Tamar had learnt to distrust .

'Now mind you treat them with respect,' he went on. 'A pig has the brain of a horse and a set of teeth like a shark. Sows with piglets are the worst. I've seen a man with half his leg bitten off.' He paused for effect. 'And a boar's not to be trusted neither. You don't get into a pen with a boar.'

'I wasn't intending to make a habit of it,' Holly said quietly in Tamar's ear. 'In fact, I don't much fancy pigs at all.' She seemed calmer this morning and more determined.

The pigs were kept in a rectangle of long, low buildings around a concrete yard, where a pile of manure and straw steamed aromatically in the cold, clear air. Most of the styes contained two animals, sometimes three. These were sows 'waiting to pig' as the foreman explained. The girls were to work in pairs, one penning the pigs into the corner with a yard brush, the other shovelling the dirty straw into a barrow. The boars and any sows that had piglets were to be left for the men.

Holly and Tamar took it in turns. Guarding the pigs gave the spine time to recover from the back-breaking job of mucking out. Although nervous at first, Tamar and Holly gained confidence as they moved down their allotted row. The pigs were Gloucester Old Spots, obese pink pigs with black markings like ink blots and, for the most part, they were very well-behaved. The occasional disgruntled lunge was easily deflected with the brush.

'I could get quite fond of these,' Holly said, scratching one behind the ear as it tried to chew her boot laces. 'They're quite sweet really.'

'They don't smell very sweet though,' Tamar said. She was wondering how she would ever get the stench of pig manure out of her clothes. There were still another three more days to laundry day.

The last pen held a single pig, rather smaller than the others. 'I wonder why she's on her own?' Holly asked.

'Perhaps she's bad-tempered,' Tamar said, warily. It was her turn to corner it. But the pig obediently stood against the wall when Tamar flourished the brush.

Suddenly the foreman came running up to the stye door. He was white faced. 'You're not supposed to be in there,' he said. He had a pitch fork in his hand as he pushed open the door. 'Move slowly and don't do anything sudden.' He jerked his thumb at Holly, indicating the door.

Tamar stayed where she was, gripping the brush shaft, every muscle tensed. In front of her the pig gave a sudden deep, shuddering grunt that resonated all the way from tail to snout. The foreman lowered the pitch fork until it was level with the pig's head. Tamar saw that he was sweating.

He nodded to her. 'Now you just walk back towards the door with me. Keep your brush down and don't take your eyes off that pig till we're out of the door.'

The pig looked at Tamar with a round yellow eye and blinked as if it was winking at her. Tamar wanted to laugh, but the fear of the man beside her was so real, she stifled the impulse. Outside the door, he leant against the wall, took his cap off and wiped his arm across his head. 'Are you mad, or didn't you hear me telling you not to go in with the boar?' he asked harshly.

'We didn't know which was which,' Holly said.

He sighed and put his cap back on. 'How they expect us to win a bloody war with a load of ignorant lasses, I don't know,' he said. 'As if life wasn't tough enough.'

'I don't think we're very popular,' Holly said, as they watched him stamping off across the yard, aiming a bad-tempered kick at one of the dogs that ran towards him.

'They just don't like having to work with women,' Tamar said. 'I expect it'll get worse next week when we get sent out to the farms.'

'I'm dreading it,' Holly said. 'But I've decided I'm not going to let it beat me.' She looked very determined. 'And I've made another decision. Will you do something for me tonight after tea?'

Tamar looked at Holly's reflection in the mirror. At the mass of red gold hair that tumbled around her shoulders like a cape. She fingered it enviously. 'Are you quite sure?' she asked for the second time.

Holly took a deep breath. 'Absolutely,' she said. 'There's no time to brush it in the morning and it attracts hayseeds and corn chaff all the time.'

Tamar sympathised with that. Her own short bob was troublesome enough. Her scalp itched permanently and there was no shampoo to wash it properly. Already its sheen was dulled by washing in carbolic soap.

'It has to go,' Holly said firmly.

Tamar nervously cut off a long curl near the front just below the level of her chin and handed it to her. 'Keep this as a souvenir,' she said.

Holly twisted it inside her handkerchief.

'I hope you're not going to regret this,' Tamar said as she made another jagged cut. She was appalled at her own lack of skill. Surely anyone could cut a reasonably straight line.

'What in bleedin' hell are you doin'?' Margie's voice said behind her.

'Tamar's cutting my hair off,' Holly said.

'Turnin' you into a bleedin' scarecrow more like! Here,' Margie held out her hand for the scissors. 'You give them to me. I'll do it. Anyone would think you were shearin' a bleedin' sheep!'

Swathe by swathe Holly's hair folded itself into a golden carpet on the floor. She looked down at it and for a moment Tamar thought she was going to cry. But then her chin came up and her lips set in a firm line. The result was surprising. As the long tresses were detached, Holly's remaining hair curled itself under, hugging the shape of her head like a coating of silk. Her face looked bigger, her cheekbones more prominent, her eyes huge. It wasn't the same person who stared back from the mirror.

'There now!' Margie said. 'What d'you think of that?'

'She looks really nice,' Tamar said, meeting Holly's eyes. 'You're obviously an expert.'

Margie grinned. 'I used to be a hairdresser in Liverpool before I went into the clubs.'

'My mother will hate it. But I don't care.' Holly smiled back.

'Thanks Margie.'

'Don't mention it.'

'We get our placements tomorrow. Where d'you suppose we'll be posted?'

'We're goin' into the hostel,' Margie said. 'Couldn't bear to be out in the middle of nowhere and we can still all be together. It's much more fun.'

'I asked for a farm,' Holly said, looking up at Tamar. 'I told the supervisor I wanted to be with you. Do you mind?'

Tamar didn't know whether she did or not. Holly was something of a liability. If they were sent out together, Tamar knew she'd have to spend half her time looking after her. But then, Holly was never going to survive on her own and she was so determined. 'Of course I don't mind,' Tamar said.

On the Thursday morning after Walter's departure, as Anna was washing her brushes in the studio, there was a thump on the door. It was pushed open almost immediately and two policemen stepped inside. One of them had a piece of paper in his hand. 'We're looking for a Miss Anna Weissmann,' he said.

'That's me.' Anna looked at the two men and then out of the window at the police car parked on the quayside. Memories of Sadie's accident flashed into her mind. 'What is it? Is something wrong?' Her heart came up into her throat. Had something happened to her mother or her grandparents while she was at the factory?

'We've received information that you are a non British subject.' The policeman recited the words as if reading from a script. 'As an alien you are required by law to register and according to our records, you haven't registered.'

'When did you come to England?' the other policeman asked.

'About four years ago.' Anna felt dazed. 'Who's been telling you all this?' She thought of the posters on every bill board encouraging people to spy on each other, remembered the spurned Alicia, the girl at the factory. Someone was no doubt feeling self-satisfied at having done their patriotic duty. She was in no doubt that it would be a woman. Anna made a face. Spiteful, self-righteous bitch!

She was allowed to collect her bag and coat. It would just be a formality, she told herself, but her stomach churned inside her. Why hadn't she taken her mother's advice and anglicised her own name as well? But the thought was rejected as soon as it came into her mind. She propped a note on the table in case anyone came to find her. 'Police have taken me to register as an alien.' Fear took hold of her as she propped the note up against the easel and her hands trembled so much her fingers could hardly hold the paper.

They took her to the main police station in the city centre and Anna was told to queue up with a number of other people. There seemed to be a lot of foreign nationals. When she finally got to the head of the queue, a friendly looking woman in a greeny brown uniform was sitting at a desk filling in forms.

'You'd better give me your details,' she said brightly, and drew a note pad towards her. 'And then we can decide whether you're a friendly alien or an enemy alien.' She smiled optimistically.

When Anna gave her name and told the woman how to spell it, she looked up and asked 'Is that a Dutch name?'

'No,' Anna said automatically, before she had time to stop herself. The woman waited. Anna went very cold. 'It's German,' she said at last.

'Oh dear,' the woman pulled a wry face. She brightened up when Anna gave her mother's nationality but then she asked 'And your father?'

'German.' The moment Anna said it, she regretted it. Why couldn't she have lied? Anna held her breath.

'Oh dear,' the woman said again. She looked down at her papers and then up again. 'Have you ever lived in Germany?'

'Yes,' Anna said reluctantly.

'I think you'd better see Major Carson,' the woman said. She got up and went away. Anna could see her chatting to someone in a back room.

The major was a thin man with a narrow moustache on his top lip. He kept Anna standing on the other side of the desk and asked a lot of questions about her father and the length of time she'd spent in Germany. Anna began to feel afraid. 'My mother brought me back about four years ago.'

'I'm afraid that makes no difference to your position. In Britain, you see, a woman takes her nationality from either her father or her husband. So, since you aren't married, you're over sixteen and you haven't been naturalised, technically you are a German national.'

'But that's ridiculous! My mother's English; I live here. Isn't that English enough?'

'Not quite.' His lips thinned into a tight, straight line. 'You are an enemy alien and I'm afraid we're going to have to send you to a place of safety while we investigate more fully. We will need to talk to your mother and your case will be put to the Internment Tribunal.' He put his signature to a piece of paper as he spoke and rang a bell on the desk. Orders were given. Anna was taken down stone steps, put into a vacant cell and the steel door was locked behind her.

There was nothing in the room but a mattress on a metal frame and a bucket. A spasm of fear rose into Anna's throat as she looked at the bare walls enclosing her, the small, high window, the locked door. Anna clenched her fists to stem the rising tide of panic that threatened her. Everything usual and ordinary had gone. It was as if she had woken up and found herself among the surreal metaphors of dream, where nothing was what it seemed and everything was treacherous.

PART IV

THE REAL THING

1940 – 41

'All art constantly aspires towards the condition of music. . .
To burn always with this hard, gem-like flame, to maintain this ecstasy, is success in life.'

Walter Pater
The School of Giorgione

CHAPTER SIXTEEN

It was dark by the time the transport van deposited Tamar at Holme Farm, but the full moon illuminated everything like daylight. The farm at the bottom of the lane was a miserable collection of buildings in a shadowy hollow. A square stone house stood at the corner of the yard in the shadow of a barn, facing the gate. Tamar could see that the entrance porch leaned to one side as if blown by the wind. Inside the open door, the kitchen ceiling was so low Tamar could put her hand up to touch it. The old plaster bulged in places where it had sagged on the lathes and two muslin-covered lumps of bacon swung on steel hooks embedded in it. Nearer to the fireplace, a pair of filthy blue overalls steamed from another and in the centre a tarnished brass oil lamp threw a flickering, uneven light across the ceiling.

Most of the chimney wall was taken up with an enormous patent range that dominated the room. The steel mantle shelf – as high as Tamar's head – had a dirty paper frieze under its collection of old biscuit tins, an assortment of bills tucked behind two clocks – one of which had stopped – gloves, ration books, yellowing photographs and scorched kettle holders. In the wall beside it was a cracked green cupboard and drawers. The doors hung open on sagging hinges and Tamar could see shelves lined with old newspaper, and a muddle of linen and china. On the other side of the range, a wooden settle was built out into the room, and three cats slept on the greasy velvet cushions safe from the draught coming from the door behind her. The air in the room, despite this influx of fresh air, was fusty and the sunken flagged floor struck damp into the soles of Tamar's shoes through the thin, trodden-out carpet.

Between the fitful glow of the oil lamp and the flickering firelight, Tamar could see a woman standing in the middle of the floor holding a loaf of bread. 'Mrs Heslop?' Tamar asked. There was the faintest movement of the head that might have been a nod. She was a skinny, wispy woman with mousey hair faded almost grey, scooped up into a hair net. Her skin hung slack on her bones and quivered when she moved. Her long, bony face had a timid, exposed quality and her thin, upper lip was deeply creased, like the frill of a petticoat. She seemed startled by Tamar's appearance at the door.

'You are expecting me, aren't you?' Tamar asked.

Mrs Heslop nodded, more definitely this time, still holding the loaf of bread in her hands, half-way to the table.

Tamar put her case down just inside the door and laid her coat over it. 'Can I give you a hand with the tea?'

A quiver passed through the woman, then her lips parted and words slipped nervously out as though escaping against her will. 'You can set the plates,' she whispered. Her head inclined towards the wall cupboard. Tamar obediently opened the door and took out three odd, and not very clean, plates. She brought knives and forks out of the drawer and these, too, felt greasy under her fingers.

Mrs Heslop put the bread on a board on the table next to a saucer of butter. Tamar, tired after the journey, sat on a chair and watched her swing the kettle off the fire to stand on the hotplate of the range before taking down a big cast-iron frying pan to hang on a metal hook over the flames. Then she took down one of the hams, unwrapped the muslin, carved off three thick slices of what looked like pure fat and tossed it into the sizzling pan. The kitchen filled with acrid stife.

A hidden door behind the settle opened and Tamar could see the top of someone's cap. There was the sound of boots being removed and the cap was lifted and placed on a hook. The man who came into the room was thick-set, with a deeply weathered face and red veins in his cheeks and nose. He was almost bald, white-skulled where the cap shaded his scalp from the sun, but had incongruously generous eyebrows which grew out horizontally and vertically like wiry vegetation. Tamar found it difficult not to stare. He was wearing an old tweed jacket, a ragged pullover stretched over his belly and the most derelict trousers Tamar had ever seen.

'Aye', he said, on seeing Tamar sitting beside the table. 'I see you've come. About time.' He grunted and sat down, pulling a farming magazine across the table towards him and propping it up against the pot of jam and moving the lamp to illuminate the page.

His wife, unacknowledged, collected three eggs from a bowl on the sideboard and cracked them into the pan with the bacon. Tamar, wanting to be useful, picked up the teapot to take it to the kettle.

Mr Heslop lifted his head. 'You.' He pointed a finger at her. 'You sit down. You're here to help me. Not her.' He jerked his head towards the fire. 'She's got nowt to do but look after us. Easy bloody life n'all, lying about the house all day.' And then he went back to the Farmer's Weekly.

Tamar sat down, feeling very uncomfortable, and presently a plate was put in front of her with one slice of bacon fat and a slimy looking egg, sliding around the plate in blackened lard. A thick slice of bread was carved off the loaf for her. At least two days old, Tamar thought, feeling it between her fingers. She ate as best she could, seeking out the pinker bits, disguising as much of the fat as she could stomach with pieces of egg and bread. She was ravenous.

After tea Mrs Heslop cleared the plates. Tamar rose automatically to help and was quelled by Mr Heslop's eye. She sat and stared at the fire, listening to the sounds of running water and clashing dishes in the scullery, and wondered how she was going to live in this atmosphere of bleak hostility. But at least Holly was arriving the following day. There would be company. And maybe, once they had made friends with Mrs Heslop, things would get better.

As soon as she could, Tamar asked to go to her room. She was tired, she said. If they didn't mind, she would go to bed and read. Mr Heslop took a watch out of his pocket. 'Aye. Well, mind you don't read too long. We keep early hours here to save on candles. And I want you up at half past five for the milking. Have you got an alarm?'

Tamar nodded, but her heart sank. Half past five! She followed Mrs Heslop up the awkward wooden stairs, almost blind with weariness and disappointment.

The bedroom was at the back, where the roof sloped down almost to the ground. The window was small and low, cramped between the floor and the eaves, and the air struck cold and damp against Tamar's skin. There were two single iron bedsteads on either side, pushed against the walls. A mahogany wardrobe stood near the door on the only wall that was full-height and there was a washstand and mirror and one bedside cupboard. There was a half burned candle stuck into a saucer beside the bed which Tamar lit from the one Mrs Heslop was carrying.

'Goodnight,' Mrs Heslop said in a trembling whisper, and Tamar heard her footsteps going slowly downstairs again.

Standing in the middle of the bare, cold room without so much as a hot water bottle, Tamar found it difficult to suppress the tears that had been close behind her eyes ever since she left Lily's. 'There's a war on,' she told herself sternly. 'Nobody expects to be comfortable.' She unpacked her suitcase, put Edward's and Sadie's portraits on the bedside cupboard, laid out her work clothes for the morning, set the alarm and then, wrapped in her greatcoat Tamar lay down in the clammy bed and tried to sleep.

Memories of her weekend at Lily's crowded into her mind as she lay shivering in the dark. She had hoped to spend time with Anna and it had been a considerable shock to go to the Cotteslow's house and be told that Anna had been interned. Her mother had been distraught. Couldn't Tamar do something, she had asked? The only thing that Tamar could think of was to write to George. He was in the army and perhaps he would know who to approach. It didn't make any sense to lock Anna up. What did they think she was going to do? Spy for Hitler? But when Tamar considered it, that was presumably what they did think she might do. At Mrs Wiseman's request, Tamar had gone down to the studio Anna had shared with the German painter and packed up all her belongings – paints and canvases – to be brought back by a friend of Mr Cotteslow in a borrowed van.

Afterwards Tamar had gone to have Sunday lunch with Edward's family. The Antonellis had made such a fuss of her, and his mother seemed to regard her already as part of the family. 'Why don't you call us Mam and Dad?' she kept saying. 'I do wish you and Edward could have got married before he went away.' Tamar knew that she should have been glad to be so welcomed, so included, but their possessiveness had made Tamar feel uneasy and she wasn't sure why. Now, she would have given anything for some of that warmth.

'What is this place?' Anna asked her military escort as she climbed down from the lorry. The camp was composed of a series of rusting Nissen huts connected by flagged pathways inside a barbed wire enclosure. The huts had a deserted, semi-derelict air, but the fencing wire gleamed new and the guard post at the entrance still smelt of creosote.

'It used to be a TB sanatorium until a few months ago,' the corporal said grudgingly. He'd been unwilling to talk about anything since they left Newcastle. Perhaps they weren't supposed to talk to enemy aliens.

The locking of the gate behind them unnerved Anna as much as the mention of TB. She wondered where all the patients had been taken (were they mysteriously cured by war?) and whether tuberculosis could be caught from the furniture. But when she was escorted into the hut that was to be her home for the foreseeable future, there wasn't a great deal of that anyway, and what there was gave the impression of having been thrown out of an old boarding school. The whole place had a temporary, makeshift feel to it. They were going to be moved to a proper camp, somewhere down south, Anna had been told at the police station, as soon as it was finished. Until then, they would have to make do.

Anna had been allocated to hut seven – the female dormitory – a long, draughty building with a bare floor and six scuffed metal bedsteads on each side of the room, making twelve in all. Between the beds was a dented locker with chipped paint, a wooden chair and a cupboard for clothes. Anna had never lived communally before and the idea revolted her, but only three of the beds had been made up, the rest still had blankets folded in neat piles on the exposed mattress ticking. She chose a bed at the far end, in a corner, directly in the draught between the door and the window. It would be worth suffering a little cold air, for the benefit of privacy.

When the corporal left, the other occupants of the dormitory came forward to make themselves known. One of them was an elderly German nun with a face like crumpled tissue paper and small damp eyes, who bowed but said nothing. The nun was plump and pale and had the same sour odour of human sweat and woollen underclothes that Anna remembered from her visit to the Convent school in Tynemouth. 'This is Sister Perpetua,' the woman standing next to her explained. 'She has taken a vow of silence.' Sister Perpetua gave another little bow of the head before she sat down again on the hard chair beside her bed and picked up the small, leather-bound book she'd been reading.

The woman who had spoken was also elderly, though much thinner and more energetic. The sinews of her neck showed through the thin, creased skin that hung in folds from her jaw. There were gold rings on her fingers and her tweed suit looked expensive. 'I am Frau Friedrich,' she said, shaking Anna's hand. 'My husband and I have a butcher's shop in Durham. Our daughter married an Englishman after the last war, and we came here to be near her and our grandchildren. When the police came for us, they asked us why we had never become British citizens. But what difference would it have made?' She seemed utterly bewildered. 'We are the same people. With a different coloured passport we would still be German.' Anna made sympathetic noises. 'Now I worry that people will loot our shop and the house before my daughter can come to look after it. This is a terrible thing! An insult to us.'

The third occupant, Grisel, was a well-made blonde girl in her early twenties who explained that she'd come to England to do a year's teaching and then decided that she couldn't go back to a country run by Nazis. 'I was in Hamburg on Kristallnacht,' she told Anna. 'I saw the bonfires, people smashing shops and houses. There was a disabled student – very Jewish-looking – though I don't know if he was a Jew. They kicked him to death. It made me feel sick. How could I go back?'

'And you?' Frau Friedrich asked Anna. 'How do you come to be here?'

'I don't know. I think it's because I was born in Germany and my father's German. My mother being English didn't seem to count.' She found it difficult to shake off the conviction that she was living in a nightmare and would wake up at any moment to find herself in bed in her room at home with her mother calling up the stairs. 'What's it like here?' Anna asked.

Frau Friedrich shrugged. 'Cold. Uncomfortable. Like being in prison. I have already sciatica from these hard beds. And I worry about Herr Friedrich's bronchitis. They make my husband sleep in another bed as if we were not married.' Her voice was sharp with incredulity. 'In forty years we have never been separated. Never!' She repeated emphatically.

'It's difficult to keep your spirits up,' Grisel said. 'Mostly the soldiers aren't too bad, but there's one – a woman – who never misses any opportunity to make our lives hell.'

'You will meet her when we go to the mess hut for our evening meal,' Frau Friedrich said with a grimace.

Private Huyton had a square, heavy-jawed face and small, mean eyes. Her body was similarly disproportionate – with a large bust straining the buttons on her uniform shirt, narrow hips and short stubby legs. Anna thought that even if she hadn't been warned about her, she would still have disliked the woman on sight.

'Right, you lot!' She shouted, as if dealing with unruly children. 'Line up.'

Everyone shuffled into a queue for the food being served from catering size pans on a trestle table. There were boiled potatoes and a grey, rather lumpy slop flecked with orange that Anna eventually recognised as boiled mince and carrots.

'The food will not kill you,' a voice behind Anna said, 'It will nourish the body, but it does nothing for the soul.' She turned to look at the man standing behind her. He was shorter than she was, balding, with very dark eyes shielded by metal-framed, half-moon lenses balanced on the bridge of his nose. He had one of the most elaborate moustaches Anna had ever seen. His black suit was neat, but shiny and beginning to whiten at the seams. 'Dr Wilhelm Blum,' he said, giving a little formal bow.

'Fraulein Anna Weissmann.'

'I am not an ordinary doctor, I must tell you,' he went on as if anticipating a question. 'If I was I do not think they would have sent me here. I would have been too useful.'

'Then what kind of doctor are you?'

'Of the mind, my child, of the incorporeal substance we call the mind. I was lecturing at the university here when this unfortunate war began.'

They had reached the head of the queue and held out their plates in turn to have the food ladled carelessly onto the white china where it looked if anything, even less appetising. There was a film of grease on the meat that left a tidemark on the plate. But it smelt savoury and to Anna, who hadn't eaten since breakfast, very welcome. She followed Dr Blum to a table where the three women sat with three other men. One, she guessed immediately, was Herr Friedrich – a small red-faced man who sounded slightly asthmatic.

'This is not meat,' he said to Dr Blum as he sat down. 'This would be an insult to any animal.'

'It's muck!' someone said derisively. 'Scrapings from the abattoir floor.' The man who spoke was much younger than the rest – Anna thought in his late twenties or early thirties. He had shaggy dark hair and a rough outdoor face.

'That is Herr Brunner,' Dr Blum said. 'He is a trawlerman from Kiel.'

Brunner nodded brusquely to Anna. 'I had the misfortune to be shipwrecked and the further misfortune to be rescued by the English.'

'My father was in the merchant navy when he was young,' Anna said. 'He was the ship's cook. But then he left to run a guest house when my grandparents became too old.'

'What did you say your name was?' Brunner asked. He was staring at her in a way that made her feel very uncomfortable.

'I didn't. It's Weissmann. Fraulein Weissmann.'

'That is a yiddish name is it not?'

Anna said nothing. Brunner gave her a strange look and then picked up his plate and went to sit at another table.

'Don't take any notice of him,' Grisel said. 'He's a Nazi. He should keep his politics to himself.'

'He is entitled to his opinions,' Frau Friedrich said phlegmatically. And then to Anna; 'Are you Jewish?'

'Only partly.'

Dr Blum smiled. 'There is no such thing in Hitler's Germany. Even a small amount of Jewish blood provokes anti-semitic rage.'

Frau Friedrich leant across the table and tapped peremptorily with her fore-finger. 'We will not start one of these conversations, if you please. I will not listen to anyone who speaks ill of the Reich Chancellor. He has taken the guilt from our shoulders. Germany is no longer a second class nation and at last we can hold our heads high among other nations.'

'Not much use in here though, is it?' a quiet voice said from the other end of the table. A very thin, ascetic looking man with curly grey hair was sitting next to Grisel. He waved his fork as if to illustrate the point.

'This is Herr Froebel,' Dr Blum said, giving a little bow in his direction. Anna did likewise and received a slight inclination of the head in reply. 'He is a musician – a violinist.'

'I teach.' Herr Froebel said firmly. 'That, apparently, is my offence – to corrupt the youth of England with German music.'

Private Huyton banged a spoon against a metal plate and everyone leapt up to clear the tables and place their dirty utensils into buckets to be carried back to the kitchen.

'We have to take turns to cook and wash up,' Grisel whispered. 'You'll get your rota tomorrow.'

'Now,' Private Huyton shouted. 'Everyone to their tables. There'll be silent recreation until bed time at ten o'clock.'

Dr Blum and Herr Froebel went over to the other table where someone was opening a box of chess pieces. Sister Perpetua took out her little book which Anna could see now was a volume of devotions. Her lips moved as she read and every now and then she closed her eyes in silent contemplation. A radio was clicked on and Anna heard an immaculate voice announce, 'This is the BBC Home Service broadcasting from Alexandra Palace.' It seemed odd that her mother and grandparents were probably sitting in the parlour at this moment, listening to the same programme.

Private Huyton placed a basket containing balls of khaki coloured wool on the table in front of Anna, and then produced two knitting needles and a pattern. Anna stared at them in disbelief. Grisel and Frau Friedrich had already taken bundles of half knitted garments out of their bags. 'We're supposed to knit gloves and socks for the troops to put into Red Cross parcels,' Grisel said.

'I can't knit,' Anna said in English, fixing Private Huyton with a challenging stare.

The WRAC seemed a little nonplussed at being addressed with such perfect fluency in her own language, but soon recovered. 'Then you'll have to learn,' she replied. 'Idle hands make mischief.'

'I'm not going to be idle,' Anna said. 'I have my own work.' She opened her bag and took out her sketch book and pencils.

'What's that?' Private Huyton asked sharply.

'I'm studying painting. I have to practise.'

Private Huyton's lips thinned, but she said nothing.

'There will be trouble there,' Frau Friedrich said as she walked away. 'She does not like to be crossed.'

'She will not like it that your English accent is better than hers,' Grisel said shrewdly.

Anna supposed that, compared to Private Huyton's Yorkshire drawl, it was. That gave her a feeling of great satisfaction. She found her pencil tracing the exaggerated outlines of Private Huyton's figure, her short legs and bureau-shaped bust. To complete the caricature she made her face more oblong than it was, her eyes smaller and more menacing, sketched a whip in her hand and wrote the letters 'Kommandant' across the top pocket of her army jerkin.

'That is good,' Grisel said, chuckling as she looked over Anna's shoulder. 'Let me show it to the others – they'll love it!'

'Don't let her see it,' Frau Friedrich warned as Anna detached it from the book. 'Or you will be in trouble.'

'I don't care if she does,' Anna said.

'No talking over there!' Private Huyton shouted.

'*We're in the most isolated, bleak place you could ever imagine*,'

Anna wrote to George on a sheet of sketch paper, '*At the mercy of a natural sadist. She takes a perfect delight in pettiness. We're controlled and watched every minute of the day as if we were children at school, or dangerous criminals. There's no discrimination in the camp between Nazis and anti-Nazis either and I fear that could lead to trouble. One of the men went to sit on another table when he knew I had Jewish blood. There are several of the men who seem pro Hitler, but the government are mad if they think any of us women are a risk to national security. An elderly nun, a housewife, an anti-nazi student and a half jew – what danger do they expect from us? Apparently we aren't allowed torches to find our way from the hut to the toilet in the night in case we use them for signalling and they read our letters and censor them. I expect half of this to be crossed out and I just hope you don't find yourself in the punishment block for corresponding with me! Are you allowed to have a relationship with a dangerous enemy alien?*'

Anna lifted her head and looked at the blacked out windows of the mess, at Private Huyton standing with her arms folded beside the door and longed to be back in North Shields, in Lily's living room, listening to the gramophone with George and Tamar. She wondered where they were and what they were doing and hoped that they were in happier circumstances than she was.

The next morning Tamar was barely awake as she pulled on her boots and her coat and followed Mr Heslop out of the back door. The cold hit her face like a freezing wave of sea water, making Tamar catch her breath and close her eyes. In the clear early light, Tamar could see what had been hidden in the dusk of the previous evening. Behind the farmhouse a low wood darkened the rise of the land and then higher up, fields bumpy with rocks and rushes, walled in against the wild land that extended beyond. There were crags and waterfalls, looming close in the frosty light and above them the flat-topped mass of the high range of hills that stretched away southwards. Tamar's heart lurched. She had not expected to be so near to the hills.

There was only one farm beyond the Heslops – a big white

building with a stone turret and a cluster of outbuildings behind it, perched on a little plateau looking out across the Solway Plain, sheltered by trees. Although it was so early, smoke already curled invitingly from its chimney. Tamar wondered who lived there, with such views, and thought enviously of the fire that burned in the kitchen range.

The concrete byre was harshly lit by the paraffin lamp hung on a hook from the ceiling. Heslop pointed to the feed bins and a pile of turnips in the barn next door. One scoop of corn into each trough and a couple of handfuls of turnip chips. He indicated what looked like a mangle. Tamar had to put the turnips in a hopper at the top and turn the handle to chop the bits into a basket underneath. Some of them were soft where they had been frozen and then rotted in the heap. The stench of fermenting swede filled the barn.

As soon as he'd shown Tamar what to do, Heslop snatched up an ancient lady's bicycle that leant against the barn wall, jumped on it and pedalled off across the yard at top speed, his head lowered over the handlebars against the wind. 'Come on dog!' he yelled, 'You lazy bugger!' From the doorway the silent shadow of the collie detached itself from the darkness and loped after him reluctantly.

Tamar scooped and mangled, scooped and mangled – her stomach hollow and sick from working without so much as a cup of tea – until all the troughs were filled. She could hear Heslop yelling 'How! How!' and whistling to the dog. Then the big-boned Ayrshires began to slither and sway up the yard and into their accustomed stalls. Tamar had to duck out of the way of the pointed horns to fasten their neck chains. In the background she heard the clatter of a milking machine engine reluctantly firing and dying. She could hear Heslop swearing and swinging the starting handle again and again. At the third attempt it coughed and fell into an erratic rhythm.

Tamar blundered through the milking in a half conscious state, aware that she was sworn at for being slow, but too cold and tired to care. 'Have they got any names? Tamar asked, as she unchained the cows, patting some of the quieter ones to encourage them out of the byre.

‘Don’t be daft!’ Heslop said. He didn’t need to explain – his scandalised expression spoke for him. They were commodities – milking machines. If Heslop treated his animals decently, if not with kindness, Tamar thought, it was probably because a well fed animal attracted a better price than a poor one.

By the time the cows were back in the field and the milk safely poured into churns and dumped at the farm gate for collection, the sun had lifted over the horizon – a dramatic pink glow beneath black bars of cloud in the east. It was more than two hours since Tamar had got out of bed and as she pushed open the kitchen door the smell of frying eggs made her light-headed.

By lunchtime she was exhausted, having mucked out the byre, fed the fifty hens the Heslops were allowed to keep by the War Agricultural Committee plus another fifty in a shed in the wood that the ‘War Ag’ knew nothing about. Then the eggs had to be washed and graded; the biggest into trays to be black-marketed to the Lakeside Hotel, medium size for the War Ag, and the smallest into buckets of isinglass to preserve them for home consumption. Lunch was a rather tough rabbit stew with onions in a pale, floury gravy that had a fatty, rather sickly aftertaste, even when mashed up well with potatoes and boiled swede, but Tamar was so hungry she felt she could have eaten anything.

Holly arrived at three, waving cheerfully from the gate as the van drove away.

‘I was beginning to think you’d changed your mind,’ Tamar said as Holly laid her soft, scented cheek against her own. ‘I was afraid you weren’t coming.’

Holly looked apprehensively at the dirty yard and uncared for buildings. ‘Is it as bad as it looks?’

‘Not what we’d hoped for.’ Tamar tried to make her face bright. ‘But it’ll be much more fun now you’re here.’

The little room under the eaves seemed cosier already as Holly’s careless belongings spilled from her suitcase over the bed and every other flat surface.

‘I brought all the new winter clothes my mother bought me before rationing came in. You never know when we might need something smart.’

‘The jumpers will come in handy!’

'And I brought a pair of fur-lined driving gloves my father was given years ago and never wore. He'll never miss them.'

Tamar could hear Heslop shouting from the yard. 'I must go. I'm supposed to be helping sort some calves. I'll be in the yard if you want me.'

'Tamar, I'm dying to go to the lavatory! Tell me where it is before you go.'

'It's outside round the back. I'll show you.'

She took Holly down the flagged path beside the barn and indicated a wooden door, slightly off its hinges. 'I'm afraid it doesn't shut properly. I'll stand here and keep watch for you.'

'Thanks.' Holly disappeared inside while Tamar waited. After a while she put her head out of the door, looking completely perplexed. 'Are you sure this is the right place, Tamar?'

Tamar was laughing so much she could hardly speak. 'Haven't you ever seen an earth closet before?' She leant against the wall and wiped her eyes. 'No, I don't suppose you have! Just lift the red lid and sit on the round wooden hole. It smells a bit, but it's all right.'

'And there isn't any toilet paper!'

'That's what the newspapers are there for – you're supposed to tear bits off. If you want the proper thing, we'll have to buy our own.'

'But where do you wash your hands?'

'I don't think they do. We'll have to go into the back kitchen or the dairy and use the sink.'

'It's disgusting.' Holly looked near to tears. 'Oh, Tamar, I don't think I can live with this.'

Worse was to come. When they were getting ready for bed, Holly found the chamber pot in the bedside cabinet. Tamar could see her looking at it.

'That's for the middle of the night, so's you don't have to find your way across the yard in the cold and the rain.'

'But I couldn't . . .' Her face was flushed bright red. 'Not in this room . . . with you here . . .' And then she began to cry, kneeling on the floor with her head against the bed.

Tamar came over and knelt beside her. She put her arm around

Holly's shoulders. 'It'll be all right. You'll get used to it. It just takes time.' Her heart burned for Holly as she thought of her own need for privacy. But at least she had had some practise – all those years of sharing with Sadie. Holly had never been to boarding school, had never had to share.

CHAPTER SEVENTEEN

'Why me?' Anna asked the Captain. It was her second morning in the camp and she had requested an interview, to try to establish their reasons for holding her. 'Why only me? My brother hasn't been interned and he's got exactly the same blood as myself. A German father and an English mother.'

'Ah, but your brother was born in England and he's too young to be a security risk.' The Captain was a man in his forties. He had a weary, disappointed air about him, which Anna thought probably had something to do with being posted to the camp. It could hardly be a desirable commission. Anna suspected that he was a recruit, since his uniform was stiff and new despite the scraps of coloured silk stitched above the breast pocket – relics of a war in which he had taken a more active part.

'Then why am I considered a security risk? My father may be German, but his family are Jewish and they're no friends of Hitler.'

'I'm afraid I am simply here to implement the decision of the Internment Tribunal. In a war, any information that might be passed on that would be of use to the enemy is a danger to national security. That is why you are here. Anyone who has links with Germany or who might be recruited by the Fifth Column is suspect. This is not a prison, or a concentration camp. Simply a place of safety until the war is over.'

'And suppose it isn't over soon? Supposing it goes on for years and years? I'm only eighteen . . .' Anna could hardly speak for emotion, thinking of all those years and years of her young life that might be lost.

The Captain was unmoved. 'There is an appeal committee – if your family feel that you have been interned unjustly, they can apply to them for a review of your case. I didn't make the rules, I simply enforce them. Now, if you'll excuse me, I have to get on.' He waved his pen towards a tray piled with paper.

Anna stood up and left. She felt utterly without hope.

In the days that followed, that feeling of hopelessness increased. Everything seemed pointless. In the morning she peeled buckets of potatoes and carrots, and in the afternoon she walked round and round the perimeter fence to try to stimulate her sluggish circulation. It took exactly nine minutes, and the view on the other side of the wire never varied. In an easterly direction, rough fields ran down to a line of trees with the suggestion of buildings beyond. West and north the land ran up to moor and the kind of sky that suggested space and distance. The road came in from the south and there was a grand entrance, as if to an estate, and lodge houses where some of the staff lived. The landscape was flat and featureless and its lack of interest only added to Anna's depression.

Her feeling of being caged like an animal was exacerbated by the way she was treated. Private Huyton seemed to have a personal vendetta against Anna that made her wonder whether the cartoon she'd so recklessly drawn on that first evening had been shown to her. Anna was being given the worst jobs on the rota – cleaning the toilets, scrubbing the mess floor, peeling vegetables in freezing water. By the end of the first week her hands were chapped and raw and she found it difficult to hold her pencil for drawing. 'It's not fair,' she said to Dr Blum in the mess hut, 'I've counted the days on the rota and I'm doing twice the number of cleaning details as everyone else. The woman's a sadist!'

'See how shallow her forehead is?' he replied quietly. 'She has no imagination. That makes you her superior. You can imagine how she feels and thinks, but she can never put herself in anyone else's place. This is how people become cruel.'

The worst thing to be endured in the camp was the boredom. Some of the internees had formed a committee and made an attempt to take responsibility for organising their activities from their captors. One of the men had been a PE instructor and he was detailed to arrange a daily physical fitness programme inside or out depending on the weather. The men had a chess club and another group had begun to dig a vegetable plot which, it was proposed, would provide them all with fresh produce and improve their diets. None of these occupations appealed to Anna.

The mess was the only warm space. There was a stove there, and in the evenings they could listen to the wireless and read books which had either been donated or left behind – cast-off romances, Agatha Christie and boy's own adventure stuff. Some of the internees had books of their own they'd been allowed to bring in. Dr Blum lent her Thomas Mann in German, but Anna found it too difficult. 'I'm not much of a reader,' Anna told him.

Sometimes Dr Blum played whist with Herr Brunner, who was the only one of them who was openly anti-British. 'I'd kill the buggers if I had a gun,' he would say, shaking his fist at the young soldier on guard duty, who fortunately didn't understand German and – unlike Private Huyton – didn't expect them to be silent. 'One day I'm going to escape and take a boat to Bremerhaven. I'll show them who's boss.'

'And where will you get a boat?' Herr Friedrich asked. 'This is wartime.'

'I know where you can get fishing boats. Any time. You take them out and nobody asks questions. I would take you, but you are all too cowardly to come with me.'

Another man at the table stood up and shouted, 'Shut your mouth, you bloody Nazi, or I'll shut it for you.' A chair was kicked over as several others sprang to restrain him and the soldier on guard duty raised his rifle with an expression of panic on his face.

'It's a great mistake,' Grisel said quietly into Anna's ear, 'to put fascists and communists in the same camp.'

Anna's great release was in drawing and her sketch book was filling up rapidly. '*You're going to have to send me another one pretty soon,*' she wrote to her mother. '*It's the best Life class I've ever been to – people have nothing else to do but pose for you.*' There was Frau Friedrich asleep in her chair – mouth open and glasses askew; Grisel frowning as she turned the heel of a sock; Sister Perpetua masked in silent prayer; Dr Blum bent over the chess board with his head on his hand. She drew the furniture, the bleak perspectives of the dormitory, buckets of peeled vegetables, and the intricate patterns of barbed wire. As she moved her pencil over the paper, she was astonished to find that a surge of delight pulsed through her.

'It makes me feel a different person,' she told Dr Blum, who had taken to walking with her round the perimeter fence in the afternoon.

'There's an old Chinese proverb. If you have only one mark, you must spend fifty pfennigs on a loaf and fifty pfennigs on a lily. That's because you have within you, not one, but two selves to feed. The anima and the animus. People think of it as feminine and masculine, or body and soul, because this is how we divide the world, but it is more complex than that.'

'In Germany the fact that I was half English and half German never seemed to be a problem. But since I came to England I've always felt that I was two people. I call them English Anne and German Anna. They have conversations inside my head. Particularly since the war started. I'm on both sides at once. Almost as if I was at war with myself.'

'It's not easy to have a double heritage,' Dr Blum said. 'The secret of health is to have the two in balance.'

'I don't know how I could ever achieve that without painting. It's as necessary to me as breathing.'

'That is because it comes from the creative soul that is neither Jewish nor Christian, German nor English. It is your very self; your essential essence. You must nurture it.'

'It's hard to do that in here. I've always thought I was a strong, determined person who could surmount any obstacle that came my way. But this is something else. I feel trapped, claustrophobic, panicky, all the time. I can't sleep either. I have such terrible dreams.'

'We have all been taken from our safe, ordinary lives. We are all afraid.' His voice was very comforting. 'You are not alone. What you must do is to find a way of surviving from day to day until all this is over. We must all try to live just one day at a time.'

Anna looked up at the sky, at the vast expanse of it and the clouds scurrying eastwards on the wind towards the German coast, and wondered if her father too looked up at it and thought of her. Was he being confined in the same way? That he had been taken to some kind of camp seemed no longer in doubt. It was ironic that they were both being held by opposite sides. Would they ever be together again?

'It's hard to be optimistic,' she said to Dr Blum, 'when tomorrow could bring so many dreadful things.'.

~~~~~~~~~~~~~~~~~

On Saturday morning after milking, Heslop grudgingly gave them what was left of their pay after deducting bed and board. A grubby, creased ten shilling note, eight shillings counted out reluctantly into their open palms and then, after a wait during which Tamar did not flinch but stood with her hand out, expectantly, he dug deep into his jacket pocket and with a sigh produced the sixpences. Tamar felt she had won some kind of psychological battle. If she had dropped her eyes, or her hand, or showed any sign of hesitation, she was sure the sixpence would have been withheld.

'What shall we do?' Holly asked, tossing her head back at the clear sky, where a few optimistic white clouds floated like small blobs of meringue. Everything had begun to look edible.

'I'm going to walk down to the village shop to get something to eat,' Tamar said. 'There must be things that are off-ration.' Their precious ration cards had been given to Mrs Heslop so that she could feed them, and it made Tamar furious that so far not a single item had been purchased for their consumption. What did the Heslops do with the coupons? Certainly none of it came to the table.

'I feel like asking for my card back,' Tamar said. 'Then we could buy our own rations.'

It was over a mile into the village from the farm, but it was a pleasant walk on such a fine day. The spring sun had a definite warmth in it as it fell across their shoulders. Tamar could almost smell things growing. A small weasel ran across the road to hide in the stone wall and as they turned a corner a big buck hare bounded out from a gate and ran down the road in front of them before leaping the gate into the next field. Tamar felt a rush of pleasure as the walls gave way to hedgerows sweet with primroses
~~~~~~~~~~~~~~~~~

and flowering sloe.

A girl came whizzing round the corner on a bicycle, her brown hair blowing in the wind behind her as it escaped from the beret she was wearing. She slowed down when she saw them and stopped, propping the cycle with one leg. 'Hello', she said cheerfully. 'I'm Maggie.' She held out her hand which they shook in turn and told her their names. 'I'm the postgirl,' she explained. 'But there's nothing for you today. You're the new land girls up at Holme Farm aren't you?' Before Tamar could do more than nod Maggie had mounted her bicycle again. 'Cheerio, I'd better be off. My mother'll kill me if I'm not back for my ten o'clocks.'

'People are so friendly here,' Holly said. 'If the Heslops weren't so miserable, I'd really like it.'

The village was only a cluster of farms and cottages grouped around a crossroads.

There was a signpost but it had no arms. 'How are you supposed to know which way to go?' Holly said.

'I think it's to confuse the Germans if they invade.'

'You don't suppose they will, do you Tamar?'

'They've invaded everyone else! So I suppose we've got to be prepared.' Holly looked so worried Tamar felt bound to add, 'but it won't happen.'

There was only one shop in the main street between the blacksmith's and the Farrier's Arms. It had a post office sign outside but when the girls went in they found it was a parlour shop. It was like going into someone's front room, except that there were shelves and cupboards everywhere piled with cartons and tins. A whole shelf of almost empty glass jars contained the remnants of what had once been a comprehensive stock of sweets. Across the middle of the room was a large oak counter supported on trestles with weighing scales and a large blotter. There was an iron safe in the corner and a stool with headphones resting on it beside a small telephone switchboard. A middle aged woman was sitting in an armchair unravelling a jumper and winding the wool up into a ball. She got up as they came in.

'Morning girls. What can I do for you?' She stuck the ball of wool onto a pair of knitting needles and came towards the counter.

Tamar's nostrils were quivering with the smell of new bread. A wicker basket under the counter was filled with crusty loaves dusted with flour. Tamar pointed to it. 'I'd like one of those please.'

'Me too,' Holly said behind her.

'No need to ask where you've come from,' the woman said with a laugh as she gave them the loaves.

The bread felt warm and soft in their hands. Tamar could feel the saliva running under her tongue. 'Is there anything else we could buy that's off ration?'

The woman considered for a moment. 'I can let you have a jar of Bovril? I'm afraid there's not much else.'

They sat on the seat outside the pub and tore the bread apart, dipping it into the jar and then stuffing it into their mouths without any regard for table manners. When they'd finished they licked the crumbs off their fingers and went back into the shop to buy another loaf to keep for the next day. 'Pity we can only do this once a week!' Holly said.

On the way back from the shop they walked past a lych gate set in a high wall. Tamar had noticed it on the way down, but had been too intent on getting to the village to stop and look. It had a wrought iron arch over it with an oil lantern set in the centre. Tamar peered through the gate. The high wall enclosed an almost circular graveyard shaded with yew trees and, in the centre, one of the smallest churches Tamar had ever seen, little more than a chapel with a low square bell tower at one end. A bicycle was propped up against the wall and at the far end of the graveyard a man was mowing the long grass with a scythe, carefully swinging it over the grave mounds. The air was heavily scented with the smell of wet, cut grass.

'Let's go in and explore,' Holly said. 'It looks so sheltered and peaceful in there.'

Tamar wondered why the church had been built so far from the village. As she stood outside the church door, the fells made a semi-circle at her back and in front the valley fell away so that she could see the Solway Firth glittering below and beyond it the towering dark blue mass of a Scottish mountain range against the horizon on the other side.

Holly was examining the gravestones, some of them dating from the seventeenth century, running her fingers over worn masonry to try to decipher dates and names. Every now and then Holly would exclaim at a new discovery. 'I've found a Christopher Ellwood, 1748, teacher of psalmody. What do you think that is?' Most of the graves shared a linked heritage of interconnected names that recurred again and again. There were Braithwaites and Teasdales and Mossops and Bainbridges. 'Everyone in this village must be related to everyone else!' Holly called.

The sun beat warm from the church wall and Tamar had the most wonderfully peaceful sensation. Although she'd been brought up in cities, used to noise, she'd never really been aware of the clamour of people, the clatter of wheeled traffic and the blaring shipyard sirens that had assaulted her consciousness every day and even into the night. At least, not until this moment. Now it was as though her whole body had been aching for the silence that surrounded her. As she lifted her head to look at the sky, two buzzards circled overhead, their great wings spread to catch the thermal, and she could hear them calling to each other, a haunting cry that would drive every small animal under cover for miles. They were beautiful powerful things.

'Tamar, come here quick.' Holly sounded excited. 'Look what I've found! It's you!' She was standing in front of a big slab of sandstone and she pointed to the inscription. 'Read that!'

'Tamar Fell.' The letters were carved in flowing script. 'Beloved wife of William Teasdale of Town End House. Dearly loved mother of Alice, Elizabeth, Margaret and Henry. At peace with God. This day 11th March 1871.'

'How strange,' Tamar said.

'Isn't it!'

Tamar shivered. 'I've never found another Tamar – never mind a Tamar Fell. It's the weirdest coincidence.'

'Good morning girls.' They turned to see a man wearing a clerical collar – a slight, elderly man in a greasy black suit and old-fashioned clerical hat locking the vestry door. 'Are you looking at the old graves?'

'I've found one here with my name on it.' Tamar called back.

He came over and stood behind them, peering at the inscription over his half lenses. He had a soft, unused kind of face with big pouches under his eyes.

'Tamar Fell. Not such an unusual name around here.'

'I've never found another Tamar.'

'It's a common Quaker name. The Pennines are riddled with lead mines and the London Mining Company that owned them was Quaker. You'll find a lot of lead miners and their families in this graveyard.'

'My father was a Quaker. So, is it a biblical name? When I was little I used to think I was named after the river in Devon.'

'She was an Old Testament princess,' the vicar said as they walked back towards the gate. 'A model of female behaviour.'

'Well that's certainly not me!' Tamar laughed, looking down at her corduroy trousers and muddy boots.

'So how are you enjoying the village? You're living at Holme Farm I believe.' Unlike everyone else who mentioned Holme Farm, there didn't seem to be any sarcasm or ambiguity underlying the Vicar's remark.

'It's beautiful,' Tamar said, looking back at the churchyard in its walled enclave. 'But can you tell us why the church is built so far from the village? They're usually in the middle, aren't they? People must have the best part of a mile to go to and from church.'

The vicar was looking up at the hills beyond. 'This is a very ancient religious site,' he said. 'As far as I can ascertain from the records, the circular walls of the graveyard follow the contours of an ancient henge monument of some kind.'

Holly shivered. 'Does that mean it's pagan?'

He smiled. 'Oh yes. The Christians often built their churches on older sites. It was a way of preventing them from being used in the old ways. Quite sensible really. People still came to worship there but in the new religion rather than the old.'

'The church seems to have been built a long time ago,' Tamar said.

'A very, very long time ago. This building dates from the 13th century when St Cuthbert's desiccated body was paraded around England and every resting place was commemorated with a church. This pagan place was just the kind of site they would have chosen to sanctify with his body. People believed that miracles happened wherever it went.'

'It seems strange to think of so much history in this landscape,' Tamar said.

The vicar bent to put on his bicycle clips. 'Will I be seeing you in my congregation tomorrow?' he enquired. 'Or are you chapel like most of the folk round here?'

'You might see me,' Holly said.

He tipped his hat to them and mounted his bicycle.

'Are you really going to go?' Tamar asked as she watched him ride off towards the village.

'It's such a beautiful little church,' Holly said. She looked almost guiltily at Tamar. 'I can't manage by myself like you. I'm one of those people who needs to be able to believe in something. I like to think there's a God up there looking after me.'

All the way back to Holme Farm Tamar thought of what the vicar had said, imagining the tramping feet of Roman cohorts, the shadowy hordes of pagans with long hair and painted bodies in torchlight procession to the henge.

'Do you suppose they made human sacrifices?' Holly asked. 'I thought it was such a peaceful place until he talked about the pagans, and then suddenly I imagined all sorts of ghosts lurking in the shadow of the yew trees.'

'It's wonderful,' Tamar said. 'Just think if we could really see into the past!'

'No thanks! According to my history teacher their lives were fairly brutish. There was nothing romantic about it at all!'

'I shouldn't think it was much more primitive than Heslop's,' Tamar said.

Holly stopped in the lane, her face contorted. 'I wish we didn't have to go back.'

'So do I, but there's nothing we can do. Maybe when we get to know Mrs Heslop better things will improve.'

'I was wondering whether she'd let me do some cooking.'

'Can you cook?' Tamar asked, amazed.

'A little. Sponge cakes and souffles and things like that – we had to learn it at the ladies college. None of us could see the point really, but I do now.'

'Heslop probably wouldn't let us anyway. He told me off for helping her set the table the first night I was here. He's a horrible man.'

'We can only try,' Holly said. 'Things couldn't be much worse.'

~~~~~~~~~~~~~~~~~~

Private Huyton was on breakfast duty and, judging by the consistency of the porridge, Herr Brunner was probably in the kitchen. Anna looked at the grey sludge being ladled into her bowl and thought it probably more suited to cementing pathways than lining her stomach. Hungry as she was, the salty, lumpy mess was left to congeal in her bowl.

'Eat your porridge,' Private Huyton ordered as she prowled around the mess, pausing behind Anna's chair.

'It's horrible.' She had been meaning to pass it to Sister Perpetua, who was the only person who regularly ate everything that was put in front of her.

'You won't get anything else if you don't.'

Anna looked at the single slice of bread and marge left on the plate in the centre of the table and reached out to take it. Who was this woman to tell her what she could and couldn't eat as if she was a child?

But as Anna put the bread on the plate beside her, Private Huyton coughed and a slimy bubble of sputum landed in the centre of the slice. Anna couldn't believe it. 'That's disgusting,' she said, half turning to face the woman.

'You'll just have to eat your porridge then, won't you,' Private Huyton said with a sneer.

Something ignited in Anna's head. She moved her hand, as if reaching into the centre of the table for something and sent the bowl of porridge sliding from the surface over the woman's immaculately polished brogues. Some of the glutinous mess splashed up her stockings. There was absolute silence in the hut.

'How clumsy of me,' Anna said with as much irony as she could. 'I do apologise.'

The Private's face was crimson. 'You did that on purpose, you evil German bitch,' she shouted. 'But you're not getting away
~~~~~~~~~~~~~~~~~~

with it.' She stormed out of the mess. There was a sputter of clapping around the tables as she banged the door.

'Now you really are in trouble,' Grisel said. 'She won't let that rest.'

A few moments later the corporal from the guard post came into the hut and told Anna that the Captain wanted to see her. She was escorted to the main office at the entrance and marched in front of the Captain's desk.

'Private Huyton has told me what happened,' he said in a dull monotone. 'What have you got to say for yourself?'

'She can't make me eat what I don't like,' Anna said.

He looked completely indifferent. 'I'm afraid we can't have this kind of insubordination here. It's bad for morale. You're to be confined to the dormitory for the rest of the day. I've also been informed that you have drawing materials in your possession. I'm afraid I'm going to have to ask you to hand them over. Private Huyton will escort you to your hut and collect them.'

Anna gasped in protest, but he continued in the same bored voice. 'Drawing, or taking photographs of government installations and personnel without permission is against camp regulations as a risk to national security.'

Anna was so stunned she could say nothing. Private Huyton and the corporal were standing behind her, the Captain in front of her. She was trapped. With shaking hands she opened her bag and handed over her sketch book and pencils. Then she was marched back to the dormitory where a smirking Private Huyton made her turn out her cupboard for any other items she might have hidden – even her mattress was searched. Then they left her alone. Anna lay down on her bed and faced the wall. She had never felt such devastation and loss. Everything had been taken from her now – painting, the future she had envisaged, friends and family. How was she to live? Day after empty day stretched endlessly in front of her made hideous by the prospect of all the petty cruelties that Private Huyton would no doubt inflict on her at every opportunity.

Someone came into the dormitory but Anna didn't move. She just wanted to be alone.

It was Grisel. 'You've got letters,' she said, gently touching

Anna's shoulder. 'Two of them.'

Anna sat up and took them from her. The first was from George and sight of his cheerful scrawl made her heart leap. He was at Catterick camp, he wrote, and shortly to be made a sergeant. Tamar had told him about Anna's predicament. '*Keep your spirits up*,' he wrote. '*Sooner or later someone's going to realise you're the victim of government insanity. I'm due some leave shortly so I'll try and get up there. I can't wait to see you again. Love George.*' A series of large, crooked kisses were scratched across the bottom of the page. It was, Anna thought, probably as near as George could get to a love letter. She found George's expressions of affection oddly comforting and that disturbed her. She missed him more than she had expected.

The other envelope was in a strange hand Anna didn't recognise. When she opened it she was very surprised to find that it was from Alicia. Since the incident at the flat there had been one or two awkward, embarrassed meetings at the life class and for a while Anna had stopped going. Now Anna felt sorry for Alicia and vaguely guilty about the way she had over-reacted. But she had never expected, or wanted, to hear from her again.

'*I can't tell you how sorry I was to learn that you'd been interned*,' Alicia wrote. '*It's so unjust. The last war was the same – everything run by bureaucratic idiots! My brother has a permanent commission, and I've written to him to see if anything can be done. I can't bear to think of such a shining girl as you locked up like a criminal. There's no need to write back to me – I just wanted you to know that everyone here is on your side. The entire art college has written to the Home Office!*'

~~~

Heslop kept a nanny goat tethered in the orchard where it was allowed to munch the nettles and anything else within reach. Neither Tamar nor Holly had ever met a goat before and they were wary of her horns and her malevolent eyes. It was a relief to find that Heslop did the milking. During their second week at the farm the goat managed to chew through her tether and make a substantial fringe around the sheets on Mrs Heslop's washing
~~~

line before she was caught.

Two days later when Tamar and Holly went into the orchard they found the goat running round and round its stake, bleating as if in pain and rubbing herself against the fence posts as if she had some kind of skin disease. Heslop was bucketing the calves in the old byre. Holly approached him like an unexploded bomb. Tamar could see that she hated having to talk to him at all. 'Mr Heslop,' she said tentatively. 'The nanny goat's acting very strangely. I think she must be ill. Do you think she's got colic from the sheets?'

Heslop looked at her as if she was mad. 'She's ruttin',' he said crudely. The way Heslop used the innocent farming term made it sound like an obscenity. 'You'd best take her up to the Bainbridge's billy.' He laughed derisively and stamped off with the calf pail in the direction of the barn.

'I hate him,' Holly said. 'He makes my flesh creep. Have you seen the way he looks at me?'

Tamar sighed. 'He does that to me too. It's horrid, but I don't think there's any danger from him. He's the type who looks but doesn't touch.' Tamar hoped that she was right.

It took all their ingenuity to catch the nanny goat. After several undignified pursuits round the orchard, Holly held out a bucket of scraps meant for the dog's supper and when the goat dipped her head in it, careless with greed, Tamar slipped the halter over her horns.

It was the Bainbridge's who owned the next farm up the lane, the high, white building she could see from the yard – that much Tamar knew now, but she had never met them. She wondered whether they minded Heslop using their billy goat rather than having one of his own. 'Useless buggers!' he'd said when Tamar had asked. 'Eat their bloody heads off and good for nowt!' Once into the lane, the goat seemed to know exactly what was at the end of the journey and began to trot so quickly it took both girls to hold onto the rope. But at the farm gate she finally slipped her leash with a quick twist and tug and though they both ran, they only appeared in the yard in time to see her clear the rail of the garth at the far end, greeted by a deafening clamour of bleating.

'She's been here before,' Holly said, panting and laughing as she leant against the porch to get her breath back.

It was a big, sheltered yard with two barns on the opposite side to the house. The doors were painted red and the yard had been meticulously swept. Two calves pushed healthy pink noses over the bottom half of a byre door and a sleepy collie wagged its tail lazily as it lay on the cobbles in the sun. The house was two stories high with a steeply pitched roof and the front door was centrally placed as if it expected the house to be conventionally double fronted. But while at one side there was the traditional white farmhouse with one big window up and another down painted with black surrounds, on the other side there was a square turret built from granite blocks, rising up like a church tower. The upper windows were long, narrow slits separated by mullions but the ground floor window was a modern casement that looked as if it had only recently been put in.

'It's half castle, half house,' Holly said. 'I wonder why?'

The door was open and a fabulous smell of baking drifted out. The scent of it made Tamar feel quite faint. She tapped and went cautiously inside. 'Mrs Bainbridge?' she called.

The inner door on the left was latched open and a broad, plump woman in a floral wrap-round overall, wisps of greying hair in a fan around her pink face, came out to greet them. She wiped her hands on her overall and held them out, clasping both their fingers in a warm grip.

'You'll be the lasses from Heslop's,' she said. There was a laugh in her voice. 'No need to ask why you've come – I saw the nanny fly past!'

'That's wimmin for you!' A male voice called out from the room behind her. 'When they fix their eye on a fella there's no hoddin' them back!'

'Away wi' you, Father!' Mrs Bainbridge called back, leading the girls into the kitchen. 'You watch your tongue in front of these young ladies.'

'This is Joe,' Mrs Bainbridge said. 'My husband. And this is my brother-in-law Wilf.' She indicated a man sitting in the corner reading a newspaper. He nodded to the girls over the top of it without saying anything. Joe winked at them and said, 'Tha' won't get much out of 'im. Flayt to death o' wimmin!' Joe was sitting at the table in his shirtsleeves with a mug of tea in one hand and piece of bread in the other. He was a small, thin, weasel faced man, with skin so weathered and brown it looked like shoe leather, but his eyes were bright with humour and there were deep laughter creases round his mouth and eyes. 'How do!' he said. 'Sit thee down.' He nodded towards the empty chairs on the other side of the table, appraising them with his twinkling eyes as they moved to obey him. Tamar presumed they had passed the inspection. 'Them's ladies, right enough, you're not wrong there Mother!' he said to his wife, with an emphatic nod of the head.

Tamar introduced herself and Holly, who had suddenly become shy and silent.

'What mek o' name's that?' Joe said when she told them Holly's name.

'Tamar says it's a character in a book,' Holly said quietly.

'Oh. Books is it!' Joe said, in a tone of voice that made the entire compass of English literature irrelevant. Then he narrowed his eyes at Tamar. 'Is't tha' related to the Fells of Old Hall then?' he asked.

Tamar shook her head. 'I didn't know there were any Fells here at all until I saw the name on a gravestone in the churchyard.'

'Been Fells up at Kirkland for a long time since.' Tamar could see Joe lining them up in his mind, before bringing them into recollection. 'Though not now, mind. Old Archie Fell's son, Alec – nobbut a lad – got killed in the first war. 1918. Three days afore the armistice. But they weren't tell't till two days after. Celebratin' with relief, and then the telegram! That was a bad do, that was. The daughter married Dickson Pearson and he farms it now. So there'll be no more Fells.'

'It's odd,' Tamar said. 'I've never met anyone with the same name before.'

'It's a northern name,' Mrs Bainbridge said.

And Joe added with a wry laugh 'Down south they call them Hills.'

Mrs Bainbridge had already taken two more cups out of the cupboard and was pouring water into the teapot. 'No need to ask if you'd like a bite,' she said, putting a plate and knife in front of them. 'You won't have had much at Heslops.'

Tamar nodded. She felt almost sick with hunger as she looked at the plates of bread and scones and cake spread across the table. There was a thick slab of butter in the middle, a plate of ripe tomatoes that still smelled of the greenhouse, a bowl of sliced cucumber in vinegar and a bread board covered with thick wedges of home-cooked ham.

Joe was watching her. 'Things still bad down there then?' he asked.

Holly shuddered. 'We've been there less than a month and we're starving. I don't know how they can live like that.'

'Heslop's a greedy bugger. Allas was. Short arms, long pockets. That's him!'

'Mrs Heslop seems nice enough,' Tamar said. 'If only she wasn't so timid. She's afraid to go out of the house, even into the yard. I've tried to talk to her, but most of the time she lives in a world of her own.'

'She's never been the same since her son died,' Mrs Bainbridge said.

'I didn't know they'd had a son. He's never been mentioned.'

Mrs Bainbridge sighed and looked sadly across at Joe. 'Light of his mother's life that boy. Only child. Then he got a lift back from a dance in Dalston on the back of some daft lad's motor bike and they went straight into the back of a road roller parked up for the night. She'd never been much of a one for socialising, but she used to come down to the WI and I used to go up there for a bit of a crack occasionally. But not since. I went up once and she wouldn't open the door even. Spoke to me through the sneck hole.'

'Thowt she'd be to tek away after the lad died,' Joe said, reaching for another slice of ham and bread.

'Poor body! Living with that man would turn anybody's wits.' Mrs Bainbridge picked up the tea pot to top up their cups. 'Now you two tuck in, you're both as thin as laths.'

'Well they would be, wouldn't they?' Joe said. 'The last hired lad Heslop had, couple o' years back, climbed out o't window in the dark, rolled down't lean-to roof and scarpered. Couldn't wait six month to the next hiring. Thowt himself lucky to get out alive. Now none o't lads'll go there. That's why he applied for thee. Slave labour!' He winked. 'Still, you know where to come now when you want a good feed.'

As they got up to leave, Tamar noticed the framed photograph of a young man in uniform on the dresser. 'Is that your son?' she asked.

A shadow crossed Mrs Bainbridge's face. 'That's our Martin, Wilf's son. He's been joined up about a year. Such a clever lad. It's a waste.' There was a kind of restraint in her voice that deterred Tamar from asking more questions.

At the door Mrs Bainbridge gave them a soft parcel wrapped in greaseproof paper. 'Mind you don't let Heslop see you with that,' she said. 'It'll do for your supper.'

Going home again at a slower pace dragging a reluctant and evil-smelling nanny goat, the evening seemed colder and darker the further they walked down the lane.

'Just think if we'd been sent to the Bainbridge's instead!' Holly said.

'Don't!' Tamar could feel her eyes pricking with tears. But she wasn't going to cry. She never cried. Crying never got anything done.

~~~~~~~~~~~~~~~~~~
~~~~~~~~~~~~~~~~~~

CHAPTER EIGHTEEN

Dear Anna,

I'm writing this while waiting for a cow's afterbirth to boil in a bucket on the range for the dog's supper. The things you have to do! If anyone had told me that I'd be able to do things like this without throwing up, I would never have believed them. Holly and I watched a calf born today for the first time. It was quite a revelation. Messier than I'd expected, but also very moving. We both cried when the slippery little beast – all covered in slime – finally staggered to its feet and the mother turned round and licked it clean. Then Heslop came in and grabbed it and took it off before they'd time to get acquainted. Apparently you can't let them suckle, otherwise they won't take the bucket. So now the calf is shivering in a pen of straw bales in the barn and the cow is shouting her head off. It all seems very cruel.

Things are just as bad as ever here. I think Heslop enjoys watching people suffer. Everything's done the hard way. Instead of a separator we have to stand the milk in old fashioned crocks so that the cream rises to the top and we can skim it off for the butter churn. That's Holly's job because it's not too heavy for her. Heslop makes us take almost all the cream off, which is scandalous, because it's supposed to go to the dairy as whole milk. Heslop sells the butter on the black market to hotels and restaurants further south – it gets put on a train and sent to Preston. The same with the eggs. He has a secret hen house in the wood that the Ministry don't know about and all the biggest eggs go off with the butter. God knows what he does with the money. His wife certainly doesn't see any of it. She has a pretty miserable life. Heslop's a bully and it's time someone stood up to him. Holly and I plot rebellion when we're shivering under our blankets at night. But we can't think of anything that would be the perfect retribution – not yet anyway.

I haven't heard from Edward in ages. He's in [blacked out], and according to the news [two lines obliterated], so I hope he's going to be safely home soon. It's more than six months since I last saw him and sometimes I find it difficult to remember what he looks like. Does that sound awful?

Are you all right? I know you can't talk about the camp, but I hope it's better than being here. I'm too tired to write any more and I suspect the dog's supper is cooked – it stinks dreadfully. I'd better sign off for now. When will we ever see each other?

Love and best

Tamar

Anna folded Tamar's mutilated letter up and put it in her pocket. The second sheet of it was only written on one side and she could use that for drawing. They had left her a pen for writing letters and secretly, at odd moments during the day when she could be alone Anna had found a way of doing little sketches on the backs of envelopes or unused pieces of Basildon Bond. They were microscopic, but the discipline of scaling everything down and getting in just the right amount of detail was a challenge. It was the only thing that kept her sane now that all hope of being released immediately had gone. Her mother wrote that she had gone to the Appeals tribunal and found them less than sympathetic. Anna was of military age, had been brought up in Germany and her loyalty to her adopted country was in question. Hadn't she always insisted on using her German name? '*Apparently you even told the recruiting officer when you went to work in the parachute factory that you weren't willing to do military service,*' Mrs Wiseman wrote sadly. '*Anyway, I've been told since then that a lot of it is down to who you know. Your Grandpa's a freemason, though it's not something he talks about, and he's going to speak to someone he knows down at the lodge. Don't worry. We'll get you out of there somehow.*'

But that was a month ago and nothing had happened. The long summer nights gave no relief to Anna. She had never felt so desperate. She couldn't sleep, lying awake for hours listening to Sister Perpetua's snores and the little night sounds outside; a rodent scratching at the wooden skirting, an owl on the fence, the scrape of a guard's foot on the path, the sound of the lavatory chain being pulled in the nearby latrine. She was also finding it difficult to eat. The unappetising food stuck in her throat and refused to be swallowed. Dr Blum told her that she was suffering from depression. 'It is your mind that is ill, not your body.' Anna felt that she was surrounded by a thick grey cloud which drained everything of colour and obscured the future. She knew that she had to be able to draw and paint if she wanted to hold on to her sanity.

It was Grisel who unwittingly gave her the idea. She was talking in the dormitory after the lights had been switched off, about her home town of Tubingen. 'Some of the students at the university were so appalled by what the Nazi's were doing they went on hunger strike as a protest.'

'Did it do any good?'

'It made everyone aware of what was going on – but several of the students disappeared afterwards. Two of them, I know, were shot.'

Walking round the perimeter fence with Dr Blum the next day Anna asked how long a human being could survive without food. 'Quite a long time – weeks, perhaps months, so long as there is plenty of water to drink.' He looked at Anna perceptively over his half-moon lenses. 'This is a strange question. Why do you ask?'

'I have to do something,' Anna said. 'I can't just let them treat me like this. I feel so angry all the time because I'm powerless. I've lost control of my own life. There has to be something I can do to fight back. They wouldn't want me to die would they?'

At breakfast the next morning Anna accepted the cup of tea she was given but refused to eat anything. It was easy to forgo the mess of powdered egg congealing in the tray. At lunchtime she refused again, sitting quietly while the others ate their vegetable soup, but found it harder to resist the urges of her appetite. All afternoon her stomach ached and she felt oddly shaky. The evening meal was torture. A savoury corned beef hash with onions was being served and the smell made all the juices run into Anna's mouth. It was all she could do to prevent herself giving in to temptation – just a mouthful – just a taste. Surely it wouldn't hurt?

'What's the matter with you?' the corporal on duty asked. 'Why aren't you eating? Are you ill?'

'I'm not eating anything until my book and my drawing pencils are returned to me.'

He looked disconcerted, but said nothing.

The pain in Anna's stomach kept her awake most of the night and when she did sleep there were lurid dreams. She was standing in the kitchen at Partenkirchen and her grandmother was ladling out one of her spicy sausage stews. Anna could smell it and taste it and woke in the early morning light with her stomach rumbling dismally under her rib cage.

After breakfast Anna was summoned to the Captain's office.

'What's all this nonsense about?' he asked testily.

'I'm on hunger strike until my drawing things are returned to me. You had no right to take them away.'

'You were given a perfectly proper punishment for insubordination. And what you were doing was also a risk to security.'

'That's ridiculous!'

He glared at her. 'I am warning you that if you continue in this course, I will be forced to take strong action.'

'Do,' Anna said. 'But this isn't a prison – we're internees and we have certain rights.'

'He's a fool,' Grisel said. 'He gave in to a petty impulse when you upset Private Huyton and now he can't go back on what he knows was a stupid decision because the retreat would make him look even more foolish.'

'Good. In the end he'll have to give in. Think of the fuss if I died of starvation!'

Anna felt confident talking to Grisel, but by the end of the week she was beginning to feel shaky and disorientated. If she stood up too quickly she became dizzy and walking around made her light-headed. There were flashes of light at the edge of her vision and she felt tired all the time. The ache in her stomach was constant. The Captain had given orders that she was to be present in the mess hut for every meal and it was torture to have to watch people eating. Private Huyton lost no opportunity to taunt Anna – holding a plate of stew beneath her nose, savouring a spoonful of steamed pudding in front of her with exaggerated expressions of satisfaction. Anna thought of what Tamar was enduring at the hands of Mr Heslop and wondered what it was that made people enjoy watching other people suffer.

~~~~~~~~~~~~~~~~~~

For Holly and Tamar the days had settled into a pattern. At five fifteen the alarm clattered them awake, amplified inside a metal bucket with a tin plate on top. There was just time to roll out of bed and pull on trousers and jumpers over the top of the shirts and underclothes they slept in to keep out the early morning cold which had a bite to it even in late June. Overcoats on, scarves over uncombed hair, a splash of water in the eyes and then downstairs just as Heslop came to bang on the door at half past five. No tea – the range wasn't lit until Mrs Heslop rose at seven, so no hope of boiling a kettle. Holly experimented with leaving it hanging over the dying embers last thing at night, but it was barely lukewarm by morning.

Breakfast was sometimes porridge, lumpy and unsugared, but at least edible – the preserved eggs were often not. And then it was a gruelling routine of feeding livestock, mucking out byres and pens before lunch which the Heslops called dinner – a meal that grew increasingly repulsive as the spring progressed towards summer. There were a number of alternatives – all of them unpalatable. Rabbit was the staple food, either shot or snared, stewed or put into a pie. Tamar began to feel sick when she saw them hanging in the dairy with their heads swollen with blood and their sticky, blind eyes. Sometimes it was a doe with milk in her udders and Tamar would know that somewhere a litter of baby rabbits was starving slowly to death. Holly, who was unbelievably soft hearted, had almost given up eating at all, just picking at the vegetables on the edge of her plate. Crow or pigeon pie was another regular visitor to the dinner table, whenever Heslop had the double barrel out in the garth. The birds were bony and tough, with dark-tasting meat that stuck between your teeth. Tamar learned only to eat the pie-crust and savoury gravy.

Every Saturday on their afternoons off, Tamar and Holly went down to the bakery in the village and bought a whole loaf of
~~~~~~~~~~~~~~~~~~

bread each, eating all of it on the way home. The smell and taste of fresh bread, warm and crusty, was something to look forward to during the rest of the week. Later they would go up to the Bainbridge's for Saturday tea – a gastronomic treat that kept them going for days and Mrs Bainbridge always gave them a package of cakes and sandwiches to take home for Sunday. If it hadn't been for the Bainbridge's friendship, Tamar didn't think they would have been able to survive.

In the long light evenings Tamar took out her correspondence course and wrote essays on a rickety wooden table in the orchard. She was finding it easier than she'd expected. It was just a matter of reading and remembering. Only the maths was a struggle, but unexpectedly Holly came to the rescue. She seemed to have a natural talent for figures and happily passed on everything she knew to Tamar. 'You should have been a teacher,' Tamar told her.

Holly laughed. 'I was hopeless at school. I was the only girl in my class who actually failed their school certificate.'

'At least you make good cakes.' Tamar was munching her way through a mouth-watering slice of Victoria sponge spread with blackberry jam. Mrs Heslop had been quite happy to allow Holly to do some baking on her afternoon off and even Mr Heslop had grudgingly appreciated the results.

'Sugar's the problem,' Holly said. 'The ration isn't enough. But the Women's Institute have got some recipes you can make with honey so I'm going to experiment.'

Tamar had been astonished to find that Holly had joined the WI as well as spending one evening a week helping the Vicar's wife with parish work. She seemed more confident and, except for the gruelling work on the farm, happier.

But the news from the war front in Europe was growing steadily more depressing. Although George was still in England, Edward was on the other side of the channel, reporting on events and his letters, even though censored, made Tamar less than optimistic about the outcome. Edward's mother sent Tamar newspaper cuttings of his articles as they appeared in the local papers. The German armies were advancing, inexorably.

Both Holly and Tamar listened anxiously to radio reports of the fall of France and the evacuation of Dunkirk. Heslop was far from keen to have the radio on except for the weather forecast, so for three evenings in a row they went to the Bainbridge's to sit with Joe and his wife and brother Wilf. Wilf's son Martin was with the expeditionary force across the channel, and their anxiety for his safety matched Tamar's for Edward. After the evacuation, Tamar met the post girl at the gate every day, hoping for a letter – a letter with an English postmark that would tell her he was safe and well and somewhere not too far away. The Bainbridge's took a daily paper and Tamar scanned the lists of wounded and missing, but Edward's name was always absent.

A month after Dunkirk when Tamar collected the mail from the post girl at the gate, she realised that she had almost given up expecting any kind of communication. Something had happened to him, she was sure. He would have come back by now. But the thought of Edward wounded somewhere, taken prisoner, or even worse, didn't affect her as much as she had expected. Tamar felt curiously detached. She closed her eyes and tried to conjure up Edward's face but it was becoming increasingly difficult. He was fading in her mind, his existence more and more unreal.

She took the Heslop's mail and put it on the kitchen table and then went to give Holly her weekly letter from her father. Holly was in the stable trying to attach a silk stocking stuffed with chaff to the inside of a horse's collar to make a pad that would keep the collar away from the horse's skin. The shire mare, Jess, had a tendency to pull too hard when she was harnessed into the shafts by herself and the only collar that would fit her was too big and rubbed her shoulders raw. Flies collected in thick heaving masses on the red glistening patches of flesh and yesterday Holly had had to scrub maggots out of one wound and apply coal tar to it.

Holly opened her letter and read it quickly, then, with tears beginning to well up into her eyes, handed it to Tamar. Mr Pergavie's letters were always typed on stiff cream paper – presumably by his secretary at the shop. '*I'm sorry to have to tell you*,' it read, '*that your cousin David was shot down over the channel last week. We are all devastated, and I know you will be too. He died bravely, defending his country, though I know that is not a lot of comfort, but it is something to hold onto.*'

'It's not as though he was a boyfriend or anything like that,'

Holly said. 'But we've known each other since we were children. It seems really strange to think I'll never see him again.' A tear trickled down her cheek.

The stable door slammed back on its hinges and the girls jumped apart. It was Heslop. 'Can't leave you two minutes without you skiving off. Get your arses into the paddock and take old Ben to the smithy. He's cast a shoe. And be bloody quick. I want to start cuttin' hay this afternoon.'

Tamar groaned. 'It would be Ben.'

Holly dried her eyes on her sleeve. 'Let's just get it over with. I've never seen a horse shoe'd before.' She took the bridle and a piece of sacking down from the hook and stuffed her letter in the pocket of her trousers as they walked nervously across the yard.

Heslop got his horses cheap. Other men's rejects. But, Tamar thought, it wouldn't matter if he bought the best, a few months of being shouted at and pulled around by Heslop would make them as nervy and vicious as Ben. Heslop's thrifty stockmanship didn't extend as far as his horses. They weren't marketable produce like the other animals, but machinery to be used and abused so that he could grind as much work out of them as possible. Tamar winced whenever she saw him yank the bit roughly in their tender mouths, shouting 'c'mon, yer stubborn, bloody-minded brute. I'll teach yer who's boss!'

Jess was the best of the heavy horses, a good tempered elderly mare. But Ben was different – a big handsome Clydesdale over 20 hands high with a white blaze down his face and an innate hatred of the human race. He had a particular fear of anyone going behind his legs and if he knew you were there he would kick out. Old Joe had said he was what was called a Reister, and that he'd kicked one of the hired lads so hard he went clean over the midden wall. Holly had to put a sack over his eyes when hitching him up and get Tamar to stand at his head to soothe him. Once he was in harness he was fine. Tamar sometimes wondered what had happened to inspire such dread. But this morning, as Tamar held out a scoop of oats, Holly managed to get his bit and bridle on without too much trouble, dodging his tossing head and bared teeth.

The blacksmith looked completely dumbfounded when Holly, accompanied by Tamar with a riding whip, led Ben into the smithy yard. 'They've never let a couple of girls like you out with that animal? Bloody Heslop!' He turned away from the anvil and called through the back door,

'Ivan! Get yourself in here with the rig!'

A tall, thin, rather foreign-looking man appeared in the doorway with a coil of rope.

'He's a DP,' the smith said. 'I put in for him when my son got called up.'

Ben was no trouble until Holly tried to lead him inside the smithy door and then he started to kick and rear and it took all four of them to hold him and get him inside. As soon as they were through the door, Ivan threw a rope round Ben's back leg, tied it up to a beam and then pulled on it really hard. Tamar was amazed to see how it calmed him instantly. Ivan nodded to the girls without speaking. His hair was almost white blond and the down on his tanned arms was like gold floss. Tamar noticed that Holly blushed as he looked at her. Then his eyes were on Ben. Tamar saw how gently he stroked his flank, and listened to the flow of words in his own language, spoken softly, that brought the horse's ears up to listen even as the white's of Ben's eyes were rolling back with fear.

'Comes from a farm in Lithuania, or some such outlandish place,' the blacksmith said. 'Knows how to handle a horse right enough like, but not much cop else.'

Ivan glanced up, his eyes flashing with sudden humour. Holly smiled and he smiled back and then quickly lowered his head again.

The smith pared off the quick of Ben's hoof like slices of grey rind, holding the huge fringed hoof between his knees like the underside of a gigantic mushroom. Then, quickly, he applied the red hot shoe and the whole forge was full of the smell of burning horn. It made Tamar's eyes water and her stomach turn. Ben stood still, but his eyes were showing only the whites, his muscles trembled and small patches of white foam had formed around the base of his neck.

The smith pointed to a long scar on his rear quarter where the hair grew in different directions, like grass over a furrow. 'See that,' he said. 'Someone did that to him with a metal bar, or a nail in a bit of wood – summat like that. Horses never forgive an injury. He doesn't trust anybody, this one. And he hates iron!'

'Poor Ben,' Holly said.

'You wouldn't say poor Ben if you'd been on the receiving end of one of these!' the smith said. He had lifted up one of Ben's front hooves to inspect. 'They can deliver a punch that can break a man's skull like eggshell. You don't take risks with a horse like this. Mind you take notice!'

As if he'd been listening, Ben lurched forwards, quickly restrained by Ivan who uttered what sounded like an oath in his own language. Maggie, the post girl was standing in the door with her bicycle.

'I've got a letter for you, Tamar,' she said. 'Second post. I saw you coming down the lane with the horse earlier, so I thought you'd be here. You might not want to wait until tomorrow for it.'

Tamar's heart leaped into her throat as she took the envelope from Maggie's outstretched hand. Edward's handwriting was on the envelope, which was crumpled and grubby as if it had been in someone's pocket. There was an English stamp on it.

She went outside and sat down on the edge of the stone water trough to read it.

'My darling Tamar, I'm giving this to one of the lads who's going home in the hope that he can post it once he gets back. I can't tell you exactly where I am, but we're headed south in the opposite direction to everyone else and I want you to know that I'm safe. Don't worry if you don't get a letter from me for quite some time. Where I'm going, I won't be able to write, but I'll be thinking of you and loving you and looking forward to the day when I can see your darling face in front of me again. Dearest Tamar, you can't think how much I love you and want you. Please don't stop loving me just because I'm not there. Just knowing you're waiting for me keeps me going through the most awful moments.

We're none of us the same as we were when we started out. The first time, even the second time you kill someone it shocks you rigid and you sweat with guilt and terror and adrenaline. After that you don't think about it. You just kill. We're all murderers.

I can't tell you where I'm going or what I'm doing or when I'm likely to be back. Don't stop writing though. Send the letters to my unit and they'll get them to me when they can. Reading them will be something to look forward to. Give my love to Anna and George and Lily.

Dearest Tamar. How I do love you. Good night and God Bless.

PS I bought you a ring – a real bobby dazzler as Lily would say. There were some bargains to be had in Paris when the German's rolled in. I wish I could give it to you now, but you'll just have to wait!

Pray for me. I know you don't believe, but that won't matter. Just pray.

Edward

There was no time to think about the implications. Tamar stuffed the letter in her pocket to read again later. A truculent Ben had to be taken back to the farm, and for the rest of the day the girls were occupied harnessing the horses and hitching them to the cutting bars. Heslop took Ben into the twenty acre field and Tamar and Holly were told to cut the small field near the house. 'There's nowt to it,' Heslop said, 'you line up with the hedge and then lower the bar and gee up the bloody `oss.'

He was right. Holly took the reins and Tamar raised and lowered the bar, watching the long, sweetly scented grass fall in swathes behind the teeth. But it was bone-rattling, sitting on the uncomfortable metal seats, bouncing up and down. By the time Mrs Heslop appeared at the gate with a can of tea and some bread and marge in grease-proof paper, the base of Tamar's spine was bruised and sore.

Holly had found a tiny round nest woven from grass stalks with half a dozen pink mice in it. 'What should we do?' she asked. 'They haven't got any fur on. They're bound to die.'

'Just put the nest into the long grass by the hedge. Maybe their parents will come back for them.'

Holly's eyes were streaming from the grass pollen. 'It's only hay fever,' she told Tamar dismissively. 'I've always had it.' But by the end of the day she was wheezing painfully. Tamar felt desperately sorry for her. She'd secretly begun to wonder whether Holly really was physically fit enough to stand up to farm work. That night, as Tamar tried to ease her body into a comfortable position on the hard mattress, every bone and muscle ached in protest, and she knew that she was much stronger than Holly. She carefully re-read Edward's precious letter and then tucked it under her pillow.

'The trouble is,' she said to Holly as they lay in the fading light, listening to the branch of a tree rattling against the corrugated iron roof of the lean-to. 'Although I love him, I'm not very keen on the idea of getting married. Does that make sense to you?'

'Not really,' Holly was still wheezing, but she sounded sleepy. 'I thought if you really loved someone, you wanted to marry them and spend your life with them.'

'But I do want to spend my life with Edward – I can't imagine spending it with anyone else. It's just that there's this gap. I can't explain. As though I'm waiting for something to happen to me first. Something important. But I don't know what it is.'

She was talking to herself. From the other bed, Holly's breath came and went in the long sighs of shallow sleep.

~~~~~~~~~~~~~~~~~~

At the end of the second week, Anna was feeling too weak to make the trip to the mess hut and spent the summer days lying on her bunk. Grisel kept her water jug filled and sat quietly beside her. There were rumours, Grisel told her, that they were all to be moved shortly. Herr Brunner and two of the others were going to be deported as potentially dangerous Nazi sympathisers, and the rest were to be taken to a camp on an island – Grisel was unsure of its location. This uncertainty made Anna feel even more depressed. Two families had also arrived at the camp, Grisel said, with young children. 'What kind of country is it that puts children in prison?' she asked.

The following day Private Huyton came into the hut accompanied by a stout figure in a dark suit carrying an attache case. 'Dr Wilson's come to take a look at you,' she said. 'Up you get.'

But the doctor put a restraining hand on Anna's shoulder as
~~~~~~~~~~~~~~~~~~

she struggled to get out of bed. 'Starvation puts a strain on the heart,' he said to Private Huyton. 'I'd like to check that it's in good order first.' He listened to Anna's chest with a stethoscope, checked her reflexes and peered into her eyes with a light, before asking her to stand and walk a few paces.

'Do you know how dangerous self starvation is?' he told her. 'You could damage your health for the rest of your life. Besides the fuss and bother you're causing everyone. I've had to come all the way from Newcastle to see you, and neglect genuinely sick patients.' He re-packed his instruments in the attache case and turned to go.

'If she won't accept food by Friday,' Anna heard him say, 'We'll have to move her to the infirmary and start force feeding. That usually solves the problem.'

'What's force feeding?' Anna asked Grisel when she came back.

She shrugged. 'I'll ask Dr Blum at dinner – he might know.'

When Grisel came to bed she came across the hut and said, 'They put a tube down your throat and pour the food straight in.' She shuddered. 'I wouldn't want it to be me.'

Anna had now passed the point of hunger. She felt a floating sensation like being in a constant day dream. Nothing seemed real. She no longer had the energy to write letters, but thought it was probably a waste of time anyway. The last letter to her mother had been so heavily censored Mrs Wiseman had complained that there was nothing of it left. The content of her mother's letter made it quite clear that she was unaware of what Anna was going through. 'I don't think they want anyone to know,' Grisel said.

Two days after the doctor's visit, she came running in to tell Anna that there was a commotion at the gatehouse. A staff car had drawn up outside the Captain's office. Shortly afterwards Anna had another visitor, accompanied by the Captain, a corporal and Private Huyton. The newcomer was dressed in an extremely smart khaki uniform with a tailored jacket rather than battledress. He stared down at Anna for a few moments and then proceeded to have a conversation with the others across her bed.

'The government are relaxing the orders of course, in the light of events. We don't want a national outcry. Perhaps, in view of the circumstances? . . . It's important to keep up morale.'

They drifted away without a single word being addressed directly to Anna. She wondered if he had even realised that she understood English.

Frau Friedrich and Grisel came in almost immediately afterwards. 'One of the soldiers told us there's been a terrible tragedy. A liner sank transporting hundreds of internees to Canada. Almost everyone died. Apparently it's in all the papers.'

At three o'clock that afternoon Captain Mayhew came into the dormitory and put Anna's sketch books and her precious boxes of pencils and oil pastels on the locker. 'The Lieutenant Colonel has given his permission for them to be returned to you. I do hope that this will be the end of your silly charade. I've asked someone to bring you some bread and milk.'

One of the new women, a young blonde girl in her twenties came in with a tray and helped Anna to sit up. 'You must not eat or drink too much at first,' she said. She held up the glass to Anna's mouth as if she was a child. Anna drank the milk and then ate the slice of bread and margarine on the plate. She felt sick. Later they brought more bread and milk and a tapioca pudding. As she looked at her books on the locker she knew she should feel triumphant, but instead there was a kind of void, as if her body was saying, 'What now?'

'*I've been on hunger strike*,' Anna wrote to George. '*Because they wouldn't let me draw – but I think they became frightened I might actually pull it off – anyway, they've just given me back my things and I have permission to draw or paint provided I show my work to the Captain, Oberfuhrer Mayhew. I don't know how I'm going to survive this place. You can't imagine what it does to your spirit being penned inside a wire cage day after day. Some of the others are managing to make the best of it – and I feel ashamed that I can't. I need my freedom.*'

One Monday in early July, Private Huyton came over to the bunk house and asked for Anna. 'You've got a visitor,' she said sharply. Anna followed Huyton to the Captain's office. There in the waiting room was George, very smart in his uniform with three new stripes on his sleeve. He threw his arms wide to hug her and Anna offered no resistance. His warm, solid bulk gave more comfort than she could ever have imagined when she rested her face against the rough fabric of his uniformed shoulder. He smelt of soap and tobacco, and it reminded her of her father. George's cheek was against hers, pressing her to him and his breath was warm against her ear.

'Oh George, you don't know how good it is to see you!' Anna lifted her head to look at him. 'How did you get in?'

'I told them you were my fiancé. I got some funny looks, but they let me come.' George grinned. 'It was a hell of a job getting up here mind. It's uphill all the way from Catterick!' He offered a cigarette which Anna accepted gratefully.

A young private was standing at the door, gun on his shoulder, looking uncomfortable. 'Do they watch you all the time?' George asked.

Anna nodded. 'They think we're dangerous German spies.'

George got up and went over to the boy. 'Ha'way man! Can't you stand on the other side of the door for a bit? When I've come all this way to see my girl!' George winked. The young soldier looked at the sergeant's stripes on George's arm and then at Anna. 'She's not going anywhere,' George said. 'Do a bloke a favour?'

The lad shrugged. 'Well, I suppose it won't make much difference if I stand on the outside. I'd have to leave the door ajar mind.'

When he'd gone, George said, 'I've found a sure fire way to get you out of here.'

Anna held her breath.

'Marry me,' he said. And then, seeing the troubled expression in Anna's eyes, said, 'You could walk straight out of here as a British Citizen.'

'I don't understand. How can marrying you turn me from a dangerous enemy alien into a respectable British citizen? I'm still the same person. It doesn't make sense.'

'It does sound barmy. But it's true. I asked my commanding officer. It would have to go to the Review Committee, but he seemed to think there'd be no problem.'

Anna ran her tongue round lips too dry to speak. What was she to say?

'I wouldn't bother you much,' George went on, as if this speech was something he'd thought out carefully and learnt by heart. 'You could go to Art College and paint if that's what's really important to you. Married women don't get called up, so you'd be free to do what you wanted.' He bent to stub the cigarette out in a metal tray on the table and then grasped Anna's hand in his own. 'I'm being sent overseas next month,' he said. 'So you won't have to put up with me around for quite a long time.' He smiled crookedly. Anna thought his face had never looked so dear.

'I really do care for you George,' she said. Her lips were stiff and she found it difficult to form the words. 'But I worry that I don't love you in the way you love me. That it won't be enough.'

'Friendship's everything,' George said. 'It'll last better than love.' He said it so confidently it was easy to believe him. 'So shall I ask the committee? Will you think about it?'

Anna nodded. They smiled at each other.

Am I taking advantage of him? Anna asked herself. She knew how much he wanted her. The need was raw in his eyes; it made his hands tremble when he touched her. And she could also feel something inside herself draw back, begin to close up like a sun daisy after dark.

'The main thing's to get you out of here,' George said, suddenly very businesslike. 'If they give their permission, I'll get a special licence and organise things with your Mam.'

'How soon?' Anna asked. She would have given everything just to walk out of the door with George now.

'I don't know. I'll be due a weekend's embarkation leave before I go abroad. Maybe it'll come through in time.'

George kissed her when he left – a proper kiss and for once she didn't want to turn her mouth away. His arms felt like rings of protective steel around her. He was so dear and so familiar. It touched her to the core that George should care for her so much. It would affect his army career, surely, being married to a German?

As Anna stood behind the wire and waved him off through the fence, she felt excited and terrified all at once. Excited at the prospect of getting out of the camp, of being once more with people who cared for her, the chance to resume her studies again. And terrified by the idea of marriage to a man she cared deeply for, but felt no sexual attraction towards. This wasn't how Anna had imagined her life. It was Tamar who had said 'Of course we'll get married, it's what girls do isn't it?' In Anna's fantasies, her most private imaginings as she floated off to sleep at night, it wasn't romantic love that filled her consciousness. No handsome prince came to rescue her. And if she ever allowed herself to think of bodies, of naked flesh, the images that came most readily were those of which she was most afraid. But George was offering her security, a safe framework in which to live and the opportunity to devote her life to painting. They were such good friends. She thought of the night that George had taken her to see the Carl Rosa opera company perform Tosca. As they'd walked home afterwards she had asked him 'What was that beautiful aria, Vissi d'arte? What does it mean?'

'She's talking about living for love and art,' George had said. 'Bit like you really.' And then he'd gone on to argue that you shouldn't have to choose. Why wasn't it possible to have both?

Why can't I? Anna asked herself. Why must I sacrifice the idea of being loved in order to be a painter? Did she really need to be that single minded? Anna knew her mother wouldn't agree. She would say 'You can't have your cake and eat it too.' Which was ridiculous, Anna thought with a spurt of familiar anger. What was the point of having cake if you didn't eat it?

~~~~~~~~~~~~~~~~~~

'I was wondering if I could have my leave the weekend after next?' Tamar asked anxiously. It was difficult to find the right moment to ask Heslop anything.

'No you bloody can't,' he said. 'We're dosin' the sheep next week – Saturday and Sunday'n all. Can't have you traipsin' off.'

'But I haven't had any leave since I started here. My best friend's getting married and I have to be there – I'm her matron of honour.'

'Oh, a weddin' is it?' His voice was derisive. 'Well, they'll take themselves to hell without bein' helped to it. I can't spare you and that's that.'
~~~~~~~~~~~~~~~~~~

'You can't not go to your friend's wedding,' Mrs Bainbridge said. She was big on weddings, Tamar knew. The woman in the village shop had told her that there wasn't a wedding, christening or funeral in the entire valley that Mrs Bainbridge didn't go to. 'You just tell him your goin'. There's nowt he can do to you.'

'Supposing he complains to the superintendent?'

'He can't complain about owt! It's in the regulations.' She paused to sift some flour into the baking bowl. 'You go lass and let him fret. He'll feel the lack of you, I know that.'

'But what about Holly? I can't leave her on her own,' Tamar said. 'She's been ill ever since the hay timing. Her chest's really bad and she can't manage the heavy work. That's one of the reasons why Heslop won't let me go.'

Old Joe was sitting by the fire smoking his pipe. 'Tell you what,' he said, 'if it's just the doing up, I could give him a hand, like. First and last thing.'

'I thought you said you'd never speak to him again?' Mrs Bainbridge said.

'I never said owt about talkin' to the bugger. I can milk a cow without opening me mouth can't I? Anyways, I'd be doin' it for his father.' He turned to Tamar to explain. 'Old Heslop was a good bloke. Strict mind – the lads were all afeared of `im. But he was a fair man. Did me a gay few good turns here and there. He'd be turnin' in his grave if he saw how his son had run the place down.'

'I couldn't let you do it Joe,' Tamar was crimson with embarrassment.

'Hows't tha gan to stop me?' Joe said with a grin. 'Bye, I can't wait to see Jimmy Heslop's face when I turn up for t' milkin'.'

'You'd better go, lass,' Mrs Bainbridge laughed. 'There's no stoppin' Joe when he gets a bee in his bonnet.'

Tamar blushed again. 'It's really good of you. Anna and George are like my brother and sister, I can't let them get married without being there!'

Mrs Bainbridge tipped the cake mixture into a baking tin and flattened the top with a knife. Then she smiled at Tamar. 'We've had good news'n all.' She nodded her head towards the ever silent Wilf reading the paper on the other end of the table. 'Our

Martin's in some hospital in London. He's been injured, but he's going to be all right, the letter said. Came just this morning.'

'I'm so pleased for you,' Tamar said. 'It must be such a relief to know he's all right.'

'It surely is. There's nights I've been past myself with worry. Couldn't have lost more sleep over him if he'd been my own.'

'Mind you,' Joe chipped in, 'he's been with us since he was two year old. We brought him up between the three of us. Cheeky little bugger he was'n all.'

'You mind your language, Father, in front of the ladies!'

'At least I'm not flait o' wimmin' like that great ejit ower there.' Joe pointed his pipe at Wilf who had gone brick red. 'Has't tha ever heard him say a word?' he asked Tamar.

She shook her head, but smiled sympathetically at Wilf, wondering whether his son was as shy as he was. But no doubt she would soon find out when Martin, the apple of all their eyes, came back from the war.

As she walked back down the lane to Holme Farm, still warm and cheerful from the Bainbridge's hospitality, Tamar hoped that Anna knew what she was doing. Her letter had come as a bolt from the blue. Anna, who had always insisted that she would never get married, had agreed to do just that. Tamar took the letter out of her pocket and re-read it.

'*Dear Tamar, this is going to surprise you, but I've agreed to marry George. It's always worried me that I didn't love him enough, or in the right way, but George says all that romantic love nonsense only exists on the cinema screen. He says friendship and really liking each other are the best basis for a marriage. There's certainly enough of that. I'd always dreamt of a grand passion, but maybe that's a kind of myth. I feel so lost and confused, Tamar. Everything is so different, it's hard to know what's real any more.*

We're getting married on the 14th providing the permission comes through in time, and then afterwards I'll be a British Citizen and free to do what I want. George has agreed that we're not going to have children – at least not for years and years, until I'm established as a painter. The problem, to put it delicately, is how not to. I presume I shall have to trust George to take care of it. It seems odd to be marrying someone and feel unable to ask them something so fundamental.

Is it the same with you and Edward? Or can you talk about intimate things?'

Tamar smiled as she read the last part. It had always seemed strange to be so close to someone – to be prepared to take part in the most intimate physical acts, and yet feel embarrassed about discussing contraception, or periods. The first time she'd gone to the beach with Edward when she had the curse she remembered her embarrassment at trying to explain why she couldn't go swimming, and Edward's answering blush when he realised what she was hinting at. His sisters were both little girls and he was still quite innocent when it came to what Sadie had called 'women's things'. Then Tamar sighed, remembering that most intimate moment of all, and how, far from drawing them closer together, it had seemed only to create a distance between them. Thinking of this, and the little rubber cap in her wash bag, she realised that she could help Anna. She would send her the address of the clinic in Newcastle. Sadie's legacy would help them both.

~~~~~~~~~~~~~~~~~~
~~~~~~~~~~~~~~~~~~

CHAPTER NINETEEN

The Register office in Tynemouth was crowded. George looked very nervous in his uniform. Not smart. Somehow the heavy wool jerkin and shapeless trousers made George seem shorter and swarthier and more thick set than he really was. It was warm and stuffy in the room and his forehead shone with sweat, but George's dark face was beaming with suppressed delight. He grasped Tamar's hand in both of his and squeezed it hard, leaving a damp imprint on her palm. 'I'm the happiest man in England,' he said. 'I never thought I'd be this lucky!'

'It's Anna that's lucky! You're a good man, whoar George,' Tamar said, imitating the Geordie accent perfectly. She reached up and kissed him on the cheek, watching a blush spread across his face.

Lily was sitting in the waiting room ignoring the No Smoking sign and Anna's mother and grandfather stood awkwardly on their own in a corner. Anna's mother had put on weight recently and the way her camel-hair, pre-war coat was tightly belted over her stomach, only emphasised her bloated shape. She was wearing a black hat, almost trilby shaped with the single small feather allowed by war time regulations, and that too, balanced on top of her abundant dark hair seemed to make her look larger than she was.

There were several other couples occupying the remaining seats. 'Everyone's getting married!' Tamar joked.

'It'll be you next,' George said. 'When are you and Edward going to tie the knot? Poor lad. It's time you put him out of his misery!'

'I don't even know when I'm going to see him again,' Tamar said. 'He was in France last I heard, and he didn't come back after

Dunkirk. I got a letter from the south of France, so I presume he's still there somewhere. I worry dreadfully. It's so long since I heard anything. I used to read his articles in the paper. But even they've stopped now.'

'I bet he's been drafted into special operations,' George said. 'They're always on the lookout for people who are bi-lingual. Especially Eye-ties at the moment. My guess is that's where he is, either Italy or north Africa. Behind the lines. You won't see him until the war's over.'

George's remark left a deep hollow pit in Tamar's stomach. How long would she have to wait?

Anna was so late Tamar began to get nervous. Was she having second thoughts? George was wondering too. He was standing by the small, grimy window looking down at the streets with his hands crammed in his pockets to kill the urge to light a cigarette.

Then there were steps on the stairs and suddenly Anna was there with a man in a captain's uniform behind her like a prison escort. She was wearing a grey tweed costume that seemed much too big for her. As Tamar kissed her cheek, she thought how thin Anna had become. Her skin was blue-white like skimmed milk and her eyes were deep in their sockets as though she hadn't slept for several nights in a row. Tamar felt her hands shaking as she gripped them.

'Do I look all right?' Anna asked nervously. 'You know how I hate hats!'

'It's fine,' Tamar said. 'Just needs a little tweak.' She adjusted the velour cloche slightly to one side so that the spray of red wool toggles hung at a better angle and pulled the veiling down over Anna's forehead. 'There.' Tamar was surprised to see that Anna's eyes were glossy with tears. When George came over, Tamar noticed that although Anna gave him her hand she didn't look at him when he leant forward and awkwardly kissed her cheek.

'You're not allowed to kiss the bride until afterwards,' Tamar said playfully, in an attempt to lighten the atmosphere. The captain's presence did nothing to improve it. He stood in the doorway leaning against the door frame.

'They don't trust me not to make a bolt for it,' Anna said loudly and with considerable venom.

Tamar was relieved when the registrar called their names and they were able to go into his office and group themselves around the table. Anna seemed to have rallied a little and repeated the simple words in a clear voice. George produced a ring at the right moment and almost before Tamar had time to take it in, they were being ushered out again. The Captain shook hands with George, congratulated Anna and left.

'Thank God he's gone,' Anna said. 'I never thought I'd be propelled to the altar with an armed guard.' She began to laugh, but it wasn't a happy sound. There was an edge of hysteria to it.

Everyone queued up to kiss the bride and press their congratulations on George, but Tamar sensed a slight discomfort, a lack of real celebration. Lily and the Cotteslows were being polite to each other. 'But there's no love lost there,' Tamar decided. Even Anna and George seemed uncomfortable with each other, certainly not rapturous. Only George seemed happy, beaming and shaking hands.

'Can I see the ring?' Tamar asked, and Anna extended her fingers to show, not the traditional gold band, but a half hoop set with several different coloured gem stones.

'It's a Victorian pledge ring,' she said. 'From George's grandmother. I didn't want anything conventional. The first letter of each stone spells a word. This one says Dearest.' She flashed the tiny coloured chips. 'Diamond, emerald, amethyst, ruby, emerald, sapphire and topaz.'

'It's pretty!' Tamar said. She wondered if she would ever see the diamond ring that Edward had bought for her, and for the first time, wished more than anything that she was standing there in Anna's place.

'Where are you going to live?' she asked. 'George thought you might like to keep Lily company.'

Anna shook her head. 'Walter Suzmann put me in touch with some friends of his. They've all moved out of London till the war's over and they're staying in Seaham in an old farmhouse. I'm going to write and see if they can find somewhere for me to rent. With George's army pay and my savings I can just manage.'

'What about the Slade?'

'I never thought I'd say this, but I'm beginning to have second thoughts about that. They didn't like me and I didn't like them. Besides, evacuated to Oxford and with half the teachers called up, it wouldn't be the same.'

'I wish you luck,' Tamar said. 'At least you're following your dream.'

'You will too one day. Promise.' Anna's eyes sparked momentarily as George called her and she turned to go. 'I'll write and let you know my address when I've found lodgings.'

Anna's mother had laid on a high tea in the parlour; sandwiches, scones and even a cake, though there was no icing. She had tied a ribbon round it and a little plaster bride and groom sat on top in a circle of crystallised flowers. Anna and George cut it nervously, while Mr Cotteslow took a photograph with his box brownie. Then Anna's mother whisked it quickly into the kitchen to cut up into the thinnest possible slices, so that everyone could have a piece.

'How long before you go?' Tamar asked George.

'Monday,' he said. 'It's north Africa, though we're not supposed to know. But as we've all been issued tropical kit and they're spraying all the jeeps with desert camouflage, it's a dead give away!'

'I wouldn't mind seeing the desert. I've read about it in books and tried to imagine all that empty space. And the heat. How are you going to stand the temperatures?'

'It isn't the desert that worries me,' George grimaced. 'It's the Jerries!'

Anna and George left at five to catch the train to Whitby where one of Lily's sisters had a boarding house and was giving them a honeymoon as a wedding present. Tamar hugged them both very hard and found she couldn't say anything at all. There were no words for what she was feeling. Everyone around her was shouting 'good luck!' 'We'll be thinking of you.' 'Save yourself for Hitler,' and other more ribald comments. How long would it be before she would see either of them again? By the time she got her next leave Anna would be probably be in Seaham.

Tamar walked silently back to Heaton Street with Lily, who for once seemed to have nothing to say either. The interior of the house seemed darker than usual. All the windows were criss-crossed with tape and the curtains lined with blackout material.

'I live in the kitchen,' Lily said, stubbing her cigarette out in the sink among the washing up. 'I never go in the other room except to go to bed.'

Above her, Tamar noticed for the first time, that the cream paint of the kitchen ceiling was nicotine coloured with years of cooking fat and cigarette smoke. It was beginning to need re-decoration.

The house had a stagnant, empty feel now that everyone was gone. Lily didn't have a single permanent tenant. 'I let the front room now and then to some woman who comes up to see her husband when he gets a weekend pass, and I'm livin' on what I've got put by.'

'You could make a fortune renting rooms to people who've been bombed out,' Tamar said, but Lily just sighed and shrugged her shoulders. 'I haven't got the heart for it, pet.'

Lily was looking older. Her face was thinner, more lined, and Tamar could see the white roots of her hair where the dye was growing out. She'd stopped going out at night. 'There's no street lights, pet, and God knows who's out there lurkin' in the dark! Annie Whale got pushed down last week comin' back from the club and had her purse taken. He just jumped out on her from a doorway.'

She seemed reluctant to talk about the wedding. 'I don't like it,' she said at last, when Tamar pressed her. 'And it won't last. But you could never tell whoar George anythin'.'

'I thought you liked Anna?'

Lily shook her head. 'Oh she's a deep one, that girl. Nice enough on the surface. But all this arty rubbish . . .' Lily lit another cigarette. The kitchen was already so full of smoke it made Tamar's eyes water. 'She's only marryin' whoar George to get out of that place. It'll come to grief that will.'

Tamar said nothing. But inside she didn't agree. Anna was more complicated than that, though you'd never get Lily to believe it.

'Always thought it would be you,' Lily said. 'George always had a soft spot for you.'

It was Tamar's turn to shake her head. 'We were too much like brother and sister to be romantic about each other.' When she thought about it, George was too solid, too careful and conventional to really appeal.

The siren went off at eleven o'clock – an unfamiliar whine spiralling up into a long, bone-chilling wail. Tamar leapt up and grabbed her coat off the back of the door and reached for the torch, but Lily stayed where she was. 'They're bombin' the docks again. Poor souls!'

'Aren't you coming out to the shelter?'

Lily shook her head and poured some more gin into her glass. 'No hinny, I'm stayin' where it's warm and comfortable. You won't catch me in that place. It's cold and dark and drippin' with damp.' She gave a theatrical shudder and began to light another cigarette. 'I'll take my chance here. If my number's on it, then that's the way it is.'

Tamar didn't know what to do. The siren had stopped and she could hear the distant drone of a plane's engine. She put the kitchen light out and opened the back door. It was bright moonlight, illuminating the silver barrage balloons suspended over the rooftops. Narrow searchlight beams fingered the sky looking for a target and there was the occasional dash-dash-dash of anti-aircraft fire streaming up into the sky accompanied by the intermittent, thudding percussion of the gun battery at the top of the road. In an eerie, weird way it was quite beautiful.

'Come in or go out, will you,' Lily called from the kitchen. 'You're lettin' in the cold.'

In the morning Tamar went down to the docks. A man walking back the other way told her that one of the bombs had hit Nelson Street, three hundred yards from the shipyard gate. 'Two houses gone,' he said. 'But they were all in the shelter.' Another bomb had fallen on the south side of the river.

Nelson Street was like a demolition site. Most of the houses had had their windows blown out and people were sweeping up the glass and hammering pieces of plywood over the broken frames. Half-way down, the street was blocked by rubble and a single fire engine was spraying water over a head-high mound of bricks and smouldering beams. There was a pungent smell of gas.

Two streets further along Edward's family home was largely unscathed. One of the windows was cracked and had been taped up, there were a few broken slates in the front garden, but otherwise the house was intact. Mrs Antonelli made a great fuss of Tamar when she rang the doorbell. 'Come in, pet, come in. You don't know how good it is to see you. I didn't know you had leave?' Was there a bit of a rebuke in the last sentence? Tamar realised guiltily that she hadn't written to Edward's family for quite a while.

'It's my friend Anna's wedding. All very short notice. George is being sent overseas.'

A shadow passed over Mrs Antonelli's placid face. 'Another one gone! It's such a shame. Bertie and Tony got their papers last week.' She looked for a moment as if she might cry. Tamar put a tentative hand on her shoulder. 'It must be hard.'

'You don't know how hard pet. Three Italian men from Wallsend were interned last week – one of them even had a lad in the army. I'm terrified they'll come for Joe.'

'Surely not?'

'We're hoping it'll come to nothing, but with Mussolini declaring war and Churchill telling the military to "collar the lot", I'm not holding my breath.'

'If they intern him how will you cope with the ice-cream business?'

'We've had to close it down – you just can't get the stuff to make it – and with the boys gone . . .' She took a handkerchief out of her apron pocket and whisked away a tear, quickly turning her back on Tamar to put the kettle on.

'What are you going to do?'

'We've turned the ice cream parlour into a café. There's a lot of service people down there now and plenty of trade. The problem's getting the supplies. Coffee's gone – it's all chicory and dandelion roots now. My husband won't drink the stuff! It's the same with everything. A lot of it comes in the back door if you know what I mean.' She turned round and tapped her finger against the side of her nose. 'But what can you do? You have to make a living somehow.'

'I don't know how you manage. How do you get any sleep? The bombing round here looks terrible.'

'Every night pet – sometimes even before it gets dark. But Mr Antonelli's put electric light in the shelter and proper bunk beds and we go in there every night so's we're not getting up and down with the sirens. He's even put a carpet in. It's almost as good as the house!' She attempted a laugh but it ended in a sigh.

'There's something I've got to show you,' she said, wiping her hands on her apron. 'Something that came last week. I've been worrying and worrying, thinking about writing to you, but I didn't want to put it in a letter.' She took a brown envelope from behind the clock and took out a folded piece of paper with a regimental heading. The wording was very simple. *'Dear Mr and Mrs Antonelli, we regret to inform you that your son, Private Edward Luciano Antonelli, has been reported missing behind enemy lines. We will, of course, let you know if there is any further information.'*

'Do you think he really is missing?' Tamar asked. 'I had a letter that implied he was being sent somewhere quite secret – George said possibly North Africa or Italy – and he said I wasn't to worry if no one heard from him for a while because he wouldn't be able to write letters.'

'I don't know pet.' She sighed again. 'But you'd think his regiment would.' Nothing more was said. Mrs Antonelli made a cup of tea while Tamar told her about her work on the farm and Anna's wedding. Then, as Tamar stood up to go she asked, 'Will you light a candle for him pet?'

Tamar didn't know what she meant, but then she saw Mrs Antonelli looking towards the shrine on the sideboard with its plaster Madonna and surrounding saints. Above it on the wall hung a bleeding Christ on the cross. Tamar nodded, though her whole body shrank from it. The figures were so tawdry and tasteless – the Madonna so sentimental. But she quelled her rebellious feelings and took the thin candle that Mrs Antonelli handed her. She lit it with a match and then fitted it onto one of the spikes on the metal stand in front of it. Mrs Antonelli crossed herself and began to murmur the words of a prayer, 'Hail Mary, mother of God . . .' Tamar bowed her head feeling numb and sad. *'Pray for me,'* Edward had written. '*I know you don't believe, but just pray.*'

'If there is a god, somewhere up there,' Tamar prayed inside her head, 'I hope he's looking after him.' And then she thought what a selfish, hopeless wish it was. How could any god look after all those men, women and children out there and choose that one be killed and another saved? What kind of deity would do that? Only a cruel monster.

Tamar was glad to get back on the Penrith train again, though it was difficult to leave Lily. She wouldn't even come to the door to say goodbye. 'I've waved too many people off, hinny.' She gave Tamar a consolatory kiss on the cheek. 'Now you take care of yourself and don't let them work you too hard. Those beautiful hands of yours are in a dreadful state.'

In the twilight of the unlit carriage, Tamar looked down at her fingers and remembered the days when she'd massaged her hands with lanolin and gone to bed in cotton gloves. Now, they were chapped and calloused, the nails broken and ingrained with the brown stains of ammonia. They would never be the same.

'This is the happiest day of my life,' George said. 'Come here.' He put his arms around Anna and leant over to place his open mouth on hers. His warm hard body pressed against her, pinning her to the mattress. Anna felt herself go rigid under him in spite of herself. It was all she could do to resist the urge to push him away.

George felt her stiffen. 'What's the matter?' He lifted himself up on one elbow so that he could look at her. She could see his face in the almost dark – anxious, swollen with longing. 'Look, I know I haven't done this before – not with anyone, but I'll be gentle with you. I promise. I've waited for this, such a long time.'

He ran a hand in a soft caress down her breast and then across her stomach to her groin. Anna couldn't prevent herself from shuddering. 'It's no good George, I can't. I just can't.'

'For God's sake, Anna. We're married now. I thought you cared for me?'

'I do care for you George – probably as much as I can ever care for anyone. It's not that.'

Anna forced herself to say it out loud, in the dark. 'I'm frightened . . . frightened of men. When I was a child – before I left Germany . . . I was attacked by some boys.'

'Nazis?'

Anna nodded. 'I suppose that's really what they were – but at the time they were just boys I went to school with. One of them . . . they pushed me in the privy . . . he shut the door . . . and then . . .' Anna turned over and buried her face in the mattress and felt as though she was going to be sick.

'Did he rape you?' George asked quietly. 'Is that what it was?'

Anna couldn't say anything. When George touched her cheek with his fingers, his hand came away wet. He lay back on the pillows and stared at the ceiling. Anna could feel his disappointment. 'It's all right, Anna,' he said in a tired, flat voice. 'I'll wait. It doesn't matter. It'll come right in the end.'

A few moments later he got up and put on his pyjamas to go to the bathroom and when he came back he kissed her shoulder and curled up on the furthest edge of the bed where he quickly fell asleep. Anna felt let down, empty. She had rejected him, yet perversely now, she wished that he had not accepted the rejection. She wished he had taken her in his arms and cuddled her and warmed her with his passion until all her resistance melted away. Part of her wanted him. The other part was afraid. 'The only thing I'm afraid of,' Anna thought. It was a long time before she could go to sleep.

When she woke in the morning, George's arm was around her and she could feel his warm body pressed against her back. He was awake, she could tell, but she continued to feign sleep keeping her body relaxed and her breathing shallow. When his hands moved to caress her breasts, so lightly, delicately, she clamped her teeth together and curled her fingers tightly into her palms. He's going away tomorrow, she told herself, to the other side of the world, perhaps even to be killed. You owe him this. You owe him.

When he turned her over so that he could lie on top of her, parting her thighs with his hand, she offered no resistance, but there was a stone at the pit of her stomach – cold and hard and obdurate. Anna felt it inside her – an impediment that would not dissolve.

But George was past the point of any control. His face red, distorted with passion, mauled her face with hot open lips, and he grasped her breasts with his hands as he pushed inside her. He was clumsy with desire, and despite his attempts at gentleness, made her gasp with a sudden sharp pain which George seemed only to acknowledge as a sign of passion. He moaned and pumped and writhed over her, lost in a concentrated, focussed world which did not include Anna. She watched from a distance as she allowed him to use her body to sate his own need.

Then suddenly he pulled away from her and collapsed on top of her again. She could feel his penis hard against her stomach, jerking like a trapped animal until it became limp and still. She was touched that even in his passion, he had thought to protect her, to honour his word about not having children.

George raised his head to look at her. 'Are you all right?' he asked. He was smiling, his eyes sleepy and content. 'Thank you for letting me,' he said, with such touching gratitude it made Anna want to cry. He kissed her gently first on one cheek and then the other. 'You don't know what it means to me, after all this time,' and then, haltingly. 'I know you don't like it much now, but you will in time. Lots of blokes say it's the pits the first time, but after that you sort of get the hang of it and it comes right.'

Anna said nothing. She closed her eyes.

George kissed her nose. 'It will, you'll see!' He rolled over onto his side of the bed and dozed off.

Anna pulled her nightdress down and carefully mopped up the sticky patch on her stomach with the cotton frill. She felt as used and dirty as she had in Germany all those years ago. Please God, George was right and it would get better. It will get better, Anna said to herself. It must. Then without warning, tears poured down her face and she had to bury her face in the pillow to prevent herself from sobbing aloud. I am really fond of him, she heard her own voice saying in her head. But it isn't enough. It isn't enough.

CHAPTER TWENTY

When Tamar walked up the lane from the bus stop, Holly was waiting for her at the gate. 'Thank goodness you're back!' she said as she kissed Tamar's cheek. 'I don't think I could have stayed here for another night on my own. I've been trying to sleep with the chair jammed under the bedroom door handle.'

'Why? What happened? Was it Heslop?'

'The first night you went away I woke up about two o'clock. It was bright moonlight and at first I just thought it was the moon shining on my face. But then I heard a noise on the landing outside the door, a kind of scuffling noise, but very quiet. And then after a while it came again. It sounded like an animal, and I thought maybe one of the cats had been left in and come upstairs. So I opened the bedroom door and there was Mrs Heslop on the landing in her nightdress with her hair all hanging down, like a ghost – I could see her quite clearly in the moon light. She was looking at me – looking in such a way. Oh Tamar – you should have seen her eyes!'

'What did you do?'

'I said, "Are you all right Mrs Heslop?" And she made a kind of mewing sound and turned away as if to go back to her room and as she turned,' Holly paused and shivered. 'As she turned something slid out of her hand and clattered onto the wooden floor. I looked down and it was the carving knife from the kitchen drawer!'

'What happened then?'

'She bent to pick it up as if it was the most normal thing in the world and then she went downstairs. I wondered whether I should wake Heslop, but then I thought, nothing's really happened. It was just so strange. I wondered if she was going to kill me in my sleep.'

'I think she's more likely to kill Heslop.' It was Tamar's turn to shudder. 'We can't go on living in this atmosphere, Holly. I could hardly bear to come back.'

'I'm glad you did,' Holly said. 'I couldn't spend another night here alone.' She shrugged her shoulders as if shaking off a bad dream. 'Did you have a good time at the wedding?'

'Yes and no.' Tamar didn't feel like telling Holly about Edward being reported missing just yet. As they crossed the yard she asked. 'So what else has been happening since I went away?'

Holly went rather pink. 'You remember Ivan, the DP at the smithy? I'm going to teach him English. What do you think?'

Tamar tried very hard not to smile. 'That'll be good,' she said. She wondered what Harold Pergavie would make of his precious daughter falling in love with a Lithuanian refugee?

~~~~~~~~~~~~~~~~~~

When Anna got back to North Shields from Whitby after her honeymoon there was an emotional reunion with her mother. Anna found herself hugged to within an inch of her life. 'Well, at least you're Mrs Kennedy now – I don't have to worry about you being locked away again,' Mrs Wiseman said as she released her.

'George says I can still keep my own name for painting.'

Mrs Wiseman's smile faded and was replaced by a look of anxious disapproval. 'Are you sure that's a good thing Anna? As a married woman to keep your own name? You haven't even got a proper wedding ring. What'll people think?'

Anna grinned. 'Probably that I'm living "over the brush" as Gran would put it. They can think what they like. It's between George and me. Anyway, what about film stars? They don't change their names when they get married.'

Mrs Wiseman had no answer for that.

Frankie seemed to have forgotten who Anna was. He stood in the corner of the kitchen sucking his finger and couldn't be coaxed out even for a sweet, running to hide behind his mother's legs when Anna approached him.

'Give him time. They have short memories at that age.'
~~~~~~~~~~~~~~~~~~

'How's Gran and Grandpa?'

'Your Grandpa's down town for an ARP meeting. He's out almost every night fire-watching now. The bombing's been bad recently and it's expected to get worse. He thinks Hitler's softening us up for an invasion.'

'God! I hope not.'

'Your Gran's upstairs resting. It's not doing her any good all these nights in the shelter. She's very confused. Get's night and day mixed up. It's a bit of a worry. Last week she thought the insurance man was the Fuhrer – he has a little moustache – and she went for him with the floor sweeper. Fortunately he has a sense of humour.'

Anna went upstairs to look at her old room. It had an uninhabited air about it and every square inch of floor space was crammed with canvases and boxes rescued from the studio. Anna picked up a palette caked with old paint – so beyond redemption it would have to be thrown out. Many of the brushes were in the same condition. It reminded her of how hurriedly she had left. At the back, propped on the chest of drawers where she had left it, was Walter Suzmann's portrait. Anna stared at the face in the painting and then went to look in the mirror, but the face that stared back at her didn't seem to be the same person at all. Had she changed so much in six months?

There were a couple of letters on her bedside table – one from a cousin of her mother's congratulating her on her marriage, the other from Walter.

'So,' he wrote in a thin, elegant German script. *'You have finally married your "fond friend"? I hope as you say in your letter that his love for you will be a healing force in your life. You have had more than your fair share of its opposite.*

You wrote to ask my advice on what you should do now you are free again to pursue painting. My friends in Seaham would be very glad to see you, but they are talking about moving to Cornwall where it is warmer and more peaceful. I'm glad that you have had second thoughts about the Slade. I have never thought it the right place for you. They teach a set style – you can always tell a Slade painter – whereas you have your own already formed and it would be a pity to change it. After the war I think you should go to Paris – you will learn more in a year there than three at the Slade.'

Down in Shields Anna stood and looked at the crater where their studio had stood. There was nothing left. She had not expected such devastation. In almost every street around the dockyards the walls of houses stood crazily erect among water-filled craters and mountains of rubble. In one of them someone's clothes waved to her as they hung in an upstairs cupboard no longer accessible. Fire grates glared down, robbed of hearths and floors, and picture frames still hung askew, far out of reach. Everywhere there was a smell like burning meat that clung to her nostrils and made her feel nauseated.

'*There was a woman crying because she'd lost her cat,*' Anna wrote to Tamar in her weekly letter. *'It's like an image of hell from some medieval old master. I know I should be drawing and painting it – and I will one day, but just now I can't bear to look at such man-created ugliness. I'm going to take Walter's advice to go to Seaham for a while. I haven't had a night's sleep here since I came back and my nerves are like razor wire. The sound of the guns and the bombs is unbearable – it goes right through you and your breast bone vibrates with it. I've written to Walter's friend and asked if they can find me somewhere and I'll let you know my new address when I've got it. I wish we'd had more time to talk at the wedding. Are you well? Are you happy? Have you managed to tame the beastly Heslop yet?'*

Anna left her letter unfinished to go down to Lily's to collect George's gramophone and records. 'She's only stuffed them in a cupboard,' George had said at the station. 'You might as well have the use of them while I'm away.' He'd paused and sighed and then said, ' I wish you'd live with me Mam.'

'Look, George, I know Tamar gets on with her really well, but Lily and I are too strong minded to share a roof with each other – we'd fall out in no time.'

George had accepted it good-naturedly. 'I know she's not easy.' Then he'd kissed her and climbed aboard the train.

Today Lily was in a talkative mood. She made tea, pouring a generous tot of gin into her own, and broke open a pack of cigarettes. Anna thought she must be lonely in an empty house. Frightened by the intensity of the bombing, Lily's temporary lodger had just left. 'I'm writing to Tamar,' Anna said. 'I thought you might have some news for her before I close the envelope.'

'Nothing, hinny. Every day's the same. Planes keepin' you awake all night, then half the day queuin' for food and the other half workin' out what to do with it. How're we supposed to make a meal with a piece of cheese only big enough to bait a trap? A man came round yesterday and told me I should dig up my back yard and grow taties. I told him where to go, I can tell you! Went off with a flea in his ear. Askin' questions about how many rooms I had an'all. Said I might have to take a family. Nosey bugger.'

Even though it was early in the evening and broad daylight, Anna heard the familiar whine of the air raid siren. It made the hair rise on the back of her neck. 'Not in daytime, surely?'

'All hours of the day and night, hinny.' Lily shook her fist at the ceiling as the engines roared overhead. 'Bloody Hitler!'

'We'd better get into the shelter,' Anna said getting up to put on her coat. 'Come on Lily.'

'I'm stayin' where I am, pet. You're not gettin' me in that dark hole. I'd spend me life in there if I went every time the siren goes off.'

'Then at least let's go somewhere safe in the house.' Anna had read the leaflets that her grandfather had brought home advising families not to go into the cupboard under the stairs, but to push the kitchen table up against a wall and crawl under it. There was the sound of aero engines, very close and then a strange whining noise followed by a heavy crump. The house shook. Bombs, she'd been told, were dropped in sticks. Where would the next one fall?

'This is too close for comfort,' Anna said as the droning increased in pitch. Her hair was crackling with static electricity. 'Under the table Lily – now! Quick!' She dived underneath herself and grabbed Lily's legs, tugging her down against her will. There was a moment's silence and the sound of rushing air. Then the kitchen exploded around them and everything went black.

~~~~~~~~~~~~~~~~~~

Anna's handwriting was on the envelope that Maggie handed Tamar through the barn door. She and Holly were bundling
~~~~~~~~~~~~~~~~~~

sheep fleeces for the collecting wagon and they stank of lanolin and the peculiar, clinging odour of their excrement. Tamar sat on a bale of wool and opened the letter – a typically Anna missive in bold italic script that made Tamar smile. But then as she read further a little cry of grief escaped her and she clapped her hand over her mouth.

'What's happened Tamar?'

'It's Lily! She's been bombed. A whole string of them dropped right across the street. Lily and Anna were under the kitchen table and had to be dug out.'

'Are they all right?'

Tamar laughed unsteadily. 'Anna says that when the firemen asked Lily, she said, "It'll take more than a couple of Jerry bombs to rattle me!" But Anna sounds very shaken. They were trapped for four hours apparently. Lily's had stitches in a cut on her head and she's got a black eye. She's staying with a neighbour at the moment. Apparently there's nothing left of the house at all.'

She found it difficult to imagine. The living room where they had spent so many happy nights listening to George's gramophone – the bedroom she had shared with Sadie. The house in Heaton Street had become her home and now it was gone. Then with an almost physical pain, Tamar remembered the hat box – all Sadie's letters and keepsakes. She had put them aside to read at some time in the future, but somehow there had never been the right moment, and there had been no feeling of urgency. They would always be there. Now they had gone with the house and any chance she had of finding out about Sadie's family history – perhaps even to read letters from her dead father – was lost. Tamar couldn't stop herself from weeping.

Holly put her arm around her. 'I'm so sorry Tamar.'

Heslop was standing in the doorway leering at them. 'Every time I turn my back you two are skivin' off cuddlin' each other like a couple o' toms. Come on you lazy buggers. I want that lot ready by milking time not the middle of next week!'

'Leave us alone,' Holly said sharply. Tamar had never heard her use that tone of voice before. 'Can't you see she's upset? Her house has just been flattened by a bomb!'

Heslop was unperturbed. 'Animals don't wait on bombs nor

owt else. They'd still need milkin' n' feedin' if the king of England was here. So get a bloody move on!' He turned and slammed the barn door to behind him.

'He's right, Holly,' Tamar dried her eyes on a corner of her shirt. 'Life has to go on. And at least Lily's alive. I used to worry about her in that house with the bombing. She would never go in the shelter. She's been lucky.'

After supper Tamar went out into the orchard and just stood under the trees looking up at the stars. They shone so very brightly here. The Milky Way looked like a drift of snow across a path; Venus so bright it was like car headlamp low over the fells. In the silence Tamar could hear the goat munching in the long grass, the clink of a cow's chain in the byre. The idea that somewhere, not very far away people were at that very moment being killed or maimed by bombs seemed crazy.

A plane engine droned in the distance. Tamar listened without any of the fear that drove everyone in Heaton Street running for the shelters, praying their houses were still there when they got out. Here they were out of range of Hitler's bombers. Only once about a month ago, a young Luftwaffe novice had got lost trying to find Manchester and had been forced to shed his bombs over Shap Fell before he ditched in the sea. It had been cited as an incidence of sod's law that one of the bombs had fallen down the chimney of the only building in the whole desolate area – a roadside café, which had been blown to brick dust. It had aroused great hilarity and curiosity.

Tamar felt guilty that she should be having such a peaceful time, when everyone else seemed to be suffering. She was also aware that without Sadie she was lonely. It was a strange feeling – like being the only tree left standing in the middle of a field, isolated and exposed. Sometimes Tamar tried to imagine her father, but it was difficult. When he smiled out of the photograph, the corner of his mouth was just a little bit crooked and his hair was springy and dark like hers. But she had no idea whether he was short or tall, quiet or introverted (not an introvert, surely with Sadie?) And his personality was a mystery. He looked nice. Not at all like Sadie's usual taste in men. Tamar thought of the hat box, shredded into confetti by the bomb and all the papers and letters she had never had time to read, and wept.

It took Anna three trips on the bus to take all her equipment to Seaham. Walter's friends had written to say that they were leaving, moving south, but that one of the cottages they'd rented still had six months left of the lease, and would she like to take it over? The cottage was fully furnished and by the time she'd introduced all her personal belongings, easels and canvases, there was scarcely a square inch of bare floor to walk on. For Anna the peace and privacy was bliss. For the first time in months she slept alone, undisturbed by sirens or any human sound. Once when she woke with the moon on her face, she heard the faint drone of aero-engines flying north and shuddered to think of the suffering they were going to inflict. Those hours spent in the rubble were still a raw memory. She could taste the mortar dust in her mouth, feel the pressure of the bricks against her body, pinning her against the wall. For a while she had been afraid that she would suffocate, but as she tried to quell her panic she had begun to realise that there were little currents of air drifting across her skin from minute holes in the wreckage. Her worst fear had been gas, which she could smell clearly. She remembered thinking how lucky it was that Lily had just finished boiling the kettle and the cooker was not alight at the time of the blast. Anna had just been able to reach Lily's shoe-less foot with her right hand, relieved to find it warm and still moving in response to her touch, but they had been unable to talk to each other. Those four hours had seemed like eternity.

Too tired to dwell on it for long, Anna turned over and slept again, waking with autumn sunlight spilling into the room. She picked up a couple of apples from the kitchen table, crammed her sketchbook into a bag and set out for the shore. There on the rocks she stared out over the sea and drank in its infinitely changing surface, rejoicing in the space around her – space that meant freedom. The wind on her skin made her feel alive again. She stayed out most of the morning, coming back only when she felt hungry. There was a letter on the mat in George's handwriting.

'I can't tell you where I am, or what I'm doing,' he wrote, *' so I don't know what the point of writing letters is. I can't even talk about the weather because that might give you a clue. The food's terrible. I'm sick of bully beef and biscuits, which is all we seem to have. Sometimes, if we can find them locally, we get eggs which we fry on the mudguards. What took most getting used to was the flies! They crawl over you even when you're asleep. Some smart alec said a fly can lay a million eggs a year, and I believe him. But you get used to them after a bit, on your face and your hands and your food – you just wave them off and carry on.*

Only plus is, Jimmy Blacker from Shields is in the same company and we play cards when there's nothing going on, and talk about the times we had back home. It's odd being a sergeant – some of the lads in the ranks are much posher than us. Managed to find an old gramophone in the suekh that still works. We had to file down a few nails for needles. I got a copy of Aida and Jimmy went one better with our Gracie singing Ave Maria, which is grand. It's amazing what you can get with a bit of baksheesh.

We play football to keep fit – our company has two good teams. They've put me in goal because I can't run fast enough. Some of the lads are really good and we beat the Aussies last week.

How's the painting? I like to think of you putting brush to canvas – it seems such a peaceful occupation. I imagine you painting flowers, trees, green fields – what I'd give for some of that right now.

See you one of these days

Your loving George.

It was such a good letter. Had she made a mistake by marrying George? She loved him like a brother, or a best friend. But was that really the right kind of love for marriage?

On Anna's fifth day in the cottage a man arrived at her front door, tapping lightly and then pushing it open to stand in the passageway. He was tall and grey haired with a slightly military look even though he was wearing civilian clothes – an expensive camel coat and homburg hat. Anna was struck by his beautiful leather shoes as he sat down on the chair in her cluttered front room and crossed his legs. He refused tea.

'I've got a proposition to put to you,' he said without preamble.

Anna's heart was in her mouth. Surely they weren't going to put her back in the camp?

'We're looking for fluent German speakers to monitor German radio broadcasts.'

She shook her head quickly. 'I don't want to be involved in anything to do with military operations. I worked in a parachute factory, but that was saving lives, not taking them.' Then, in case he misunderstood her motives she added, 'I'm not pro-Hitler, just anti-war. And after the months I've just spent in the internment camp I don't feel too well disposed towards the British government at the moment. I just want to be left alone to get on with my own life.'

'That might not be possible for much longer. As a British citizen you won't be exempt from conscription. At present married women aren't being called up for military service, but that state of affairs won't last much longer. There's a chronic shortage of personnel.'

'I'll take my chances.'

'You might want to change your mind when I tell you what I know.' His voice was very smooth. 'I have information concerning your father.'

Anna's heart went cold.

'He was taken to a labour camp at Buchenwald in 1939 and as far as we're aware he's still there, being forced to work in an armament's factory. I don't want to distress you, but information is coming out of Germany that Jewish families are being transported to concentration camps where they are being subjected to the most inhuman treatment. There are suspicions – only suspicions I must stress – of genocide. If there are any means by which this war can be brought to an early conclusion, they would be justified. I know that you are in a difficult position. You don't want to harm your own people, and you have no particular reason to feel loyalty towards the British. But I would urge you to think carefully.' His voice became softer and even more silky. 'There is also the possibility of invasion. If German forces were to invade Britain, what do you think would happen to yourself, to your mother and brother? Don't you think you have a responsibility to protect them too?'

Anna's throat was dry. She asked unwillingly, 'What would I have to do?'

'Listen to German radio broadcasts on the open airwaves and translate. Then, if you had the aptitude, you would also be trained in coding and de-coding other radio traffic.'

'Why me? One moment I'm an enemy alien and the next I'm being asked to do something highly confidential?' Anna's voice was bitter.

'We've been investigating your background. I'm afraid your internment does seem to have been rather over-zealous. As things stand at the moment you would be classified as a Jewish refugee and accorded special status. Unfortunately the initial policy was to make a broad sweep – in war time it's better to be safe – so many people's lives depend upon it.' He smiled apologetically and Anna felt a spurt of rage that her life had been so carelessly disrupted. The man held out a card. 'I would urge you to think carefully about this. When you have made up your mind, perhaps you would telephone me on this number?'

After he'd gone, Anna walked down to the harbour and clambered out to sit on the outermost point watching the waves. The tide was coming in and the green swells were breaking in great white walls of water over the rocks and around the base of the light house. Above her the sky seemed to go on forever into infinite space. It was hard to consider giving up this freedom, but on the other side of the sea her father was confined to a labour camp in conditions of the utmost degradation. Brigadier Mostyn-Soames had made it seem like blackmail – anything she could do, he had implied, might help her to free her father earlier. By entering the war effort she could help her family. How could she refuse now that *that* seed had been sown in her mind?

~~~~~~~~~~~~~~~~~~

The lime spreaders came in September and the air was filled with caustic dust. Tamar's eyes and mouth were red and sore. The men doing the spreading were white all over – their skin and clothes and hair. Only their eyes – little reddened pin-points – showed through and when they talked their mouths were dark
~~~~~~~~~~~~~~~~~~

red holes in the white mask. Tamar wondered how they could stand the pain. The lime affected Holly more than the hay pollen had. She coughed all the time they were there and even after they'd left she couldn't shake it off. Sometimes she would wake in the night and cough and cough and cough till her throat was raw, occasionally asking the darkness 'You don't think I'm going to get TB like my Aunt do you?' Tamar, wide awake on the other side of the room, would pull on her woollen socks, wrap herself in her greatcoat and tip-toe down to the kitchen for a cup of hot water. No honey or lemon to be expected here, (when had she last seen a lemon?) but a teaspoonful of blackcurrant jam and another of vinegar, according to the magazine she'd read, was just as good.

Getting back into bed with cold feet from the damp flagstones was difficult and Tamar lay awake for a long time listening to Holly determinedly trying to suppress the painful cough. When the alarm jangled them awake at five thirty they were both exhausted. Tamar wondered how they could possibly survive a winter here. Were other land girls having it so hard? She made up her mind that when the supervisor came on her six month visit to check that they were all right, she would tell her what it was really like and ask if they could be moved.

But, the week after the lime spreaders left as Tamar was mangling turnips for the evening milking, a bolt snapped and the handle came off the turnip cutter. Sighing, but inwardly relieved to be able to give her back and arms a rest, Tamar walked across the yard to the stable, which also served as a tool shed and where she knew Holly was cleaning the horse tack. As she approached the door she could hear Holly's voice saying, 'No, please! Oh please don't. Leave me alone!' Tamar began to run. Just inside the door Heslop had Holly pushed up against the bench and his hand was inside her shirt as he grunted and pressed himself against her. Holly was struggling, but her strength was no match for his.

Tamar felt anger exploding inside her head. She picked up the first thing she could lay her hand on, one of Ben's harness chains and without stopping to think, slammed it across the back of Heslop's jacket. He shouted with pain, staggering backwards and spinning round to face her.

'Leave her alone you brute,' Tamar was breathing hard, the chain still in her hand, 'or I'll hit you again.' She glanced across at Holly, pulling her shirt together with trembling hands. 'Get into the house, Holly. I'll be there in a minute.'

'Yes,' Heslop said scornfully. 'A pair of upper class toms aren't you. Can't wait to be at it. Bet you're in bed cuddlin' up together all the time. What you want is a real man 'atween your legs. That'd sort ya!'

'Well it isn't going to be you,' Tamar said. She felt icy cold. 'You lay a finger on either of us and I'll kill you.' She noticed there was blood trickling from the lobe of his ear where the end of the chain must have caught him above the collar of his jacket. Unnerved by the strength of her desire to hit him again, Tamar forced herself to drop the chain back on the floor and fled.

Mrs Heslop was nowhere to be seen when she went into the house. Probably hiding in the dairy. Tamar had found her in there several times, biting her nails and staring out of the window. Why didn't she leave? Tamar thought. Why did she stay with such a monster?

Upstairs Holly was packing clothes into her suitcase. She was crying and shaking. Tamar put her arms round her. 'It'll be all right, Holly. Did he hurt you?'

She shook her head. 'God knows what would have happened if you hadn't come, though. It makes me feel ill to think about it.'

Tamar got her suitcase out from under the bed and began flinging her clothes into it, the photographs from her bedside cabinet, the books for her course work. She could barely get the lid to close. 'We'll go to the Bainbridge's,' she said. 'And tomorrow I'm going to contact the County Supervisor and ask to be moved to another place. We've stayed here too long Holly. We should have made a stand earlier.'

When they went downstairs Mrs Heslop was cowering in the corner of the kitchen, twisting her apron in her hands. Tamar went over and put a hand on her arm. It felt stick thin, like the limb of a bird. 'We're going now I'm afraid. I caught your husband in the stable mauling Holly.'

The woman gave a little cry and her body trembled under

Tamar's hand. 'I'm sorry,' she said. It was barely a whisper. 'I've tried to keep him off. I know what he's like.'

'Why don't you come with us?'

She shook her head.

'There are people who would help you.'

Again that movement of the head. 'You go. You've been good girls.' She gave a shaky smile. 'You go.'

There was no alternative but to leave her there. The yard was deserted and there was no sign of Heslop at all as they trudged up the lane to Crow Hall puffing and panting with their cases..

Joe was standing outside the front door when they arrived. 'Well, I'll say this,' he chuckled. 'You lasted longer'n them hired lads!'

In the warmth of the kitchen Tamar told them what had happened and Holly wept against Mrs Bainbridge's apron. 'Poor lass,' she said. 'He's a filthy, filthy, man. Shouldn't be trusted with young lasses.'

'I wouldn't trust him with a heifer,' Joe said forcefully. 'The man wants puttin' down.'

'Tamar hit him with a harness chain,' Holly said, mopping up her tears with one of Joe's white Sunday handkerchiefs.

'She did what?'

'I'm afraid I did – it was the nearest thing to hand.'

'He who takes the readiest, never wants!' Joe started to laugh. 'I hope you hit him hard. Bye gum, I wish't I'd a seen it.'

The door sneck clicked up and the door swung open behind them. Tamar turned her head. For a moment the space was empty and then a tall fair-haired young man on crutches hobbled into the room.

Mrs Bainbridge stood up. She pulled a chair round towards the fire. 'This is our Martin,' she said. The pride in her voice was unmistakable. 'Got home just last night.'

Martin paused. He smiled at each of them in turn. 'Don't tell me,' he said, 'But you're the land girls I've been hearing so much about. Holly and Tamar, isn't it?' His manner was as open and friendly as the rest of the family, but his accent was less broad. He had startling blue eyes, the colour of wild cornflowers. When he looked at Tamar she felt a tremor pass through her whole body.

'How do you do,' Holly said, walking towards him and holding out a hand. He let go of his crutch to clasp it briefly. Tamar forced herself to do the same, but was scarcely aware of what she said, only his eyes and the warm, firm grip of his hand.

'How's your leg?' she managed to stammer.

'Better than it was.' He eased himself down in to the chair his aunt had drawn out. 'They say I'll be jumping over five barred gates again in a few months.' He grinned and Tamar felt herself flushing crimson.

'He's lucky to be alive,' Mrs Bainbridge said. 'Laid on the beach with his leg in pieces for two days waiting to be taken off. Thank the lord he can't go back.'

'Can't you?'

Martin shook his head. 'They've invalided me out. I've got a piece of shrapnel in my back as well, which they couldn't take out because it's too close to my spine. That's the war over for me I'm afraid.'

'Any news of that fiancé of yours?' Joe asked Tamar.

'No word. Just that he's missing.'

'Don't go pestering the girl, Father. And let's get some tea going afore you starve to death blathering.'

'Are you sure it's all right to stay tonight, Mrs Bainbridge?' Tamar looked across at Martin. 'I can't get hold of the supervisor until tomorrow.'

'Of course it is, lass. You don't fret yourselves. You can have the lile bedroom at the back. I'll give you the sheets and a couple of hot water bottles to air it out and you'll be right as rain.'

Later, after an enormous tea, lying in a comfortable bed between clean sheets, her toes tucked under the hot water bottle, Tamar felt as if she'd emerged from a nightmare. But she was aware of a difference in herself, a new strength. So many things had happened to her in the past few years, and she had somehow coped with them all. It gave her new confidence that she could deal with the future, whatever it held. She had once envied Anna her confidence and determination but perhaps she had more of it herself than she had realised.

Holly was lying on her back looking at the ceiling. She was very quiet.

'Are you all right, Holly?'

'Yes. Just relieved that it's over.'

'Has he done that before?'

'Once or twice. Today was the worst. I never said anything because I felt so ashamed. I just tried to keep out of his way.'

'You should have said something. They would have moved us sooner.'

'I didn't want to fail. I didn't want us to have to leave because of me.'

'It wasn't failing, Holly. You don't have to submit to that kind of treatment.'

'I can't bear the thought of all the fuss and having to go back to my parents. They'll say "I told you so," and they won't want me to come back.'

'Do you still want to be a land girl?'

'I love the animals. Especially the horses. But not the heavy work. I can't lift bales like you Tamar.'

Tamar lifted her arm up and examined it in the light of the oil lamp. 'Who's going to find me attractive with muscles like this?'

'Martin does. I could tell the way he smiled at you.'

'Don't be silly Holly. Anyway, I'm engaged to Edward.'

'He might not come back,' Holly said in a very soft voice. 'Have you thought of that?'

Tamar ignored her. 'How are things with you and Ivan?' she asked.

'He's very nice.' There was a smile in Holly's voice. 'And he speaks really good English now. He's started going to Church on Sundays with me, though he says it's not like the church at home. He says they have pictures and candles and incense and lots of singing. It sounds wonderful.'

'Have you told your parents about him?'

'Not yet. There's nothing to tell. Not really.' Tamar thought she detected the faintest hint of hesitation in Holly's voice.

There was the sound of stockinged feet on the stairs. 'Here's Joe and Mary coming up to bed. I think we'd better put the lamp out.'

As she passed the door Mrs Bainbridge called out 'Good night girls, I hope you sleep well,' and then her bedroom door closed.

Tamar turned down the wick and the chintz wall paper faded into darkness.

~~~~~~~~~~~~~~~~~~

Joe drove Tamar down to the Post Office to telephone the supervisor after breakfast and two hours later Mrs Simms arrived at Crow Hall in a mud spattered Ford. Mrs Bainbridge made her a cup of tea while Tamar and Holly patiently explained why they had had to leave.

'The man's not fit to keep pigs,' Mrs Bainbridge said, putting the cup down on the table beside a plate of newly baked scones, 'Never mind lasses!'

'Things do seem to have been very bad.' The woman sighed as she stirred her tea. 'But of course we don't always know these things when a farmer asks us for help. I can only apologise and say it won't happen again. I'll be going to see Mr and Mrs Heslop to collect your ration cards and explain why we won't be sending anyone else. The problem is, what do we do with you now?'

She gazed at them distractedly.

'Holly's really good with horses,' Tamar said. 'Has them eating out of her hand. But she's not up to heavy work – she has a weak chest.'

'Well, let's see. I might have a word with Lord Nithsdale – he breeds horses for the military and it's a beautiful stud. He's got a market garden on the estate as well. It's just possible he might need some extra help. Whether he can take both of you, I don't know.'

'Is it far away?' Holly asked anxiously.

'About five miles. Would that do?'

Holly looked relieved and Tamar knew she was thinking about Ivan.

'Would it be possible to have some leave?' Tamar asked. 'I've only taken thirty six hours since I came here, and my home's been bombed out. I'd like to go and see that everyone's all right.'

'How long would you need? A couple of weeks? It would give me time to get your placement arranged. I'll write you out a travel warrant anyway. It's Newcastle isn't it? What about you Holly?'

She shook her head. 'No. If I go home and tell them what it's
~~~~~~~~~~~~~~~~~~

been like they'll never let me come back. I'd rather start my new job first.'

It was decided that Holly would stay on at the Bainbridge's for a few more days until she could be moved to Nithsdale Hall and that Tamar would join her after her holiday.

When Mrs Simms had left, Tamar wandered out, through the gate, to look at the view. Below her, lay the whole of the Eden valley with the river like a silver snake running through it. On the other side the mountains of the Lake District made a jagged dark blue edge against the sky and northwards she could see the glitter of the estuary with the Scottish hills behind it.

'Beautiful, isn't it?' a voice said.

Tamar jumped. Martin Bainbridge was sitting quietly on a stone trough against the wall.

'I didn't see you there!'

'I can't get enough of looking at it. Can't believe I'm home yet.'

'Was it awful?'

'Hellish. If I hadn't seen it I couldn't have imagined that human beings could do those sorts of things to other human beings. Growing up on a farm sort of hardens you to death and having to kill animals. But that was something different.'

Tamar went to sit beside him on the trough. 'It's hard to think that's all going on somewhere while everything's so peaceful here.'

'Are they sending you somewhere else?'

'Possibly to Nithsdale Hall, but I don't know where that is.'

Martin pointed along the river valley. 'Do you see where it bends and another river comes in?' Tamar nodded. 'There's a clump of trees in the angle of the bend. That's Nithsdale. A very posh spot. You'll like it there.'

'I'm glad I'm not going far away. I love it here. There's so much history in this landscape. I like to imagine all the people who've been here before.'

'Do you see that stone?' Martin pointed to the lintel above the barn door. 'That's a standing stone they dug up out of the field when they built the barn. There must have been a whole circle of them once. And some of the other stone in the tower is

Roman.'

'So are there Roman ruins here somewhere?'

Martin laughed. 'You're standing on them. These flat terraces that fall away in front of the house are called the Hanging Gardens of Mark Anthony.'

'Like Babylon?'

'Not as romantic as that – probably just cultivation terraces, or so the county archaeologist says. You like history then?'

'Love it.'

'Well then. When I get my legs back in working order I shall have to take you up the Maiden Way.'

'What's that?'

'It's an old Druid trackway that goes up the side of Kirkland Pike,' he pointed to the hill behind the house, 'to an enormous pagan stone monument called Meg's Cairn. Tell you what,' he grinned at her. 'Will you climb to the top of this hill with me before Christmas? That'll give me something to aim for.'

'It's a date.' Tamar found herself smiling back – grinning like an idiot. He was so comfortable to be with. She was going to have to be careful. There was Edward to consider. It was a good thing she was going away for a couple of weeks.

~~~~~~~~~~~~~~~~~

Lily was sitting in Mrs Whale's cluttered front room beside a roaring fire with her feet up on the fender. She looked smaller and shrunken. Older.

'I'm sorry about the house,' Tamar said. 'What are you going to do?'

'Stay where I am hinny. Annie and me have had our differences over the years, but she's a canny woman and we'll get on just fine.'

This wasn't how Tamar remembered her talking about Mrs Whale, but she let it pass. 'Was there anything rescued?'

'Not a scrap pet. All blown to bits. And by the time I was on my feet again, anythin' worth havin' had gone to the looters. There were some clothes, too filthy to wear, but nothin' else. Can't say what's under the rubble, but it'll all be spoiled by the
~~~~~~~~~~~~~~~~~

water.'

Tamar was very glad that she had taken her most precious things with her, Sadie's silver hair brush, the pot pourri dish and the little book of Charles Carter's poems. But the contents of the hat box grieved her. She had hoped one day to find out the truth of Sadie's past. All she could remember was the address and the names of Sadie's parents on her birth certificate. Rosie Libby and Harland Tomlinson, 3 Headland Cottages, Looe, Cornwall. That at least was something. And her own birth certificate was carefully tucked in her writing case.

'Have you seen much of Anna?' Tamar asked.

'A bit. I have to say she's been very good since the bombin'. But she's in Seaham now and the buses aren't that reg'lar.'

'I'm going over there tonight to stay with her for a day or two. I'm really looking forward to it.'

'You could do with a holiday, pet,' Lily said. 'Brown as a gypsy you may be, but you look fairly worn down. A good night's sleep and plenty of home cookin's what you need. But you won't get that from whoar Anna.'

'At least you've graduated to "whoar Anna" and you're not the German Girl anymore,' Tamar said when Anna opened the cottage door to her. It was a tiny fisherman's dwelling with two rooms on either side of a passageway, a kitchen in a lean to at the back and a closet at the end of the garden. Anna was using one of the rooms as a studio and the other contained a double bed, a table and dining chairs as well as two arm chairs. They were all crammed in so tightly it was hard to walk between them. It was filthy too. Anna obviously didn't do much housework.

'It isn't my thing,' she said, waving apologetically at the disorder. 'I try to keep the dust down, but it always ends up like this. It's like trying to bail a leaky boat – as fast as you chuck it out the water comes back in.'

They opened a can of spam and ate it between slices of bread without butter. 'I hate the taste of marge,' Anna said. 'It reminds me of the camp.'

'Have you made up your mind what you're going to do? You said in your letter you'd been asked to do some kind of war work?'

'Top secret. One minute I'm a dangerous German alien who has to be locked up, the next I'm being asked to spy for the government. There's no logic to war at all.'

'Are you going to do it?'

'He told me they'd located my father. Apparently the Germans keep lists of everyone they've taken to the labour camps and you can get them through the Red Cross. He's in somewhere called Buchenwald. They work in some kind of factory apparently, making military engines. That's all they could tell me. If anything I can do would contribute to ending the war quicker and getting him out of there, then I'm willing to do it, providing I don't have to fight.'

'Let's go out for a drink,' Tamar said. 'Didn't I see a lovely little pub down on the harbour when I walked up?'

Anna had changed. She'd lost weight and had her hair cut in a boyish, twenties-style bob. The straight dark mass, contrasted against her white skin gave her a rather gamine look. She was wearing a red, hand-knitted waistcoat over a man's white dress shirt and a pair of loose, black twill trousers. A yellow and blue scarf was knotted like a cravat at her throat. What worried Tamar most was the gauntness of her face and the troubled, almost nervous look in her eyes. Tamar had never seen Anna anything but confident and self possessed. She could only surmise that the internment camp had affected her more than she could have imagined.

'I think I was wrong to marry George,' Anna told Tamar as they sat in the window seat over a glass of beer. 'It was a stupid, stupid mistake when I was at a low ebb.'

'Anna! How could you do that do George?' Tamar was angry in spite of herself. 'You know how much he loves you. I couldn't bear to see him hurt.'

'I know. I know. You couldn't be as cross with me as I am at myself.'

'What are you going to do?'

'I don't know. I'm too fond of him to want him to suffer. But I keep thinking, what if I'm just confused? It's difficult with him being so far away. How can you know what you really feel for someone when they're not there?'

Tamar looked at the set of her lips, compressed in a fine line of anxiety, the doubt in her usually fearless eyes and wondered where the old Anna had gone. How could she make a mistake like that? Anna who had always known where she was going; who talked so knowledgeably about love and human relationships? If Anna could get it wrong, what hope was there for anyone else? Herself included.

Anna was twisting her ring round and round on her finger as if trying to make up her mind about something. Then she looked up and flushing slightly, said. 'It's not really George, so much. . . It's the sex thing. I hate it.'

'I can see that must be hard.'

'I don't know whether it's him or me and there's no one who can tell me. Have you and Edward? You know . . .?'

Tamar nodded and felt herself blushing brick red. 'It was a bit disappointing, but I could sort of see that it might get better with practice. I didn't dislike it.'

'Have you heard any news of Edward yet?' Anna asked.

'No. If he's a prisoner, we won't hear anything until the end of the war.'

'That could be years away. Are you going to wait for him?'

Tamar looked down into her drink. 'I have to. I promised.'

'But?'

Tamar sighed. Trust Anna to know that there was a but. 'I've met this man. I've only known him about forty eight hours, but it's as though I've known him all my life.'

'Love at first sight.'

'No. Not at all. This is something much more primitive. A kind of knowledge. When we look at each other – it's as if we read everything inside each other's heads. It's frightening. I'm not in love with him yet, but I could be if I let myself. And I don't think I'm strong enough to resist. If I want to stay faithful to Edward I ought to run away from him as far as I can go.'

'You need to get away – take a holiday Tamar. Have you thought about it?'

'I've sometimes thought of going down to Cornwall to see if I can find any of Sadie's family. My family. I'd like to try and find out the truth.'

'You might not like it when you find it.'

'But at least I'll know who I am. Everyone has some kind of family history – I only have the stories that Sadie told. Perhaps she invented it all, who knows? The only fact I can be certain about is that she was born in Looe in Cornwall in a fisherman's cottage. I'd like to go and have a look.'

'So why don't you? You've got Ida's money, so you can afford it.'

'Maybe I will. You're right. I need to get away from everything. I'd like to find out if my grandmother is still alive. She can't be that old – if she had Sadie in her twenties, she'd still only be about sixty. I still find the idea of relatives quite strange. And they might not want to see me. Otherwise why did Sadie never keep in touch with them? Why did she lie about them?'

This was a question Tamar had asked herself again and again without getting a satisfactory answer. She drained her glass and changed the subject.

'I'm fed up of talking about me. What are you going to do?'

'Join the services probably.' Anna sighed. 'That seems to be my fate. Every time I've tried to follow the path I want to go down the way's blocked. I sometimes think I'm simply not meant to be a painter. I swore I wouldn't get married and here I am – Mrs Kennedy. I swore I'd never join the armed forces and here I am accepting the fact that I'm probably going to be doing some kind of war work. I hate it, Tamar. But there doesn't seem to be anything else I can do.'

'This is what war has done to us. All our dreams and desires have been pushed aside to make way for other things. But they're only postponed. The war won't last forever and then we'll get our ordinary lives back.'

But Anna shook her head gloomily. 'Our lives have been changed forever.'

'Anna! You mustn't give up. Promise me. You mustn't let go. There will be a way.'

Anna gave a wry smile. 'Funny isn't it, not so long ago it was me urging you to go all out for what you wanted. Now you're doing it to me.'

‘Let me buy you another beer.’ Tamar stood up to go to the bar. ‘And then let’s talk about something more cheerful.

PART V

FORBIDDEN DREAMS

1941-2

I must not think of thee; and, tired, yet strong,
I shun the thought that lurks in all delight –
The thought of thee – and in the blue heaven's height,
And in the dearest passage of a song.

Alice Meynell – *Renouncement*

CHAPTER TWENTY ONE

When Tamar arrived in Liskeard, after a long and exhausting train journey, it was raining. In the absence of a wind it fell out of the dusk in a relentless stream, pouring off the station roof and gurgling down hidden gutters. Despite her umbrella, Tamar's feet and legs and the arm that carried her suitcase were soaked by the time she reached the entrance.

'How do I get to Looe?' she asked the ticket collector.

'There's no buses this time of night.' He jerked his head towards the solitary taxi sitting at the kerb. 'Tom's waiting for somebody, but maybe he'll pick you up on the return.'

'Will it be expensive?' Tamar had no idea how far it was.

The man shrugged impatiently, already reaching for the next ticket. 'You'll have to ask him,' he said.

Tamar approached the ancient ford and tapped on the driver's window. It was wound down about an inch and a draught of warm cigarette smoke drifted out.

'I need to get to Looe,' she explained. 'Can you take me?'

'I've got a fare to take to Polperro, but if the gentleman don't mind, you can hop in the front and I'll drop you off on the way.'

The passenger, a middle aged man in a business suit, arrived just at that moment and to Tamar's relief, had no objection to her sitting with the driver. He climbed into the back, reclined on the seat and lit himself a cigar.

It was cramped in the front seat with her suitcase on her lap and the sodden umbrella between her knees. The whole inside of the car steamed with condensation as the moisture dried out of her clothes. Tamar was too tired to start a conversation, but rather surprised that the driver said nothing either to her or to his other passenger. If this had been a northern cab, she thought with a flash of humour, their entire life's history would have been prised out of them in the first mile. People here were perhaps more private. She wondered whether anyone would be willing to talk to her.

'Where are you wanting to be?' the cab driver asked, as they began to descend into a valley, winding down towards a collection of houses around a small harbour.

'I haven't got anywhere to stay yet,' Tamar confessed. 'I thought I'd find a bed and breakfast somewhere in the centre.'

He grunted and then after a moment said, 'You could try Molly's place on Harbour Road. She takes in visitors and it's clean and cheap.' He glanced across at Tamar's coat and her shabby suitcase. 'You'll not be wanting the Headland Hotel, I'm thinking.'

Tamar was too grateful for the suggestion to resent the implication. By the time she was dropped in Harbour Road the rain had intensified. The tide was up and the sea water heaved and slapped onto the quay to mingle with the rain water streaming down the gutters to meet it. The double fronted white and blue house had a card in the window which said 'Vacancies'. Tamar knocked twice and the door was opened by a petite woman of about fifty with tightly permed hair and bright cerise lipstick. She was wiping her hands on her apron.

'What can I do for you, dear?' she asked and then, without giving Tamar time to reply said, 'Silly question, with you standing on the step with your luggage. Come inside out of the rain.'

Bed and breakfast was seven shillings and sixpence; dinner two and sixpence extra. Tamar agreed to the latter. 'I expect I'm too late for dinner tonight,' she said.

'I'm afraid so, dear. But I could do you a sandwich? Or fry you up a nice kipper?'

'If it wouldn't be too much trouble.'

'Oh, it's not a question of trouble,' Molly said. 'You're paying for it, dear.'

The room was fussy, with chintz curtains and covers and crocheted lace doilies on all the surfaces. It smelt rather damp but it was clean, and the bed, piled with pillows and quilts, looked luxurious compared to Tamar's bleak iron bedstead at Holme Farm.

'So what brings you here, dear,' Molly asked as she laid Tamar a place at the pine table in the kitchen.

'I'm looking for my grandmother.'

Molly's eyes glittered with curiosity. 'I wouldn't have taken you for a Cornish girl.'

'My mother was born in Headland Cottages. I never knew them, but her parents were called Rosie Libby and Harland Tomlinson. Do the names mean anything to you? My grandfather was a fisherman.'

'Harland Tomlinson.' Molly put down the fish slice she was flattening the kipper with. 'No, dear. The name doesn't mean a thing. But you can ask my husband when he gets back from the Blackamoor. Jimmy's a fisherman and there isn't a man between here and Plymouth he doesn't know.' She turned the kipper over. The stife was prickling Tamar's eyes.

'And your grandmother was a Libby did you say?'

'Yes. I was hoping she'd still be alive. My mother died a couple of years ago when she was only thirty four, so my grandmother wouldn't be so very old now.'

'There's a big family of Libby's round here – all of them related, so I expect she'd be one of them. I don't recollect a Rosie Tomlinson though, but I don't know everyone in Looe. I'm not a native, dear. Came down from London in service and met Jimmy and stayed.'

Tamar's heart jumped at the mention of domestic service. Molly might be able to answer her other questions. 'Is there a big house near here called Ruthen?'

'Ruthven Manor do you mean? It's a bit out along the cliff towards Polperro. Lovely place.'

'You don't know who owns it do you, or anyone who worked there?'

'I know who used to own it. That was the Tremaines. Very big family. Gone now of course. Old Mr Tremaine ruined himself gambling and womanising and then shot himself with a twelve bore. The inquest said it was an accident – caught his foot on a tree root and the gun went off. But that was only a cover up. He and the coroner used to drink together at the Headland Hotel. Everyone knew Mr Tremaine couldn't face the shame of being bankrupt. Mrs Tremaine went off to live with her married daughter – somewhere up north and it was all sold up. A London doctor owns it now, but it's been requisitioned by the military.'

That was all Molly seemed to know. Tamar had hoped to talk to Jimmy about her grandfather, but it was ten o'clock and he'd still not come back from the pub. Tamar's head drooped as she tried to hold it level and her limbs ached for the waiting bed upstairs. Molly gave her a hot water bottle and a mug of warm milk with honey stirred into it.

'Not that you'll want anything to help you sleep by the look of you. And you can talk to Jimmy in the morning, dear,' she said as she pushed Tamar towards the stairs.

Anna locked the cottage door and reluctantly put the key under its stone. The owner had said she could continue to rent it for another couple of months which would allow her time to transfer all her belongings. She hated leaving the freedom that this cottage represented.

A royal naval transport was waiting for her at Scarborough Station and she was quickly driven up the cliff road and out across moorland – the sea on her right, the moor rising on her left. Then the road ran through an avenue of beeches with a high stone wall on one side. After about a mile, they turned in through wrought iron gates guarded by two armed soldiers and drove up a long curved driveway shielded by rhododendrons, ending in a gravel sweep. The house, revealed round the final bend, was ugly Victorian gothic, with ill-proportioned windows and oddly placed turrets that seemed to have no purpose but decoration. Incongruously, there was an anti-aircraft gun emplacement on the front lawn with sandbags piled up around it and another soldier sitting on the grass smoking a cigarette.

Inside the front door, far from the military order that Anna had expected, there was a kind of homely chaos. Boxes of files were stacked in the hall among coats and boots and a bag of golf clubs. Through a doorway, Anna glimpsed an over-decorated drawing room crowded with assorted arm chairs. A large Labrador lay in a patch of sunlight on the parquet.

A young Wren was coming down the stairs, a dark slim girl with a rather architectural face. 'Are you the new recruit?' she asked.

'Anna Weissmann Kennedy.'

'Oh good. We're expecting you. Come upstairs and I'll show you your room.'

Anna toiled behind her up four flights of stairs – each one progressively narrower and shabbier.

'We've put you in the tower,' the girl said. 'The room's tiny. But at least you'll have it to yourself. There are just too many people. It's like the old woman and the shoe.'

The room was smaller than Anna could have imagined – the door opened against the bed and there was space only for one chest of drawers with a mirror above it. Set into the thick circular wall were a series of narrow slit windows of diamond-paned white and blue glass. Through one of them Anna could see the sea glittering in the distance. Through another, a network of aerials, masts and wires, stretched behind the house across the fields. Her uniform was laid out on the bed – a dark blue skirt and jacket, white shirt, black shoes and stockings. When the girl had left, Anna put it on. She was no longer an individual now, but a rank and number. She was glad it was the navy, that at least would please her father. A typed note on the chest of drawers informed her that dinner was at seven and she was free to 'get her bearings' until then. Commander Forbes would see her after dinner in the library.

Anna went out into the garden. Everything had an autumnal look about it – the trees turning yellow and red – a dusting of fallen leaves on the lawn and spiders' webs glittering with rain like scraps of muslin flung over grass and shrubs. An elderly lady was standing at the edge of the lawn with a shallow basket on her arm and a pair of pruning shears in one hand. She was wearing knickerbockers and a faded leather jerkin. Something about her seemed familiar. She turned as she heard Anna's footsteps behind her.

'Miss Bateman!' Anna's heart leapt with delight. 'It is isn't it?'

'Anna! My dear girl. How wonderful.'

Anna felt herself firmly clasped in a pair of wiry arms and kissed on both cheeks. 'What are you doing here? I wrote to you in Germany, but Papa said you'd gone away.'

'The politics became impossible, so we moved to France, to the Auvergne. It was quite a wrench after so many years. But we'd only been there a year or so when even France became unsafe. My brother-in-law told us to come home. We packed up straight away but even so we were almost too late. It was such a struggle! The roads north of Paris were almost impassable. There were so many refugees – people wheeling huge bundles on bicycles – their children sitting on the cross bar. We even saw someone with a dining table on a pram. We got one of the last boats out of Calais. It was a very near thing. I'm so glad your mother decided to bring you back to England when she did. We tried so hard to persuade her that it was necessary. Did your father join you?'

'He's in a labour camp.'

'My dear girl, I'm so sorry.'

Anna thought that Miss Bateman had aged dreadfully. Her hair was white and had thinned so that her pink scalp showed through. 'Where's Miss Beatham?'

'In London, working for the Ministry. I'm afraid my lungs won't stand up to the city smog – never could abide it anyway. Barbara comes up here when she can.'

'Are you working here too?'

'No. Not at all. This is my family home, but when it was requisitioned I was allowed to stay on in the lodge. I look after the grounds and generally help out. Brigadier Mostyn-Soames is my brother-in-law you see,' she added almost as an afterthought. 'I worked for the government during the first World War so they think I'm perfectly secure.' She gave a little laugh and then said, 'Now tell me what's been happening to you? I know that you were interned – such nonsense – my brother-in-law told me.' She saw Anna's look of surprise and went on, 'When he saw that there was a girl from Partenkirchen on the list he asked me if I knew you. I was pleased to be able to help. It must have been very difficult for you.'

Anna told her about the camp and her struggle to study art.

'You poor child. But at least here you'll get time to paint. It's very peaceful and there's not much else to do when you're off duty. We can work together if you like, though I fear you'll be far ahead of me by now.' She said it regretfully. 'I've heard of Walter Suzmann. He was one of the Bauhaus group. If he's been teaching you . . .'

She took Anna down to the lodge and showed her rooms crammed with pretty furniture rescued from the main house, the walls crowded with pictures. Miss Bateman beckoned Anna towards the sitting room. 'We bought some paintings from a man sitting on the side of the road – he wanted to buy a ticket to America. Come and see.'

On Miss Bateman's sitting room wall, a small abstract glowed like a jewel against the faded wallpaper. 'It's a Derain,' she said, 'Do you know about him? He's a very underestimated painter. And this,' Miss Bateman said, moving through to the dining room, 'This is the best of all'. Above the sideboard a group of purple horses cavorted in a forest of ochre and blue. 'Franz Marc,' Miss Bateman said. 'One of the Blaue Reiter school. I don't know how its owner could bear to part with it. There was a small Picasso too, just a sketch in oil, but we didn't have enough francs. Someone would probably get a bargain when its owner became desperate enough. People over there were selling everything they had in order to get the money to leave. Everyone still remembers what the Germans did in the Great War – the pillaging and looting, people's houses stripped bare. It seemed terrible to profit by their misfortune. But at least here they will be appreciated.'

Miss Bateman showed Anna a rather ramshackle building at the back of the lodge that had been used as a potting shed. It had big windows and a roof light. 'I winter the geraniums in here,' she said. 'But you could use it as a studio if you wanted to. I'm sure we could find a paraffin stove for the coldest days – it's one of the advantages of being a military installation – you can always get things.'

'I'm glad I agreed to come to Harwood,' Anna said as she prepared to go back to the main house. 'I so very nearly didn't. I've always wondered what happened to you and where you'd gone.

When you didn't reply to my letters I feared the worst.'

Miss Bateman kissed her cheek. 'You must come here whenever you like. And now I must write to Barbara – she will be so pleased to know that you are safe.'

At dinner Anna met her fellow operatives. She guessed there were about twenty people around the big table and there were others in the radio huts who would – so Anna was told – be fed at a later sitting. The Commander, at the head of the table, was a handsome fresh-faced man in his early forties, probably the most senior person at the table, Anna thought, examining the gold braid. She had been told that only English was to be spoken at the dining table, but a medley of accents assaulted her ears, from the most plummy English to heavy eastern European tones she couldn't place. There were only three other women; the girl she had met earlier, a plump fluffy girl in her twenties with a slightly Scandinavian look, and a dark quiet woman about ten years older. Although her English was perfect, there was something about the way this woman clipped her words when she spoke that made Anna think she might also be German or possibly Swiss.

After dinner Anna went as instructed to the library. It was a small comfortable room with a roaring fire. The Commander sat behind a huge leather-topped desk with an impressive array of telephones on it. He stood up as Anna came into the room.

'Welcome to Operation Epsilon,' he said, shaking her hand firmly. 'Do sit down. I see you've already signed the official secrets' act, so we don't need to go through that. You do know that you must never talk to anyone – not even your husband – about what we do here?'

Anna nodded.

'People's lives depend on your silence.'

'What does Epsilon stand for? Or shouldn't I ask that?'

'It's the Greek letter E. E for Ear,' he smiled. 'That's what we are – a gigantic electronic ear monitoring all the radio traffic across the North Sea. You must report for duty tomorrow at 9 am. You'll be given some routine translation work and put on the rota for listening duty. The rest of the time is yours to do as you please.'

'I'm a painter,' Anna said. 'And I'm trying to continue my

studies in spite of the war. Is there any objection to my drawing and painting here?'

'So long as you don't draw the radio equipment or the personnel or anything else that would help the enemy if it fell into their hands.' He smiled. 'I used to do the odd watercolour myself before the war. But there isn't the time now.'

He stood up and Anna realised the interview was at an end. He held out his hand. 'Good luck,' he said. 'I hope you enjoy your stay with us.'

The documents Anna was asked to translate into English the following morning were boring and highly technical. There were two words she'd never come across before – both occupying almost the whole width of the page. The dark woman who had been at the dinner table the night before was sitting at a desk on the other side of the room. Seeing Anna frown, she got up and stood behind her shoulder. 'What's the problem?' she asked in German.

'I don't know what this means, or that.'

'It's a manufacturing term, I think. Four different words all put together – just put the meaning down literally and let them work it out. You'd need to be an engineer to know what the jargon meant.'

The woman introduced herself as Kirsten Heidegger.

'I guessed you were German last night,' Anna said as they walked back across the lawn to the house for lunch. 'When did you come over?'

'I'm Austrian actually. My father was in the government but he was shot for having anti-Nazi sympathies. I got involved in refugee work – I was one of a group of people who accompanied a train load of Jewish children back to England. War broke out while I was here – so I suppose I'm lucky – I might have been trapped on the other side. Given the work I was doing, I'd probably have been shot like my father or sent to one of the camps.'

'Was your mother English? I noticed last night how fluently you speak the language.'

'My grandmother. But my mother died when I was small, so I spent a lot of time here as a child. She more or less brought me up.'

For an hour after dinner, Anna had her first experience of listening. In a dark quiet hut, concealed in the wood behind the house, were rows of radio sets with illuminated dials pulsing with life. Anna was shown how to put on the headphones and spin the dial until she had a contact. The supervisor, a young naval radio officer, told her to try a particular frequency. 'We usually monitor this one. It's a patriotic music programme,' he said, 'but the announcer's good at giving out useful information. Have a listen and write down everything he says, including the titles.'

The music was very familiar. It brought back memories of sunny Fest days at Partenkirchen where the town band played tunes just like these in the market place. If she closed her eyes she could see the fat accordion player who had a pork butcher's shop, and a very cheeky boy with a trumpet whose father was the town clerk. But as a child it had been the Glockenspiel that fascinated her most as the hammers flew to and fro across the polished wooden keys.

Just then the music stopped and a man began to speak. Anna's hand almost froze on to the pencil she was holding. He had the most beautiful voice she had ever heard, warm and resonant. He pitched the words like music. She had never heard German spoken like that.

'Now for all our gallant young men, serving their Fatherland, we have something to lift the heart and make you dream of wives and sweethearts left at home. Brigitte Soderstrom will sing the lament from Tristan and Isolde by our own incomparable composer and patriot, Richard Wagner.'

Anna copied the words down. 'What am I listening for?' she asked.

The operator smiled. 'They never tell us that. It goes to the code department. We're not just listening to German radio to find out what's going on over there. We have agents using the broadcasting network to relay information to us.'

'Is he one of them?'

'I couldn't tell you even if I knew, which I don't.'

'So is everyone here listening to European radio stations?'

'Some of them, but we're also monitoring coded traffic between military sources – ship to ship and ship to shore communications, German agents reporting home – that kind of thing. You have to have a very high security clearance to do that.'

The beautiful voice belonged to a man called Michael Schmidt, Kirsten told her at breakfast. Anna could have listened to its hypnotic qualities all night every night. But he broadcast only twice a week. As she listened and transcribed in the days that followed, Anna thought she could begin to detect a pattern to his announcements. Some of them were different – there would be a phrase that didn't quite fit, a word out of place. Sometimes it would be a homely statement – such as 'I hope you're having better weather at the front than we are having here.' A lot of what he said was propaganda – that much she did know. Alarming statements about the success of the German war machine. 'We shall crush the Bolsheviks like vermin under the heels of our German boots.' 'We are all fighting for the glorious future of the Fatherland and God is with us.' Somehow Anna couldn't quite equate the owner of this beautiful voice with such sentiments.

'They do say the devil has the most seductive voice of all,' Kirsten said, smiling. 'He who seems most fair, may yet be foul.'

'Is that a quotation?'

'It is. You have my Grandmother to blame for that. Her favourites were Goethe and Milton. I'm afraid they're both way above my head.'

~~~~~~~~~~~~~~~~~~

Tamar woke with no memory of actually getting into bed at all. A watery sun was lighting the edge of the curtain and the only sounds outside were the slapping of waves on stone, the cries of the gulls, and the distant growl of a boat engine. She got up and dressed, feeling more optimistic than she'd done the night before. Downstairs, a grey-haired, very weathered looking man was sitting at the kitchen table in braces and shirt sleeves eating a kipper, reading a newspaper propped up against the tea pot.

'I've put you in the parlour, dear,' Molly said as Tamar went to pull up a chair. 'There's only you this morning, so you can have it all to yourself.'

'Oh. You shouldn't have gone to all that trouble. I'm quite
~~~~~~~~~~~~~~~~~~

happy to have my breakfast here.'

'Well,' Molly hesitated, looking doubtfully at her husband. Tamar sat down beside him to settle the argument.

'Jimmy,' Molly said, putting her hand on his shoulder to get his attention. 'This is the young lady I was telling you about.'

He grunted and held out a rather kippery hand for Tamar to shake.

'I don't know what to give you for your breakfast,' Molly said. 'There not being any eggs, and bacon rationed. You'll not be wanting another kipper.'

'Just toast, please.' Tamar didn't think she could face eggs again after the Heslop's. Hungry again this morning she ate her way through three slices of toast with margarine and blackberry jelly.

'You've got a healthy appetite for a lass,' Jimmy observed.

Tamar blushed. 'I'm a land girl. I suppose all that physical work does make you want to eat a lot.'

'A land girl! You're just a slip of a thing,' Molly said. 'You don't look as though you'd last five minutes.'

Tamar blushed again and turned to Jimmy, now silently eating his way through the potato scones his wife had just put in front of them. 'Molly said you might have known my grandfather, Harland Tomlinson. He was a fisherman and they lived in Headland Cottages. His wife was called Rosie. Rosie Libby.'

Jimmy finished his scone and licked the crumbs off his thumb and forefinger. 'Harland,' he said thoughtfully. 'Yes, I remember him. But it was a long time ago, my love. He died in . . . let me see,' he counted on his fingers, 'about fifteen years back it would have been. There was a big storm, just about this time of the year and there were two boats out there that didn't come back in. Terrible loss of life that winter. He was a good man, Harland, straight. Had his own boat, but no luck with women.'

'What about his wife, Rosie? Do you remember her?'

'Ah, well. . . Your grandmother was it? Bit of a flighty one that. I'm sorry if that's not to your liking, my love, but that's what the lads always said.'

'Do you know if she's still alive?'

He shook his head. 'No. I'm not sure if I ever met her. 'Twas only Harland that I knew.'

After breakfast, Tamar wandered out into the town. She felt instantly at home. The fishing boats lined up against the harbour wall, the nets and creels piled high on the quay, the seagulls swooping and screaming. But the wind was kinder and the air warmer than the banks of the Tyne. She asked directions at the post office and was told to cross the river and follow the road along it in the direction of the sea and then to fork left up towards the cliff.

Headland Cottages was a terrace of two-up-two-down black and white houses tucked into the shelter of the cliff facing across the harbour mouth. There were neat lace curtains at every window and geraniums on the sills. Tamar held her breath, gazing out to sea for a moment to gain courage. Sadie must have stood here as a child, staring out to catch sight of her father's fishing boat heading home. Had Sadie kept contact with her mother after she left? Did she know that he had been lost at sea? If she had, then no knowledge of it had been passed to Tamar. How was she to disentangle the truth of Sadie's past from the false history she had constructed for herself?

Tamar knocked sharply on the door of number three. There was no answer. After the second knock, Tamar thought she saw a twitch of lace in the next door window, so she decided to knock at number four.

A young woman about Sadie's age opened the door. 'I hope you're not selling anything,' she said.

'I'm sorry to bother you, but my grandmother Rosie Tomlinson used to live next door and I'm trying to find someone who might have known her.'

'Well it won't be me,' the girl said. 'I've only been here for a year and she's been dead longer than that.'

Tamar's face dropped. This was not what she had expected.

'I know who would be able to tell you though.' The girl explained that she had worked in the local shop before her marriage and knew most of the customers by sight. 'Old Rosie used to come in with Alice Cummings – they were very good friends – and she's still alive as far as I know.' The girl thought for a moment. 'She lives up the road in one of the lodges to the manor.' She pointed to a path that zig-zagged up the headland beyond the houses.

'Thank you,' Tamar said, concealing her disappointment. 'I'm very grateful.'

The door was briskly closed the moment she turned away. Tamar got the impression that people didn't welcome strangers here and wondered whether Mrs Cummings would be equally unwilling to talk.

Although it was late in the year the cliff top path was still lined with gorse in yellow bloom and there were little clumps of purple ling sheltering between stones. As the path gained height, Tamar could see the grey hulls of warships, just discernible in the sunlight out to sea. There were two freighters beating their way out of the channel towards the Atlantic and the hulls of several small fishing trawlers. Then the path diverged. A smaller path turned to the left inland, and the cliff top path continued on past a new concrete pill box piled up with sand bags. A young soldier was sitting on them smoking a cigarette. 'Nice day,' he said.

'At least you've got a good view.'

He grinned. 'Boring bloody posting though. This isn't what I joined up for.'

'I'm looking for Ruthven Manor. Am I going in the right direction?'

He stood up and pointed along the smaller path. 'Just up there about quarter of a mile.'

Tamar thanked him and turned her back to the sea. Over the brow of the headland a wall came into view. It was very definitely an estate boundary. The brickwork was neat and well maintained and it was high enough to keep people out and to prevent them looking in. About a hundred yards further along the wall, there was a stile – a flight of steps leading to two metal bars set into the top of the wall between ornamental stones surmounted by carved pineapples. Unable to resist the temptation, Tamar climbed over and found herself in a thicket of overgrown rhododendrons – their large, dark green leaves still dripping from the overnight rain. A winding path brought Tamar out onto an unkempt lawn – the grass obviously unmown all summer and now laid flat by autumn storms.

In front of her was the house – a long low construction of red brick with mullioned windows and spiralling Elizabethan chimneys. It was very beautiful in the mellow autumn sunlight. Behind its roof Tamar could glimpse the spire of a church and when she turned her back to it the sea lay glittering where the garden fell away towards the cliff edge. She saw at once how Sadie would have loved it. Had she slipped into the grounds as a child to wander dreaming among the rhododendrons? Did she imagine herself living here so often that it became real? That's what I might have done, Tamar thought.

A military landrover was parked on the gravel, but there was otherwise no sign of occupation. No one stepped out to challenge her as she made her way down the drive to the little lodge she could see at its entrance. When Tamar knocked on the door it swung open at her touch and a quavery, but still authoritative voice inside called 'Come in! Come in!'

There were only two rooms opening from the narrow passageway – a bedroom on the left with an old fashioned high bed, and the living room to the right where a lively coal fire burned in the grate and an elderly lady with very white hair was sitting in a wing chair holding a cup of tea in a shaking hand.

'Mrs Cummings?'

The woman didn't respond immediately. She stared at Tamar as though looking at a ghost from the past. Tamar waited patiently.

'You'd better tell me who you are,' Alice Cummings said at last. 'You remind me of someone, but I can't properly recall who it might be.'

'My name's Tamar. Tamar Fell.' She held out her hand but the woman didn't take it. She nodded towards the armchair on the other side of the fire and Tamar sat down.

'So that's what you call yourself,' she said.

Disconcerted, Tamar began to explain the purpose of her visit. 'I came to Cornwall to look for my grandmother Rosie Tomlinson, but I've just discovered that she died. The next door neighbour told me that you were friends, so I hoped you might be able to tell me something about her.'

There was another silence while Mrs Cummings continued

to look at Tamar. A great deal was going on behind her eyes. She seemed to be assessing Tamar, or making up her mind about something. 'Rosie,' she said after a lengthy pause. 'Well, she worked with me at the Manor for over thirty years, so I suppose you could say we knew each other pretty well. I was the housekeeper here and she came in and did the daily work – she didn't need to – she just liked to get out of the house and with her husband away so much – you know about him? – she was on her own a lot. But of course after the Tremaines left things changed and the doctor didn't need any extra help, but we stayed friends and she came in for the spring cleaning and whenever they had a house party down from London.'

'You must have known my mother Sadie?'

'Oh yes.' Another pause. Then, cautiously, 'Did she send you?'

'She died in an accident about two years ago.'

A sigh. 'That's sad. Just as well Rosie's already gone. It would have broken her heart all over again.'

'What was Sadie like when she was a child?'

'Oh a beautiful little thing – but a devil mind – into everything she was. Like the nursery rhyme. When she was bad she was very, very bad. Just like her father really.'

'Harland?' Tamar was confused. 'I thought – I was told by someone who knew him that he was a good man and that it was Rosie who was the flighty one. Well, that's how they put it anyway.'

Mrs Cummings laughed. She lifted the cup out of her lap and put it down on the little side table with a trembling hand. 'I can see you don't know very much.' She leaned forward confidentially. 'Rosie never said a word, but it was bound to cause talk. The idea that Harland – that big rough man – could father such a picture of perfection as your mother was difficult enough to credit especially after being married so long without so much as a twinkle in the eye. Rosie was pretty, especially when she was young, but Sadie was out of another stable altogether. And when she and Pamela Tremaine stood together, well, there was something about the eyes . . . but it's best not to comment on a likeness if you want to keep your job. Let's just say this, dear, if

Harland Tomlinson fathered that angelic sprite after twenty years of barren marriage it would be a miracle.'

Tamar said nothing.

'Your mother was up here all the time when she was a girl. She and Pamela were more or less of an age – about a year's difference. They did everything together, except they didn't go to the same schools. Pamela went away to some posh college for young ladies and old man Tremaine paid for your mother to go to a school in Plymouth as a weekly boarder. Oh – he did his duty by her as he saw it, but it gave her ideas above herself. Poor girl, how could she be content with marrying some local fisher lad after that? He had her trained as a secretary and she used to work for one of the solicitors in Liskeard. Poor Sadie. I remember she kicked up such a fuss because she couldn't be invited to Pamela's wedding. She might have been her friend, but when it came down to it, as far as the Tremaine's were concerned, she was just the daily help's daughter.'

Tamar's mind was reeling. 'How did she meet my father?'

'You want to know about the Fells? Well, I'll tell you. There were three of them – the brothers anyway. I think there were sisters but they never came here.'

'What were their names?'

'Well, there was William – he was the eldest. He married a girl and went off to drive an ambulance in the Great War and got blown up by a shell. And then there was Robert – very serious he was – a barrister or something, probably a judge by now I shouldn't wonder. He married Pamela just before the bust up. A very swanky wedding – over a hundred guests – champagne on the lawn – seven courses for dinner – quite a do to cater for. I had to hire in twenty extra staff. None of it paid for of course. It nearly bankrupt the butcher in Liskeard. I couldn't hold my head up round here for years after.'

'And James?'

'Now he was the youngest. His mother's darling. Proper mollycoddled. Mrs Emily was only here twice – once for the wedding and then when your dad and Sadie ran off. You'd have thought she was the Queen Mary the way she behaved. Poor Rosie. The shame of it was terrible.'

'I read one of Emily's letters to my mother.'

Mrs Cummings sighed. 'Yes, Sadie got no sympathy from that direction.'

Tamar hesitated and then asked tentatively. 'She said that James died just after they were married. But it's not true is it?'

'No dear, though I'm sorry to have to say it. But it's better to have the truth. You mother may have called herself Mrs Fell, but she and James were never married. Mrs Emily saw to that. They went off together, but of course she wouldn't give him any money and so he soon came to heel. I don't think your mother got much – a bit here and there.'

'Did my father ever see me?'

'I don't think he did, though I couldn't swear to it. His mother made him promise never to see Sadie again and knowing her she'd keep him to it. He got married you know – about ten years ago. It was in the London papers that the doctor brought down. I took one for Rosie to see. Daughter of a big publisher the paper said. What's happened to him since, I don't know.'

The thought that her father might be alive somewhere made Tamar feel giddy. The fire was too hot. She moved her chair back a little. Some lines from one of the poems in Sadie's book sprung into her mind. She had read them so often she knew almost all of them by heart.

Truth it is you must beware of.
Fatal shafts – who dare's embrace?
Merit is there in dissembling;
Masks become its Gorgon face.

Knowing the truth was one thing. Living with it was another. Whoever wrote those lines had known that. 'My mother talked about an elderly man – I think he must have stayed here. A poet called Charles Carter?'

Mrs Cummings smiled and her eyes looked distant as though remembering things a long time ago. 'Oh yes. Mr Carter. A lovely gentleman. Eccentric of course, but then you expect that with a poet. Used to wander round the rhododendron walk talking to himself.'

'He gave Sadie a book of his poems.'

'Yes, he was quite taken with Sadie. She'd have been about

thirteen or fourteen I suppose. Gave Rosie quite a turn. But I used to tell her it would be all right – he was a lovely man.'

Tamar stood up, feeling the need to be out in the fresh air.

'I'm sorry,' Mrs Cummings said. 'I haven't even offered you a cup of tea – you can make one yourself if you pop in the kitchen. I've got arthritis in my knees, so I'm not so good at getting up and down.'

'It's all right, thank you,' Tamar said.

'You have a look of your father,' Mrs Cummings said. 'That's what struck me when you came in, though I couldn't place it until you said your name.'

'Is there anything I can get you before I go?' Tamar asked.

'No dear, I'm quite comfortable. Come again if you want to. I don't see so many people now. It's not like it used to be.'

'Thank you for telling me everything. I've always wondered about Sadie's family and why she didn't talk about them and now she's dead there's no one else I can ask.'

'She must have had a struggle, your mum. But you're a credit to her, I'll say that. It's a pity Rosie isn't here to see you. Pamela and Robert wanted to adopt you after you were born, you know.'

'Did they?'

'They didn't have any of their own – at least not then. But Sadie wouldn't have it. Rosie offered to bring you up as well, but your mother wanted to give you a better life than she'd had. Said she'd manage. Not that she ever did. Always writing and asking for money she was. Rosie washed her hands of her in the end. She and Rosie were too alike to get on – peas out of the same pod. Such a row they had the last time Sadie was down.'

She stopped as if she'd said too much and Tamar had to prompt her to go on. 'What did they quarrel about?'

'Rosie called her a hussy and worse. She had a terrible temper when she got worked up. And then Sadie flew at her – "You've no right to point the finger," she was shouting and then she brought up that bit about people in glass houses. Well, you can't talk like that to your own mother, even if it's true.'

'I think Sadie must have brought me with her that time,' Tamar said. 'I can remember an old lady with grey hair and I've always wondered who it was.'

'Oh that wouldn't be Rosie dear. Not then. You're thinking about Sarah Libby, Rosie's mother. She was a lovely lady. Sadie was very fond of her grandmother. She used to look after you a bit when you were little – at least until she died.'

'Thank you for telling me all this,' Tamar said. 'But I'd better go now. You must be tired.'

'Oh talking doesn't tire me. I don't see enough people these days. Not like it was. The manor's empty now. It's been requisitioned, but the military haven't moved in yet. Would you like to have a look around?'

Tamar felt her blood quicken with anticipation. 'I'd love to. Wouldn't they mind?'

'What they don't know won't hurt. I've still got a key.' She pointed to a single large key hanging from a hook under the mantle shelf.

Tamar let herself in the back door which opened into a lobby lined with coat hooks and boot racks. There was an empty wall cupboard that looked as though it might have contained guns and a row of bells above it with the names of the rooms they served. On the right a door opened into a vast kitchen. On the left was a billiard room, the table covered with a cloth. A big, baize lined door in front of Tamar opened into the front hall and a blaze of light from the long windows and the glass panelled front door. An oak staircase with a heavily carved balustrade curved upwards towards an upper landing. Tamar felt a thrill of excitement. This was the house with twenty bedrooms and a tennis court that Sadie had talked about. The air was completely stagnant, as if it hadn't been disturbed for a long time. Opening a panelled door on the right Tamar found herself in what must have been the drawing room. Long casement windows looked across the lawns to the sea. They were frosted with salt from the prevailing wind. The furniture was huddled under dust sheets – pale islands on an ocean of dusty floor boards. The carpet was rolled up beside the wall and there was damp in one corner where the wall paper bulged. Mirrors and pictures hung under anonymous calico shrouds. Tamar stood in the middle of the room and tried to imagine how it had once been. This was where her mother had met James Fell, where she had fallen in love with him and been cheated out of marriage by an accident of birth. And this was where, if Tamar had read the story right, her real grandfather had lived with his wife and his legitimate daughter. Poor Sadie. Suddenly the past was peopled with relatives. An uncle who was a high court judge; an aunt who was also her mother's half sister; and a father who might still be alive with a wife and children in London.

CHAPTER TWENTY TWO

Anna was due her first weekend's leave and it was a relief to go to Seaham and spend two days sitting quietly on the rocks by herself. She packed up her painting materials and managed to bring most of them back with her. Miss Bateman helped her to set them up in the shed. It felt good to be hammering frames together and stretching canvas over them. Then she could begin priming them and sketching out her new ideas on the blank expanse of white. There was a collection of ancient bicycles in the old stable block and during off duty hours Anna often borrowed one and cycled down to the cliffs to spend precious hours with her sketch book. She sometimes took the Commander's dog with her for company and he splashed happily through streams and thickets of wild broom while she drew. For the first time in months, perhaps even years, Anna felt if not happy, then at peace. So much of her time had been spent in battling against obstacles towards her cherished goal, to be placed in this comfortable limbo gave Anna a marvellous sense of release. The war had swept her off in other directions, and there was no point in resisting its flow. Perhaps like Walter, she should be content, just for a little while, to record what was happening. '*Painting is a language*,' he had written in his last letter. '*Use it to talk about what you know*.'

That night after her shift, she had gone to her room and from memory begun to draw the scenes of devastation she had witnessed in the streets of Shields. She had an idea in her mind for a big abstract where the slabs of wall with gaping windows and their collages of wallpaper, fire places and cupboard doors could be painted with their full surreal power. That was what this war meant – not the clash of army on army in some far away country, but the destruction of innocent people's lives, their houses and their children.

The night shifts were the most intense, twiddling the knobs, scanning the air waves, hoping to stumble on clandestine communications, listening for coded phrases. Once as Anna listened to one of these unintelligible, carefully enunciated messages, the line crackled and the broadcaster stopped in mid transmission and then began again, talking 'in clear'. 'Schnell! Schnell!' He was shouting. The panic in his voice made Anna's skin prickle. 'They are coming, it is too late! Tell Clara for me . . . Tell her that I love her. . . .' There was a clattering sound and the line went dead. Anna sat frozen to the spot until Kirsten came over and put her hand on her shoulder.

'It happens,' Kirsten said. 'Too often. I wonder sometimes how they can do it when the risks are so great.'

That morning during breakfast there was a buzz around the table and the Commander was looking unusually serious. Anna, preoccupied with the memory of what she had heard, was quiet. Someone down the table was saying, 'Of course his cover's bound to have been blown – such a pity. They're trying to bring him out.'

'What's been happening?' Anna asked Kirsten.

'One of our agents, I think. I don't know who exactly – we never know their names. There was a huge flurry of radio traffic yesterday, so I guessed something big was going on. What you heard last night was probably part of it. I suspect the Germans have broken one of our intelligence networks.'

Anna tried to put it out of her mind, but the terror in the man's voice as he had cried out across the air waves kept coming back to her.

Tamar and Holly were billeted above the stables at Nithsdale Hall in accommodation designed for grooms. It was almost as basic as it had been at Holme Farm except that it had electricity and the atmosphere was more cheerful. The work was just as hard. As well as cleaning out the stables and feeding the horses, Tamar's duties included working in the market garden, harvesting vegetables and earthing up leeks. It was backbreaking and she missed the contact with the animals. Picking potatoes was particularly tedious and required large numbers of people, so prisoners of war were brought in from a local camp by lorry every day to help. Tamar was surprised how friendly and easy going they were. One of them – an Italian looking man in his forties, kept bringing her little gifts – a sprig of hawthorn berries picked from a hedge, or a bird carved out of a piece of wood with his penknife. They were always accompanied by a formal bow and a few words in a language she didn't understand. His kindness embarrassed Tamar, but she knew it would be churlish to refuse. She put the little offerings on her window sill. It was hard to imagine that these men, until their capture, had been engaged in trying to kill George and Edward and Martin. How did war turn ordinary, nice human beings into monsters?

The food was better at Nithsdale Hall than at Holme Farm. They grew all their own produce and the huge kitchens were used to mass catering. There was homemade bread, milk puddings and vast stews of meat and vegetables and barley. Heslop's unending diet of rabbit stew became a mere memory. But it was all less friendly than Tamar had expected – most of the people had worked here since before the war and their families had lived on the estate for generations. Tamar was conscious of a feeling of 'us and them'. They were in awe of Holly's accent and her finishing school manners and nicknamed her 'Lady P.' Tamar kept her head down, as she always tried to do in difficult situations, and worked quietly on. She no longer wrote to Edward – if even his regiment didn't know where he was, what would be the point? And she tried not to think of Martin Bainbridge.

It was the lorry driver who brought the POW's who told her about the dance.

'Are you girls going to the dance on Saturday?'

'What dance?'

'At Kirkland village hall. The young farmers are getting it up. Should be good.'

It was a long time since Tamar had been dancing, or even to the cinema. She was tired of spending every evening studying. She needed to have a night out.

'I'd like to go,' Tamar said to Holly, 'All work and no play makes Jill a very dull girl.'

Holly was also keen – a trip to Kirkland meant an opportunity to see Ivan. The problem for Tamar was how to get there. Holly had the use of a bicycle. But Tamar had never been on one in her life.

~~~~~~~~~~~~~~~~~~

Anna was in the shed, deeply engrossed in painting when the door opened behind her and a male voice said; 'I am so sorry to disturb you.'

Anna closed her eyes and every nerve of her body trembled. When she opened her eyes again a man was standing in front of her. A blonde haired Aryan with blue eyes and the strangest face she had ever seen. His features were too irregular to be handsome – the mouth too large and slightly crooked, the nose a little larger than it should have been, his eyebrows thick and encroaching, but the brightness of his eyes and the way he smiled made all that irrelevant. It was an arresting face. 'I'm sorry if I'm interrupting you,' he said again.

'So you're the patriotic music person,' Anna said, laying down her brush. 'I've been listening to you for weeks.'

'But not any more. My patriotism was put in doubt.'

He came and stood behind her, looking at the canvas. 'That is beautiful – in a savage kind of way. You have caught something – the essence of conflict perhaps. It is big egos that start wars, but little people who have to fight them. I sometimes think that patriotism is a great evil.'

'How did they get you out?'

'Through Denmark and then a fishing boat. But perhaps I shouldn't tell you that – you might be a beautiful German spy.'

'With a father in a concentration camp?'

His face changed in an instant and he put his arm around her shoulders. 'I'm sorry. I didn't know.' The intimate gesture seemed to come quite naturally to him. 'Miss Bateman sent me to fetch you for a cup of English tea. I had heard about this habit, but it's the first time I've been to England and I am devastated to discover that there is not a drop of coffee to be had anywhere.'
~~~~~~~~~~~~~~~~~~

Miss Bateman had laid out scones and jam and tiny sandwiches rather pink in the middle which Anna suspected contained some kind of fish paste. 'Gentleman's Relish,' Miss Bateman corrected her. 'It's very difficult to get at present. Fortnum's is not what it was.'

All the time she was eating, Anna was watching Michael. He had a natural confidence, and it was no surprise when he said, 'I used to be an actor before the war, that's why they put me into broadcasting.' His blue eyes sought out Anna's. 'Tell me your history?' he demanded and so, after a glance across the table at Miss Bateman, Anna launched into an account of her life in Partenkirchen, her subsequent escape, her ambitions, the internment camp and her hunger strike.

'It was *that* that brought my brother-in-law to you,' Miss Bateman said. 'He said you must have a great deal of courage. When I told him I had known you, I didn't realise that they would send you here. It was one of life's happy conjunctions, I think.'

Michael was looking at her again and Anna had to drop her eyes and occupy her hands with folding her napkin. 'I'd better get back to my painting if I want to get any more done before dinner. Thank you for tea.' What to say to Michael? Platitudes? But he solved the problem by getting to his feet, clicking his heels together and bowing over her arm in a ridiculously old fashioned way that made her laugh.

'I look forward to meeting you again, Frau Weissman Kennedy,' he said with another mock bow.

At dinner that night Michael sat at the top of the table next to the Commander and the Brigadier – who had arrived late – surrounded by the more senior personnel. Anna, among the junior operatives, ached to listen to their conversation. She wondered if Tamar had felt like this when she met Martin? Every fibre of her body was constantly aware of his presence in the room. She watched his hands – his beautiful hands – and listened to the tones of his voice through pauses in the general conversation. How was it possible to fall in love with someone's voice, without knowing them as a person?

'What are you doing?' Holly asked a few days later. She was leaning on the orchard gate, laughing.

'Learning to ride a bike,' Tamar said. She stopped for a moment to get her breath back. 'At least on the grass if I fall off it doesn't hurt so much.' She kicked off with her foot again and managed to wobble for about ten yards before tipping over again. 'I thought if I could ride, we could go to the village dance together on Saturday at Kirkland. The head gardener said I could borrow this bike if I wanted to. It's old and rusty, but it works.'

By Saturday Tamar was able to make an unsteady circuit of the paddock, only having to put her foot to the ground occasionally.

'It's only five miles,' Holly said as they set off. 'And at least it's not raining.'

It had been a struggle to find anything to wear. Moths had attacked Tamar's best wool skirt, and her favourite yellow dress with the little blue butterflies felt uncomfortably tight. With so much physical work and stodgy food, she had gained weight. Holly was suffering too. She had squeezed into a beautiful lilac coloured wool dress, but the underarm zip refused to close and she had had to put a cardigan over the top. Tamar looked at her last new coat – now three years old and fraying at the cuffs. The next time she was in Newcastle she would have to spend some of her precious clothing coupons on a new one. Tamar rejected it for her land army greatcoat. They were cycling after all.

The fresh air felt very strange on bare legs more used to corduroy leggings and woollen boot socks. Holly's mother had sent her some silk stockings – no rationing for the Pergavie's evidently, but she had wisely decided not to risk them – 'It would be dreadful if they snagged on the pedals.' They had thought of using gravy browning to simulate stockings, but the cook could not be persuaded to part with any, and experiments with eye pencil created such wandering lines on the backs of their calves that in the end they abandoned any attempt at deceit.

The village hall was a ramshackle wooden structure with a corrugated iron roof. By the time Holly and Tamar got there it was crowded. The band up on stage consisted of an accordion, a couple of violins, a pianist and a drummer. When Tamar and Holly arrived they were playing a Scottish number but no one had begun to dance. Ivan, standing shyly in a corner near the table where tea and soft drinks were being served, came forward smiling to claim Holly as soon as they had taken off their coats at the door.

'I'm going to teach him English dancing,' Holly said. 'Will you be all right?' She looked anxious.

'Don't worry about me,' Tamar said. 'I'll be fine.' She tried to sound confident. There were several people from the village that she recognised, but there were also a great many strangers. Tamar felt very isolated. She accepted a glass of ginger beer and sat down in a corner where she could watch people coming and going. Almost immediately the door opened again and through the press of people she saw Martin Bainbridge come limping in. Maggie went to greet him, throwing her arms round his neck and Tamar's heart began to do strange things inside her rib cage.

He chatted to Maggie for what seemed a very long time and then, looking round the room, saw Tamar and smiled. She smiled back and a few moments later he came limping across and sat down beside her.

'What happened to the crutches?' she asked.

He grinned broadly. 'I threw them away. I can get around just as well without them. I'm not planning to do any dancing though.'

The caller invited everyone to choose their partners for an eightsome reel, and Tamar could see Holly and Ivan joining the circle hand in hand.

Martin had noticed too. 'Your friend seems very taken with our DP.'

'Very. I don't know what her parents will say when they find out.' It seemed extraordinary to be sitting here with Martin, talking to him as easily as if she'd known him all her life.

'Don't let me stop you dancing,' Martin said. 'I don't want to spoil your evening.'

'I'm not really very good at it. I'd much rather talk.'

'So tell me about the fiancé that Joe mentioned. Are you really engaged?' He lifted up her bare hand as if checking for the ring.

The touch of his fingers made Tamar tremble.

'It was sort of unofficial. I was only seventeen, but he wanted me to be engaged before he went away and I couldn't really say no, could I, when he was going off to France?'

'No, I don't suppose you could.' Martin put her hand back in her lap. 'How long since you've seen him now?'

'Over a year. I can't even remember what he looks like. I have to keep on looking at his photograph to remind myself. And what about you?' she asked lightly, hoping it didn't sound too pointed a question. 'How many broken hearts are there in this village on your account?'

He laughed. 'Not many I'm afraid. There was a girl in the WRAC's when I was doing my basic training, but it sort of petered out. It was a wartime thing. I take after my father really – not much of a one for women.'

'Has Wilf always been so shy?'

'So they tell me. How he ever got to marry my mother's a mystery. The family joke used to be that she was the one who did the proposing. It's probably true.'

'It must have been dreadful for him when she died.'

'I don't think he's been the same since. I don't remember any of it, being only two at the time. She bled to death having a baby and the baby died too. Nothing the midwife could do and by the time the doctor arrived it was too late. Aunt Mary said they had to burn the mattress. And since then we've all lived at Crow Hall. I suppose it was lucky that Aunt Mary and Old Joe had no kids of their own. I was thoroughly spoilt.' He grinned. 'What about your parents – you never mention them?'

'My father disappeared before I was born and then my mother died in an accident two years ago.'

'Haven't you any other family?' Martin sounded surprised.

'Not that I know of. My grandparents are dead now. I think my father had brothers and sisters but I've never met any of them.' Tamar hesitated. Better to tell him now and get it over with, so that if it mattered to him, it wouldn't be so dreadful. 'I'm illegitimate,' she said. 'He never married my mother.'

Martin smiled. 'Well, it's nothing to be ashamed of. The way Aunt Mary puts it, "A bairns a bairn no matter who its father is."'

Tamar stifled a sigh of relief. 'She's lovely. I don't think Holly and I would ever have survived Heslop's without her.'

The band were just striking up a slow number, and couples were moving closer together. Tamar noticed that Ivan already had his arm round Holly's waist and her eyes were shyly raised to his. Martin touched Tamar's hand. 'Do you fancy a turn round the floor? I think I could probably manage a slow shuffle.'

Tamar nodded. Martin tried to get out of the chair and then laughed as his stiff leg refused to cooperate and Tamar had to haul him up. Then his arms were round her and she could feel the strength of his muscles, breathe the very masculine odour of sweat and Aunt Mary's green soap. When Tamar closed her eyes the music seemed very far away. They were alone on the dance floor, just herself and Martin. His face was resting against the top of her head and she could feel his warm breath through her hair.

'I'll give you a lift home,' Martin said after it was over. 'I've got the landrover. It'll be a while before I'm up to cycling. Your bikes can go in the back with old Bert.'

'Who's Bert?' Tamar asked. Holly was hanging back in the shadows standing very close to Ivan. Neither of them seemed to be aware of anyone else.

Martin untied the canvas at the back and a huge ram poked his head out. 'He's my excuse. The government won't allow us to use our farm fuel allowance for private trips, so if anyone asks, I'm on business.'

'How do you get him to stay there?' Tamar stroked his nose and he playfully butted her hand.

'He was a family pet – Joe gave him to me when I was ten – he's a bit past it now, but he likes riding about. Joe feeds him bottles of brown ale to keep him going. He's still out there at tupping time wanting to do his bit.'

It was difficult to prise Holly away from her lingering farewell with Ivan, but eventually the bicycles were loaded and both girls climbed into the cab. Tamar was glad to be driven back. Cycling uphill already tired in the moonless dark would not have been fun. Martin drove slowly, the slits in the blackout over his headlamps illuminating only a small area of road in front. They hadn't gone far when they were flagged down by two policeman at the side of the road, their bicycles propped against the hedge.

'How do Martin!' The younger of the two said as he slid open the window.

'Business a bit slack tonight, Alec?'

The policeman grinned. 'Spot check. Just makin' sure there's no one about as shouldn't be. There's a POW escaped from the camp.'

'Out for a jaunt, are we?' the older man asked, peering in at Tamar and Holly.

'Just taking a ram down to Nithsdale and I thought I'd give these two girls a lift home.'

'Can I see your papers please. Just routine.'

Tamar and Holly dug their identity cards out of their bags, but he nodded without really looking at them. Then he went round the back and peered in at Old Bert.

'Funny time of night to deliver a sheep,' he said.

Alec winked at Martin and slapped his hand on the door, signalling him to move on.

'I was at school with him,' Martin said. 'Lucky I knew him or I might have had to answer a few more questions.'

When they reached the stable yard at Nithsdale Hall, Martin said, 'Come to Sunday lunch. Mam misses you. What about you Holly?'

'I'm sorry, I promised Ivan we'd cycle up to the Tarn.' Tamar could almost hear her blushing in the dark.

'You'll come then Tamar?'

She looked at him and then nodded. She laughed suddenly. 'It'll give me plenty of practice on that wretched bike! My shins are already scraped raw.'

~~~~~~~~~~~~~~~~~

On Saturday night after dinner Michael said, 'What do you do for night life here?'

'There isn't any,' Kirsten said. 'It's too far into Scarborough – you can get there, but there's no late bus back.'

'What about transport?' Michael nodded his head towards the
~~~~~~~~~~~~~~~~~

jeeps parked on the gravel sweep outside.

'We can't take one of those without permission.'

'Why not? Who else can drive?' Michael looked round the small group in the sitting room. Anna shook her head. Kirsten said, 'Michael! You mustn't!'

'We can't spend Saturday night cooped up in here – I refuse.'

Anna found herself in the front of the jeep with Kirsten, while two of the other radio operators climbed into the back. Michael free-wheeled it down the drive, stopped under cover of the rhododendrons, lifted the bonnet and did something to start the engine. He waved confidently to the guards, who obediently opened the gate and then they were bumping along the Scarborough road with Michael at the wheel.

'If we're caught,' Kirsten said, 'we'll be court-martialled.'

'Where's your sense of adventure? Anyway, they'll blame me and there's nothing they can do. What do you say Anna?'

'I think you're mad! But you're right, it's time we had some fun. Since the war began everything's been so deadly serious.' She tried to remember the last time she'd had a night out with friends – probably the drink with Tamar before she'd come here.

They parked the jeep on the sea front and then by common consent headed for the Victorian bulk of the Grand Hotel. The terrace doors were open to let in a breeze and music leaked through the black-out curtains with stray beams of light. In the bar, Michael ordered cocktails.

'I'd like one of those,' Anna said recklessly, pointing to a pink concoction in a shallow glass. 'It looks like something from a film.'

'It's gin and bitters,' Michael said. 'But for you, it has to be a Black Russian.'

'What's that?'

'It has vodka in it and it's lethal,' Kirsten warned. 'Don't let him lead you astray. Didn't I tell you the devil has the most alluring voice?'

The bar was full of uniforms. 'Perhaps we should all start talking in German,' Michael said. 'Make them think that the invasion has begun.' He gave a mock Nazi salute as the bar man handed over the drinks and received a very strange look in return.

'You are wicked,' Anna said. 'We could be shot. First you steal a jeep, and now you plan to start a riot.'

He smiled at her and she felt her heart contract.

In the ballroom the orchestra was going full swing and the floor was crowded with couples. Michael claimed Kirsten for a foxtrot and Anna watched them stepping effortlessly out, wishing that it could have been her.

'Care to dance?' It was David, one of the young men who'd come with them.

'I can't fox trot to save my life,' Anna said. 'My feet get tangled up.' She smiled to sweeten the refusal. 'I think you'd better ask someone else.' The next time she looked she saw him on the dance floor laughing with a pretty blonde girl in a chintz dress. Anna stood against the wall just inside the door, feeling rather lost and wondering if she'd been sensible to come.

But after the fox trot the band leader announced a waltz and there was Michael standing in front of her holding out his hand. 'If you are German, you must be able to waltz,' he said.

'I've never learned to dance. They tried to teach us at school but it was useless. I've got two left feet.'

'It's easy. Just follow me.' He put his arm around her waist and began to count as he swept her out onto the floor. 'One two three, step, one two three, turn, one, two, three . .'

Anna was so conscious of his body close to her, of his arm around her that she could do nothing but follow.

The wailing of the air raid siren cut through the music and brought Anna out of her reverie with a jolt. Michael's arm held Anna still while people milled around them heading for the exits.

'Do you want to go to the shelter with the others? You should.'

'Are you going?'

Michael shook his head. 'I'm heading for the beach. If I have to die, I want to die in the open, not caged in a cellar with dozens of other people.'

'Me too. I've been buried alive once by a bomb – I don't want it to happen again.'

Michael led her through the doors onto the terrace and down the steps that led to the beach. There was a big half moon illuminating the sea and the wet sand left by the retreating tide.

'We're much safer out here. Wouldn't it be ironic if we were killed by a bomb dropped by one of our compatriots?'

'So why aren't you in the air force or the army? How did you avoid it?'

'I failed the medical. I had rheumatic fever when I was a child and it left me with a heart murmur. It saved me the trouble of becoming a conscientious objector. I would have made a terrible soldier anyway – I hate being told what to do and following rules and regulations.'

They were walking along the hard damp sand, watching the spent waves slide up the beach towards them like liquid glass in the moonlight. Above them, somewhere out at sea they could hear the drone of aircraft engines.

'What about your family?' Anna asked. 'Are they involved in the war?'

'My parents are actively against it. But my sister is married to a captain in a panzer division and that gives us all credibility.'

'What will happen to them now?'

'I told my parents that if I was ever exposed they were to denounce me publicly. I'm the black sheep of the family.' He turned towards her, caught her hand and smiled. 'Now tell me about you. Why are you so sad? You should be a free spirit, but you're not.'

'My life seems completely dislocated. I married someone by mistake and don't know how to get out of it without hurting everyone I care for. I've more or less had to abandon studying art and I've just spent months in an internment camp being treated as an undesirable alien. I don't know who I am or where I'm going at the moment.'

The droning engines had become louder, but Anna, looking up into the sky, couldn't see the planes. On the cliff tops, over to the right and the left anti-aircraft guns began to open fire, sending staccato lines of tracer into the sky.

'It seems incongruous, doesn't it,' Michael said softly. 'Among such beauty.'

When they went back to the jeep after the all clear, Kirsten and the two other men were waiting for them. The drive home was hazy. Anna was sitting in the middle of the front seat between Kirsten and Michael. She wasn't used to drinking and three Black Russians had left her feeling rather indistinct and not completely in control of her body. She could hear herself giggling. The men in the back were singing popular songs and she and Kirsten joined in. She wasn't aware of having dozed off but woke to find her head on Michael's shoulder. The jeep had slowed to approach the gate. 'Now you will all have to be quiet,' he was saying.

The guards peered into the vehicle with a torch, checking faces, passes and uniforms, and then swung the gate open for them to go through. Half way up the drive Michael killed the lights and slowed the engine to a crawl. He parked it in its original position with scarcely a sound. The most difficult part was getting out of the jeep and shutting the doors quietly.

In the house the lights were off and the sitting room was deserted. Anna had imagined a hostile reception committee, but it seemed that no one had noticed their departure. 'You certainly have the luck of the devil,' Kirsten said to Michael. 'If I'd done that, I'd have been discovered straight away.'

'I haven't enjoyed myself so much for months,' Anna said. 'Perhaps it's the element of risk.'

Michael smiled at her. 'Perhaps that's what I miss. Life seems very dull without it.'

'Life's certainly not going to be dull while Michael's here,' Kirsten said as they went up to bed.

Anna said nothing.

CHAPTER TWENTY THREE

It was like old times having lunch with the Bainbridges – Joe's jokes and stories, Wilf silently smiling in the corner, Mrs Bainbridge pressing food on her as if afraid that Tamar would die of starvation before her very eyes. But today Tamar was nervous. She was very conscious of Martin's presence. He sat beside her on the wooden settle and throughout the meal he kept asking her questions about herself as if he genuinely wanted to know and every now and then she felt his eyes turned towards her. Tamar found them disconcerting. He had very penetrating, knowledgeable eyes. After lunch Martin suggested they go out for some fresh air, and Tamar agreed, hoping that no one noticed the flush that coloured her cheeks.

'I'd better help with the dishes first though,' she said.

But Mrs Bainbridge wouldn't hear of it. 'You go and enjoy yourself. You'll not work on your day off!'

'Land girls get male privileges,' Martin said as he hobbled out into the yard. 'Waitress service and no washing up.' He opened the gate into the garth where the goats grazed and let Tamar go through before he shut it behind them. 'I wanted to show you the Roman stones in the tower. Can you see up there?' He pointed up the wall where Tamar could see several square blocks of dressed masonry with letters and figures on them.

'What do they say?' she asked.

'One's a grave stone. It says "To the Gods the Shades. Claudius Maximus". He was probably a soldier sent to guard Hadrian's wall about twenty miles north of here. The one next to it has bits of a quotation from a Roman poet called Catallus. The archaeologist said it might have come from a bath house.'

'There must have been quite a settlement here once, then.'

'Maybe. Or perhaps just a rest house for travellers. There were hotels even in Roman times.'

'It's always puzzled me why your house has a tower like a castle.'

'That's because it's a Bastle house – it was fortified to protect the owners from border reivers back in the sixteenth century.'

'It's as old as that?'

Martin nodded.

'It gives me a good feeling being amongst so much history – layers and layers of it. All those people. Holly thinks it's spooky, but I think it's comforting.'

They had just finished having tea when Mrs Heslop walked into the kitchen. Her eyes looked wild and there was a trickle of saliva running down her chin from the corner of her mouth. There was blood on her hands and her apron, but she said absolutely nothing; just stood there in the middle of the floor smiling at them. It was unnerving.

Mrs Bainbridge was the first out of her chair. 'Joe. You'd better go down and see what's up. I'll look after her.' Already she had a protective hand on Mrs Heslop's shoulder and Tamar saw her wrinkle her nose at the rank smell that came from the woman's hair and clothes. She looked as if she had neither washed nor changed her clothes for weeks. 'Now, Ada. Come and sit down. I'll make us both a cup of tea. Joe'll go down to the farm. Don't you worry.'

Tamar and Martin went with Joe, rattling down the track in the landrover to Holme Farm. The yard was eerily quiet. All the doors were open – the byre empty and clean, so the cows had obviously not been in for their evening milking. Tamar could hear them lowing plaintively from the bottom field. The barn too was empty, a creel of sliced turnips stacked against the wall. Across the yard a horse whinnied. 'That's Ben,' Tamar said, recognising its tone.

In the stable Ben was standing quietly, his halter still attached to the hay rick, but he was sweating profusely, his skin twitching as if tormented by invisible flies. He was lifting his rear legs restlessly, shifting his weight from one to the other. Tamar could see that his hooves were clotted with dark straw, then as she looked down she saw Heslop's familiar clogs wrapped in sacking protruding from the straw at an odd angle.

'Don't look,' Martin said, pushing Tamar back towards the door.

'Ben would never let anyone walk behind him,' Tamar said. She put her hand over her mouth.

'Heslop wouldn't be daft enough to do that,' Joe said. He looked very pale. 'I'll bide here a bit,' he said, 'and you two get down to the phone and ring the doctor. Better have the police n'all. Tell them there's no hurry. By God, this is a bad do!'

It took half an hour for the policeman to cycle up from a neighbouring village. Doctor Harrington arrived first in his canvas-topped Alvis and pronounced Heslop dead. 'There'll have to be an inquest,' he said. 'But it should be merely a formality. There's no doubt about the cause of death.' He took a nervous look at the horse Joe had moved into a neighbouring stall, still rolling the whites of his eyes.

When the policeman had regained his breath after the long uphill bike ride, he agreed with the doctor. 'Of course you'll have to get the horse put down. Soon as possible I'd say.'

Tamar gave a gasp of protest. 'It wasn't the horse's fault.'

Martin put his arm around her shoulders. 'Once a horse has killed, you can never trust it again.'

'And he was a vicious brute 'afore,' Joe said.

'Ben was ill treated. The blacksmith said he'd been hit with a metal bar, or a spike or something.'

'I'm afraid he's got to go,' Martin said. 'It's the best thing for him. He couldn't ever be trusted.'

'Who found the body?' The policeman wanted to know.

'His wife,' Tamar said. 'She's up at Crow Hall with Mrs Bainbridge.'

'Then I'd better go and get a statement from her. Poor woman.'

'You'll be lucky to get the time o' day,' Joe said. 'She's gone off her rocker!'

Martin insisted that Tamar get in the doctor's car with the policeman. 'You don't want to see what happens next,' he said.

Mrs Heslop was still sitting in the fireside chair at Crow Hall, gripping the tea cup in hands crusted with dried blood, and smiling vacantly. Both the doctor and the policeman asked her gentle questions, but she failed to respond. It was as if she had retreated into another world.

'I'm afraid the shock has affected her mind,' Dr Harrington said.

'It wasn't in good shape 'afore that,' Mrs Bainbridge said tartly. 'She's been walking the lanes in the middle of the night these last few weeks – off with the fairies! I don't want to speak ill of the dead, but there's not a thing that man's ever done to get help for her.'

The doctor took a white envelope out of his bag. 'I'll give her a sedative.' He looked at her dirty clothes, her unkempt hair. 'Then I'll have to take her down to Carlisle. A couple of nights in hospital and we might be able to assess her condition.'

'She'll be for the Garlands,' Mrs Bainbridge said. 'Should've been there months ago.'

Tamar shivered at the word. No one wanted to see anyone committed to the mental asylum. 'I feel guilty now about leaving. Perhaps if we hadn't left her alone . . .'

'Don't you go down that road, lass,' Mrs Bainbridge said brusquely. 'Anyways, they do wonders in there with this new electric shock treatment. Now, you go down to Holme Farm and pack her a bag. You know where everything is. We'll get her in the car and come down to pick it up.'

The doctor stirred the powder into half a glass of water and held it to Mrs Heslop's lips, coaxing her to drink. She obeyed him like a child.

In the yard two other vehicles had parked outside the stable – the undertaker's hearse and a second landrover. A strange man was leading Ben out into the yard with a piece of sacking over the horse's eyes. Horrified, but unable to move from the spot, Tamar watched as he put a round metal object to Ben's covered forehead. There was a dull retort and the horse's body crumpled and thudded down onto the cobbles. Tears spurted down Tamar's cheeks as she turned and went into the house.

It was even more dirty and disorganized than she remembered.

The sink was filled with unwashed dishes, two cats sat on the table among gnawed rabbit bones and crusts of bread. Tamar made her way upstairs and entered the Heslop's bedroom for the first time. She felt like a trespasser. It stank like an animal's lair – of unwashed humanity and the sour odour of stale urine. Stooping to look under the bed, Tamar saw that there were two full chamber pots, one of them covered in pale scum. Retching, she went to the window and dragged it open to let the cold fresh air into her lungs.

A layer of dust, like lint, clung to every surface. Sadie had called it 'slut's wool'. On the dressing table the circular crocheted doilies and pink cut-glass dishes and candle holders had been unmoved for a long time. A framed photograph of a cheerful good looking young man stood on the mantelpiece. This, at least had been regularly dusted.

It felt wrong to be going through Mrs Heslop's drawers. They were surprisingly orderly. Neat, clean underwear was carefully folded in piles, handkerchiefs and stockings, two pretty blouses Tamar had never seen her wear. Tamar's own hands had made imprints in the thick dust on the drawer handles, so it was a long time since they had been opened. She took two cotton nightdresses, underwear, a grey pleated skirt that looked barely worn and a lilac twin set she found in the bottom drawer. She packed a brush and comb from the dressing table, but although she looked carefully, Mrs Heslop didn't seem to possess either a flannel or a toothbrush. Last of all, she put the photograph of Mrs Heslop's son on the top of the bag.

When she went down to the yard, the doctor's car had drawn up outside the door. Tamar handed the bag to Mrs Bainbridge sitting in the back with Mrs Heslop asleep against her shoulder. 'I'll be back by supper time, lass. You'll know what to do.'

Tamar waved them off sadly. 'What'll happen to Ben now?' she asked Joe. Both the vet and the undertaker had gone and the horse's body lay sprawled on the cobbles in an undignified heap.

'The knacker man's to come for it. No time to worry about that now mind. These cows'll be to milk.'

As Joe spoke, Heslop's herd of Ayrshires came running into the yard as fast as their distended udders would let them, with

Martin limping behind.

'I'll see to the chickens and the goat,' Tamar said. She grabbed a bucket from the dairy and headed for the garth, wondering how she was going to manage to milk the animal. But there was no need. When she reached the gate the nanny was standing with her legs straddled, still dripping mucus and blood, licking the new-born kid lying in the grass. As Tamar watched, the kid began to struggle to its feet and after several unsuccessful attempts, began to stagger towards its mother's swollen udder. Tamar smiled in spite of her sadness. On a farm somehow you were caught in the cycle of life and death, continually turning. Heslop and Ben might be dead, but cows needed to be milked, hens to be fed, and at any moment a new life might be born. It put death into perspective.

The following morning Mrs Simms pulled up in the yard at Nithsdale Hall and asked Tamar if she'd be prepared to work at Holme Farm again. 'Not to live in the house,' she added hurriedly. 'I couldn't expect that. But the farm has to be run until the animals can be sold off – if that's what Mrs Heslop wants – no one can do anything until she's well enough to make a decision. That's the dilemma. Apparently she's had some kind of breakdown. It could take months.'

'Where would I stay?'

'Mr and Mrs Bainbridge have agreed to have you as a boarder. They're going to try to manage the two farms between them and if they have you as well it should be possible. You know the animals and the routine.'

Tamar was thinking of Martin. Of being under the same roof. She wanted it, badly, but at the same time, she was afraid.

'It's such a tragic affair,' Mrs Simms was saying. 'Will you do it?'

Tamar nodded.

'I didn't feel I could say anything else,' she wrote to Anna later. *'Have you ever had the sensation that you were meant to do something?'*

'I'm in love with you,' Michael told Anna.

They were standing in the garden underneath the big yew tree that marked the entrance to the rose walk.

'How can you be sure? We've known each other for less than a week.'

'I knew the first time I saw you. Normally one would wait a decent interval of time before declaring oneself, but this is war – there is so little time – tomorrow I might be sent away again – it's important to live as passionately and completely as you can. If I'm killed tomorrow I want no regrets that I might have done this or that.'

'I'm not free to love you,' Anna said. 'I married someone before he went away. It was a stupid mistake. I didn't know that I could ever feel like this.'

'In war all normal morality is suspended. What is your English saying – "all's fair in love and war"? You can't ruin your life for a promise made in ignorance of what real love is. It will destroy you.'

Anna could say nothing. Michael took her face in his hands and looked at her for a few moments and then he put his lips against hers. As he kissed her Anna felt herself respond with such passion she had to pull herself free. 'I wish I'd met you first,' she whispered.

'It's not too late,' Michael said. 'You mustn't spoil your life because of one mistake. You do love me don't you?'

'Yes.' Anna felt that the word was being wrenched out of her.

'Then we should be together for whatever time we have left.' He ran his finger lightly down her cheek. 'I will come to your room tonight after your shift. If the door's locked I will know that you don't want me. But if it's open . . .'

Anna shivered, but he kissed her again, his lips gently exploring hers and she didn't want him to stop. 'I've got to go – I'll be late for my shift.' She turned and ran down the path towards the radio hut without glancing back.

When she finished work Anna went to her room and locked the door. She stood leaning against it for a moment breathing heavily. It wasn't just because she was married to George. She felt ashamed to admit it, but it was the strength of her feeling for Michael that kept her from letting him in. It was a passion that seemed to threaten her whole future, because she knew that if she gave way just once it would overwhelm her. Anna took off her clothes and crept shivering between the sheets. The cold was not just outside, it was inside her too. 'Like the child taken by the ice queen in the fairy tale,' Anna thought, 'I've been pierced by a splinter of ice.' But what if Michael was right? Perhaps love like this came only once in a lifetime – the all-consuming passion she had once dreamt of. It would be criminal to turn such love away. All her life she would think, 'What if?' and she would never know. Slowly Anna got out of bed. She stood trembling for several minutes in the cold room before she finally turned the key in the door.

A few moments later it creaked open and Michael came softly into the room. She heard the rustle of his clothes hitting the floor and then he slid into bed beside her. His body was warm as he put his arms around her and kissed her neck. She was drowning in warmth, letting herself sink into soft sand. Cool unfamiliar fingers skimmed the surface of her skin, the thin, sensitive skin on the inside of her fore-arms, her thighs, the bony intervals of her spine. Michael's lips were soft too and his mouth was open and welcoming.

Tentatively, Anna touched his hair, the firm flesh of his buttocks, ran her hands over his shoulder blades. Her senses were going wild. She gasped as cool fingers played with her nipples sending spasms of shock to the base of her spine. Anna's toes curled and she felt as if her stomach and her groin were on fire. Did Michael feel this too? Boldly, beyond caution now, Anna let her fingers stray to the springing, coarse triangle of fuzz between his legs, the pulsing hardness of his penis and heard him gasp at her touch. Then his mouth fastened on Anna's breast, while at the same time his fingers found Anna's most secret place, flicking and fluttering. With a stifled cry, Anna abandoned herself to the crazy music her body was now playing and as she did so, she felt the hard, cold, resisting place inside her stomach melt away.

Martin collected Tamar and her suitcase from Nithsdale the following day. She and Holly hugged each other goodbye. 'You'll have to come and stay,' Tamar said. 'Come on Saturday nights and then it won't be so far to go and see Ivan.'

She and Martin said very little on the drive up to the farm. It was the thing Tamar liked most about him, that it never seemed necessary to make small talk. He carried her case up to the room for her and then lingered. 'I used to have this room when I was a kid. My grandmother was alive then. When she died Joe and Mary moved into her room and I got the big room at the end.'

Tamar had opened her case and begun to unpack her books. Martin picked them up and looked at them. 'You like poetry?'

'Very much. My friend Anna bought me that one.'

He picked up another. 'Intermediate mathematics?'

'I'm studying for my school certificate – the exam's in May.'

'And what're you going to do if you get it?'

'Well, before the war I wanted to be a librarian. I'd still like to do something like that – but who knows when the war will end.'

'They're talking about paying for people who've served in the forces to undergo some form of training afterwards – university, teaching, that kind of thing. I might get to finish my university course.'

'Were you at university?' Tamar was surprised.

'I'd just finished my first year when war broke out.'

'What were you studying?'

'Classics. I know that seems odd, growing up on a farm here. I was the first child in the village to win a scholarship to the grammar school. Mary and Dad and Joe were all determined I should have my chances. Aunt Mary kept saying – you never know when the bottom's going to drop out of farming. On marginal land like this, it's all a risk, you need something to fall back on. I got a scholarship to Oxford,' Martin blushed deep red. 'But I didn't enjoy it very much. Too much snobbery and cynicism.'

'Will you go back afterwards?'

'I don't know. Part of me thinks I should and part of me says I belong here and this is where I should stay.'

'Rooted in one dear perpetual place.'

'That's Yeats isn't it?'

'It's called Prayer for my Daughter. When we did it at school it seemed to sum up everything I ever wanted in life. I used to think, supposing my father had written something like that for me.'

'Do you know who your father is? Or is that a rude question?'

'The family come from Winterings in North Yorkshire. I think his brother's a high court judge – I know that much – and apparently my father got married to a publisher's daughter about ten years ago and it was in the society column of the Times. But I don't know where he lives.'

'If his brother's a judge, his address would be in Who's Who. There's probably a copy in the library. His brother would know where your father was. Do you ever think of contacting him?'

'Sometimes, when I feel a bit down. But then I think – he's never come to find me or shown any desire to contact me, so what would be the point?'

'He might not have known where you were.'

Tamar thought about what Mrs Cummings had said about Mrs Emily Fell and the letter she'd sent Sadie and thought that might possibly be true. Should she write to her father and give him the opportunity to make contact?

If Tamar had thought that proximity and the ordinary routines of daily life would dull the strong feeling of attraction she had for Martin, she found that she was wrong. Every moment she was in his company over the following days deepened the feeling of belonging. As they walked up and down the lane to Holme Farm they talked about books and history, the landscape, childhood memories. Tamar didn't want these conversations to stop. If she touched him accidentally when picking up buckets or carrying a calf, the physical contact left a mark like a burn on her flesh. There was a growing together, a bond that was strengthened by every moment they spent with each other. I mustn't feel like this, Tamar told herself a dozen times a day. But every day that passed intensified her feelings. Sometimes she felt physically ill with the effort of suppressing them.

Tamar wondered if Martin felt it too. There were little glances and kind actions that convinced her that he did, but then Maggie would come to the gate with the letters and she would see him talking to her, laughing with her, animated and easy going, and Tamar would feel as if some wild animal was clawing at the inside of her stomach. Maggie had taken to lingering when she came with the post and she would often stay for a cup of tea.

'Always had a soft spot for our Martin,' Mrs Bainbridge said. 'They've been going around together since they were at school.'

Was she trying to tell her something? To warn her? In bed at night every detail of their conversations would go round in Tamar's head, but there was no one Tamar could talk to about her feelings. Anna's letters had become vague and unilluminating. Anna wasn't allowed to write about her job or the people she was working with and her letters were very short. Tamar was sure something was going on in her personal life that she wasn't talking about. And Holly was spending most of her time with Ivan – worrying more and more about what her parents would say if they knew about her relationship. Tamar wondered whether it would last – it was after all Holly's first love affair and Ivan, as a refugee, would no doubt be going back to his own country after the war.

One Tuesday, during the weekly trip to the auction mart in Penrith, Tamar went into the library to change her books and looked up Robert Fell's entry in Who's Who. Mrs Cummings had been right – he was a high court judge.

'Are you going to write to him?' Martin said when she told him.

'I suppose so.' Tamar didn't know what to do. She wanted to know about her father more than anything, but she was afraid. What if there was no reply? Supposing they thought that all she wanted was money? Supposing Robert Fell threw the letter into the waste paper basket without telling her father about it? Supposing her father simply didn't want to know?

That evening after supper, while Mrs Bainbridge darned socks by the fire and Joe and Wilf dozed on the settle, Tamar sat at the table with Martin and began to compose the difficult letter. 'How on earth do you address a judge?' Tamar asked him. 'I can hardly write 'Dear Uncle Robert.'

'I don't know. I think judge's are lords or justices, maybe both, but I'm not sure.'

'*Dear Sir*,' Tamar wrote. '*I would be grateful if you could give me any information you may have about my father, your brother James Fell. Is he still alive? My mother, Sadie, told me he had died, but I discovered recently that he had married and was living in London. I have no intention of intruding on his new life in any way, or asking for money – I am very well provided for and engaged to be married. But I would like just once in my life to see him, to know who he is and something about him. It seems strange to have a father I have never met. Does he even know that I exist? Much of my mother's relationship with him is a mystery to me and I would like to know the truth. I would be grateful for any help you could give me.*'

The following morning Tamar gave it to Maggie with money for the stamp and then tried to forget that she had sent it.

~~~~~~~~~~~~~~~~~

Anna lay on her back on the sand, listening to the hushing sound of the waves withdrawing over the rocky shelf. Michael, lying on his stomach beside her, was sifting sand restlessly between his fingers. The cliffs near Harwood Hall were steep, but there was a precipitous path down to the cove where a crescent of sand was exposed at low tide and the rocks sheltered them from the cold on-shore wind.

'So why did you become a spy against your own people?' Anna asked. 'I could understand it if you'd been on the wrong end of the racial purity laws like me, but you're as Aryan as they come.'

'It took a long time. You don't just decide to betray your country over night. It was just little things at first – things you notice when you're growing up but you don't work out what they mean. My father was, is, a doctor – a very good one. He always treated everyone equally, regardless of whether they could pay or not. I remember one of his friends asking why he had Jews among his patients and he said "Why not? They get sick the same as anyone else." But shortly after that the government made a law that forbade him to treat them – Jewish people could only go to Jewish
~~~~~~~~~~~~~~~~~

doctors.'

'And did he obey it?'

Michael shook his head. 'One night there was a knock on the kitchen door and my mother went out and a woman was there on the steps all wrapped up in black with a child under her coat. A very sick child. I remember my father insisting that they came in and putting the baby on the kitchen table to examine it and my mother shaking her head and saying "It's too much of a risk. Think of your family Gerhardt!" But my father took no notice and after dark there were always people at the back door. It didn't really mean anything until I went away to drama college and became interested in politics. That's when I began to think seriously about which loyalties are most important – country, family, or the human race. Have you ever thought about what the world would look like if the Fascists were allowed to win?'

'I've never thought about it in the way you have. My first instinct was to have no part of it and just concentrate on painting. Personal things were too confusing and painful. I thought I could solve the problem by being ruthlessly single-minded. But I just became depressed and confused. There are too many conflicts.'

'You're in a special position Anna. You can look at this war from both sides – the German and the English. You're not just a painter – you're a woman and an ethnic jew. Don't fight these things. Use them.'

'What are you going to do after the war? Will you go back to being an actor?'

'I dream about having my own theatre company – or maybe even going into films. But it all seems too far away. It's difficult to imagine a time "after the war". What about you? What are you going to do?'

'Find out what's happened to my father first, then I'm going to study to become the best painter that I possibly can. Maybe in Paris if I've got enough money.'

There was a silence and then Michael said, 'You know I'm going back to Germany soon?'

'Michael!'

'They'll give me a new identity and a new job in a different location and it will all start again. Except this time, I'll be imagining you listening to me every time I make a transmission.'

Anna put her hand up to his face. 'I can't bear to think of you putting yourself at risk like that.'

He drew her into his arms and Anna responded passionately. She let him undress her, oblivious to the cold, feeling the kiss of the winter sun on her bare skin, the rough tweed of his jacket against her stomach. As his love making became more urgent she didn't want it to stop, and soon she was so lost to desire that she thought of nothing but the rhythm of their bodies, pulsing together on the sand, fitting so neatly together that they might have been made for each other. So this is what all the fuss is about, she thought as she gasped against his shoulder. This was what wrecked marriages and careers and made people take absurd risks. She looked up towards the top of the cliff towering above them – supposing someone had been watching? And she thought of the little rubber cap lying unused in its cardboard box in the drawer in her room. It was too late to go back now. George would be devastated. Tamar would never speak to her again. Her mother would be furious. But nothing mattered except this one glorious moment.

Martin's leg continued to improve daily with plenty of exercise. One clear sunny Saturday in December with a warm winter sun and the frost glittering on the hill tops, Martin said, 'How about walking up the Maiden Way with me? We might not make it to the top and back before it gets dark, but we'll get far enough to get a view.'

Tamar put on her boots and an extra jumper under her greatcoat, wrapping a scarf around her neck.

'It'll be nithering up there,' Mrs Bainbridge said. 'You want your head's examined, the pair of you.' She pushed a knitted balaclava into one of Tamar's pockets and a greaseproof parcel of scones and cake into the other.

And then they were on the path, climbing higher and higher. The valley floor fell away beneath them and the fields and rivers were already vague and distant in the frosty haze. As they sat on a rock to get their breath back, the stone walls lurched crazily across the landscape below, mapping it into patterns.

'They're almost vertical!' Tamar said. 'How could anyone build walls like that? Look, that one's climbing over a boulder!'

'They tell stories, these walls,' Martin said. 'My father built some, and old Joe, and my great grandfather probably built a few more and his father before that. That's my family history you can see down there, going back and back.'

'I can't imagine what it must be like to have lived for so long in the same place.'

'Makes me restless to see other places, do other things, sometimes.'

'You wouldn't ever leave here would you?'

Martin shrugged. 'Who knows. I don't want to be like my Dad. Wilf's never been anywhere or done anything. He spent his honeymoon in Morecambe and hasn't been off the farm since, except to go to the auction mart.' Martin smiled down at her. 'I've always fancied Rome. When the war's over. What would you say to a Roman honeymoon Tamar?'

Tamar's eyes were wide with shock. The tremor ran through her body like a convulsion. She realised that she wanted, more than anything, to say yes. She blushed and looked away. Martin took her hand and squeezed it, saying nothing. There was nothing to say. She was engaged to someone else, after all. But his touch, the rough, warm skin of his hand, made her tremble. As she got to her feet she stumbled and Martin caught her.

'Careful,' he said. 'I don't want you breaking any bones.'

Tamar clung to him instinctively, feeling the soft cloth of his jacket under her fingers, and under the cloth his warm body, taut-muscled with physical work. When he kissed her, clumsily, unpractised, she thought she would die. If he had laid her down in the heather, there and then, and taken her she knew she could not have resisted.

But Martin opened his arms and let her go. They looked at each other and then looked away. Nothing needed to be said. Hand in hand they walked up to the cairn on the summit of the crag and Tamar picked up a stone and placed it on the pile.

'My own little bit of wall building,' she said.

'I want to marry you,' Martin said, as they began to descend the path, back to the farm.

'You know I'm promised to someone else.'

'You were only seventeen. It wasn't fair to tie you down at that age. And you haven't seen him now for nearly two years.'

'But I promised him. How can I just ignore that? Especially if he's languishing in some foreign camp expecting to come back to me when the war's over.'

'He may be dead.'

'I know.'

'Do you love me Tamar?'

'You know I do. More than anything.'

'You can't marry another man feeling like that.'

'But I've got to tell him first. Just think what it would be like if he came back and found me married to someone else.'

That night after supper Tamar went out into the orchard and gazed up at the new moon bright in the frosty sky. What kind of life would she have had with Edward? Tamar couldn't see clearly. Her life in Heaton Street in those rows of houses above the polluted reaches of the river Tyne had gone. It was impossible to go back now that she had moved on. North Shields was no longer her home. On the other hand, Tamar could envisage her life with Martin, rooted, like a green laurel, in this one, peaceful, beautiful place. She belonged here, in this house. It fitted her like a protective shell. But one day Edward would come back. Tamar was absolutely certain of that. And what was she going to say to him when he did?

~~~~~~~~~~~~~~~~~~

When Anna came out of the hut after finishing her translation work, Michael was waiting for her at the end of the rose walk. He looked serious and a little sad. 'Let's take a picnic and go down to the sea,' he said. In the dining room they raided the sideboard – piling slices of cooked ham between bread rolls provided for the soup and pocketing a couple of tomatoes. Anna put her sketch pad into her bag and then they wheeled their bicycles through the lodge gates and onto the track to the cliffs.
~~~~~~~~~~~~~~~~~~

'Isn't it odd,' Anna said as they pedalled side by side, 'that you can always sense the sea even before it appears? The quality of the light changes and you just know the land is going to end.'

'After the war, I must take you to Jutland,' Michael said. 'When I was a child we used to spend our holidays there. It's all sea and sky and the light is amazing. You would love to paint there.'

The tide was in so there was no point in climbing down to the cove. They sat on the coarse grass at the edge of the cliff, buffeted by the wind.

'I've just been given my orders,' Michael said.

Anna's heart thudded against her ribs. 'When?'

'Tomorrow. I'm not supposed to tell anyone. But I couldn't go without letting you know.'

'Have they told you where?'

'Not yet.'

'Oh, Michael!' Anna felt such utter despair she could hardly breathe.

'I know.' He put his arm around her. 'Let's not lie to each other,' he said, stroking her hair. 'Let's not pretend we don't know the risks.'

'If you didn't come back,' Anna whispered. 'I don't think I could bear it.'

'You'd have to, because there would be no choice. If one of us dies the other has to go on living, or it's all been worthless.' He smiled briefly. 'But I'll try to stay alive. I've got every reason to want to survive.'

'At least we've got one more night together,' Anna said.

They were both very quiet for the rest of the afternoon. The impossibility of saying everything she wanted to say kept Anna silent. They ate the rolls and ham and Michael lay on the grass, his head propped on his hand, looking out to sea, across to Germany. Anna took out her sketch pad and drew him as he lay there, preoccupied with his thoughts. She knew better than to talk to him when he looked like that – it was as if he retreated beyond a wall of glass and she couldn't follow him. Whatever he had been through – whatever he was facing – he would never share that with her. He didn't seem to be afraid, but there was a whiteness about his mouth, and a certain rigidity in his movements that she noted and understood.

All through dinner Anna was conscious of people talking and laughing around her, sharing a merriment she couldn't feign.

'You look very serious tonight,' Kirsten said.

Anna tried to smile. 'Just a bit down,' she said. 'A touch of the blues.'

It was Anna's listening shift from nine to eleven and every moment felt like forever. Two hours out of their last few hours together. There was so little time left. When she came out of the radio hut, she looked for Michael underneath the yew tree where he usually waited for her, but he wasn't there. Nor was he in the sitting room. A solitary radio officer was reading the newspapers with his feet up on the coffee table. 'Have you seen Michael?' Anna asked. He lifted his head briefly. 'No, sorry.'

Anna ran up the stairs and along the forbidden corridor to Michael's room. It was a disciplinary offence to be found in the men's wing, but Anna was past caring. She tapped on Michael's door, but there was no answer. Her heart pounding with panic and disappointment, Anna made her way back to the main staircase and then up to her own room. The door was ajar. She pushed it gently and there was Michael asleep in her bed, clothes thrown on the floor. Almost dizzy with relief and longing, she quietly took off her own and slipped in beside him. He woke as she pushed him over to make room for her body on the narrow mattress and he turned to fold himself round her, his limbs warm and heavy from sleep. He smelt slightly of whisky. A half empty bottle of malt sat on the bedside table. Anna sat up and poured herself a glass. The golden liquid burned her mouth and then exploded in her stomach. She could feel the warmth of it spreading outwards, dispelling her anxiety and relaxing the hard knot of tension that had gathered in her stomach.

'I got in such a panic when I couldn't find you. I thought for some reason you might have been forced to leave early without saying goodbye.'

'Maybe that would have been the best thing. Goodbye's are too painful.' He took the glass out of her hand and put it on the table and then pulled her down onto the pillow. He looked at her with such intensity that Anna felt uncomfortable.

'Why are you looking at me like that?'

'Because I can't take a photograph of you with me where I'm going and I want to remember every single inch of you.'

He kissed her, much harder than Anna had been used to. She could taste the whisky on his mouth. Then he began to caress her with firm hands, sculpting her body, moulding, kneading, making her gasp with pleasure, rousing her to a pitch of desire greater than anything she'd experienced before. He rolled her nipples between his tongue and the roof of his mouth, his fingers fluttering between her legs and she began to orgasm spontaneously – her whole body arching and quivering against him. Then he entered her and began to rock her to and fro on a roller coaster of delight that began slowly but gradually gathered speed, both moving in absolute harmony. The climax when it came was like a star burst – pleasure rippled through Anna's skin to every corner of her body.

'I love you,' Anna said to the darkness.

'And I you.' Michael's voice was sleepy and indistinct.

It was the last thing Anna remembered. When she woke up the room was bright with daylight and the bed was empty. With a cry of disappointment, Anna jumped up. A page torn from her sketch pad was propped on the chest of drawers.

'My darling Anna, when you read this, I'll be gone. I've written my parents' address on the back and I want you to promise that if anything happens to me you will go and see them in Berlin after the war. Will you? I don't know when we'll be together again. I can't bear to leave you, but I couldn't respect myself if I didn't. If the navy move you before I come back, leave word with Fraulein Bateman. We must always be able to find each other in the chaos of war. What we have doesn't come to everyone. Auf wiedersehen mein Liebchen. Ich liebe dich.'

Anna was seized with a violent pain in her stomach like cramp. She had to sit down on the side of the bed, doubled up with it, biting her tongue so's not to cry out. Michael had gone, and she didn't know when, or if, he would be back.

CHAPTER TWENTY FOUR

A fortnight later, Holly arrived at Crow Hall in floods of tears. 'I've had a letter from my father. He says that my mother's ill and I've got to go home.'

'Oh, Holly I'm sorry. Is it serious?'

'He says she's been getting more and more depressed for weeks and now she just stays in bed all the time. Tamar, what am I going to do? I want to stay here. I love being at Nithsdale and I want to be with Ivan.'

It was Mrs Bainbridge who answered. 'It sounds as if you ought to go and see how your Mam is. Ten to one the sight of you'll cheer her up no end, and then in a couple `o weeks she'll be right as rain.'

'They'll find a way of stopping me coming back,' Holly said. 'I know they will.'

'If your mother's really ill, surely your father can pay for someone to look after her?' Tamar thought it was ridiculous for someone like Harold Pergavie with so much money, to expect his daughter to come home to nurse her mother. 'You've got to learn to stand up for yourself,' Tamar said. 'After all you managed to find a way of joining the land army, you'll find a way of getting back.'

'I've got to,' Holly said desperately. 'Absolutely got to. Ivan and I are planning to marry – after the war when I'm twenty one. I can't let my parents separate us and they would if they knew about him.'

'Then you mustn't let them!' Tamar insisted.

A week later she and Ivan waved a weeping Holly off on the bus with promises to come back as soon as she could arrange it. Tamar had no confidence in Holly's strength of will to resist parental pressure, but she hoped that Holly's promises to Ivan might stiffen her resolve. He looked thoroughly miserable as the bus drove off down the lane and out of sight.

When Tamar cycled back up to Crow Hall there was a letter from Anna waiting on the kitchen table. How many weeks was it since she had last written? Tamar tore it open expectantly and then almost let it fall from her fingers as she read the first line.

'*Edward's home*,' Anna wrote. '*I saw him yesterday when I went through to see my mother. He seems pretty knocked up. By the sound of it he spent months in hiding and then trying to get back to England. He asked a lot of questions about you, so I gather you haven't seen him yet. Did you tell him about Martin? What's going on?*'

Tamar's heart pounded. How long had Edward been back in England? And why hadn't he written to her? Not so much as a note to even let her know he was alive. Something was badly wrong. Had he already found out about her and Martin? But even as the thought occurred, Tamar knew that it wasn't likely. She would have to go and see him. She needed to know how she would feel when she came face to face with him and she would have to tell him that she couldn't marry him.

'What's the matter?' Martin asked. He was in the barn forking hay onto a trailer. Tamar handed him the letter and waited while he read it. His expression changed – he looked almost nervous as he handed it back. 'What're you going to do?'

'I'll have to go and see him, find out what's wrong. I can't understand why he hasn't written to me, or come in person.'

'Maybe things have changed for him too.'

'Then he should have told me straight away. Moral cowardice isn't something I'd have thought Edward capable of.' She was perplexed.

That evening Tamar wrote a stilted little note to Edward at his parent's address.

'Anna told me you were back. I'm glad you're alive and not in some awful prisoner of war camp. Your mother must be over the moon. There are things we need to talk about. I'm going to try to get a weekend pass and come over to Shields next week. You can leave word

with Lily where we can meet – she's living with Mrs Whale at the moment. If I don't hear from you I'll come down to your Mum's.'

Tamar sucked her pen for several minutes wondering how to end it and eventually wrote, *'looking forward to seeing you. Tamar.'* That at least would prepare him for the change in her feelings.

It was a long week. Tamar hardly slept, worrying about the coming interview. What could she say? How would she feel when she saw him? She would have liked to talk to Martin about it but he was behaving very oddly. His usually sunny disposition had been translated into bad-tempered moods. On the morning she was due to leave he was nowhere to be found. Tamar almost cried. 'He's worried lass,' Mary said as she helped Tamar out to the landrover with her case. 'He thinks you might not come back.'

'That's ridiculous!'

Mary kissed her on the cheek. 'I know that and you know that. But they do say love is blind.' She laughed as Tamar blushed bright red. 'Go on with you. Get yourself sorted out and come back and make him a happy man.'

As the landrover jolted her down the lane to the bus stop, Tamar wished she had Mary's degree of certainty. There was a terrible doubt at the pit of her stomach. Supposing all her feelings for Edward returned the moment she saw him?

'Your Edward came round,' Lily said, almost as soon as Tamar had come through the door. 'I hardly recognised him hinny. He's a different bloke. Still handsome mind, but lookin' about ten year older.'

Tamar still couldn't believe that there'd been no response to her letter, but if he'd been round to see Lily then at least he'd received it. 'Did he leave a message for me?'

'Yes pet, he said he'd meet you outside the Cameo tonight about six.' Lily was not easily fooled. 'You're not goin' to tell me he's been back all this time and he's not gone through to see you?'

Tamar nodded.

'No moral fibre. That's what your mother said about him. All talk.'

'I always thought she liked him?'

'Oh she liked him all right, but she was very shrewd was Sadie. "Handsome is as handsome does", she used to say when you were with him. You're not still goin' to marry him are you pet?'

'No Lily. I'm not.'

Lily seemed satisfied. She changed the subject. 'Are you sleepin' here tonight? Annie's only got the two rooms, but you can bed down on the sofa, no trouble.'

'It's all right Lily, Anna said I could use her cottage.'

'Now don't you mention her name to me!'

'Have you and Anna fallen out?'

'She came here the other day. Doesn't say a word, but I know what she's up to. I can see the light in her eyes and it isn't whoar George that's puttin' it there. I've a good mind to write to him. Poor lad.'

Tamar wondered if Lily was right. It would certainly explain Anna's strange, empty letters. If she had met someone else, she would be loath to talk about it to anyone who was close to George.

Edward had changed, Tamar thought as she walked up the street towards the cinema. He was taller and thinner and very pale. That almost girlish look that had fooled her into thinking he was younger than his age had gone. She was relieved to realise that she felt absolutely nothing when she saw him – it was almost like meeting a stranger. There was only a slight pang of regret for the loss of all that feeling. To have loved him so much and then have it reduced to this!

'Hello, Tamar,' he said and squeezed her hand, letting go of it almost immediately.

Tamar couldn't read his expression. The eyes behind those long, fringed lashes were guarded, his manner stiff and rather nervous.

'Lyons?' Tamar said, looking across at the Corner House. It seemed odd to be the one who was in charge. Whenever they'd been together before, Edward had made the decisions and she'd acquiesced.

Soon they were seated at a table in the window with tea and rather synthetic looking rock cakes. 'Holly calls them "austerity buns",' Tamar said, in an attempt to lighten the atmosphere. Edward smiled awkwardly. He pulled a packet of cigarettes out of his pocket and offered her one. She shook her head. When had he started smoking? 'Tell me what happened to you,' Tamar asked. 'Were you captured?'

'They recruited a group of us to go to Italy. We had Italian passports and could go backwards and forwards across the borders pretty freely. Even into Germany. I was an errand boy. But then it all went wrong. One of the others was captured and he told the Fascisti about the rest of us.' Edward talked as if reciting a well rehearsed script. There were deep lines of strain around his mouth and Tamar noticed that he avoided looking at her when he spoke.

'I was tipped off by one of my father's cousins and managed to get across to Elba on a fishing boat. An Italian family hid me for a while and then I was passed like a parcel across the Mediterranean and finally back to England.'

'How long have you been back?'

'A month. Three weeks being debriefed in London before I was allowed any leave.'

'A month! And you never wrote to me?'

He put his head in his hands for a moment, then looked up and for the first time met her eyes. 'I couldn't find the words to say what I had to.'

'Let's get this straight,' Tamar said. 'You were the one who wanted us to be married before you went. That your feelings might have changed I can understand. But not to tell me as soon as you could . . .'

'I didn't want to put it in a letter. I feel the most awful cad. Letting you down after what happened between us. I was so certain what I felt for you would last forever.'

'It was first love for both of us. How were we to know it wouldn't stand the strain of being separated for such a long time?'

'I've behaved very badly Tamar. You don't know how badly.' He paused to take a deep drag on his cigarette burning it right down to the stub. 'There was a girl in the family I stayed with. All the time we spent together, all the things we shared. I grew to love her. Differently to the way I'd felt about you.' He pushed the stub into the ashtray and then took another cigarette out of the packet. Balancing it between his fingers he said, 'I'm married. We were married by the local priest before I left.'

'And you were too cowardly to tell me! Well, at least she's a catholic.'

'I'm sorry,' he said. 'I didn't want to hurt you.'

Tamar felt she would have liked to hit him for the months of heartache she'd suffered torn between her feelings for Martin and her commitment to Edward. Instead she said. 'I've also met someone else. But I couldn't have married him until I knew whether you were alive or dead and could tell you to your face. I thought I knew you Edward, but I don't.'

She stood up and picked her gloves and bag off the table.

'Give my love to your mother,' she said. 'And I hope you'll be happy.'

He had risen with her and held out his hand across the table. 'No hard feelings, Tamar?'

She ignored the proffered hand. 'No hard feelings,' she said.

Afterwards Tamar took the bus down to Seaham and retrieved the key from under the stone where Anna had left it. There was a bottle of whisky in the cupboard and Tamar poured it into her tea instead of milk. There seemed no point in lighting a fire so late, so she curled up in bed fully clothed with a hot water bottle and drank the fiery brew. Her first feelings were of anger that Edward could have behaved in so cowardly a way, then of irrational hurt that he could write her so passionate a letter (he'd even bought her a ring for god's sake!) and then marry someone else a few months later without even telling her. Had he given his new wife the ring he'd bought for her? Tamar felt a moment's outrage on her behalf. But then, warmed by the whisky, she could only acknowledge her relief. She had been saved the task of telling him that she had fallen in love with Martin. They had both been unfaithful. But I wouldn't have married Martin without telling him, Tamar thought angrily.

~~~~~~~~~~~~~~~~~~

The warm summer days that followed Michael's departure
~~~~~~~~~~~~~~~~~~

meant nothing to Anna. It was as though the landscape had gone from colour to monochrome. She felt so dull and heavy she couldn't even paint. It was the same feeling she'd had in the internment camp, the same ache under the ribs. Even her food tasted strange – sometimes the smell of it nauseated her.

At Miss Bateman's suggestion, Anna had a weekend's leave and went home. Her mother was pleased to see her, but for Anna it was like visiting a foreign country. The little domestic world that enclosed her family was no longer hers. Even the house seemed smaller and shabbier than she remembered and when she opened the front door instead of the usual smell of lavender polish, she was met by a sour, unpleasant odour. Mrs Wiseman explained that it was due to her own mother's deterioration. 'She's begun to wet the bed,' she told Anna, indicating a line of sheets blowing in the sea breeze. 'I've had to give up my job to look after her, and I'm absolutely worn out.'

There was no opportunity for Anna to tell her mother about Michael, a task she dreaded, but knew that the longer she left it the harder it would be.

It had been strange bumping into Edward as she walked up to get the tram to the station. He had seemed reluctant to talk to her, rather sheepish in fact. It heartened Anna to feel that perhaps Tamar's relationships were as emotionally complicated as her own. One day soon she was going to have to tell Tamar, but she kept putting it off. It grieved her to know that she would probably lose her best friend. Tamar had always been close to George, and Lily had been a second mother to her. Through loving Michael Anna felt that she had cut herself off from everyone who had previously been important in her life. The only person she could talk to was Miss Bateman.

'Have I been appallingly selfish?' Anna asked. 'My loving Michael is going to cause an awful lot of people pain.'

'We can't always choose where or how we love, Anna. Why do you think that Barbara and I chose to live so far away from our families?' She hesitated and then hurried on. 'If we had chosen to live together in this country it would have caused them untold distress. But we couldn't live apart and I can only tell you that it has been worth it. When you find real love and companionship, it should not be lightly abandoned.'

'Divorce is so sordid. People treat you as a social outcast.'

'No one will ever know you have been divorced unless you tell them. I always think that it is very unfair. To make a mistake in love is the only mistake society seems unprepared to forgive.'

When Anna got up to go Miss Bateman said. 'Commander Forbes was here to tea while you were away. He was admiring that little seascape you painted at Seaham. He wanted to know if you would sell it to him?'

'It's not something I've thought about. No one's ever wanted to buy anything before. Should I? I've no idea how much I ought to ask.'

'About five guineas I should think. It's a lovely piece. You could sell much more you know, if you found a gallery that would take your work.'

Every night when Anna scanned the air waves she hoped to hear Michael's voice, but knew that realistically it was unlikely. His broadcasts would be encrypted, monitored by those specially trained radio operators with high security clearances. She could still hear his voice in her mind when she closed her eyes, still see his beloved face, the large ears and the ironic smile. The longing for him was like a perpetual ache.

Anna had a recurring nightmare. She was in a house – an enormous mansion – and she knew that Michael was in it somewhere. But as she ran up staircases, down corridors and through endless rooms she couldn't find him anywhere. Sometimes she could hear his voice echoing from a distant part of the house and sometimes she caught sight of his moving shadow on the wall, but he always evaded her. Several mornings she woke crying.

The strange nauseous feeling refused to go away. Six weeks after Michael left Anna forced herself to pick up her diary, scan through its blank pages and count the unmarked days since the last, faint, pencilled cross. There were too many. Nothing since a couple of weeks before the day they had made love at the beach. Anna's stomach lurched and the room tilted as she thought about what that could mean.

On her next afternoon off, Anna got the bus into Scarborough and went to the services' medical centre. She was glad that the doctor was a woman. She asked a series of questions and then examined Anna's stomach, probing deep with her fingers above the pelvis. 'I think your suspicions are probably right,' she said. 'Of course it could be some emotional upset – that can make one's periods very unreliable, but there is an enlargement of the uterus – early days, but I'm pretty certain you're pregnant.'

Pregnant, Anna thought as she walked along the sea front. Having Michael's child. The words had no reality yet.

That night Anna knew there was one task that could not be put off. She couldn't wait until George came home on leave in six months or a year's time to break her new relationship to him gently, hoping that distance had diminished the strength of his affection for her. She had to tell him now, before her condition became obvious and someone else did. He didn't deserve what she was going to do to him, but the letter she dreaded would have to be written.

'*Dear George,*' Anna began.'*Nothing I say can make this any easier. It was a mistake to marry you not feeling as I should. I know that now and I want you to be free to find someone who'll love you as you deserve to be loved. The truth is that I have met someone else and, what you will find hardest of all, he is German. I wish we could still stay friends, but I know that this will probably hurt you too much to make that possible. I wish you were at home, so that I could explain all this in person. Letters are a coward's way out aren't they? But not for me. This has been one of the hardest letters I've ever had to write.*

I don't think either Tamar or Lily will ever forgive me for what I've done. Will you?

I do love you George, but it's not the right kind of love, and it has to be for a marriage to work.'

She didn't tell him the rest of it, that ultimate betrayal, the carrying of another man's child. That would come later, but at least it would make it easy for George to get a divorce. There was a whole landscape of pain in front of Anna and she had no idea how she was going to get through it at all.

Martin met Tamar at the bus stop and the strain on his face was plain. He said nothing until they had driven out of Kirkland, but then he parked the landrover on the grass verge and turned to look at her. 'How did it go?' he asked, almost as if he was afraid of what the answer might be.

Tamar found herself smiling. 'I was so prepared for him to be angry and hurt when I told him about us, but I never got the chance. He'd got married to someone else while he was away!'

Martin laughed and his whole body relaxed with relief. 'I was afraid you'd suddenly discover that you'd made a mistake and it was him you wanted after all.'

'Idiot! I sat there wondering what I'd ever seen in him.'

Martin reached over and drew her into his arms, kissing her passionately. For Tamar it was bliss to be able to return his embrace without a single twinge of guilt.

'So we can be properly engaged now?'

Tamar snuggled her face into the angle between his neck and his shoulder. 'Yes please. I've hated having to keep it secret.' She looked up at him for a moment. 'You know what bothers me most now? The fact that I could love him so much and think that I wanted to spend my life with him and then to have it all fade away. Could that ever happen to us?'

Martin looked anxious. 'Are you trying to tell me that you're not certain of your feelings for me?'

'Of course not. It's just that I felt like that about Edward too at the time.'

'Not even the least little doubt?'

Tamar thought hard, then nodded reluctantly. 'There was the religious problem. And I didn't really want to get married – I used to tell myself that it was just that I was too young and when I got a bit older it would be all right. Whereas with you . . . I've sort of known from the beginning that we belonged together. Does that sound crazy?'

'No. It sounds wonderful.' He kissed her again, holding her so tightly she could hardly breathe. She could feel the strength of his desire for her and it both excited and frightened her at the same time. Reluctantly she pulled herself back, conscious of the public road, the daylight. She longed to give herself totally to him without reserve, but this wasn't the right time or place.

'Sensible Tamar,' Martin said wryly, ruffling her hair with his hand. 'But we'd better go home. Aunt Mary'll kill me if we're late. She was putting the Yorkshire pudding in when I left.'

It came as no surprise to any of the Bainbridges when Martin told them over lunch. 'About time n'all!' Mrs Bainbridge said and she got up and hugged Tamar and then kissed Martin.

'We've got to do some hard thinking though,' Martin said. 'About where we're going to live.' Martin had explained to Tamar that, like most family farms, he wasn't paid a set wage and he didn't know whether Crow Hall could afford to keep them both. 'I might have to take a married man's job.'

'What's wrong with you both living here?' Mrs Bainbridge asked.

But Joe said, 'Young 'uns and old 'uns livin' together – it's not a good start out. They'll want their own place.'

Wilf cleared his throat at the end of the table and everyone looked at him. He spoke so rarely, that what he said had the impact of an oracle. 'Mrs Heslop's sellin' up and goin' to her sisters.'

'That tale's been around since she went off to the Garland's, our Wilf!' Mrs Bainbridge scoffed.

'Aye, but 't land agent's car was in't yard when I went down to look at that calvin' cow this mornin'.'

'It's no good even if it is for sale,' Martin said gloomily. 'She'll want more money for it that we could afford.'

'Mebbe's.' Wilf put his pipe back in his mouth and lapsed into silence again.

'It's a good house,' Mrs Bainbridge said. 'If it was titivated up a bit. Gone to rack and ruin now, but I remember what it used to be when I was a bairn.'

'I could go and ask about a mortgage,' Martin said. 'But could you bear to live there, Tamar? After everything?'

'How much would a farm like that cost?' Tamar asked.

Joe considered for a while. 'Fifty acres of good in-bye land, then the grazin' rights and the twenty acres down at Kirkland. But it's all been let go – the bugger's taken all the heart out of the land. There's a lot to put back in.'

'How much?'

'Mebbe's five or six hundred. Mebbe less. Depends how quick she wants shot of it.'

Tamar was surprised. 'It seems incredibly cheap!'

'Land's not much in demand around here,' Martin said. 'All the little marginal farms are gradually going out of business. It's too much work to make a living on the land – people want to move down to the cities and work in the factories.'

'Once on a time,' Joe said, 'the whole fellside was full `o little farms. We're the last of them.'

Tamar said nothing.

After they had finished the evening milking at Holme Farm and the cows had been returned to the field, Tamar and Martin went inside to explore the house. Tamar walked through the rooms, trying to see them with new eyes. When she'd lived here with the Heslops, the whole fabric of the place had seemed saturated with misery. Now she could see that, cleaned and painted, the wood polished and the windows gleaming to let the sunlight in, filled with the glory of her and Martin's life together, it could gradually be reclaimed

'It wasn't always an unhappy house,' she said, as they stood in the dairy staring out of the window. She could see why Mrs Heslop had spent so much time here – the view of the hills as they caught the red glow of the sunset was spectacular. The full impact of it suddenly hit her. She could belong here, rooted in this land, her children and her children's children, on and on forever and ever. The thought of such permanence made Tamar feel dizzy. She knew it was time to broach the difficult subject, knew that she should have told Martin about Ida's legacy a long time ago.

'Would you really like to buy the farm?' she asked.

'It would make perfect sense. Most of the land joins ours, so we could work it all as one farm. And it would solve the problem of where we're going to live. The only difficulty's the money. There's never been enough at Crow Hall to put in the bank. Mary and Joe have always ploughed everything straight back into the farm. I've got my demob money and some of my army pay saved, but it isn't much.'

'There's something I haven't told you,' Tamar said. 'I had a legacy at the beginning of the war, from someone who knew me as a child. She had no children of her own and I think she wanted me to have a secure future. It came as a real shock.'

Martin looked as though he scarcely believed her. 'Are you saying you could put some money up as a deposit?'

'I've got nearly three hundred pounds.'

Martin looked stunned. 'It's a good job we're already engaged. People would think that I was marrying you for the money.'

Tamar laughed. 'It's not that much really. But more than I'd ever dreamt of. After the war I was going to use it to pay for my keep while I trained to be a librarian. I never thought of buying a farm!'

Martin put his arms around her and kissed her. 'I'll let you on one condition.'

'What's that?'

'That this farm is in both our names – no, don't argue. It's your money, and I'll inherit Crow Hall one day. It'll be a partnership – a real partnership.'

Just at that moment, in Martin's arms, Tamar felt so happy she was afraid.

Anna was painting in the shed when Miss Bateman put her head round the door. 'Would you like to come for a cup of tea? The Commander's here and he'd like a word with you.'

Anna put her brushes in a pot of water and covered the palette with waxed paper. It was a nuisance to be interrupted. What did he want? To buy another painting? Or had the medical officer told him something? Anna's heart jumped. She was aware that her present situation couldn't continue, but she'd hoped for a few more weeks of breathing space, until her condition became obvious, just a few more weeks to plan, to wait for Michael to come back. So far she had told no one about her pregnancy.

Nervously Anna accepted the cup of tea that Miss Bateman handed to her, balancing it on the little pie-crust table drawn up beside her chair. The Commander looked uncomfortable, Miss

Bateman unusually grave.

'I'm afraid I have some news which, in the circumstances, I thought better to relay to you personally before it becomes common knowledge among the other officers. I'm not unaware of your relationship with Michael Schmidt, although it contravenes naval regulations – we tend to turn a blind eye unless there are aggravating circumstances.'

Maybe this has something to do with George, Anna thought. She was being divorced for adultery with Michael. Was that a disciplinary matter?

'I'm extremely sorry to have to tell you,' the Commander paused, 'That Michael was betrayed by a fellow agent yesterday and shot by the Gestapo.'

The room swung round Anna's head. She closed her eyes. A great weight was sitting on her chest and she couldn't breathe. For a moment she thought she would be sick. Then she felt someone take hold of her head and there was a searing pain in her nostrils. Opening her eyes, Anna saw Miss Bateman holding a cut glass bottle of smelling salts under her nose.

'I'm most terribly sorry,' the Commander said. 'It's a tremendous loss for us all.'

After he'd gone Anna began to shiver. 'It's the shock,' Miss Bateman said, putting a shawl round her shoulders and chafing Anna's hands between her own. She went to the sideboard and came back with a glass. 'Here, drink this.' It was brandy. 'We brought this out of France too. It's the last of the Napoleon until after the war.'

It tasted like acid in Anna's mouth.

'You must be very brave, as he was,' Miss Bateman said. 'He would expect it of you.'

It was odd not to be able to cry.

'Would you like to stay here tonight,' Miss Bateman asked anxiously. 'You should have someone with you.'

Anna shook her head. She got up unsteadily. 'It's very nice of you, but I need to be alone. Thank you.' She didn't want to seem ungrateful, but she could hardly wait to get out of the room. This was where she had sat with Michael that very first time. The image was imprinted on her mind with total clarity.

In her own room, in the bed she had furtively shared so often with him, Anna clutched his farewell note – the only letter he had ever written to her and wept internally, though her eyes remained obstinately dry. She put her fingers over her stomach where Michael's child was growing in secret. A boy or a girl that shared his genes. She didn't even have a photograph, only the many drawings that she had made. At least she had those – could give their child a likeness.

At nine o'clock Kirsten arrived with a mug of malted milk and a hot water bottle in a knitted cover. 'The milk's from Miss Bateman,' she said, 'but this is mine. It was all I could think of to comfort you.'

Kirsten tucked the hot water bottle in beside her and then put her arms round Anna and rocked her backwards and forwards like a child. 'He was a good man,' she said, 'intelligent and funny and dedicated.'

'It was his voice I fell in love with,' Anna said. 'It was so beautiful. I just can't believe I'll never hear it again.'

'There are tapes,' Kirsten said. 'Though they get re-used every now and then. It would be highly irregular, but I might be able to find something.'

Anna clung to Kirsten as if she was drowning. 'I'm expecting his child,' she said. 'I don't know what I'm going to do.'

'Does the Commander know?'

'No one.'

'You'll probably have to leave the service, which will be a pity. We need all the trained personnel we can get. What about your family – are they likely to be sympathetic?'

'Hardly. My mother's very conventional. She reads Mrs Miniver. Having a daughter who marries one man and then turns up a year later expecting someone else's baby isn't exactly the kind of thing you can discuss with the neighbours is it?'

'I think it's brilliant. Producing a new life among all this carnage.' Kirsten fluffed Anna's pillow and straightened the blankets. 'Try to get some sleep – you've got a baby to look after, remember. Tomorrow I'll see if I can find a tape of Michael for you in the archive.'

'Thanks Kirsten. You're very good. You won't tell anyone until

I've been able to talk to Commander Forbes, will you?'

'Promise. See you in the morning.'

After she'd gone Anna lay and looked at the ceiling. Through the long sleepless night she went through every single moment that they had spent together, every single word that had been spoken, as if she was watching a film over and over. She couldn't even imagine what life would look like tomorrow, but she would have to get up as she did every day, eat breakfast, translate documents and stumble on with life, feeling as though a great part of herself had been amputated. A quotation flitted through her mind. 'Tis better to have loved and lost than never to have loved at all.' How stupid. How much better to be in ignorance than to suffer the kind of pain she was suffering now.

CHAPTER TWENTY FIVE

Tamar, throwing corn to the chickens outside the gate, saw a large black car coming up the lane. It looked vaguely like the Pergavie's car. But what would they be doing here? Could they be bringing Holly back?

'Tell Aunt Mary we've got visitors,' Tamar called over her shoulders to Martin, who was taking his boots off in the porch.

As it bumped to a halt beside the barn wall Tamar could see that the bonnet and running boards of the car were caked in mud. Whoever it was had driven a long way. The door opened and a man got out and walked towards her.

Tamar stood, rooted to the spot, staring at a mirror image of herself. The same dark hair, though his was greying at the temples, the same slate grey eyes and narrow chin.

'Tamar?' he asked. She nodded her head, her mouth dry.

'I feel ashamed,' he said as he came closer, 'that it's taken me so long. I don't even know how to introduce myself.'

'You're my father?' Tamar asked, needing to say it.

'Yes. Though I probably don't deserve the title.'

'Why have you stayed away?' Tamar couldn't resist saying it. 'Why did Sadie tell me you were dead?'

'Can we walk a little? I need to stretch my legs after so long in the car.'

Tamar put down the bucket of chicken feed and went with him up the path that skirted the house towards the open moorland. She noticed that he was wearing smart town shoes – totally unsuitable for the stony track.

'I came up to Winterings for Easter,' he said. 'And when I saw on the map how close you were, I decided to drive over. It's very beautiful up here.'

He paused and then talked on as if answering the questions that were in Tamar's mind. 'It would never have worked with your mother – it was first love – a kind of grand passion. If my mother hadn't interfered it would probably have petered out of its own accord. But she forbade me to see Sadie and so we ran off together and of course you were conceived. Marriage would have been very difficult – I realised when we tried to live together for just those few weeks, how very unsuited we were, and there was no money – I hadn't been down from Cambridge very long. I'd just started my first job and was trying to climb the career ladder.'

'What do you do?' Tamar said. 'No one's ever told me.'

'I'm a newspaper editor now, but then I was a very junior hack. Marrying Sadie would have been hard, though at the time I probably would have done it. But I allowed myself to be talked out of it by my mother. She said it wasn't necessary to do the honourable thing and that she would take care of everything and make sure that Sadie was looked after. I suppose I thought she meant an abortion. Illegal of course, but in a private clinic, if you knew the right people . . . I heard later that Sadie had had the baby and that it was a little girl. But by then too much water had gone under the bridge. I thought I'd do more harm than good coming back into your lives. My mother said she'd make sure you were provided for.'

Tamar wanted to pour out all the hurt of not having enough money to get a proper education – all those lodging houses, the hand-me-down clothes, the clandestine departures. But she didn't. All she said was, 'Sometimes we didn't even have money for the rent. And she wrote Sadie such horrid letters.'

'Did Sadie tell you about me?'

'Hardly anything. She said you'd died before I was born. She lied about being married to you. I found out the truth when I went down to Cornwall, to Ruthven.'

'Ruthven! I loved that house. Who has it now?'

'It's been requisitioned by the army.'

'We had such good times there all together when we were young. Robert and Pamela and Sadie and I.'

'Does your wife know about me? The housekeeper told me

that you'd married. She saw the photograph in the newspapers.'

He stopped. His face clouded with pain. 'My wife and son were killed three months ago in the blitz.'

'I'm so sorry. How did it happen?'

'Ironically they were leaving London – I wanted them to go up to Yorkshire while the bombing was so bad. Fiona missed the train she was supposed to be on – she was rarely on time for anything – and the next train was badly delayed. It was bombed as it sat in the station at Sheffield. If she'd got the first train they'd both still be alive.'

'How old was your son?' My half brother, Tamar thought.

'He was nine. We would have liked more children, but after Alex was born Fiona didn't conceive again.'

As James talked, Tamar realised that here was a man who, though charming, had a weakness. It was something Tamar found difficult to put her finger on; something that reminded her ever so slightly of Edward the last time she'd seen him. Perhaps it was the self-justification. She noticed, even as she revelled in his presence, that he had a tendency to blame other people for the calamities in his life. And he kept glancing at her as he talked as if shaping the story around her reactions.

'I've tried to think of it as God's will,' he went on. 'But I find it difficult to accept. Did Sadie bring you up with a faith Tamar? She was always a little heathen.'

'Then I'm afraid I take after her.' Tamar smiled ruefully. 'I think we'd better go back. Aunt Mary will have tea ready and you've ruined your shoes.'

He looked down at his feet as if realising it for the first time. 'The shoes don't matter. Are you happy Tamar?'

'Very. I live with a lovely family and I'm going to marry their son, Martin.'

'Will you like just being a farmer's wife?'

Tamar laughed inwardly at the 'just'. 'Very much,' she said. 'I feel quite at home here. Did you know there's a Tamar Fell in the graveyard?' She pointed down the hill towards the church spire.

'There were some cousins of my father's up here somewhere.'

'Kirkland Old Hall?'

'Quite possibly. I've never kept up with them – the last of the family died in the Great War.'

As they walked back down to the farm, Tamar asked a question that had been bothering her ever since Sadie died. 'At Sadie's funeral, there was a woman in a big green car. No one knew who she was and she never introduced herself. We'd put a notice in the Times and I've always wondered whether it was one of your family.'

'It was Pamela. She wrote to me afterwards. She and Sadie were good friends when they were children – things only went sour later on. Did you know about that?'

Tamar nodded. 'But why didn't she come and talk to me?'

He looked uncomfortable. 'Pamela wouldn't want to get involved. I think she went on a kind of impulse. When she wrote she said she had just wanted to know that you were all right, but that you were surrounded by friends and obviously being well looked after.'

Tamar clenched her teeth to prevent herself asking all the other questions that flooded into her mind.

It seemed incredibly awkward introducing James Fell as 'my father'. Mary and Joe made him cautiously welcome, but Tamar was aware of a change in their manner towards him. His expensive suit, his charming upper class aura put the Bainbridges at a distance. Whatever P's and Q's were, Tamar thought, they were definitely watching them. And there was something else – a slight coolness and an air almost of censure in Aunt Mary's enquiries and her unconcealed consternation that this was the first time he had ever seen Tamar.

Later, when he'd declined a bed and driven off down the lane in the dusk back to Yorkshire, Mary said angrily, 'How can you have a bairn and not want to see it? What kind of a father's that!'

'I thought he seemed quite nice,' Martin said. 'And he would have been very young when Tamar was born.'

'Older than you, actually,' Tamar said, doing some arithmetic. She was trying to be objective. 'I think he was afraid of his mother, afraid of being held responsible for Sadie and me. My mother was,' Tamar paused. How could you describe Sadie? 'She was rather demanding. Not someone you'd get a quiet life with. She liked a good time. Great fun, but exhausting.'

'Well,' Mary said firmly. 'You're more of a credit to either of them than they deserve by the sound of it.'

Tamar was painfully aware that when her father had said his goodbyes and left, awkwardly kissing her on the cheek, he hadn't said anything about keeping in touch with her, nor had he given her an address. The thought of that made Tamar want to weep, but she kept her tears in check until she went to bed where she sobbed out her grief and disappointment into her pillow. A few moments later, the door opened very quietly and Martin tiptoed into the room and slid into bed beside her. Tamar tried to turn her face away, but Martin wouldn't allow her to, clasping her tightly against his chest. 'I guessed you'd be upset,' he said. 'He wasn't what you expected, was he?'

'In some ways.' Tamar dried her eyes on the corner of the sheet. 'But I suppose I expected him to be really glad to see me and that there'd be a big emotional scene. But it wasn't like that. He seemed just to want to justify his actions – guilt, I think. His wife and son were killed by a bomb, so I'm the only child he has left. He seemed very cool and distant.'

'Does that sound like someone else you know?' Martin asked softly into her hair.

Tamar choked on a laugh. 'My friend Anna accused me of being like that. But I'm not really – I just have this terrible sense of privacy, of keeping my feelings to myself.'

'Well, I'm tired of keeping my feelings to myself.' Martin's hands had strayed and were gently stroking her back. 'I want to make love to you. The only problem is, I don't want to take risks and I don't have anything, if you know what I mean.'

Tamar kissed him, allowing all the warmth of feeling inside herself, all her need to be loved flow through her body towards him. Then she pulled away. 'At the risk of being thought a tramp, I do have something.'

Martin looked surprised and then laughed. 'If I'd known that, I wouldn't have waited so long.'

Tamar was blushing in the darkness. 'Can you give me a few moments to go to the bathroom?'

'I can give you a few more minutes, but only a few mind!'

As she slid out of bed, he grabbed the hem of her nightdress playfully and pulled her back to kiss her again. 'I want to marry you soon, Tamar. Not in some dim distant future. All this "after the war" business is crazy. Will you?'

She slipped out of his arms and said, 'After my school certificate next month?'

'Is that a promise?'

Something else was bothering Tamar. Something else that she should have confessed to Martin a long time ago. She said hesitantly, 'You know that I'm not a virgin? I let Edward – the night before he went away. I'm sorry.'

'I'm not. It makes it easier. And I wouldn't expect anything from you I couldn't give myself. I'm not a virgin, why should you be?'

When she came back from the bathroom Martin had put the quilt and pillows on the floor. 'The bedsprings creak dreadfully,' he whispered. We don't want Joe and Mary to know what we're up to, do we?'

Standing there naked, half lit by moonlight, Tamar was struck by the beauty of his body. She went willingly into his arms and lay down with him among the quilts. The strong capable hands that she had watched restraining animals and wielding tools slipped off her nightdress and caressed her body. There was no hesitation or embarrassment or guilt with Martin as there had been with Edward. He wanted her and he made his pleasure obvious when she shyly touched him, moving her hands across his back, stroking the fine blond hair on his sun-burnt arms. His happy enjoyment of sensuality fuelled Tamar's desire and she gave herself to him as completely as she had often dreamt of doing. This time there was no pain, only spasms of pleasure that left her gasping with delight.

Afterwards he stroked her hair and held her close. 'I've got to go back to my own room,' he said regretfully after a while. 'Aunt Mary's got old fashioned ideas of morality. We don't want to be caught.' He kissed her again. 'It's got to be June,' he said. 'I can't wait any longer than that or I'll go mad!'

Kirsten's optimism was unjustified; there were no tapes of Michael's voice. Anna felt absolutely desolate without him. She hadn't realised that it would be so hard to carry on with her ordinary, daily life. Nothing seemed to have any meaning. Even the baby seemed unreal. It was difficult to imagine that her body contained a new life, unfurling inside her like a plant. Her breasts had swollen and the waistband of her skirt had to be let out with a loop of elastic, but apart from that she felt little different. Anna had not dared to tell anyone other than Kirsten at the base, not even Miss Bateman. The services, she knew, were not sympathetic to what everyone referred to as 'war babies'. She supposed that as a married woman – technically at least – they might treat her differently. But the end result would be the same; she would have to leave. How was she to pay her way and feed a child? George's army wage was still being paid to her, but Anna couldn't bring herself to spend any of it. She was paying it into an account to give back to him when he returned. He'd written a short note to say that he was being given compassionate leave to come home. She felt sick at the thought of having to confront him. It puzzled Anna, as she cried herself to sleep on her pillow at night, that something that had been so right and so beautiful, could have hurt so many people and made her feel so wicked.

Kirsten was the only person Anna confided in. 'Would your mother look after the baby afterwards,' she asked, 'so that you could come back to work here? People with your skills are very much in demand, and you're going to need to earn money.'

'I'm not expecting any help from my mother. I wrote to her a couple of weeks ago and I've heard nothing back. She'll be absolutely horrified.'

'People often react badly at first. But then when they've had time to think, they soften. You're her daughter after all. Whatever you do, you'll always be that.'

Anna had little confidence that this would be true. She still hadn't written to Tamar, but she was sure that George would and Tamar would be bound to side with him and with Lily. They occupied the moral high ground after all. Anna was resigned to the loss of her best friend, although it hurt more than she could have believed possible. When Tamar's letter came, she left it unopened for two days, dreading what it might contain. But the contents were completely different.

'*Dear Anna, this is going to surprise you, but I'm getting married on the 10th June. I know that's short notice, but it's got to be fitted in before the hay timing. Can you get leave to be my bridesmaid? No time for dresses or anything like that – you'll just have to wear your uniform. It'll give it a suitably war time feel! There's just you and Holly and I've decided not to be given away. The vicar says it isn't necessary and I couldn't think of anyone I'd want – except George and he's in Africa. My father sent me a cheque as a wedding present (guilt money?) and offered to do the deed, but I declined. I decided that he'd given me away years ago, when I was a child, and I didn't want him to do it again. It's odd but now that I've met him, the thought that I might not have any more contact with him doesn't bother me so much.*

Sadly Lily's not going to be there either. I had a short note which was very difficult to decipher. She says she left the farm when she was twelve and swore she'd never set foot on one again. I've promised to take Martin to see her next time I'm in Newcastle.

I don't know how I'm going to get everything done in time. My exams are the week before the wedding and there's going to be an inquest into Heslop's death. We all have to give evidence and I'm dreading it. How are you? Why haven't I heard from you? I do hope you're going to be there. Come earlier if you can and we can catch up on all our news.'

Tamar had never been in a court room before and found the dark wooden panelling and rows of wooden pews highly intimidating. The Coroner sat in a plain chair at a table below the judge's bench, and Tamar was relieved to find that witnesses were expected to give evidence at a lectern rather than climb up into the witness box.

'We have come here this morning to enquire into the circumstances surrounding the death of James Arthur Heslop, aged fifty two years, at Holme Farm, Kirkland in the county of Cumberland.'

Tamar searched the seats around her, packed with the inhabitants of the village, but Mrs Heslop was nowhere to be seen.

Joe was called first to give an account of how they had found him lying in the stall. Then it was Tamar's turn to take the oath. She had worked on the farm, the Coroner asked, and must have formed an opinion of the horse's temper?

'Ben was dangerous,' Tamar said. 'We were all afraid of him. The blacksmith said he'd been ill treated and he used to lash out if you went behind his back legs unexpectedly. He was all right if he could see you.'

The policeman and the doctor both made statements and then a list of Heslop's injuries was read out. They were horrific and made Tamar feel sick. Martin squeezed her hand. The doctor was then interviewed about Mrs Heslop, who had been certified as unfit to attend and the policeman confirmed that he had been unable to obtain a statement from her. It was all over much quicker than Tamar had expected.

'I feel quite satisfied,' the Coroner said, 'that this is a simple case of accidental death, and should serve as a warning to all those who work with animals. It is too easy to become blasé about one's personal safety. Mr Heslop clearly underestimated the risks. A moment's carelessness cost him his life.'

But there was still an element of doubt in Tamar's mind as she listened to the verdict. What role had Mrs Heslop played in this? Clear in Tamar's memory was Holly's description of her standing in the upstairs passage holding a knife. Had she perhaps gone to the stable that day and startled him with her wild behaviour? Tamar could imagine Heslop shouting, perhaps stepping inadvertently backwards to get away from her and then the horse lashing out. Was that it?

'No one will ever know what really happened in the stable that day,' she said to Martin as they stepped outside to wait for Mary and Joe.

'Poor woman,' Martin said. 'I used to play with their son when I was a kid. Johnny was a good lad, but Heslop used to take his belt to him at the least thing. I've seen him beaten black and blue just for slopping a bucket of milk. It wasn't a nice way to die, but if anyone deserved it, Heslop did.'

Tamar shuddered.

'Anyway,' Martin put his arm round her shoulders. 'Let's think of more cheerful things. You're going to drag me round the shops in a minute to buy furniture and a wedding ring and then afterwards we're meeting Mary and Joe at the George for a slap up lunch.'

'And *then*,' Tamar said, 'I'm going home to revise. I've got my exams on Thursday don't forget!' There was a hollow pit in her stomach when she thought of them. This was what she had worked so hard for, the goal she had set herself. But now that it had come she was terrified.

The Commander gave Anna two weeks leave, and accepted her claim to have 'personal problems' without questioning it. She took the train up to Newcastle and went first to her mother's, her hand trembling as she put her key in the door. Grandpa Cotteslow was in the kitchen pouring himself a cup of tea when she went in. There was no sign of her mother, but the back door was ajar as though someone had just slipped out into the garden and there were two cups on the table.

Mr Cotteslow straightened up when Anna came in and faced her belligerently. 'I don't know how you've got the nerve to come here after what you've done,' he said.

'Well, you'd be one to talk, wouldn't you,' Anna could feel her temper rising and couldn't prevent it all tumbling out. 'Such a pillar of the community. Lily told me about that woman you had down in shields. A herring girl! How many years was it? You're just a hypocrite.'

'Cheeky bugger! You always did have a lip on you. Well, I'll tell you this hinny, you may be my grand-daughter but I don't have to have you in the house. Just shut the door after you when you go.'

Anna didn't bother to argue. She picked up her bag and her jacket from the hallway and left.

Mrs Wiseman was standing anxiously beside the front gate. 'I couldn't bear to listen. I'm sorry Anna. If I had my own place it would be different. But I can't have you here because of him, and I can't leave because of your gran. You do understand, don't you?'

Anna nodded wearily. She kissed her mother on the cheek and said, with a confidence she didn't feel; 'Don't worry. I got myself into this mess, so I suppose I'll get myself out of it. I'm going to Tamar's for her wedding and then back to Yorkshire. I'll let you know what happens after that.'

~~~~~~~~~~~~~~~~~~

Tamar went to the Grammar School in Penrith to take her School Certificate, sitting in a hall with forty other students all younger than herself. It felt strange to be among so many school uniforms again. When the teacher looked at his watch and said 'You may start writing now,' Tamar could hear panicky intakes of breath in the silence around her as the papers were turned over, followed by the frantic scratching of pens. She briefly touched Sadie's four leaf clover in her pocket – the good luck charm that Edward has once refused – took a deep breath and began to write. Every word she put down was a blow struck for independence – the culmination of all those years of struggling to educate herself through one school after another, with Sadie barely able to afford the uniform, let alone pay fees for a Grammar School. How much easier it would have been if her father had paid for her, how different her future might have been. But how much sweeter to have done it all by herself. Just to be here in this hall seemed an immense achievement.

Martin was waiting for her outside in the landrover when she came out. He had two week-old calves wrapped up in sacking in the back. He leaned across and kissed her as she climbed into the cab. 'The little heifers are a wedding present from Dad. Good exam?'

'I hope so. There wasn't anything I absolutely didn't know. But I've no idea what the pass standard is.'

'You won't have to worry. Not after all the work you've put in!'

'I'm not going to count my chickens.' Tamar touched the four leaved clover in her pocket again and let herself wish.
~~~~~~~~~~~~~~~~~~

'You once said you wanted to be a librarian,' Martin said as he started up the engine. 'Are you going to regret becoming a farmer's wife instead?'

'My father asked me something very similar. But I don't think so. When I thought about being a librarian it was because books were the only things that gave me real pleasure, but now I've lived in the country and worked with animals and I love it. It feels absolutely right. Being a librarian's a job, working on a farm is a way of life.'

'The war's done that for me,' Tamar went on, staring through the windscreen to where the dark green shapes of the Pennine hills were beginning to rise above the houses as they drove out onto the main road. 'Someone once told me that war spoils your life and ruins your chances and for a long time I thought that was true. But it's been the opposite. If it hadn't been for the war I would never have ended up on a farm and I wouldn't have met you.'

Martin reached across and put his hand over hers. 'I wouldn't hold you back, you know. If there were things you wanted to do. But you're right, a farm's a way of life. I just need to be sure you're not going to regret things.'

Tamar looked over the seats at the two moist noses pushing their way out of the sacking. The calves would both need feeding the instant they were back at the farm, and tucking up in a bed of warm hay, but it wasn't a chore. She loved the feeling of their rough little tongues sucking on her fingers as she lowered their mouths into the bucket of milk. And they were *her* calves – hers and Martin's. She put her hand on his knee. 'I'm sure,' she said.

~~~~~~~~~~~~~~~~~~

There were two letters waiting for Tamar when she got back to the house. One was from Holly, the other was inked all over with military stamps and had George's familiar scrawl on the envelope. It was four or five months since Tamar had heard from George, a month since she had written to tell him of her engagement to Martin. She opened Holly's letter first.

'*Thank goodness you wrote*,' Holly began. *'I'm going crazy with*
~~~~~~~~~~~~~~~~~~

boredom here and your wedding's a good excuse to get away. I'm hoping the WLA will have me back. I had a long talk with Daddy yesterday and I think he's resigned to me going. But it will be a wrench for Mummy. I haven't told either of them about Ivan and I feel dreadfully deceitful. But how could I? I sort of hinted to Daddy that there was someone I liked, so it won't come as too much of a shock when I do tell them.

About the wedding. I know you haven't had time to save up enough coupons, but you simply can't get married in a wartime regulation suit Tamar. They're so ugly! It's got to be a dress, so I've been down to the shop. Everyone was so pleased for you. Miss Timms asked to be remembered. Anyway, Daddy's organising something – I just hope I've remembered your size right. I'll bring it with me when I come and it will be my wedding present to you. I've bought a short summery dress in a kind of pinky violet crepe de chine to follow you down the aisle in. Is that all right? It's going to be such fun, and I'm really looking forward to meeting your friend Anna.'

It made Tamar smile. Holly was right, the idea of getting married in a tailored suit didn't appeal, and the lack of clothing coupons was obviously not a problem if you were a Pergavie. It was immoral and Tamar supposed that she should disapprove. But everyone seemed to be finding ways to get round war-time regulations – Heslop's secret hen house in the wood, Martin's extra pig at the back of the stable, the Antonelli's black market food supplies, even the Bainbridges had lambs that died of natural causes in the books, but were actually butchered and roasted. This was how people survived.

George's letter was short and brutal. *'Did you know that Anna wants a divorce? What's going on Tamar? She says she's met someone else. Talk about kicking a bloke in the teeth. I'm all to pieces and can't think of anything else. The Colonel's going to arrange for me to have compassionate leave to sort it out. God knows what sort of a mess she's got herself into. Write to me will you and tell me what's going on?*

I'm glad you're happy and that you're getting to marry your chap. I never had Edward down as a rat. Hope things turn out better for you than they have for me.'

~~~~~~~~~~~~~~~~~~

Tamar thought that Anna looked dreadful when she met her
~~~~~~~~~~~~~~~~~~

at Penrith station – ill and sad.

'I've been doing some last minute shopping,' Tamar said, 'so I thought we could get the bus back together. You wouldn't believe how much work a wedding is.' Tamar had expected to feel angry with her, but when she saw Anna's gaunt and troubled face she couldn't feel anything but pity.

Anna managed a smile. 'I'm not sure you'll want me at your wedding when you know everything,' she said.

'George wrote to me.'

'Oh.'

'He told me you'd met someone else and that you wanted a divorce. I'd already worked out that something was wrong. You haven't written to me properly for months.'

She let Anna climb the steps into the bus in front of her. 'Let's sit at the back,' Tamar said, 'then we can talk.' They stowed their bags and parcels on the rack and tucked themselves into the corner of the back seat. 'Now,' Tamar said. 'I want you to tell me everything.'

As Anna talked, all Tamar could feel was sadness, for Anna and the two people she cared for most in the world after Martin.

'I blame myself,' Anna said. 'I knew that it was wrong to marry him, but I talked myself into it. I was fond of him, and desperate to get out of that terrible place. As soon as I met Michael I realised what real love was. If only I'd met him first, then there wouldn't be this dreadful mess.' Anna was staring out of the window, blinking back tears. 'You know, when I was with Michael, just for a moment, I really thought I could have it all. How could I be so stupid?'

'You really think it isn't possible to be completely happy?'

'Everything has its price.'

'I never thought I'd ever see you become cynical and bitter.'

Anna laughed harshly. 'I've just lost the one person in the world I could have made a life with. I loved him more than I ever imagined possible. I'm having his child – a child he'll never see. Why should I not be bitter?'

Tamar felt the shock go straight through her. That was something she hadn't known. Then she recovered herself. 'How are you going to manage with a child, Anna? Will your mother help?'

'She would, but my grandfather won't let her. I'll manage somehow. I sold a painting recently for five guineas – if I can sell one I can sell more. Maybe enough to keep myself.'

'It isn't easy. I know what a struggle Sadie had to bring me up.'

'I'll find a way.' Anna turned to look at her. 'Why are you still speaking to me, Tamar? I know how fond you are of Lily and George. I thought you wouldn't want to know me.'

'You're my best friend Anna. How could I judge you? I know you didn't set out to hurt anyone. It could so easily have been me with Edward and Martin if things had gone differently.'

Anna shook her head. 'You're more cautious than me Tamar, you don't rush headlong into things. I loved him and I just gave in to it and now I'm having his child.' Tears were rolling down her cheeks and dampening the collar of her white, uniform shirt. Tamar took her hand and held it while she cried.

'When's the baby due?'

'Just before Christmas.' Anna blew her nose thoroughly into a large man's handkerchief. 'Isn't it stupid? I couldn't cry at all when they first told me. Now I just dissolve all the time.' She sniffed and stuffed the handkerchief into her pocket. 'What about you and Martin?' Anna asked. 'Will you be happy?'

'I'm sure of it. We've been living under the same roof for months, so I know all his bad habits – he's got sweaty feet, hates shopping and you can't talk to him before nine o'clock in the morning.' She blushed and lowered her voice. 'And I like going to bed with him too.'

'I wish George and I had done that. It would have saved a lot of trouble. I just thought – maybe it was always like that at first. Or that it was me – because of something that happened in the past.' She turned to look out of the window again, and exclaimed, 'Tamar! You didn't tell me you had mountains here!'

'Didn't I? Actually the local people call them fells – they make jokes about my name.'

'They're not like Partenkirchen – gentler.' Anna leaned forward, craning her neck for a better view. 'I didn't know how much I missed looking at mountains.'

'They are beautiful. Sometimes when I'm working in the

fields I look up and they make me feel so utterly happy – it's difficult to explain.'

Tamar had been a little anxious about introducing Anna to Martin and his family, but they seemed to like her – talking over the table through the evening meal about ordinary things as if she was a member of the family. Anna was quieter and less abrasive than Tamar had expected, remembering how confrontational she could be. But, although she still looked pale and exhausted, Anna seemed at ease with them. She even laughed at one of Joe's jokes. She's suffered, Tamar thought, and she's still suffering.

~~~~~~~~~~~~~~~~~~

Anna was surprised how happy Tamar looked – utterly radiant. Her Celtic complexion had a healthy outdoor glow and she was more animated than Anna had ever seen her. Martin too, surprised her. She hadn't expected a farmer to be so articulate and intelligent – and then she castigated herself for her prejudice. He was very easy going with a quizzical, amused expression in his eyes that mirrored Joe's. In many ways he looked more like Joe's son than Wilf's.

After supper Tamar offered to take Anna down to the farm house to show her round.

'Mrs Bainbridge and some of the local farmer's wives had a scrubbing party the other day when I was doing my exams. They did it as a surprise. The whole place looks wonderful.'

'When are you moving in?'

'Not for a while yet. We've signed the contract, but the conveyancing won't be finished for another month or two – apparently the estate has to go through something called probate – but we've got the keys already. People don't seem to worry about things like that round here. We're staying at Crow Hall until it's ready.'

'I can't get over the change in you, Tamar. You used to be so timid.'

'Not now. You should see me with a herd of cows!' Tamar's tone became reflective as they walked down the track towards the farm. 'It's been good for me being here. Martin's even teaching me to drive, though I've only driven the landrover up and down
~~~~~~~~~~~~~~~~~~

the field so far. The only thing that's worrying me is the housekeeping. Do you realise I've never had to cook or clean? I haven't a clue how to keep house. We've always lived in lodgings.'

'What'll you do?'

'Mary's going to teach me how to cook. But I've a feeling I'm not going to be too good at it. My fingers don't exactly itch to make pie crust!'

Tamar showed Anna the house with great pride. The stone-flagged kitchen with its imposing black range, the passageways through to scullery and dairy. On the other side was a Sunday parlour with a pretty Victorian grate and sash windows looking out into the neglected orchard where two goats were grazing the long grass. The room had an unused kind of feel to it and smelled of moth balls, but Anna could imagine it in the winter with the fire lit and the curtains pulled, the arm chairs drawn up to the fire.

'We're buying it with the furniture,' Tamar explained, 'But I'm spending my father's wedding present money on some new bits and pieces. I've bought a sofa and a double bed so far!'

Upstairs there were three bedrooms with polished wooden floors and faded wallpaper. The rear bedroom had a view of the hills rising behind the farm and Anna lingered for a while beside the window.

'I envy you this view. It makes me itch to paint it.'

'Are you still intending to study art?'

'Of course!' How could Tamar imagine that she wouldn't? 'There's only art left.'

'It won't be easy with a baby.'

'I know that. But I'll have to manage somehow. It's not like a job that you can choose either to do or not do, painting's my life Tamar. It's who I am. I didn't intend to have a child because I didn't think I could give it enough, but now that I am – well, the baby will be part of it – he or she'll grow up to accept what I am. I'm never going to be a conventional mother, am I? Actually I can't imagine myself as a mother at all. But you don't get a choice, do you. It terrifies me.'

'You'll know what to do when the time comes. I've seen young heifers who've never had a calf before and they seem to know exactly what to do by instinct.' Tamar paused for a moment. 'Anna, when you have to leave Harwood, would you consider coming here to stay for a while? You'll need someone when the baby arrives. You mustn't be on your own.'

Anna's immediate reaction was to refuse. 'I couldn't Tamar. It would be like playing gooseberry with you and Martin.'

'I'll have to ask him, of course, but I don't think he'll mind. We'll be out on the farm most of the time. It would be good to have someone keeping the home fires burning so to speak. Will you think about it? There'll be plenty of time to paint. And that's another thing. Look, I know you always intended to go to the Slade, but did you know that the Royal Academy's been evacuated up here? They're near Ambleside, which isn't all that far away. It was in the local papers.'

'It's all irrelevant now. Where would I get the money?'

'I'll lend it to you. There's still some of Ida's legacy left even after we've paid the deposit on the farm.'

'I couldn't take money from you, Tamar.'

'Yes you could' Tamar sounded exasperated. 'You can pay me back when you're a famous painter, after the war.'

'Will there ever be an "after the war"?'

Tamar sighed. 'It's so much part of our lives it seems impossible, doesn't it. But it will be over one day.' She put her arm round Anna. 'Don't be so negative Anna. You've got to stop punishing yourself. You've suffered enough. And anyway, just at this very moment I need your help. Holly's arriving tomorrow morning with my wedding dress and it'll be a miracle if it fits. And then there's all the flowers to do in the church and the tables to set out in the village hall – I can't believe it'll all be ready by Saturday.'

The following day passed in a blur. Holly arrived in a taxi just before lunch looking incredibly elegant. Tamar had got so used to seeing Holly in her land girl's uniform, she'd forgotten how stunningly beautiful she could look with her milk white skin and flame red hair. 'It's so good to be back,' she said as she came into the kitchen. 'I thought I was going to die of boredom!' She hugged everyone and then deposited all her boxes and packages in the Bainbridge's parlour. Tamar watched the brief, formal exchange of names between Anna and Holly, the polite smiles and wondered what they would make of each other – her two closest friends were so very different.

'How's Mrs Heslop?' Holly asked.

'Much the same. Apparently they're giving her this new electric shock treatment. Martin and I went to see her in the Garlands. She was in the sitting room, in an armchair by the window, beautifully dressed, with her hair done – not like herself at all. We talked to her but she just sat there smiling and looking straight through us. It was unnerving.'

Mrs Bainbridge served lunch and almost straight away Holly excused herself and asked if she could borrow a bicycle to go down to the smithy to see Ivan. She had to endure a volley of ribald comments from Joe about her romance and by the time she got out of the kitchen Holly's face was scarlet with embarrassment.

Tamar eventually found time to broach the subject of Anna staying with them while she and Martin were feeding the calves. 'I had rather fancied having you all to myself,' he said with a sigh. 'But you can't see your friend in trouble and not help. And I suppose if we have all those empty rooms we'll only get evacuees or something.'

Tamar kissed him. 'It'll only be for a few months until she gets herself sorted out.'

The rest of the day was spent in preparation. Anna proved adept at decoration and she and Holly between them arranged vases of delphiniums and lupins and day lilies plundered from local cottage gardens, the stately flowers rising from a cloud of cow parsley that Anna had picked in the hedgerow. They trailed ivy along the window sills of the church and tied little posies of everlasting flowers on the ends of the pews.

The kitchen at Crow Hall was almost too hot to bear from the heat of the range – stoked up for Mrs Bainbridge to bake yet more pies and cakes for the reception. Half the women's institute seemed to have been pressed into service for the feast and the vicar's wife was apparently providing some of her legendary damson wine. Someone else had made elderflower champagne.

'Who do I have to pay for it all?' Tamar had naively asked earlier in the week and Mrs Bainbridge had been shocked. 'Why no one. Everybody gets invited and they all bring something. There's nothing to pay for.'

But it seemed an enormous amount of catering. The shelves in the pantry and the dairy were stacked high with plate cakes and trifles and bread for sandwiches.

Late in the afternoon, when the men were occupied with the milking, Tamar unpacked the cardboard box that Holly had brought with her and lifted out the dress. It was ivory crepe de chine, cut on the slant so that the material clung to Tamar's body, falling away from the hips towards the floor in a wide sweep. A row of seed pearls defined the neckline and more pearls were sewn on the points of the sleeves. Tamar stood on a chair in the parlour to see herself in the overmantel mirror.

'You look beautiful,' Anna said. Her voice sounded husky and Tamar wondered if she was remembering her own wedding – the bleak register office, the awkward relatives, the ugly suit.

'What are you going to wear on your head?' Mrs Bainbridge asked.

Holly clapped her hand to her mouth. 'I hadn't thought about that – I didn't think any further than the dress.'

'Neither did I,' Tamar said. 'I've been so preoccupied with everything else. I bought a hat to go with the suit, but it won't go with this.'

'A wreath of flowers would look nice,' Anna suggested. 'What's your bouquet going to be?'

'Sweet peas from the garden. Something very informal.'

'If you're minded to wear a veil,' Mrs Bainbridge said, 'there's Martin's mother's. I've kept it in the back of the wardrobe all these years. I couldn't bear to throw it out.'

'It could be your "something borrowed",' Holly said. 'If the moths haven't got to it.'

The box was brought down and layers of tissue paper unfolded to reveal a little coronet of wax flowers – slightly crushed, and a short, lace-edged veil which had probably once been white but had mellowed to ivory with age. It was almost exactly the same colour as the dress. Anna bent the coronet carefully into shape again and then settled the veil on Tamar's head.

'Doesn't she look a treat?' Mrs Bainbridge said.

Tamar gazed at her shimmering reflection, scarcely able to recognise herself. 'I wish Sadie was here,' she said after a moment's silence.

'Your mother'll be looking down on you from up there,' Mrs Bainbridge said. 'And Martin's too, I shouldn't wonder. You're a good lass Tamar. Esther'd be glad to see you wearing something of hers.' She picked up her pinafore from the chair. 'Now you'd better get out of that frock before the lads get back from the milking. You don't want Martin to see you dressed before tomorrow.'

'He's not supposed to see Tamar in the morning either,' Holly said.

'It's all right, he's sleeping at Holme Farm tonight,' Tamar explained. 'They're all going to the Farrier's arms for a stag night. Joe's promised me he'll get him to the church all right tomorrow.'

'Who's going to be the best man?' Anna asked.

'A man called John Richardson. I don't know him very well, he's rather quiet. He's from Town End about two miles from here and he went to school with Martin.'

'What's going to be your "something blue"?' Holly asked.

'I hadn't thought of that either.'

Mrs Bainbridge smiled. 'Aye, but we had. Now just wait on a minute.' She went to the sideboard and opened one of the drawers, going right to the back to bring out a small square box, which she handed to Tamar.

'Martin wants you to have this. It came to Esther from her mother, and now it'll come to you.'

Inside the box, on a cushion of dark blue velvet, was a filigree pendant with a small blue stone at the centre. 'This is lovely,' Tamar said. She felt overwhelmed by all this generosity. Holly had once said that being loved so much was a burden, and now Tamar glimpsed what she had meant. What had she ever done to deserve such happiness? How could she ever repay what was being given to her?

'It looks Victorian,' Holly said as Tamar lifted the necklace out of the box. 'My grandmother had one very similar.' She reached out and turned the pendant round. 'Look, it has a bar at the back so you can take the chain off and wear it as a brooch.'

Tamar fastened it round her neck. 'I'll always treasure this.' She kissed Aunt Mary's soft cheek and received a hug in return. It gave her a good feeling to be wearing things that had belonged to Martin's mother. The Fell's might not have wanted her, but the Bainbridges had opened their hearts to her. She was one of them. She belonged.

Anna lay awake in the dark long after Tamar and Holly were asleep. Her uniform was neatly pressed and hung with Holly's diaphanous dress on the back of the door ready for tomorrow. It had hurt, desperately, to see Tamar standing in her wedding dress, surrounded by love and friendship, so patently happy. Why couldn't it have been her and Michael? Tomorrow was going to be a nightmare. She would have to keep smiling for Tamar's sake, while silently grieving for her own loss. It was unbearable. And then she was going to have to decide what to do about Tamar's offer of a temporary home.

Could she live here? The Bainbridges had welcomed and accepted her. Everyone was friendly and open. They were not her people, but they were good people. No one asked awkward questions. And she could certainly work here. Anna already longed to paint the brothers – Joe and Wilf – like and yet unlike, their faces, weathered by the landscape, seemed to go back in history to another age. And then the hills towering behind the house were crying out to be captured on canvas. Their craggy masses filled her with a deep home-sickness for the mountains and alpine pastures of her childhood.

I could stay here, Anna thought. For a little while. Either Walter or John Cornell would know someone at the Royal Academy that she could talk to. Then, it was as if another doorway had opened up in front of her. Everything was once more possible. And one day, in that mythical time 'after the war', she would go back to Germany with Michael's child and look for his parents as well as her own father. Tamar had found the place where she belonged; one day Anna vowed to find her own.

~~~~~~~~~~~~~~~~~~

Tamar waited outside the church door while Holly and Anna adjusted her dress and her veil.

'Do I look all right?' she asked anxiously, fingering the little coronet of wax flowers that held her veil in place. It still felt insecure, despite the hairpins excavating craters in her scalp. One tug and it would be gone.

'You look fine,' Anna said, narrowing her eyes critically.

Holly handed her the bouquet of sweet peas she had picked that morning from the garden. Anna had bound it up in ribbon with some trailing asparagus fern. Tamar's hands were trembling as she took hold of it.

The vicar was walking down the aisle of the church to meet them and Tamar could see the pale blur of Martin's face as he turned to watch from the front pew. She took a last look at the view. A light summer wind was tossing the rowan trees in the grave yard and beyond them the dark screes of Kirkland Pike rose almost sheer to the cairn at the top. Tamar remembered the first time that she and Holly had come here to look at the grave stones and how surprised she had been to find her name-sake. That was more than a year ago now. She had certainly never dreamt that perhaps one day her name too would be carved here to be found by a casual visitor. Tamar Fell, beloved wife of Martin Bainbridge. She took a deep breath.

'Are you quite sure?' Anna asked. 'It isn't worth it if you're not.'

Tamar nodded. 'Quite sure.' Her legs felt wobbly and she was light-headed with nerves. The vicar was standing in front of her and beyond him Martin was waiting at the altar steps. The organist had fallen silent, waiting for his cue. It was time to go.

~~~~~~~~~~~~~~~~~~

About The Author

Kathleen Jones was born and brought up on a hill farm in the Lake District. After spending some years in Africa and the Middle East, where she worked in English broadcasting, she returned to Cumbria where she now lives with sculptor Neil Ferber. She has four children and writes full-time.

Though best known for her award-winning biographies, Kathleen has also published poetry; 'Unwritten Lives' won the Redbeck Press pamphlet award, and her latest collection, 'Not Saying Goodbye at Gate 21', published by Templar Poetry, won the 2011 Straid Award. She has written feature articles and short fiction for a variety of national and international magazines. Her short stories have been broadcast on BBC Radio and on radio networks in Holland, Germany and Spain. She was one of the featured authors in the recent 'Save our Short Story Anthology' compiled by the Arts Council. As a journalist Kathleen has written articles and reviews for the Independent, the Guardian, the Daily Express, and the TLS, as well as magazines such as SHE and Cosmo.

Kathleen Jones regularly leads creative writing workshops for fiction, poetry and life writing. She is a tutor for the Open University, currently a Royal Literary Fund Fellow and is a regular performer at Literature Festivals in Britain and abroad. She is a member of the Alliance of Independent Authors and is an enthusiastic blogger at 'A Writer's Life'.

Further information at: www.kathleenjones.co.uk

BY THE SAME AUTHOR

Non-Fiction

Margaret Cavendish: A Glorious Fame
Christina Rossetti: Learning not to be First
A Passionate Sisterhood: the Sisters, Wives and Daughters of the Lake Poets
Catherine Cookson: The Biography
Seeking Catherine Cookson's Da
Katherine Mansfield: The Story-Teller
Margaret Forster: A Life in Books
The Lives of Others (an anthology of life-writing)
Norman Nicholson: The Whispering Poet

Fiction

The Sun's Companion
Three and Other Stories

Poetry

Unwritten Lives
Not Saying Goodbye at Gate 21

26378205R00248

Made in the USA
Charleston, SC
05 February 2014